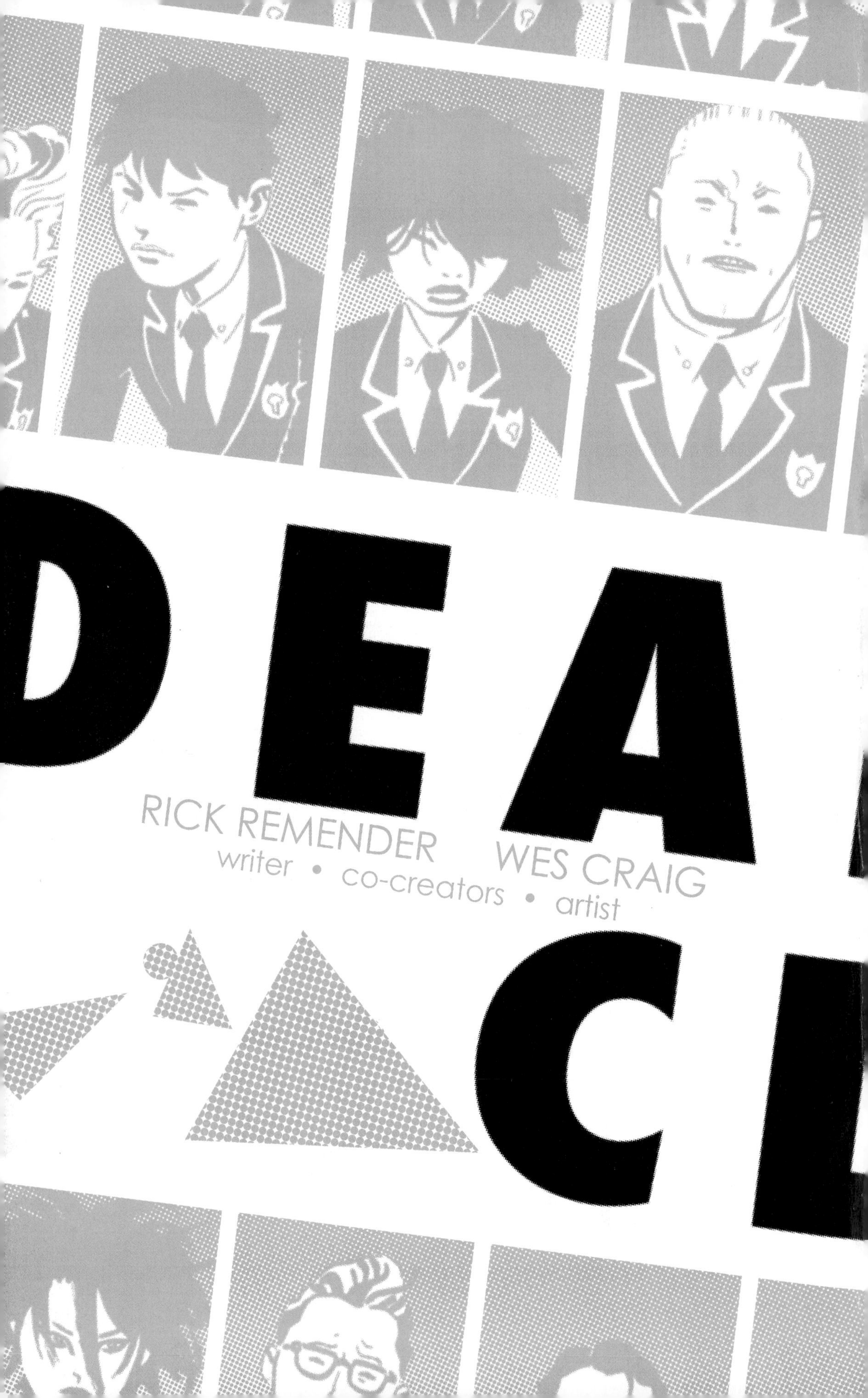
DEA
RICK REMENDER
writer • co-creators • artist
WES CRAIG
C

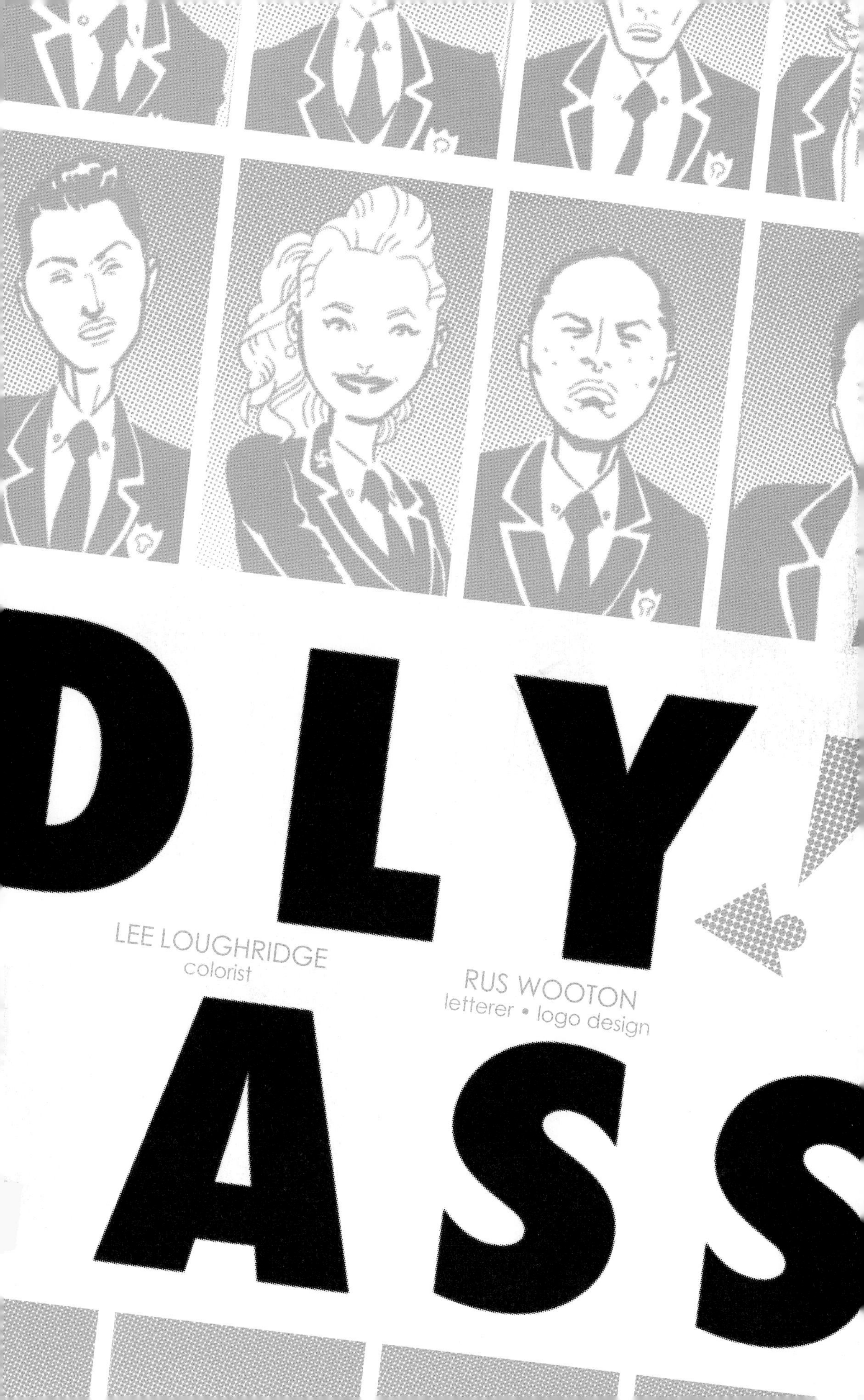

LEE LOUGHRIDGE
colorist

RUS WOOTON
letterer • logo design

IMAGE COMICS, INC.

Robert Kirkman • Chief Operating Officer
Erik Larsen • Chief Financial Officer
Todd McFarlane • President
Marc Silvestri • Chief Executive Officer
Jim Valentino • Vice President

Eric Stephenson • Publisher / Chief Creative Officer
Nicole Lapalme • Controller
Leanna Counter • Accounting Analyst
Sue Korpela • Accounting & HR Manager
Marla Eizik • Talent Liaison
Jeff Boison • Director of Sales & Publishing Planning
Lorelei Bunjes • Director of Digital Services
Dirk Wood • Director of International Sales & Licensing
Alex Cox • Director of Direct Market Sales
Chloe Ramos • Book Market & Library Sales Manager
Emilio Bautista • Digital Sales Coordinator
Jon Schlaffman • Specialty Sales Coordinator
Kat Salazar • Director of PR & Marketing
Monica Garcia • Marketing Design Manager
Drew Fitzgerald • Marketing Content Associate
Heather Doornink • Production Director
Drew Gill • Art Director
Hilary DiLoreto • Print Manager
Tricia Ramos • Traffic Manager
Melissa Gifford • Content Manager
Erika Schnatz • Senior Production Artist
Ryan Brewer • Production Artist
Deanna Phelps • Production Artist

imagecomics.com

GABE DINGER
production assistant

ERIKA SCHNATZ
production design

**DEADLY CLASS VOLUME 11: A FOND FAREWELL, PART ONE.** First printing. May 2022. Published by Image Comics, Inc. Office of publication: PO BOX 14457, Portland, OR 97293. Copyright © 2022 Rick Remender & Wes Craig. All rights reserved. Contains material originally published in single magazine form as DEADLY CLASS #49-52. DEADLY CLASS™ (including all prominent characters featured herein), its logo and all character likenesses are trademarks of Rick Remender & Wes Craig, unless otherwise noted. Image Comics® and its logos are registered trademarks of Image Comics, Inc. No part of this publication may be reproduced or transmitted, in any form or by any means (except for short excerpts for journalistic or review purposes), without the express written permission of Rick Remender & Wes Craig, or Image Comics, Inc. All names, characters, events, and locales in this publication are entirely fictional. Any resemblance to actual persons (living or dead), events, or places, without satirical intent, is coincidental. **PRINTED IN THE USA.** For international rights, contact: foreignlicensing@imagecomics.com. ISBN: 978-1-5343-2123-6

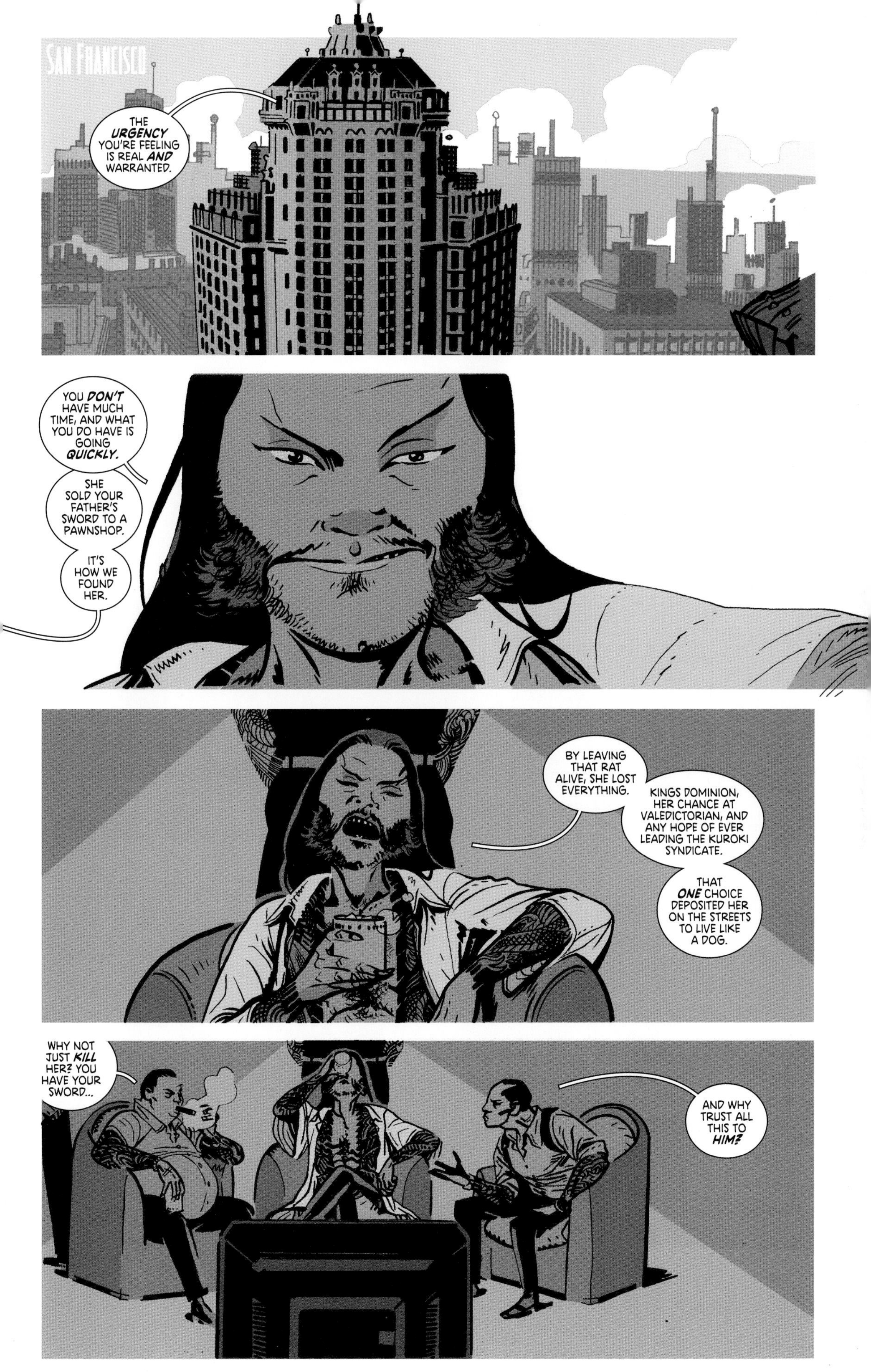
SAN FRANCISCO
THE URGENCY YOU'RE FEELING IS REAL AND WARRANTED.
YOU DON'T HAVE MUCH TIME, AND WHAT YOU DO HAVE IS GOING QUICKLY.
SHE SOLD YOUR FATHER'S SWORD TO A PAWNSHOP.
IT'S HOW WE FOUND HER.
BY LEAVING THAT RAT ALIVE, SHE LOST EVERYTHING.
KINGS DOMINION, HER CHANCE AT VALEDICTORIAN, AND ANY HOPE OF EVER LEADING THE KUROKI SYNDICATE.
THAT ONE CHOICE DEPOSITED HER ON THE STREETS TO LIVE LIKE A DOG.
WHY NOT JUST KILL HER? YOU HAVE YOUR SWORD...
AND WHY TRUST ALL THIS TO HIM?

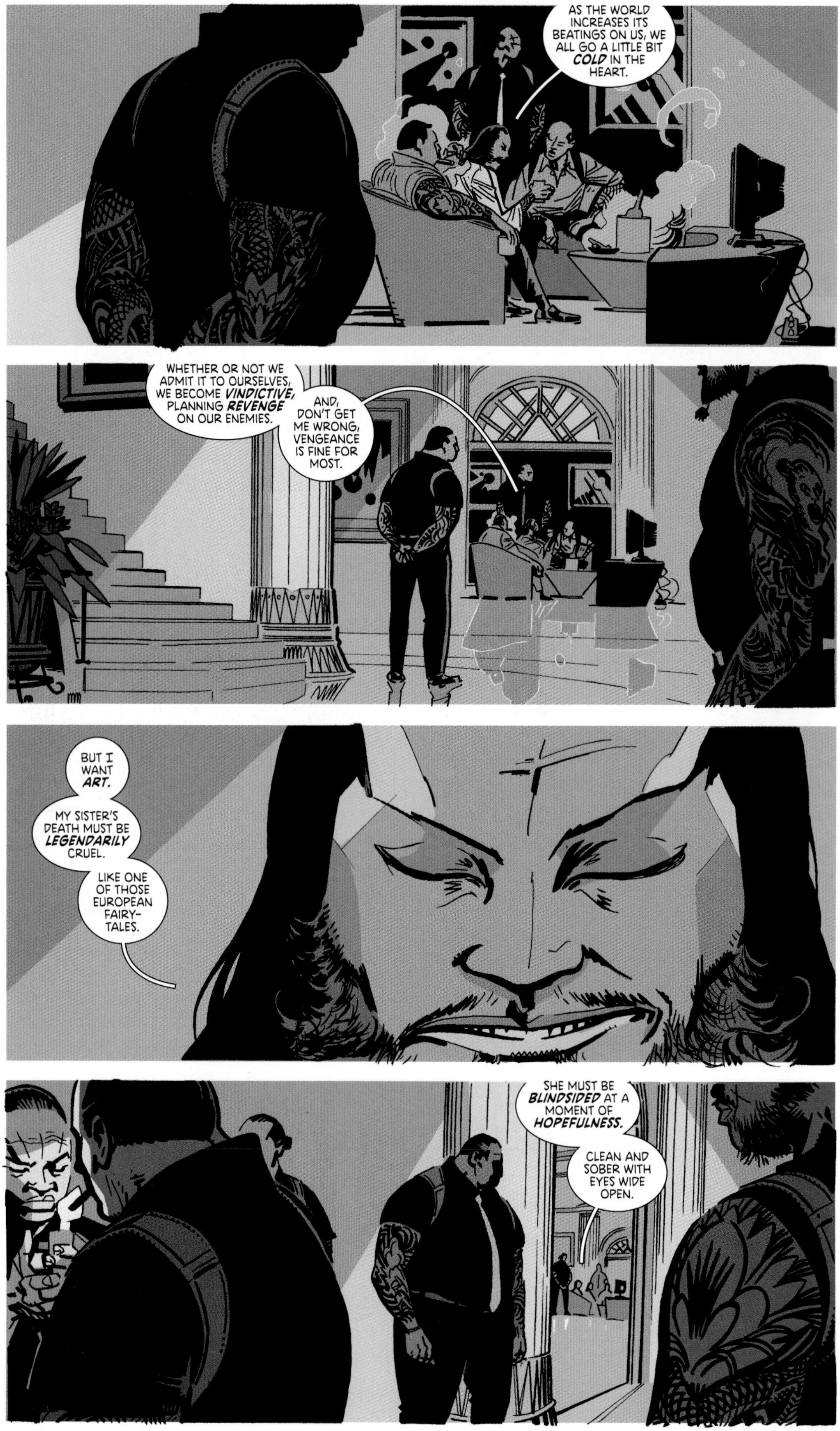
AS THE WORLD INCREASES ITS BEATINGS ON US, WE ALL GO A LITTLE BIT COLD IN THE HEART.
WHETHER OR NOT WE ADMIT IT TO OURSELVES, WE BECOME VINDICTIVE, PLANNING REVENGE ON OUR ENEMIES.
AND, DON'T GET ME WRONG, VENGEANCE IS FINE FOR MOST.
BUT I WANT ART.
MY SISTER'S DEATH MUST BE LEGENDARILY CRUEL.
LIKE ONE OF THOSE EUROPEAN FAIRY-TALES.
SHE MUST BE BLINDSIDED AT A MOMENT OF HOPEFULNESS.
CLEAN AND SOBER WITH EYES WIDE OPEN.

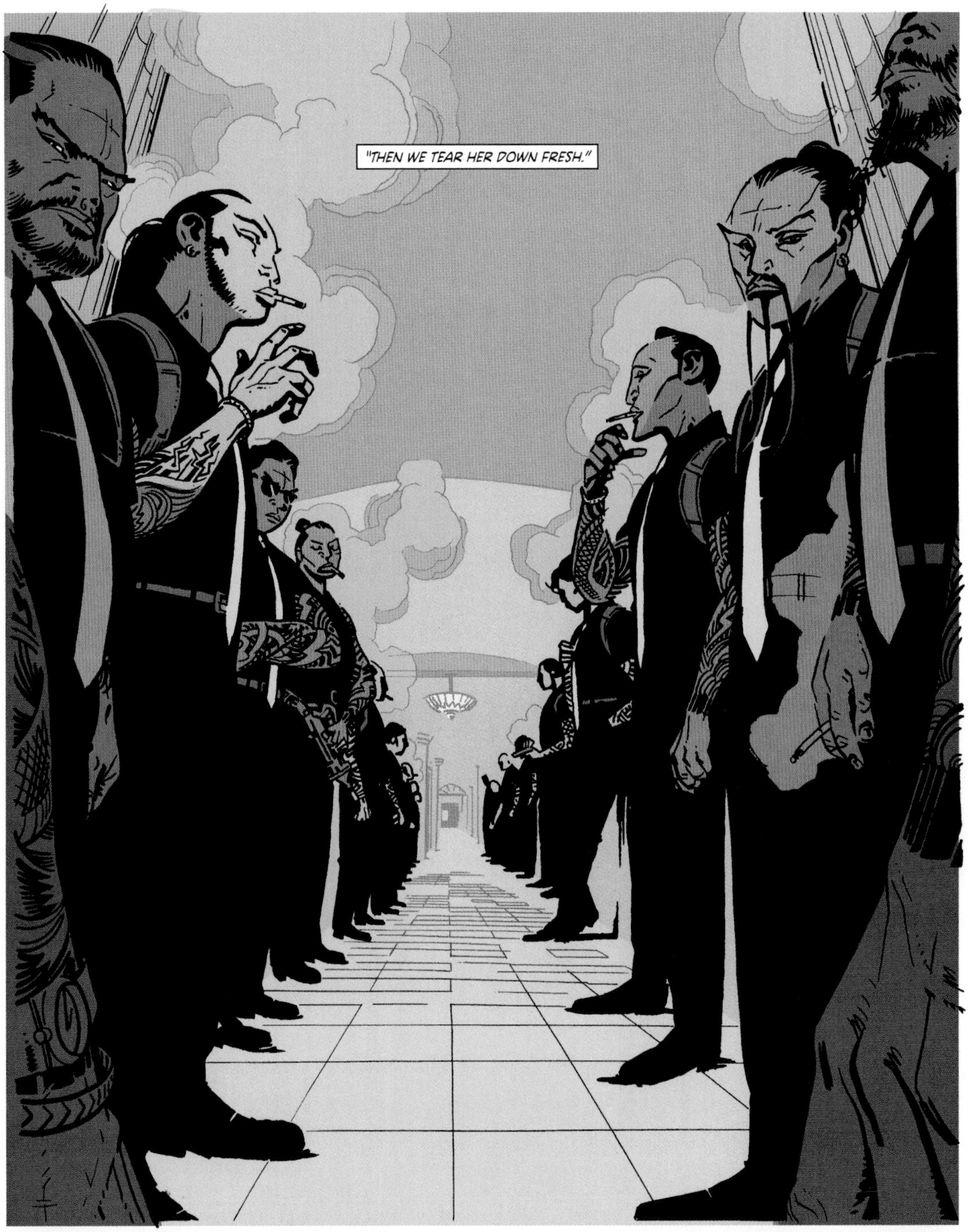
"THEN WE TEAR HER DOWN FRESH."

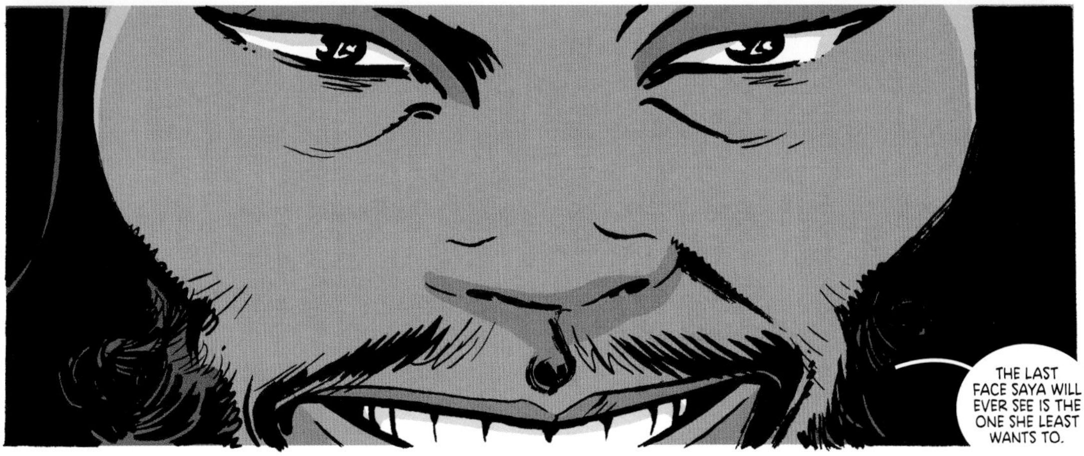
THE LAST FACE SAYA WILL EVER SEE IS THE ONE SHE LEAST WANTS TO.

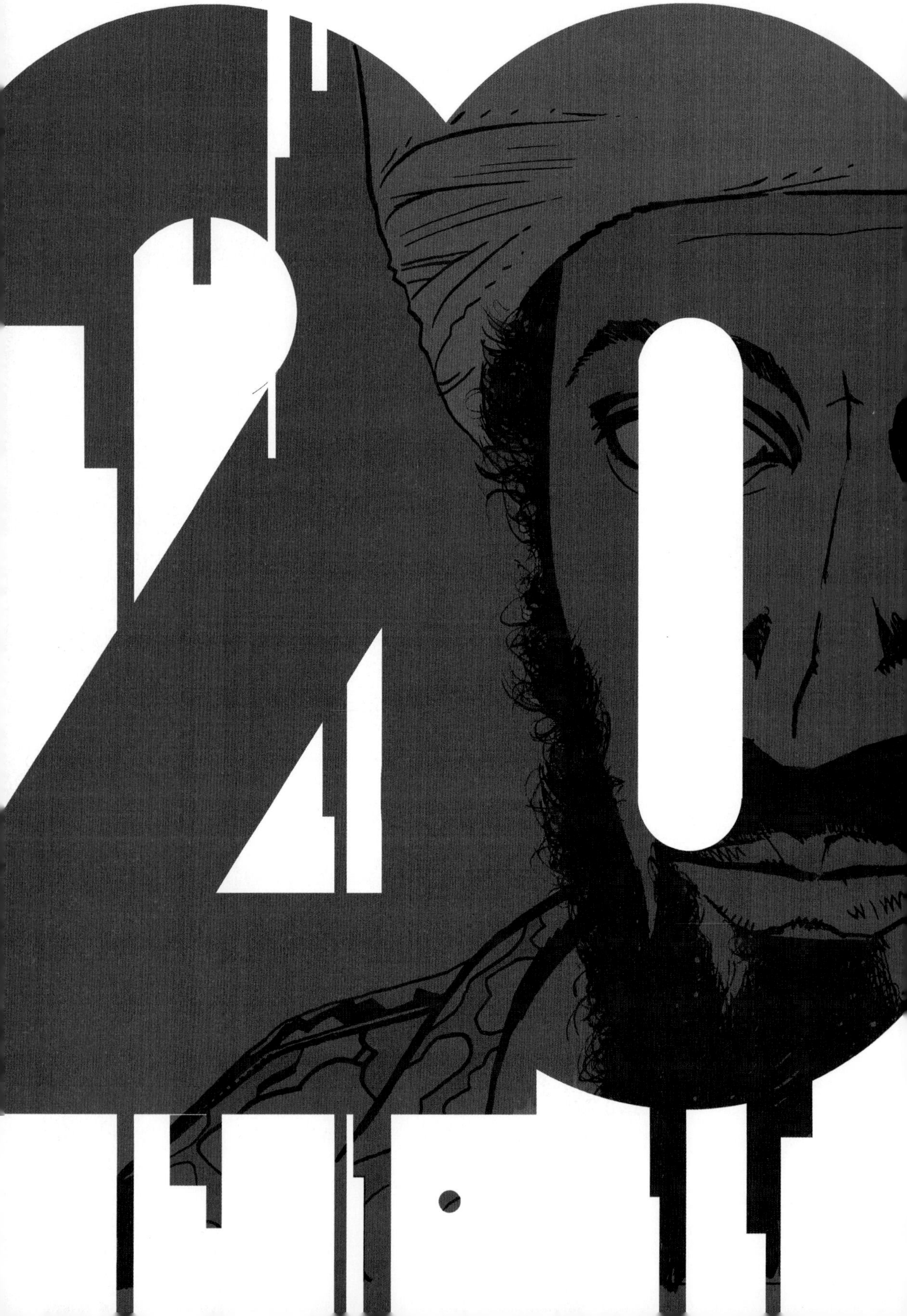

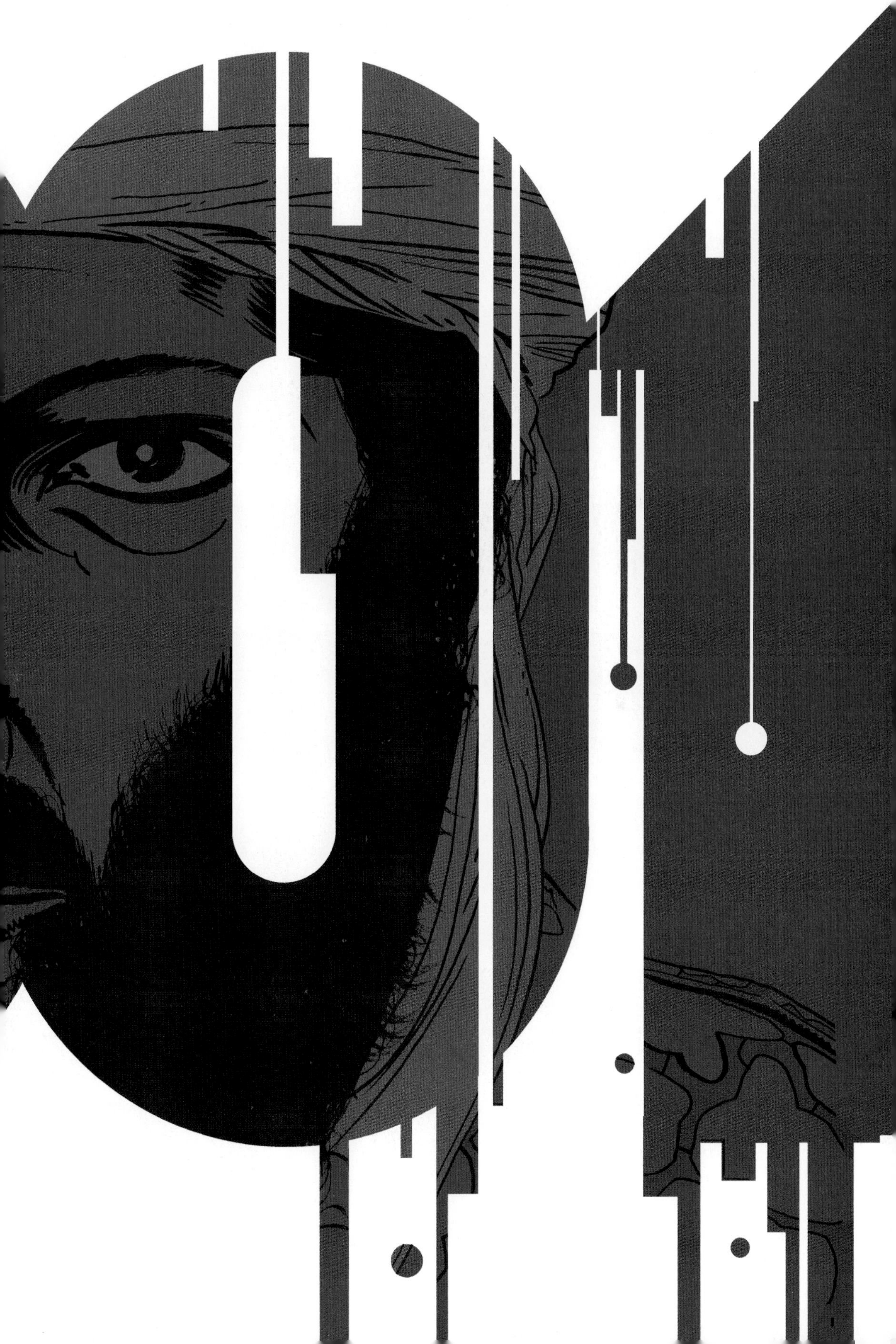

I'VE NEVER DETOXED ANYONE BEFORE.

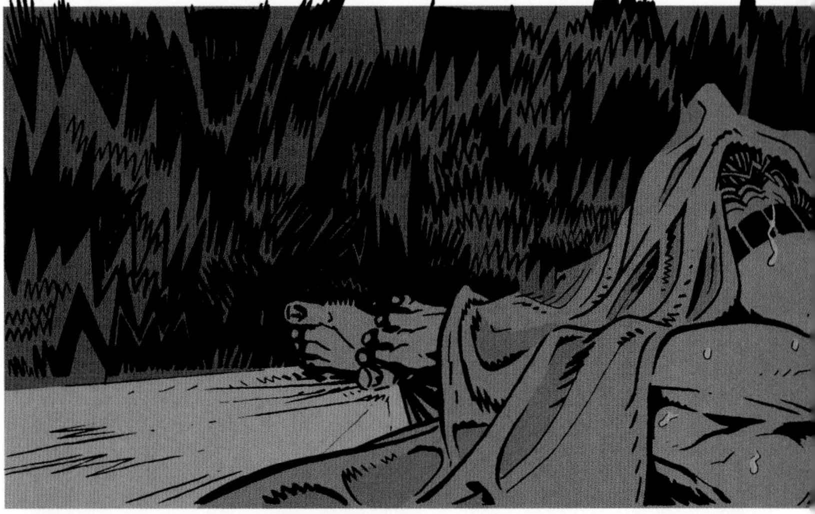

IT'S WORSE THAN THE MOVIES. IT'S WORSE THAN ANYTHING YOU CAN IMAGINE.

IN THE MOVIES THE MOST WE GET IS A **MONTAGE.**

IN REALITY, IT GOES ON FOR **DAYS.**

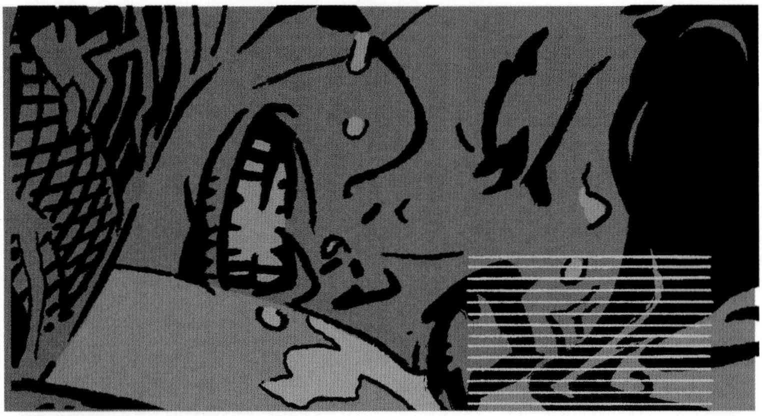

EVERY SINGLE MINUTE IS A **STRUGGLE.**

SHE WAS SMOKING THE HEROIN, NOT SHOOTING IT.

ONE THING IN OUR FAVOR.

WHEN SHE DOES MANAGE SLEEP, I INVESTIGATE HER FACE LIKE AN ARCHEOLOGIST.

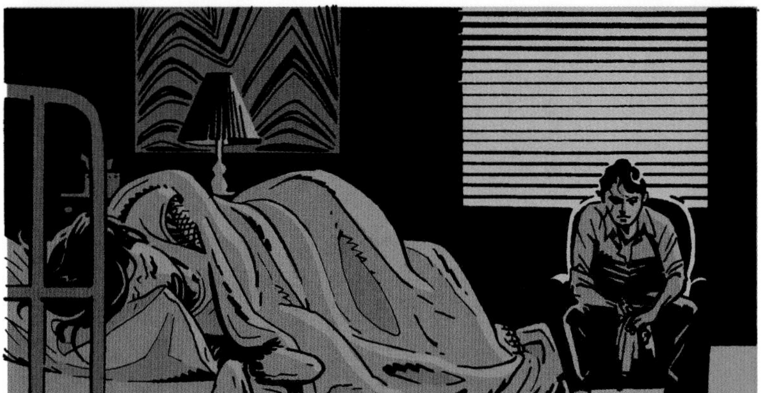

HER SKIN LOOKS THIN, INFECTED.

HER FACE PREMATURELY AGED AND WEATHERED FROM MALNUTRITION.

BUT BACK BEHIND IT ALL I SEE HER.

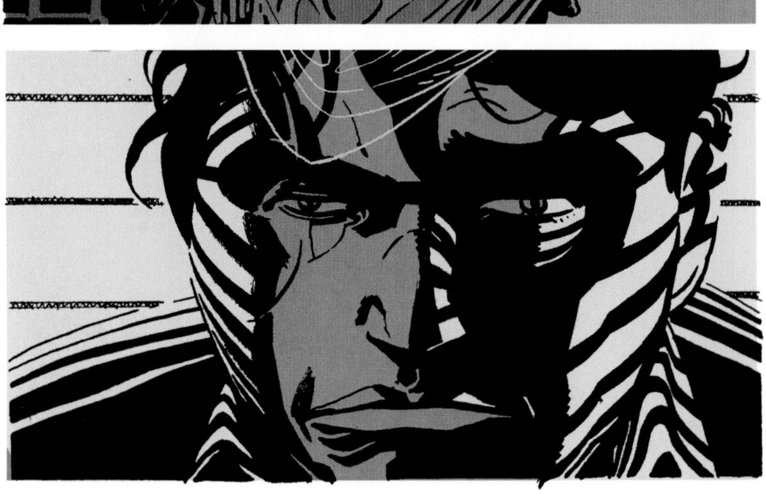

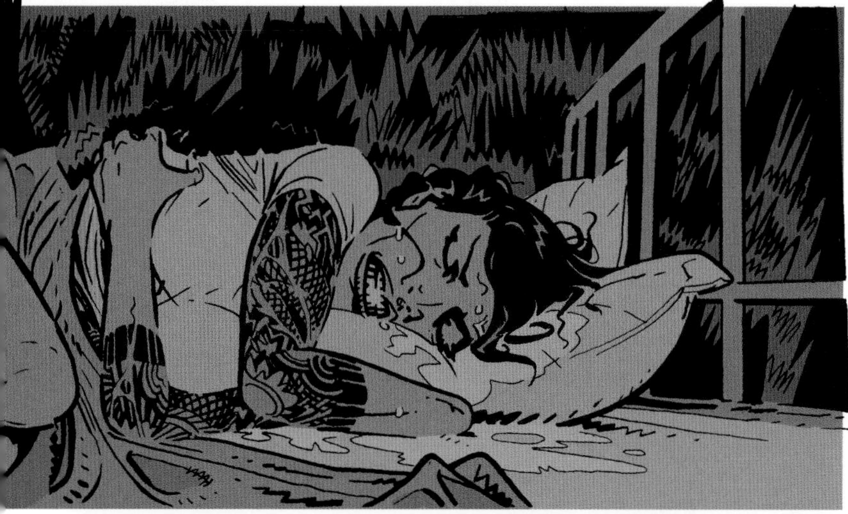

THE FIRST GIRL
I EVER LOVED.

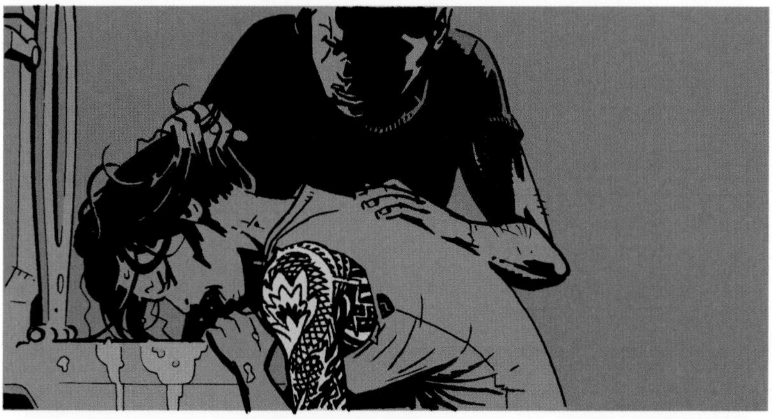

THE STRONGEST
PERSON I EVER
KNEW.

BUT LIFE IS A SERIES
OF DISILLUSIONMENTS.

THINGS THAT
YOU **THOUGHT**
WERE STRONG
ARE REVEALED
TO BE **WEAK.**

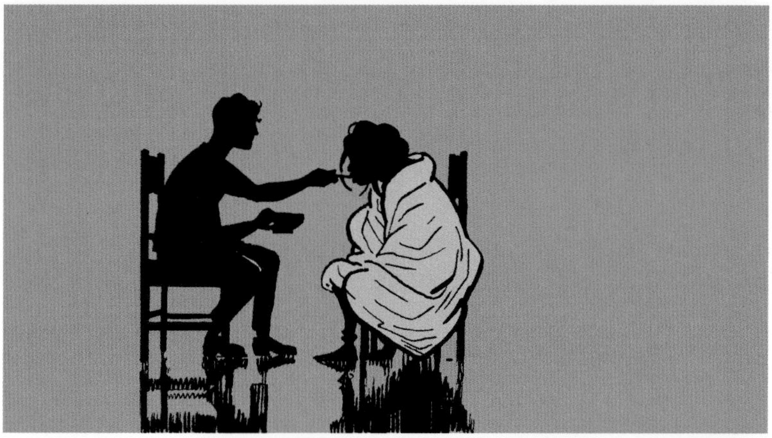

THINGS THAT YOU SAW
AS BEAUTIFUL LOOK
UGLY IN HINDSIGHT.

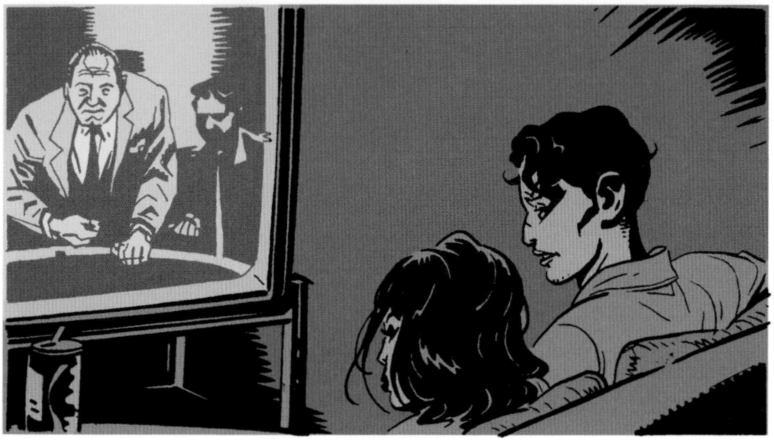

NOBODY IS WHAT YOU
THINK THEY ARE.

NOT ALL THE TIME ANYWAY.

THERE ARE OTHER THINGS
IN THERE AS WELL. HIDDEN.

THINGS THAT ARE TOO
COMPLICATED FOR YOU
TO ADD INTO YOUR
SNAPSHOT EQUATION.

YOUR BRAIN WANTS SIMPLE SOLUTIONS, EASY DEFINITIONS.

EITHER **GOOD** OR **BAD.** FUCK NUANCE.

PART OF ME WANTS TO TAKE BLAME FOR HER CIRCUMSTANCES.

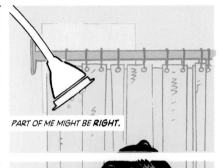

PART OF ME MIGHT BE **RIGHT.**

BUT IF SHE COULD HAVE ENDED UP HERE, SHE ALWAYS COULD HAVE ENDED UP HERE, WITH OR WITHOUT MY INVOLVEMENT IN HER LIFE.

THE TRUTH IS, I MISS HER.

ALL THESE YEARS, SHE'S ALWAYS BEEN IN THE BACK OF MY MIND.

IT'S MORE THAN JUST NOSTALGIA.

SHE'S HARDWIRED INTO MY FIRMWARE.

SHE KNEW ME WHEN I WAS YOUNG.

WHEN I WAS FINDING MYSELF.

PLAYED A BIG ROLE IN WHO I BECAME.

WE'RE ALL SENTIMENTAL FOR OLD TIMES.

THE PEOPLE FROM YOUR PAST ARE WHERE YOU FIND YOUR GLUE.

THEY ARE THE ONES WHO HAD A HAND IN THE FORM YOU TOOK.

NOTHING CAN REPLACE THE PEOPLE WHO WERE THERE AND SAW IT AND FELT IT AND UNDERSTOOD IT.

THEY ARE IRREPLACEABLE PIECES OF YOU.

THINK YOU'RE READY TO HOLD DOWN SOME FOOD?

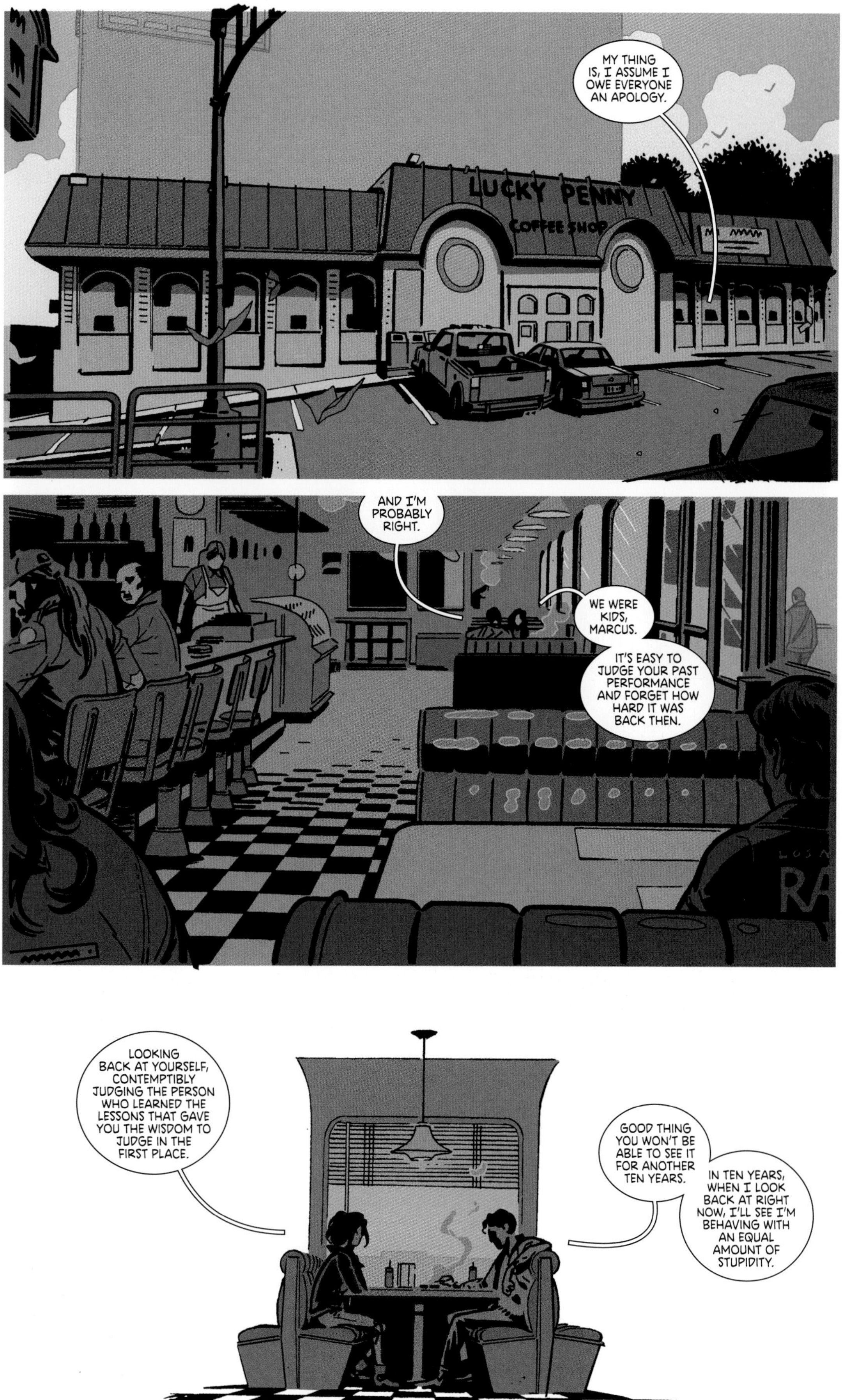
MY THING IS, I ASSUME I OWE EVERYONE AN APOLOGY.
LUCKY PENNY
COFFEE SHOP
AND I'M PROBABLY RIGHT.
WE WERE KIDS, MARCUS.
IT'S EASY TO JUDGE YOUR PAST PERFORMANCE AND FORGET HOW HARD IT WAS BACK THEN.
LOOKING BACK AT YOURSELF, CONTEMPTIBLY JUDGING THE PERSON WHO LEARNED THE LESSONS THAT GAVE YOU THE WISDOM TO JUDGE IN THE FIRST PLACE.
GOOD THING YOU WON'T BE ABLE TO SEE IT FOR ANOTHER TEN YEARS.
IN TEN YEARS, WHEN I LOOK BACK AT RIGHT NOW, I'LL SEE I'M BEHAVING WITH AN EQUAL AMOUNT OF STUPIDITY.

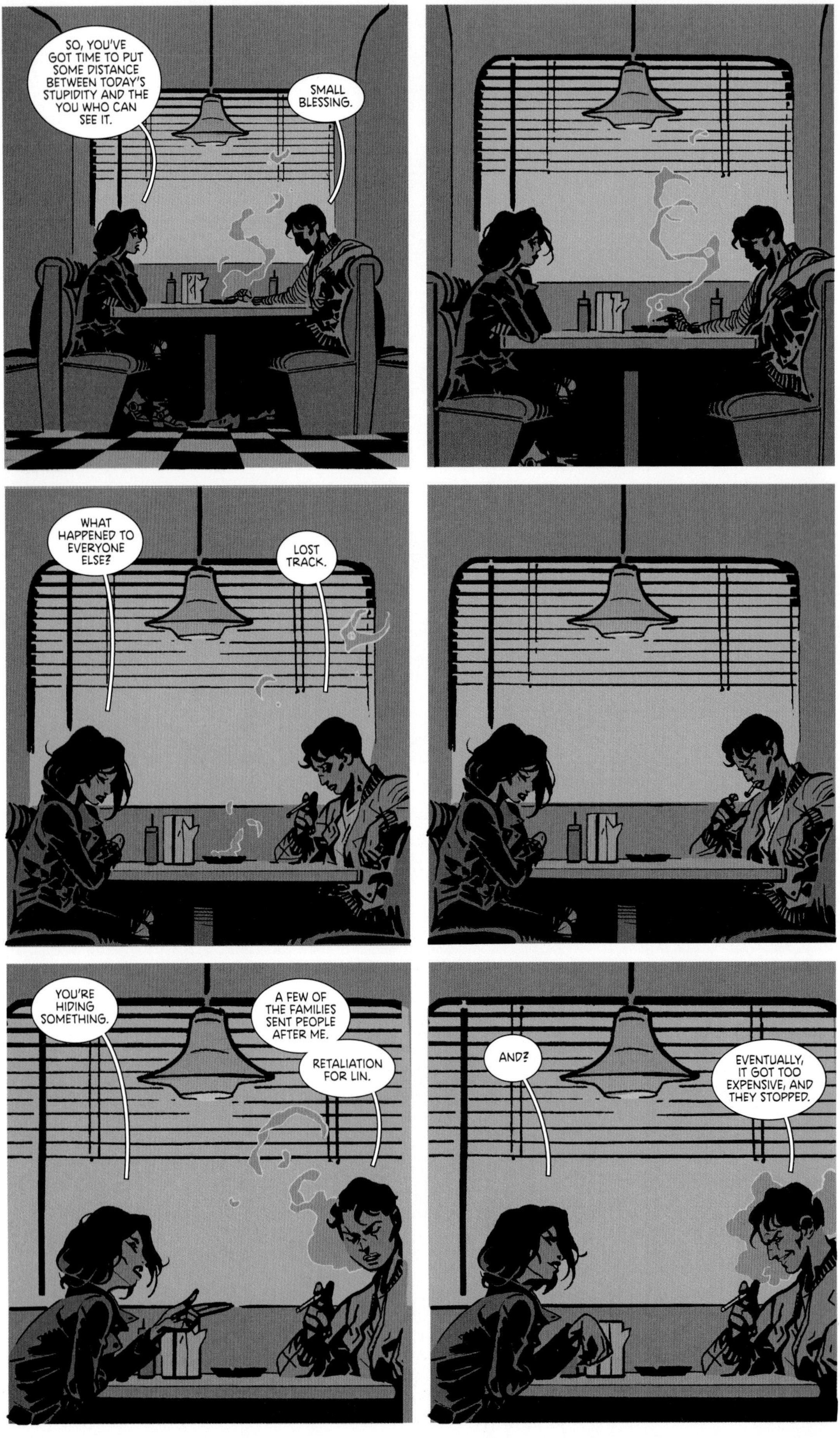
SO, YOU'VE GOT TIME TO PUT SOME DISTANCE BETWEEN TODAY'S STUPIDITY AND THE YOU WHO CAN SEE IT.
SMALL BLESSING.
WHAT HAPPENED TO EVERYONE ELSE?
LOST TRACK.
YOU'RE HIDING SOMETHING.
A FEW OF THE FAMILIES SENT PEOPLE AFTER ME.
RETALIATION FOR LIN.
AND?
EVENTUALLY, IT GOT TOO EXPENSIVE, AND THEY STOPPED.

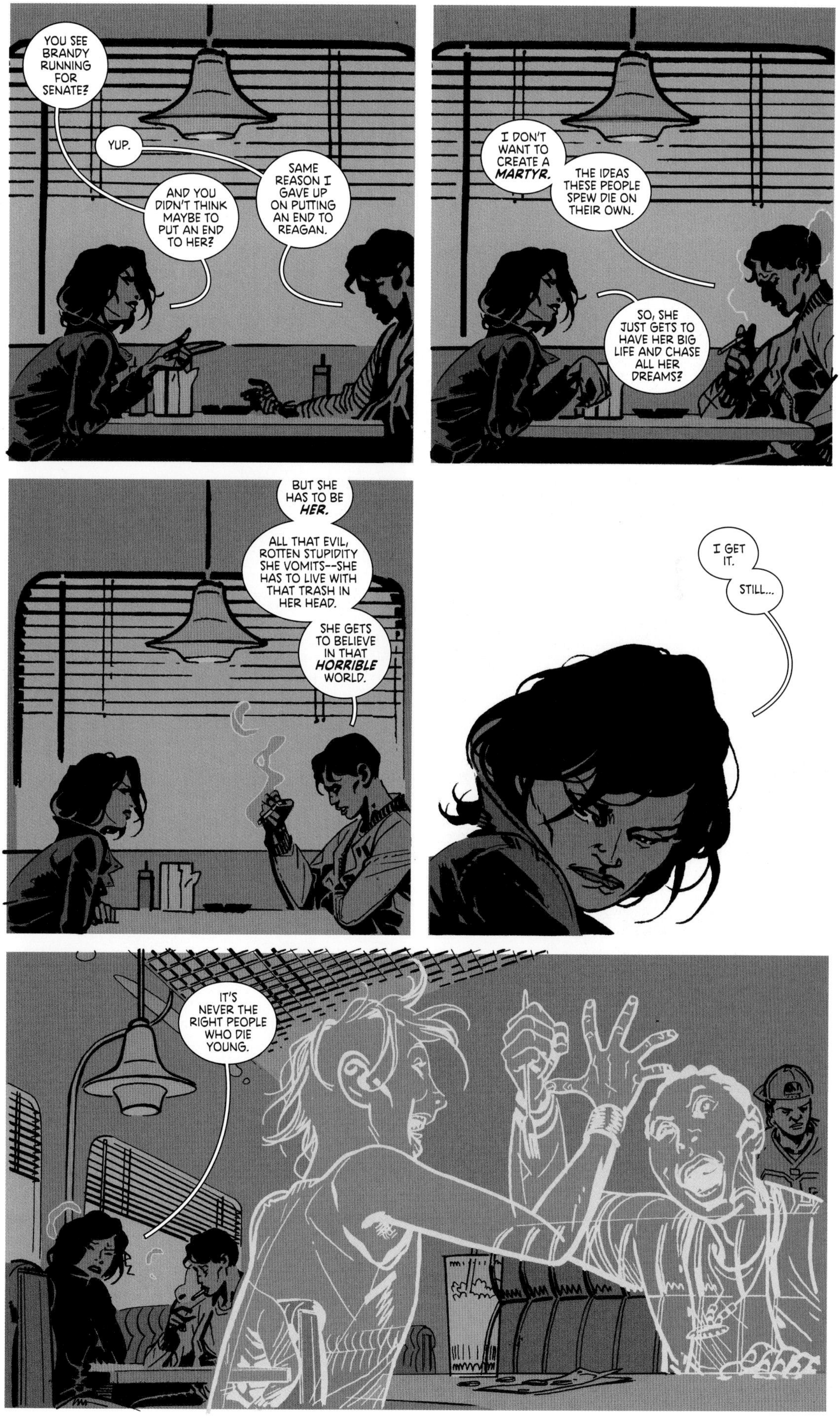

YOU SEE BRANDY RUNNING FOR SENATE?
YUP.
AND YOU DIDN'T THINK MAYBE TO PUT AN END TO HER?
SAME REASON I GAVE UP ON PUTTING AN END TO REAGAN.
I DON'T WANT TO CREATE A MARTYR.
THE IDEAS THESE PEOPLE SPEW DIE ON THEIR OWN.
SO, SHE JUST GETS TO HAVE HER BIG LIFE AND CHASE ALL HER DREAMS?
BUT SHE HAS TO BE HER.
ALL THAT EVIL, ROTTEN STUPIDITY SHE VOMITS--SHE HAS TO LIVE WITH THAT TRASH IN HER HEAD.
SHE GETS TO BELIEVE IN THAT HORRIBLE WORLD.
I GET IT.
STILL...
IT'S NEVER THE RIGHT PEOPLE WHO DIE YOUNG.

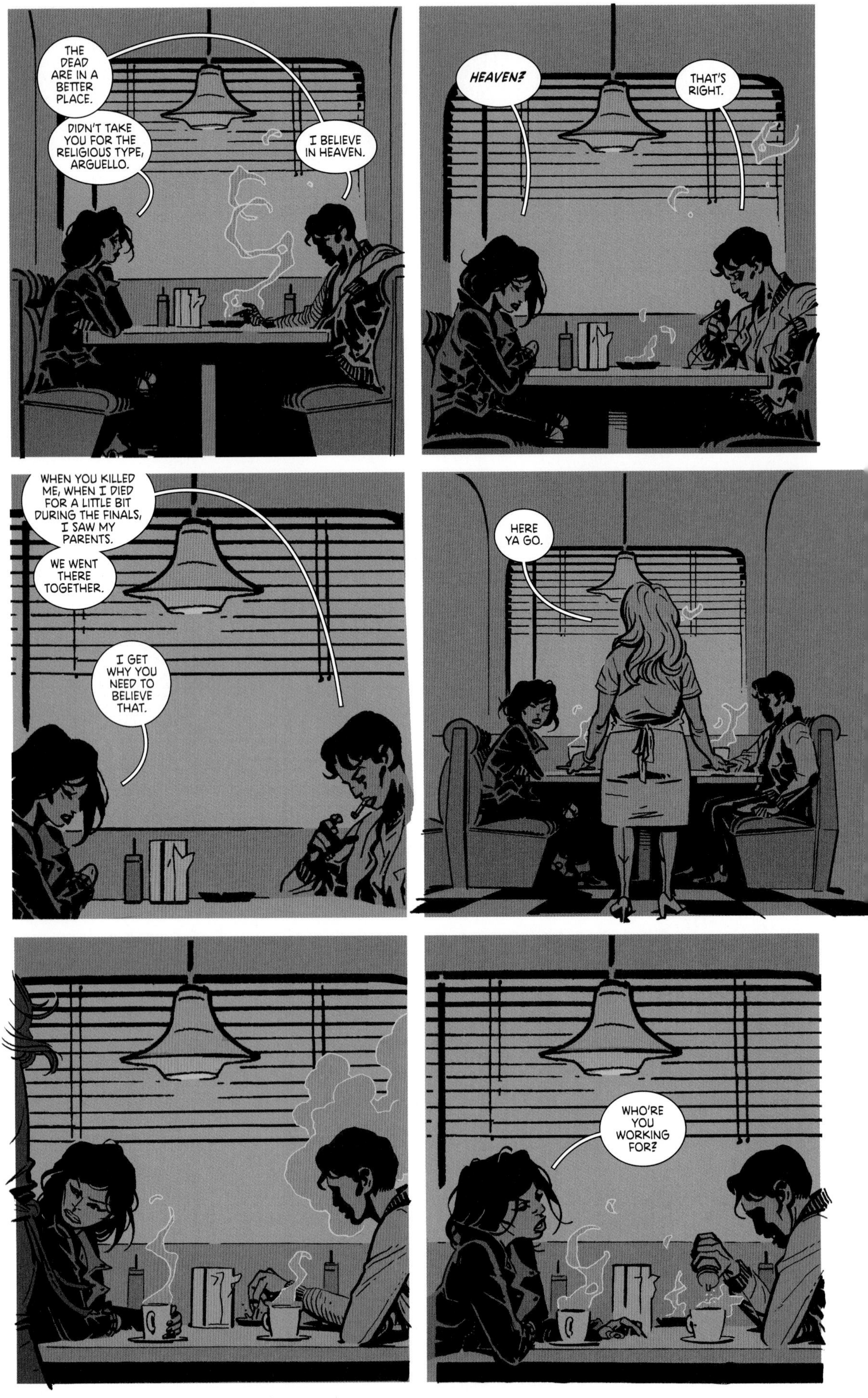
THE DEAD ARE IN A BETTER PLACE.
DIDN'T TAKE YOU FOR THE RELIGIOUS TYPE, ARGUELLO.
I BELIEVE IN HEAVEN.
HEAVEN?
THAT'S RIGHT.
WHEN YOU KILLED ME, WHEN I DIED FOR A LITTLE BIT DURING THE FINALS, I SAW MY PARENTS.
WE WENT THERE TOGETHER.
I GET WHY YOU NEED TO BELIEVE THAT.
HERE YA GO.
WHO'RE YOU WORKING FOR?

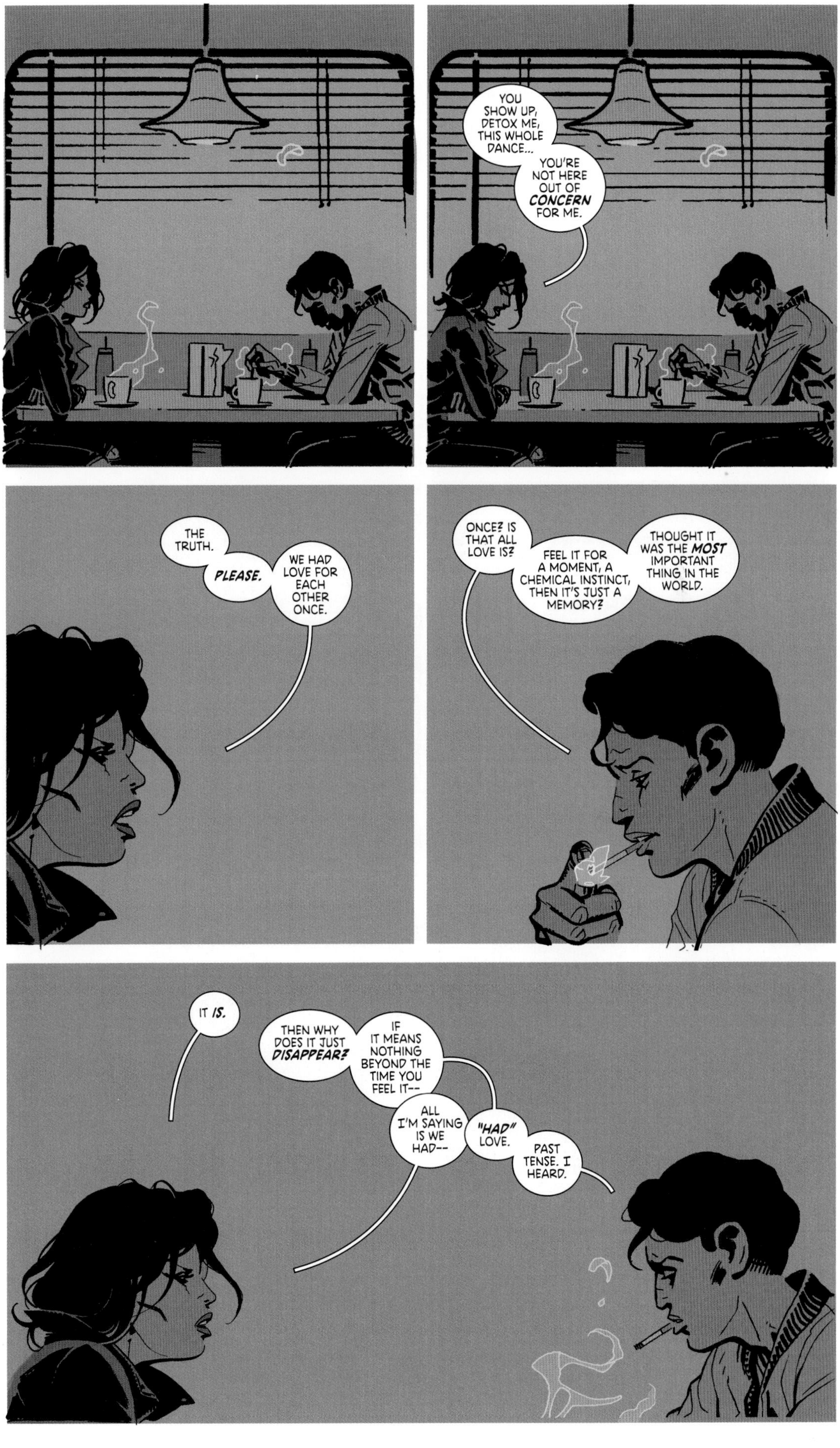
YOU SHOW UP, DETOX ME, THIS WHOLE DANCE...
YOU'RE NOT HERE OUT OF CONCERN FOR ME.
THE TRUTH.
PLEASE.
WE HAD LOVE FOR EACH OTHER ONCE.
ONCE? IS THAT ALL LOVE IS?
FEEL IT FOR A MOMENT, A CHEMICAL INSTINCT, THEN IT'S JUST A MEMORY?
THOUGHT IT WAS THE MOST IMPORTANT THING IN THE WORLD.
IT IS.
THEN WHY DOES IT JUST DISAPPEAR?
IF IT MEANS NOTHING BEYOND THE TIME YOU FEEL IT--
ALL I'M SAYING IS WE HAD--
"HAD" LOVE.
PAST TENSE. I HEARD.

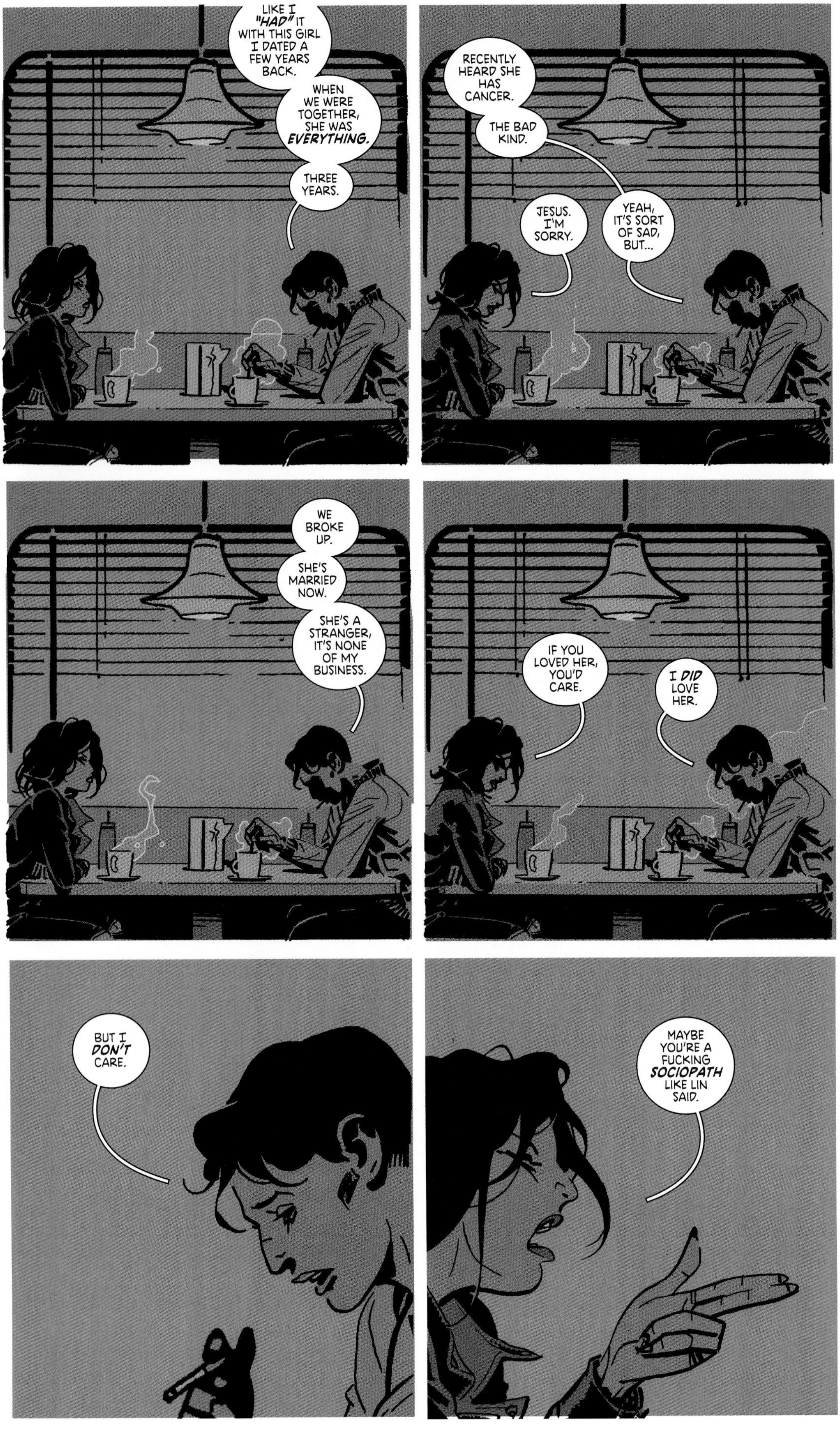
LIKE I "HAD" IT WITH THIS GIRL I DATED A FEW YEARS BACK.
WHEN WE WERE TOGETHER, SHE WAS EVERYTHING.
THREE YEARS.
RECENTLY HEARD SHE HAS CANCER.
THE BAD KIND.
JESUS. I'M SORRY.
YEAH, IT'S SORT OF SAD, BUT...
WE BROKE UP.
SHE'S MARRIED NOW.
SHE'S A STRANGER, IT'S NONE OF MY BUSINESS.
IF YOU LOVED HER, YOU'D CARE.
I DID LOVE HER.
BUT I DON'T CARE.
MAYBE YOU'RE A FUCKING SOCIOPATH LIKE LIN SAID.

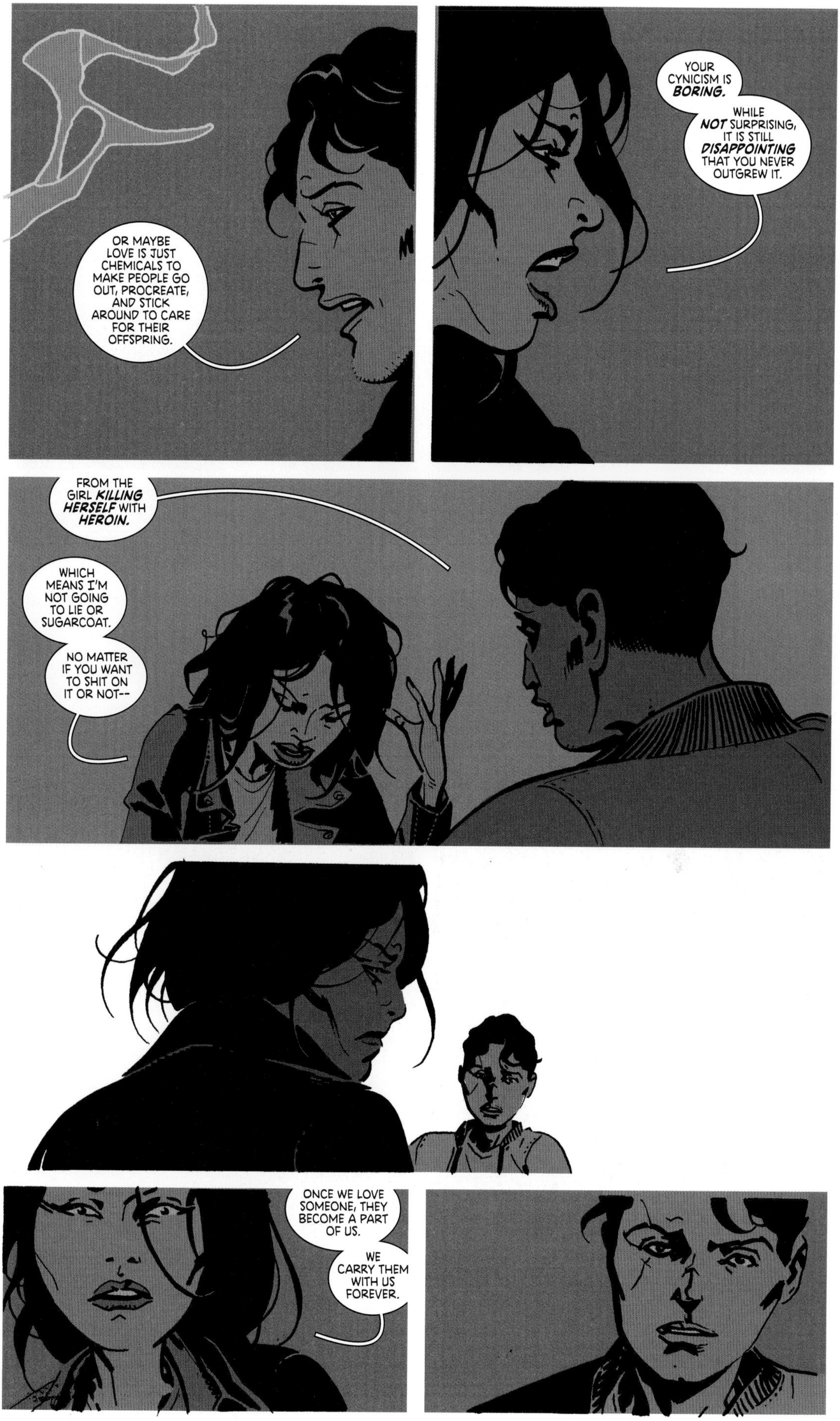
OR MAYBE LOVE IS JUST CHEMICALS TO MAKE PEOPLE GO OUT, PROCREATE, AND STICK AROUND TO CARE FOR THEIR OFFSPRING.
YOUR CYNICISM IS BORING.
WHILE NOT SURPRISING, IT IS STILL DISAPPOINTING THAT YOU NEVER OUTGREW IT.
FROM THE GIRL KILLING HERSELF WITH HEROIN.
WHICH MEANS I'M NOT GOING TO LIE OR SUGARCOAT.
NO MATTER IF YOU WANT TO SHIT ON IT OR NOT--
ONCE WE LOVE SOMEONE, THEY BECOME A PART OF US.
WE CARRY THEM WITH US FOREVER.

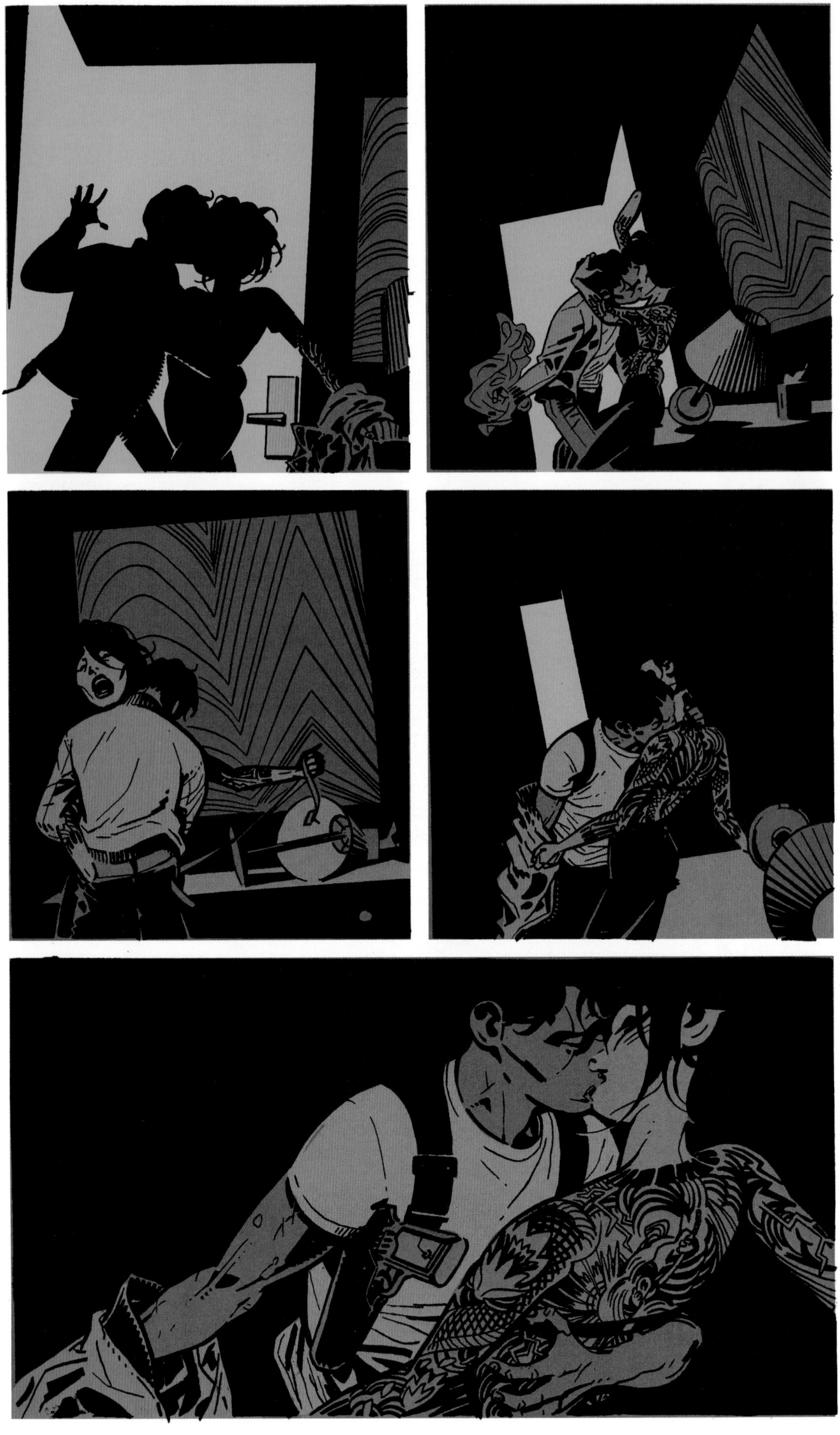

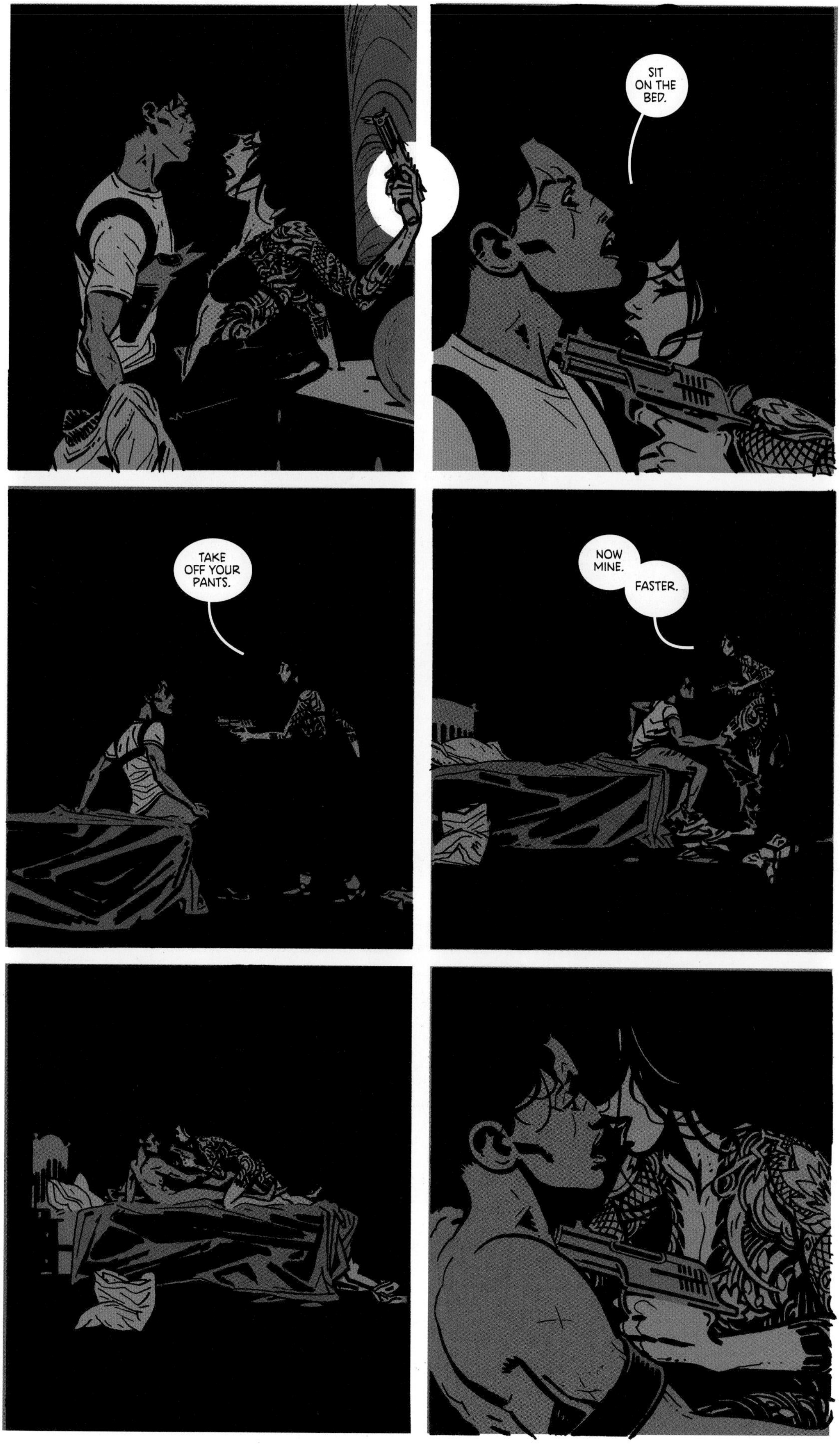
SIT ON THE BED.
TAKE OFF YOUR PANTS.
NOW MINE.
FASTER.

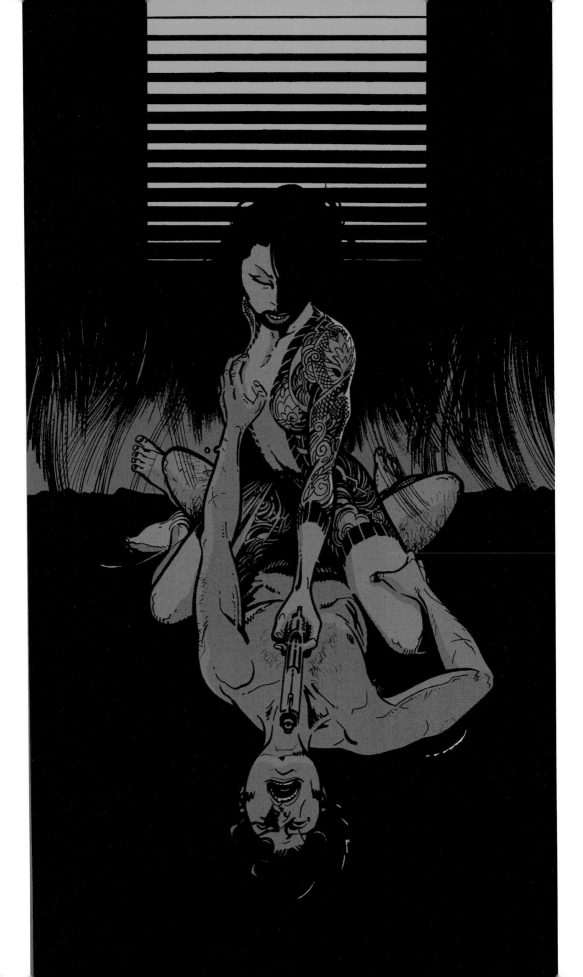

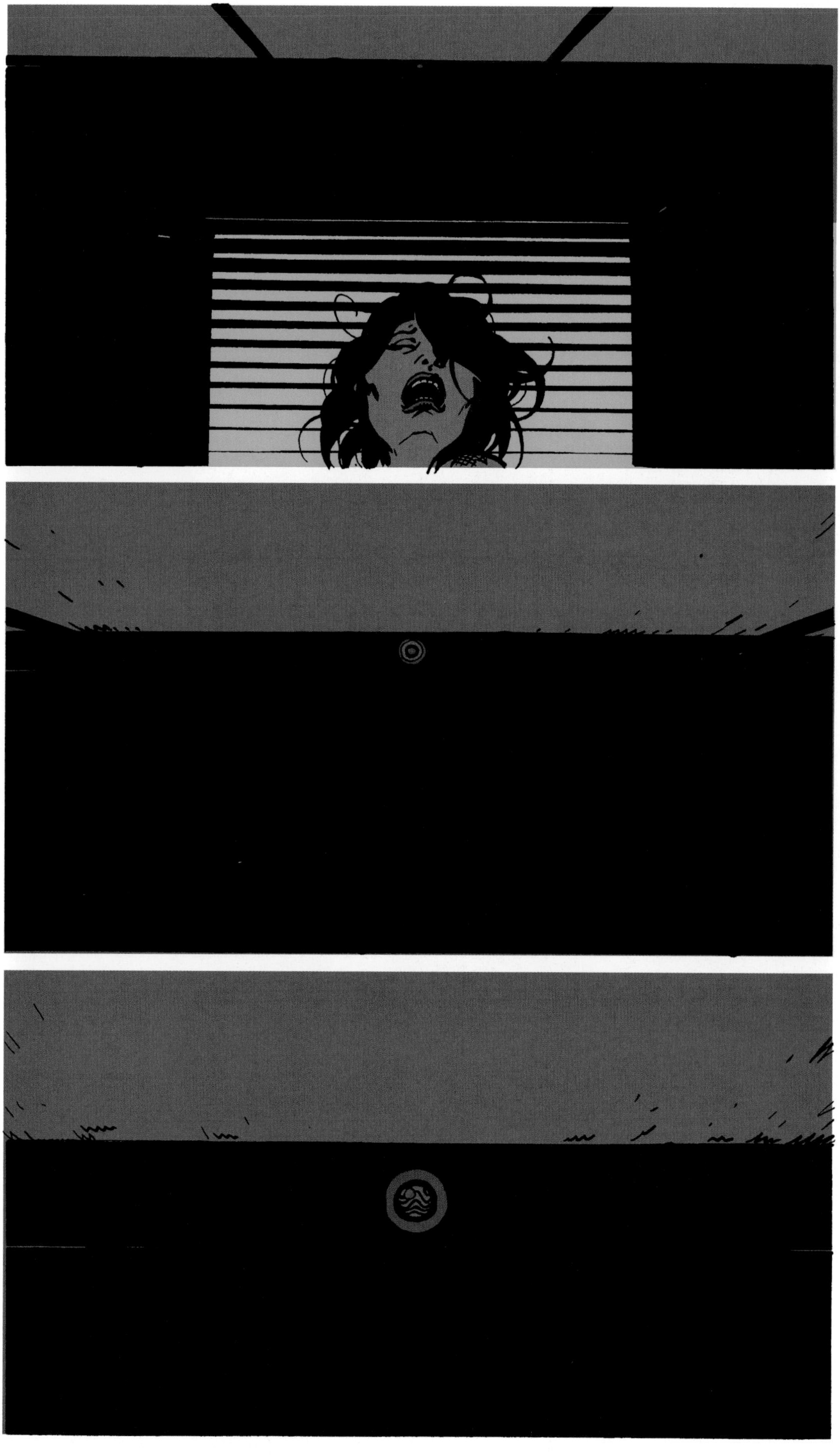

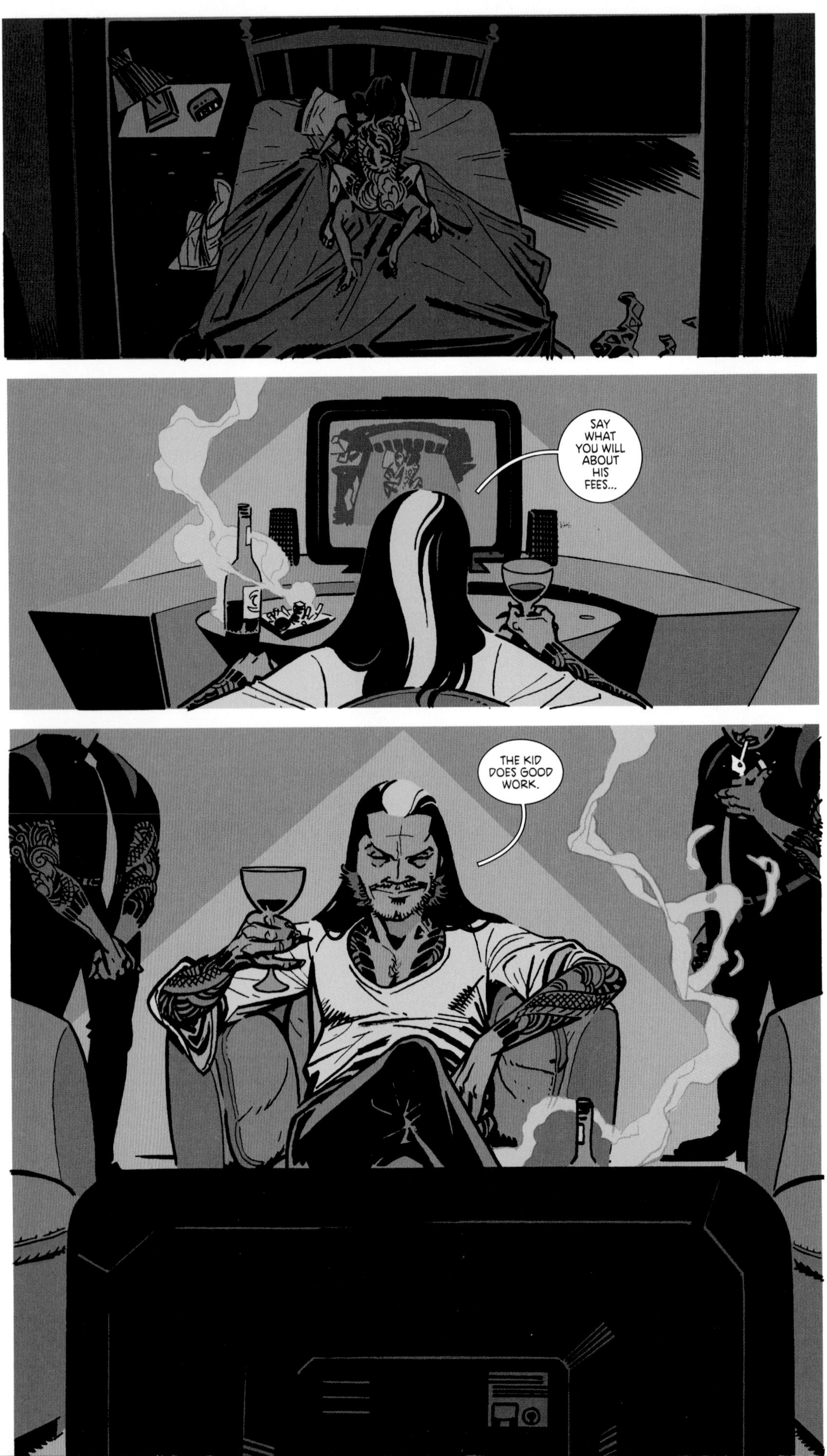
SAY WHAT YOU WILL ABOUT HIS FEES...
THE KID DOES GOOD WORK.

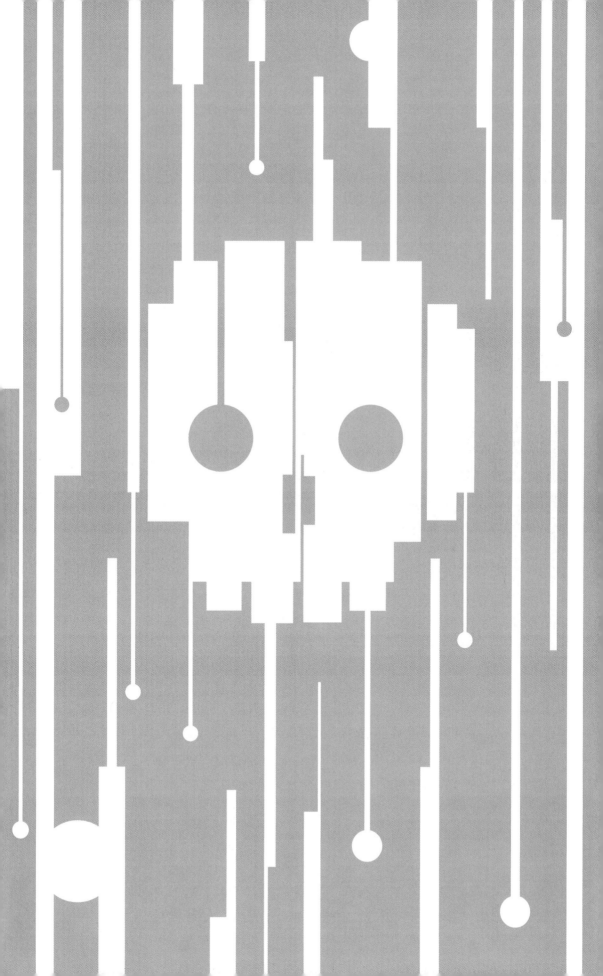

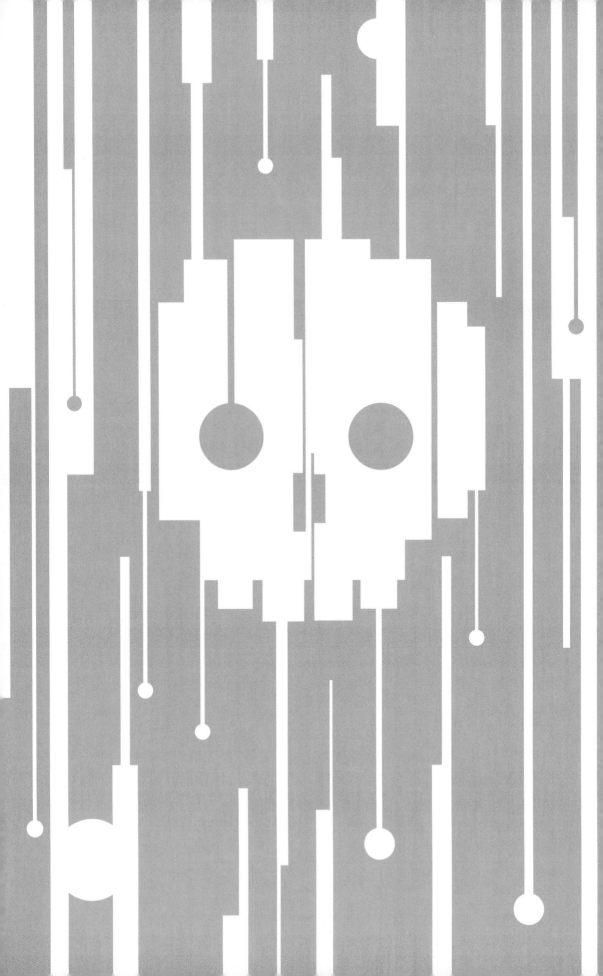

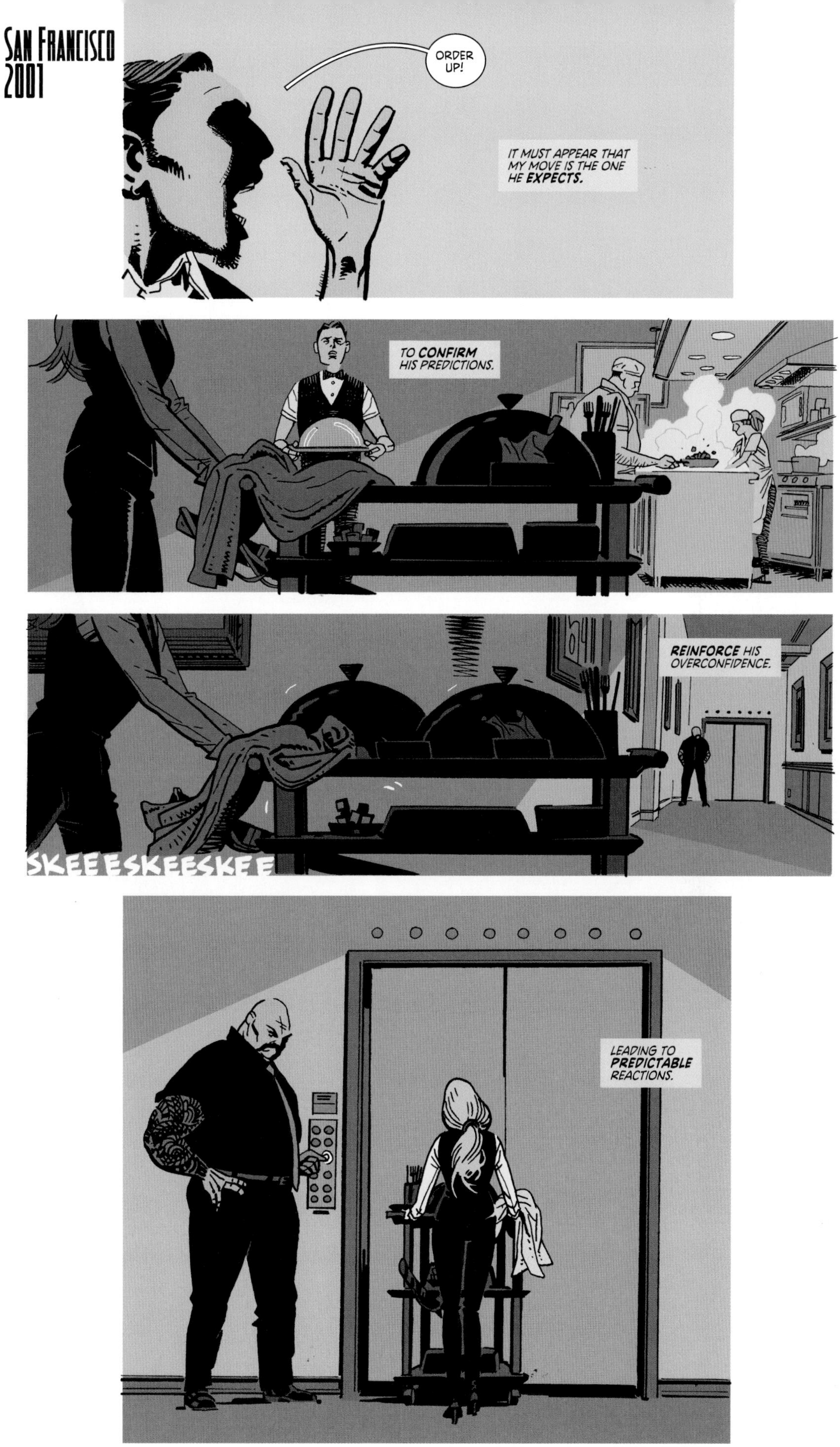
SAN FRANCISCO
2001
ORDER UP!
IT MUST APPEAR THAT MY MOVE IS THE ONE HE EXPECTS.
TO CONFIRM HIS PREDICTIONS.
REINFORCE HIS OVERCONFIDENCE.
SKEEESKEEESKEE
LEADING TO PREDICTABLE REACTIONS.

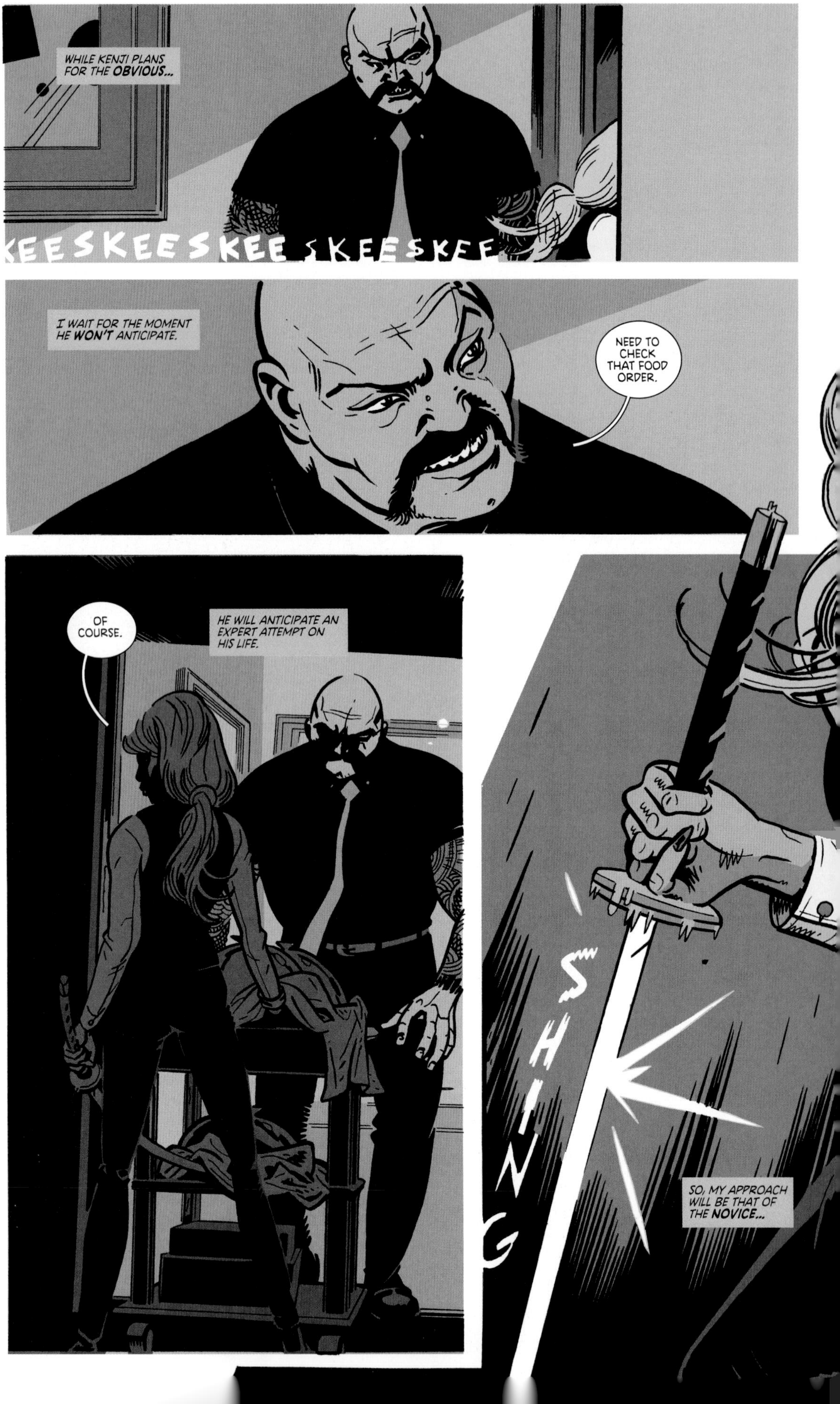
WHILE KENJI PLANS FOR THE **OBVIOUS...**
KEESKEESKEESKEESKEE
I WAIT FOR THE MOMENT HE **WON'T** ANTICIPATE.
NEED TO CHECK THAT FOOD ORDER.
OF COURSE.
HE WILL ANTICIPATE AN EXPERT ATTEMPT ON HIS LIFE.
SHING
SO, MY APPROACH WILL BE THAT OF THE **NOVICE...**

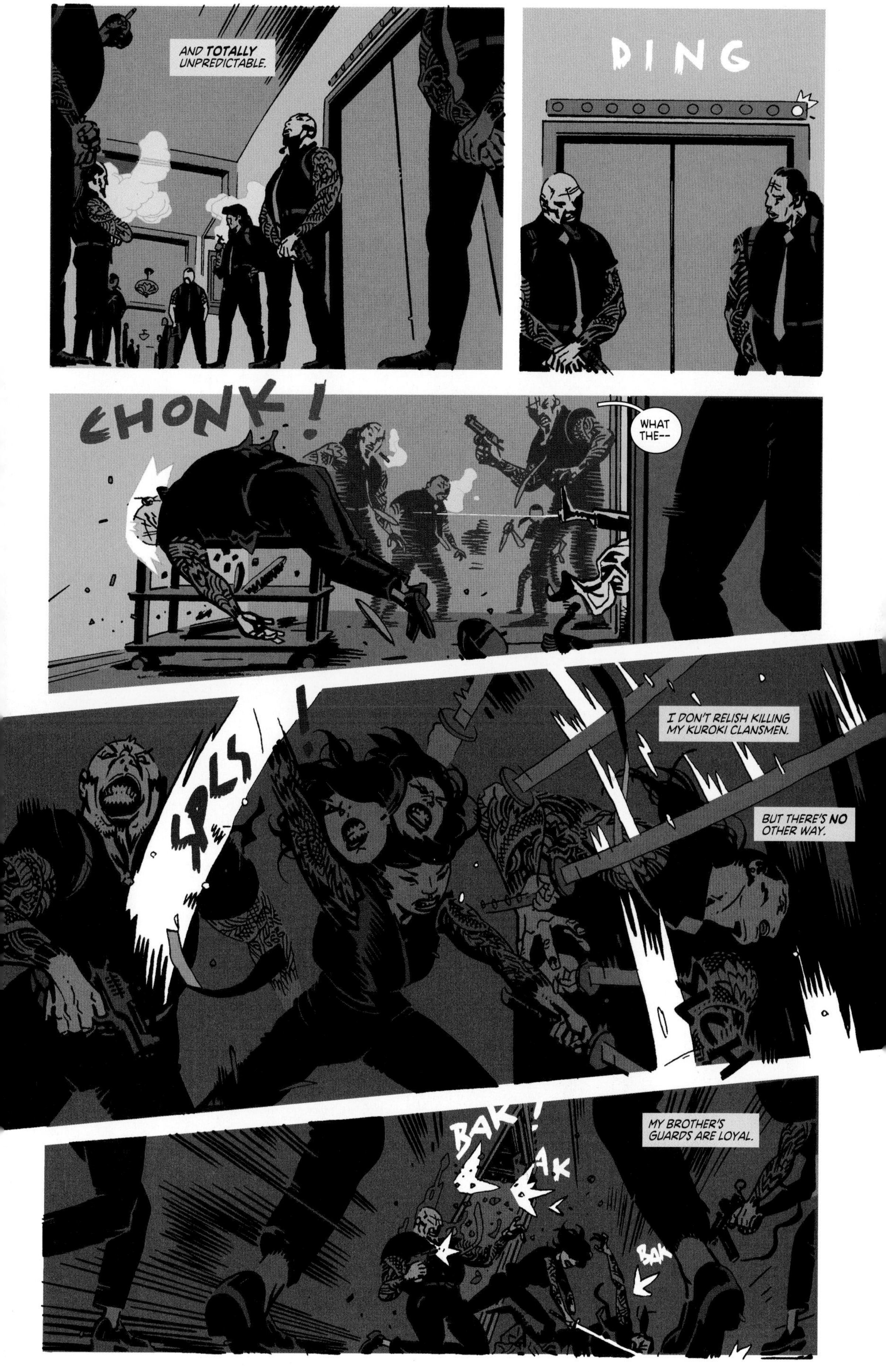
AND TOTALLY UNPREDICTABLE.
DING
CHONK!
WHAT THE--
I DON'T RELISH KILLING MY KUROKI CLANSMEN.
BUT THERE'S NO OTHER WAY.
MY BROTHER'S GUARDS ARE LOYAL.
BAK
BAK

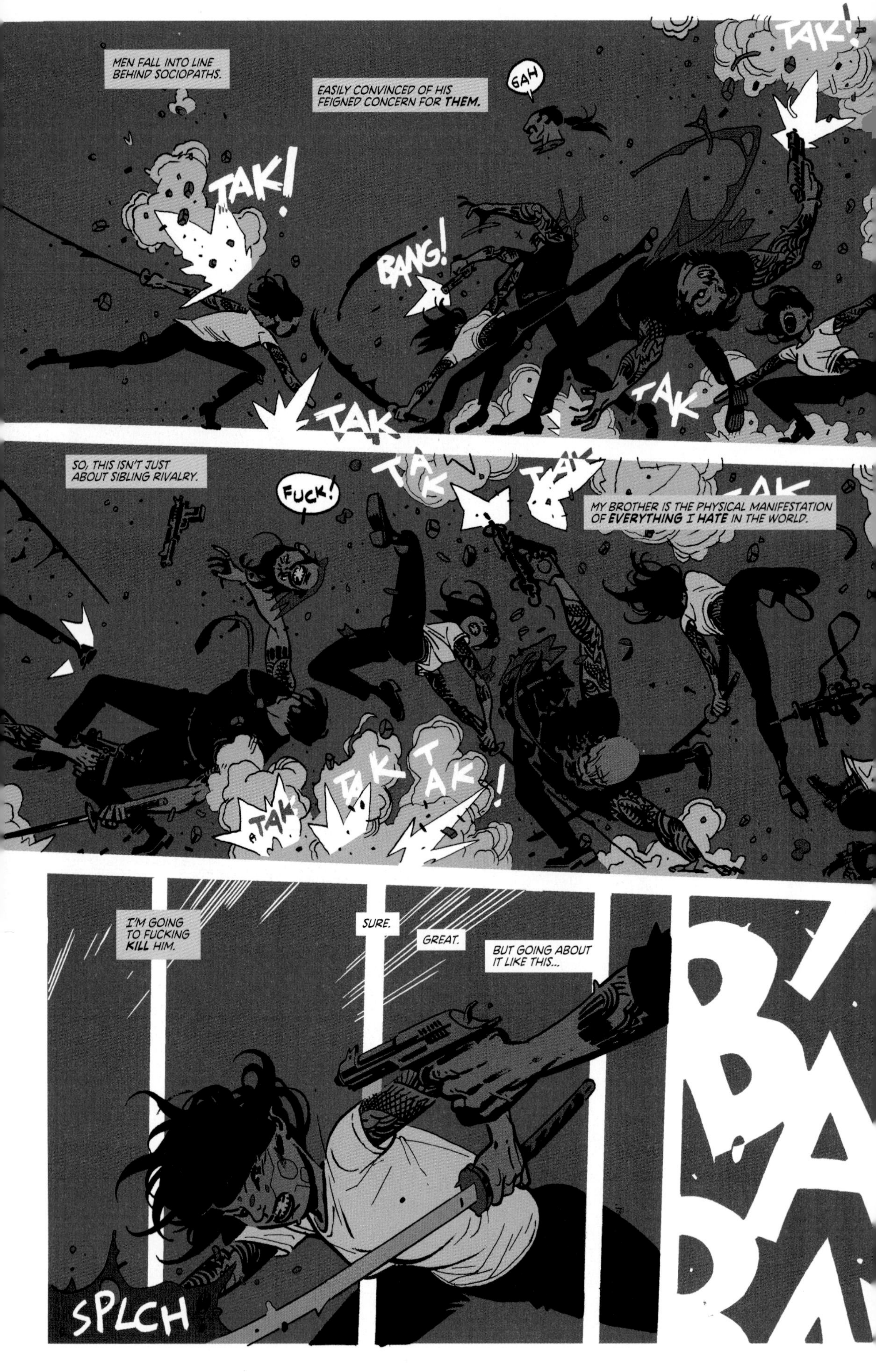
MEN FALL INTO LINE BEHIND SOCIOPATHS.
EASILY CONVINCED OF HIS FEIGNED CONCERN FOR THEM.
GAH
TAK!
TAK!
BANG!
TAK
TAK
SO, THIS ISN'T JUST ABOUT SIBLING RIVALRY.
FUCK!
MY BROTHER IS THE PHYSICAL MANIFESTATION OF EVERYTHING I HATE IN THE WORLD.
TAK
TAK
TAK
TAK!
I'M GOING TO FUCKING KILL HIM.
SURE.
GREAT.
BUT GOING ABOUT IT LIKE THIS...
SPLCH

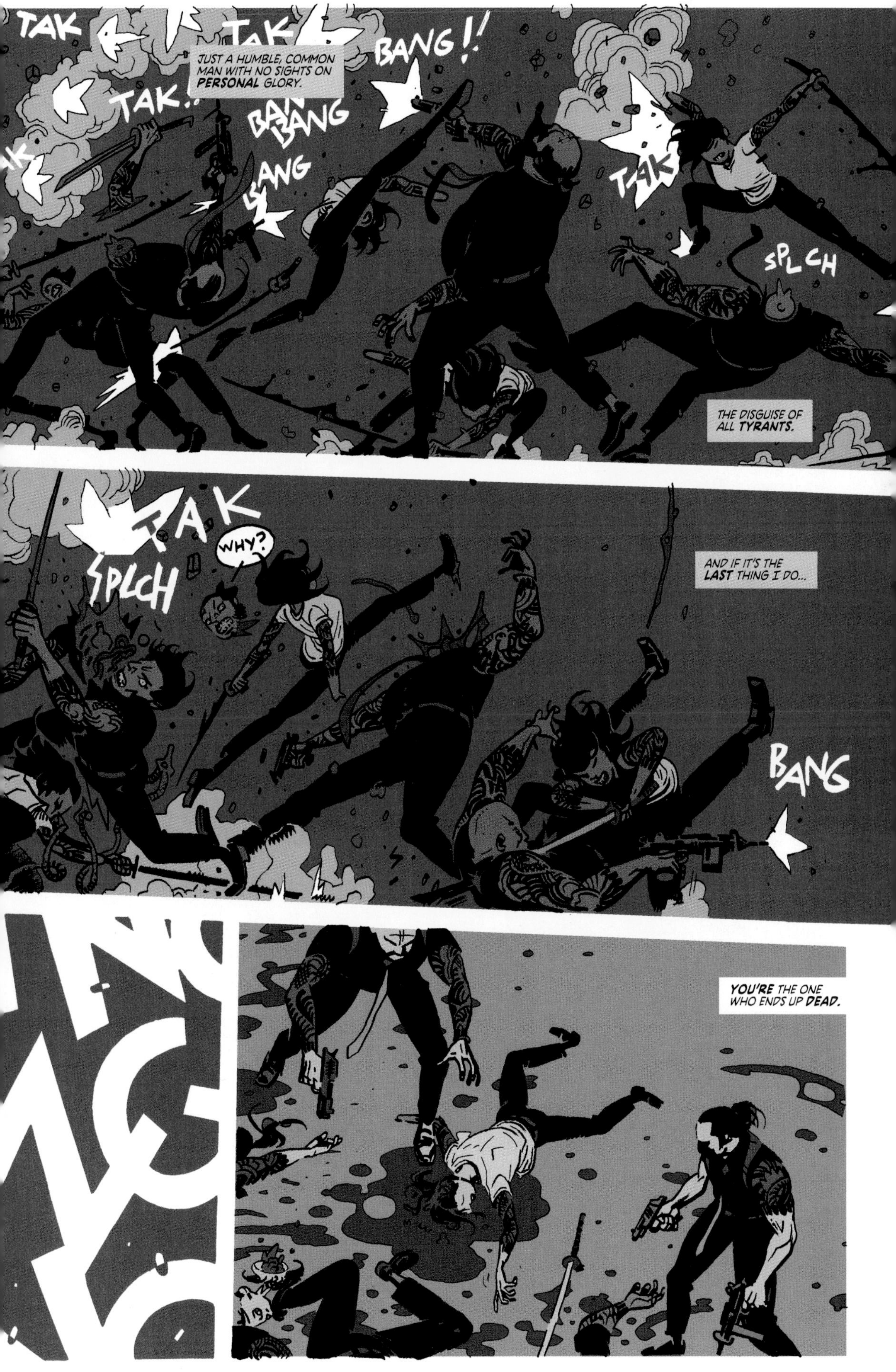
TAK
TAK
JUST A HUMBLE, COMMON MAN WITH NO SIGHTS ON **PERSONAL** GLORY.
BANG!!
TAK!!
BAN BANG
BANG
TAK
SPLCH
THE DISGUISE OF ALL **TYRANTS.**
TAK
SPLCH
WHY?
AND IF IT'S THE **LAST** THING I DO...
BANG
**YOU'RE** THE ONE WHO ENDS UP **DEAD.**

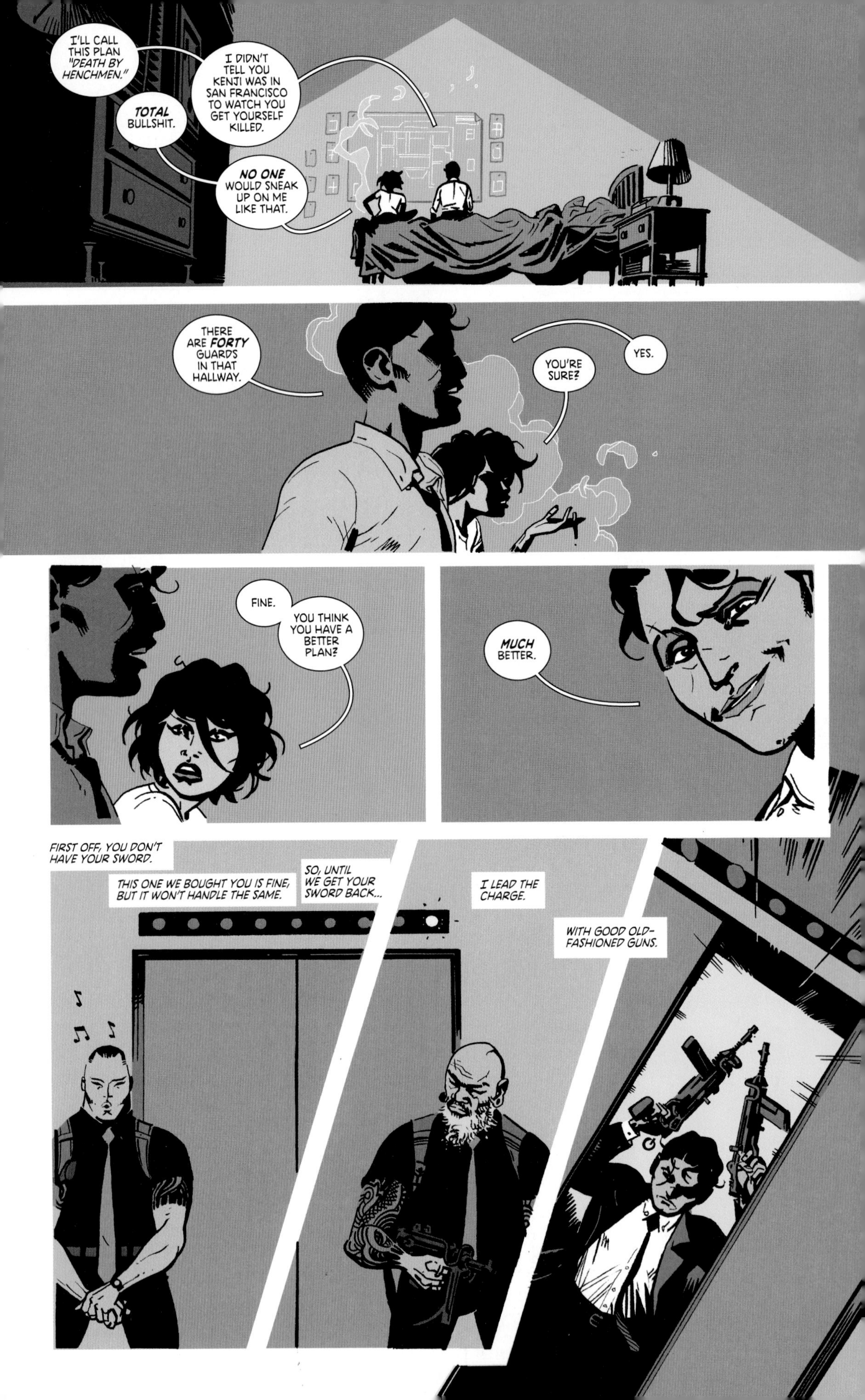
I'LL CALL THIS PLAN "DEATH BY HENCHMEN."
TOTAL BULLSHIT.
I DIDN'T TELL YOU KENJI WAS IN SAN FRANCISCO TO WATCH YOU GET YOURSELF KILLED.
NO ONE WOULD SNEAK UP ON ME LIKE THAT.
THERE ARE FORTY GUARDS IN THAT HALLWAY.
YOU'RE SURE?
YES.
FINE.
YOU THINK YOU HAVE A BETTER PLAN?
MUCH BETTER.
FIRST OFF, YOU DON'T HAVE YOUR SWORD.
THIS ONE WE BOUGHT YOU IS FINE, BUT IT WON'T HANDLE THE SAME.
SO, UNTIL WE GET YOUR SWORD BACK...
I LEAD THE CHARGE.
WITH GOOD OLD-FASHIONED GUNS.

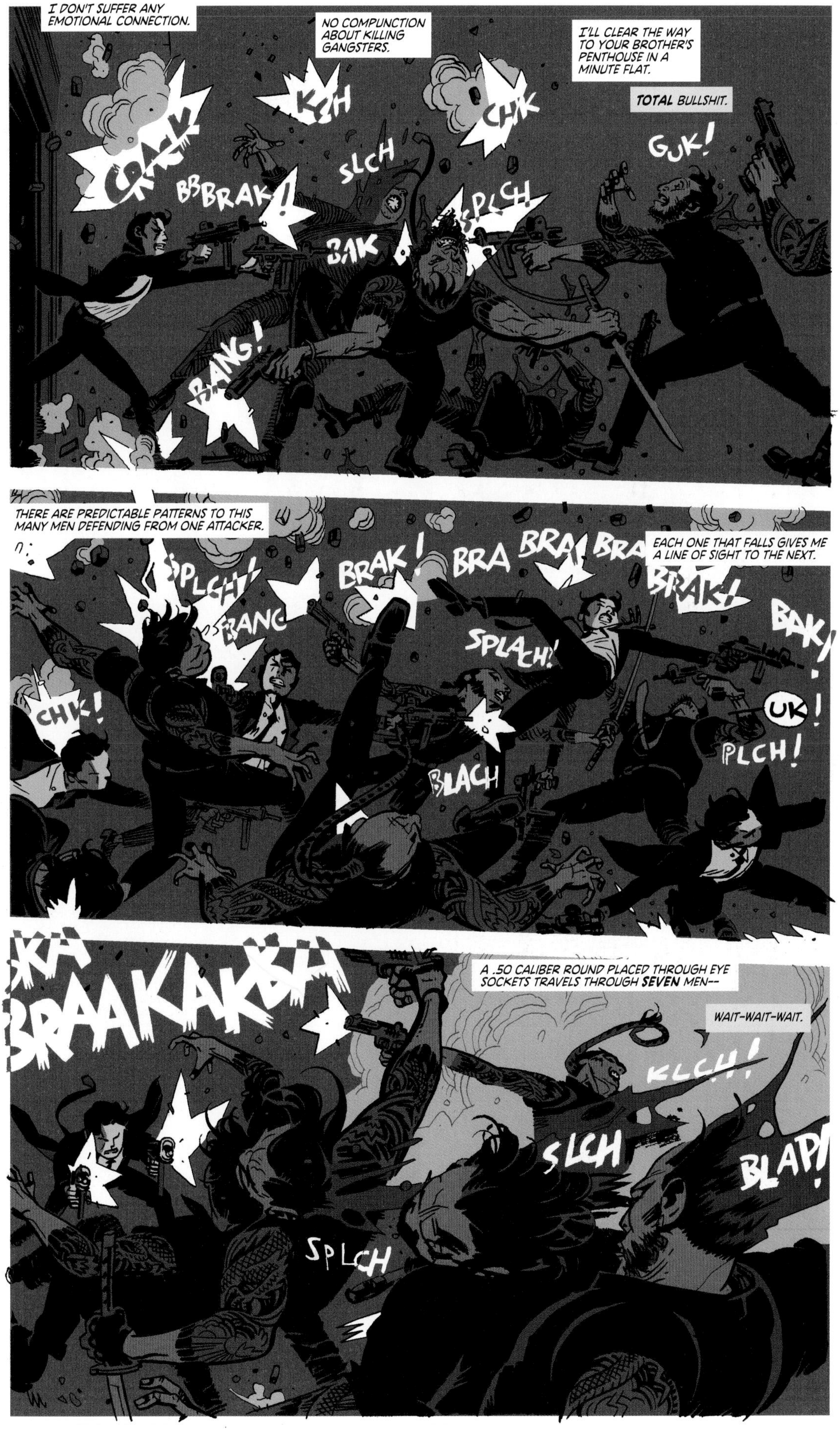
I DON'T SUFFER ANY EMOTIONAL CONNECTION.
NO COMPUNCTION ABOUT KILLING GANGSTERS.
I'LL CLEAR THE WAY TO YOUR BROTHER'S PENTHOUSE IN A MINUTE FLAT.
**TOTAL** BULLSHIT.
CHK
SLCH
BBBRAK!
SPLCH
BAK
GUK!
BANG!
THERE ARE PREDICTABLE PATTERNS TO THIS MANY MEN DEFENDING FROM ONE ATTACKER.
EACH ONE THAT FALLS GIVES ME A LINE OF SIGHT TO THE NEXT.
SPLCH!
BRANG
BRAK!
BRA
BRA
BRA
BRAK!
BAK!
SPLACH!
CHK!
UK!
PLCH!
BLACH
A .50 CALIBER ROUND PLACED THROUGH EYE SOCKETS TRAVELS THROUGH **SEVEN** MEN--
WAIT-WAIT-WAIT.
KLCH!
SLCH
BLAP!
SPLCH

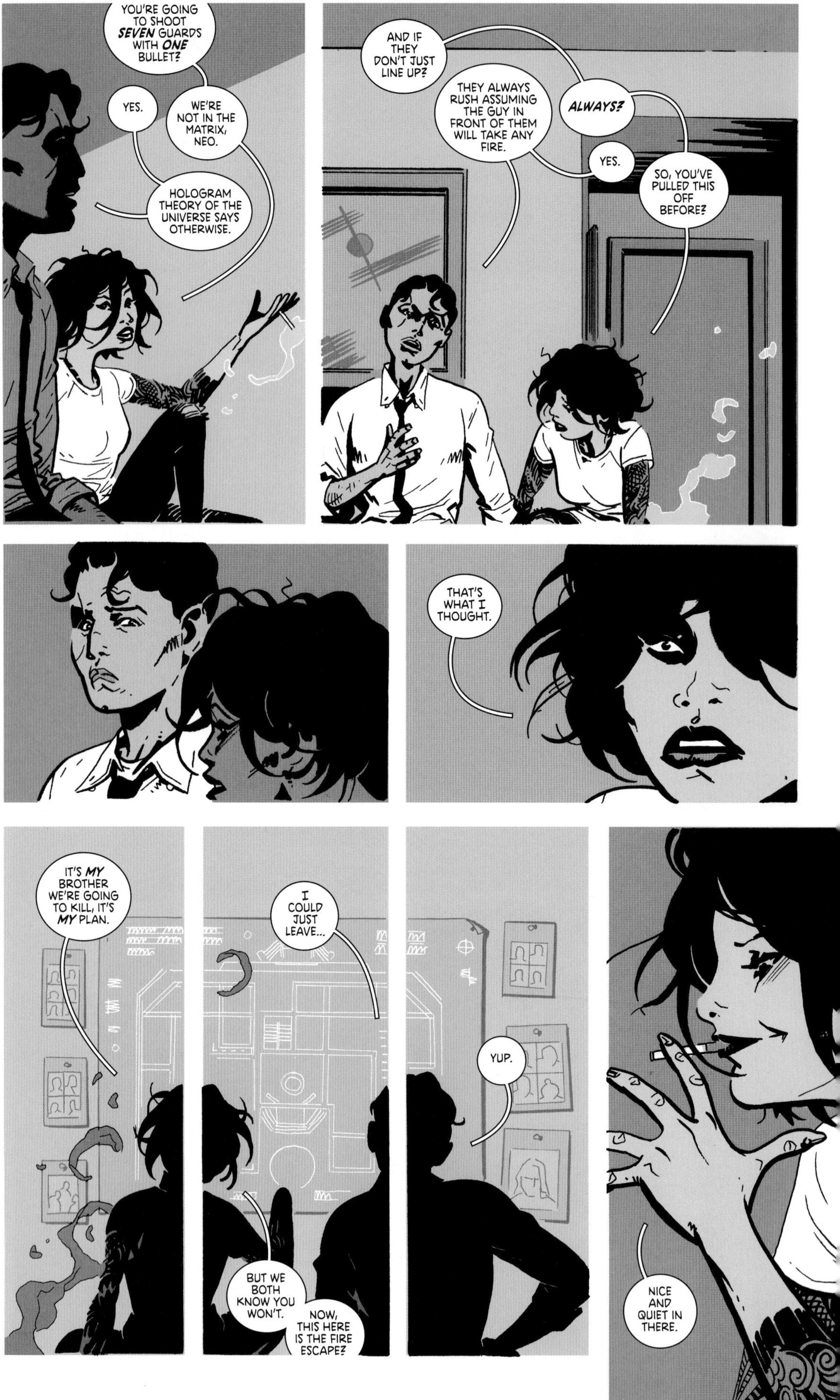
YOU'RE GOING TO SHOOT SEVEN GUARDS WITH ONE BULLET?
YES.
WE'RE NOT IN THE MATRIX, NEO.
HOLOGRAM THEORY OF THE UNIVERSE SAYS OTHERWISE.
AND IF THEY DON'T JUST LINE UP?
THEY ALWAYS RUSH ASSUMING THE GUY IN FRONT OF THEM WILL TAKE ANY FIRE.
ALWAYS?
YES.
SO, YOU'VE PULLED THIS OFF BEFORE?
THAT'S WHAT I THOUGHT.
IT'S MY BROTHER WE'RE GOING TO KILL, IT'S MY PLAN.
I COULD JUST LEAVE...
BUT WE BOTH KNOW YOU WON'T.
NOW, THIS HERE IS THE FIRE ESCAPE?
YUP.
NICE AND QUIET IN THERE.

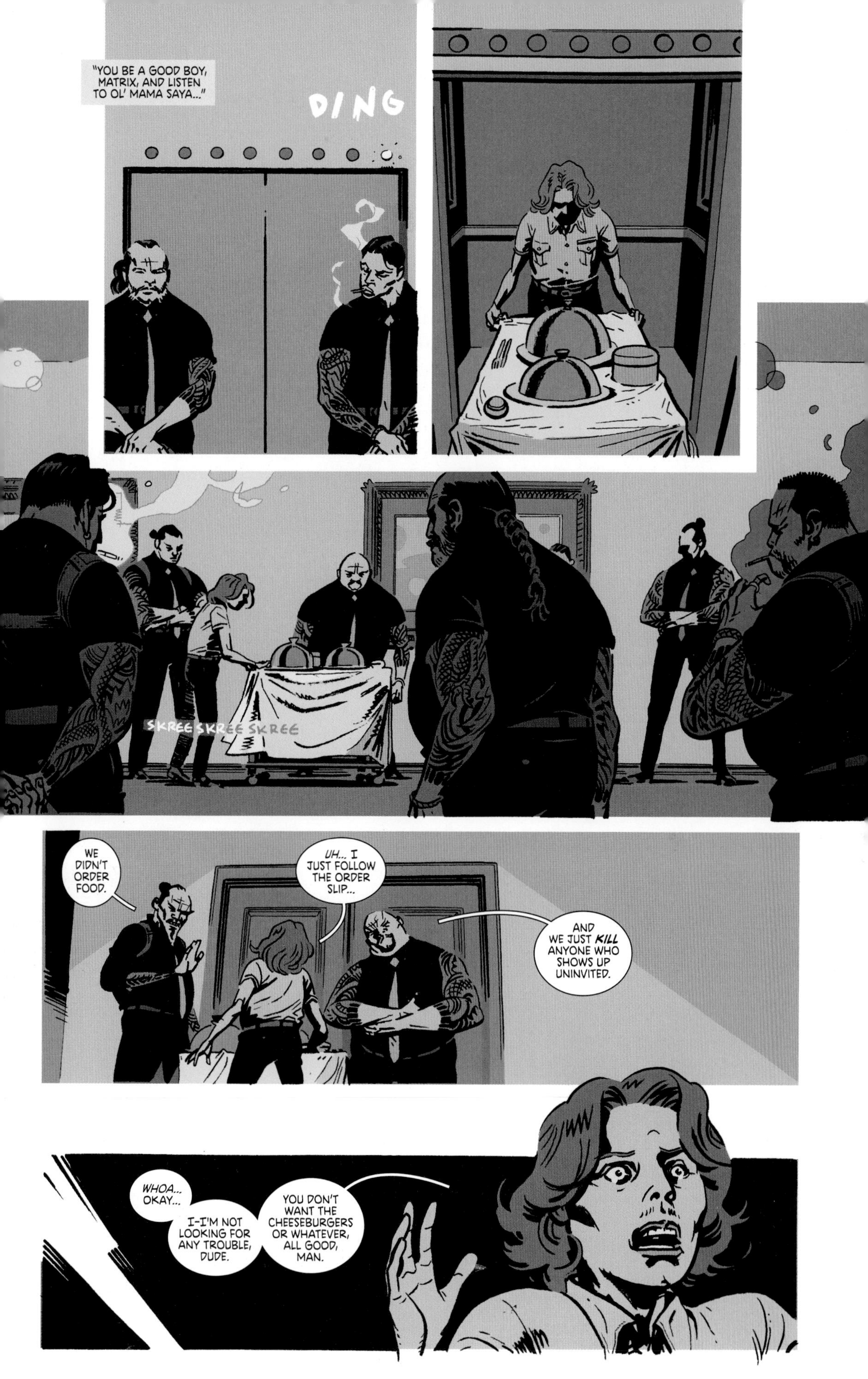
"YOU BE A GOOD BOY, MATRIX, AND LISTEN TO OL' MAMA SAYA..."
DING
SKREE SKREE SKREE
WE DIDN'T ORDER FOOD.
UH... I JUST FOLLOW THE ORDER SLIP...
AND WE JUST KILL ANYONE WHO SHOWS UP UNINVITED.
WHOA... OKAY...
I-I'M NOT LOOKING FOR ANY TROUBLE, DUDE.
YOU DON'T WANT THE CHEESEBURGERS OR WHATEVER, ALL GOOD, MAN.

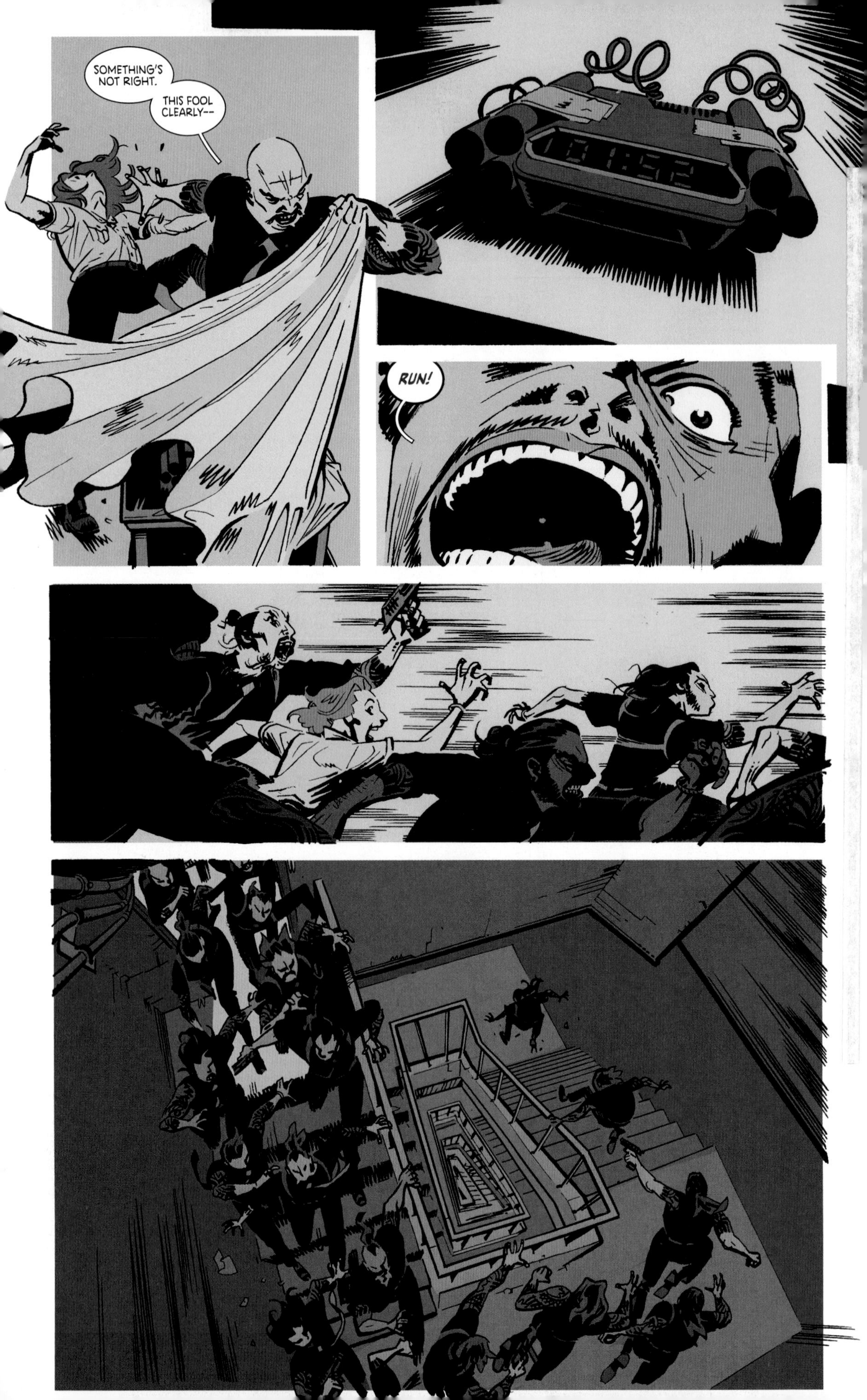
SOMETHING'S NOT RIGHT.
THIS FOOL CLEARLY--
RUN!

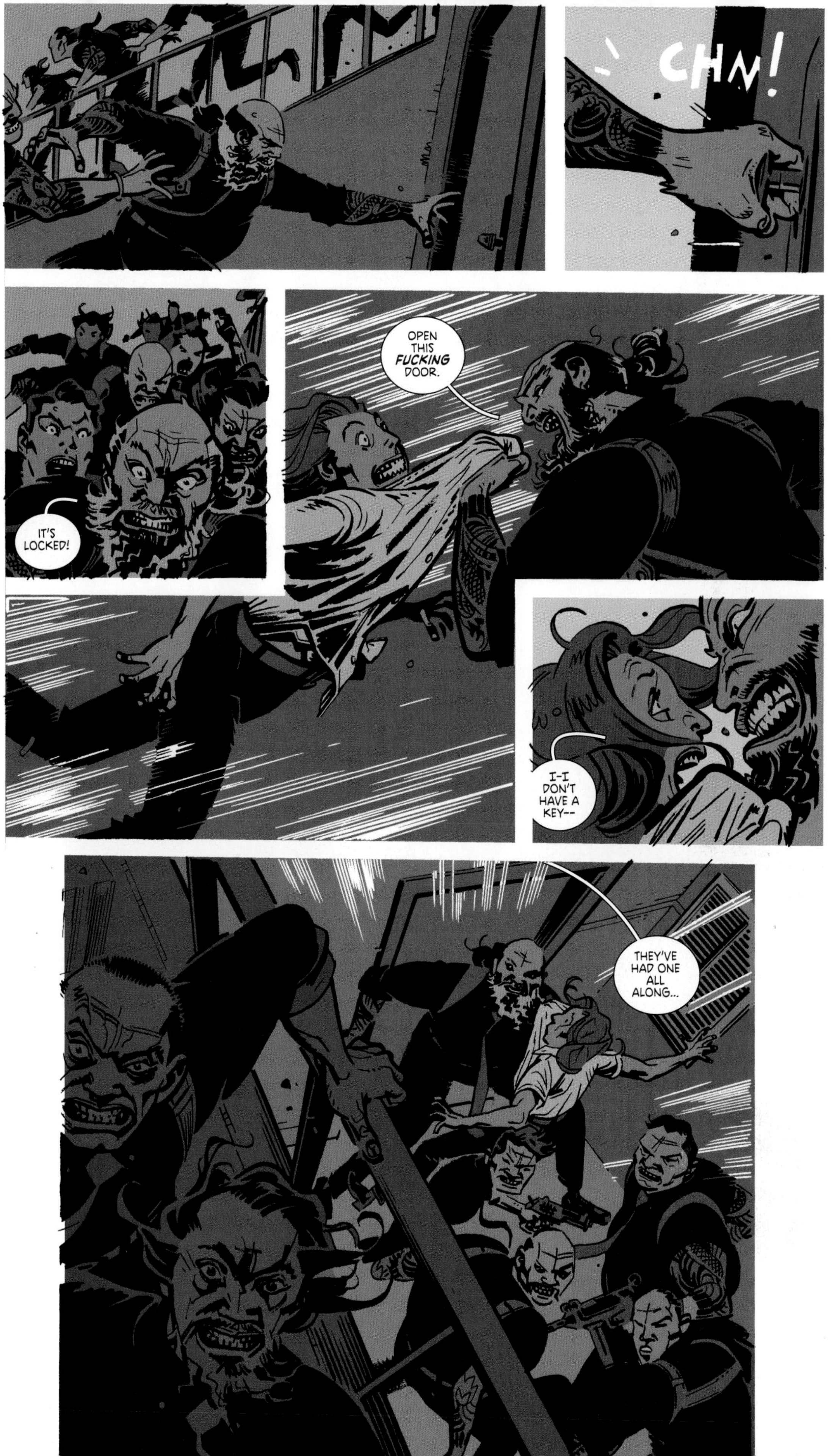
CHN!
IT'S LOCKED!
OPEN THIS FUCKING DOOR.
I-I DON'T HAVE A KEY--
THEY'VE HAD ONE ALL ALONG...

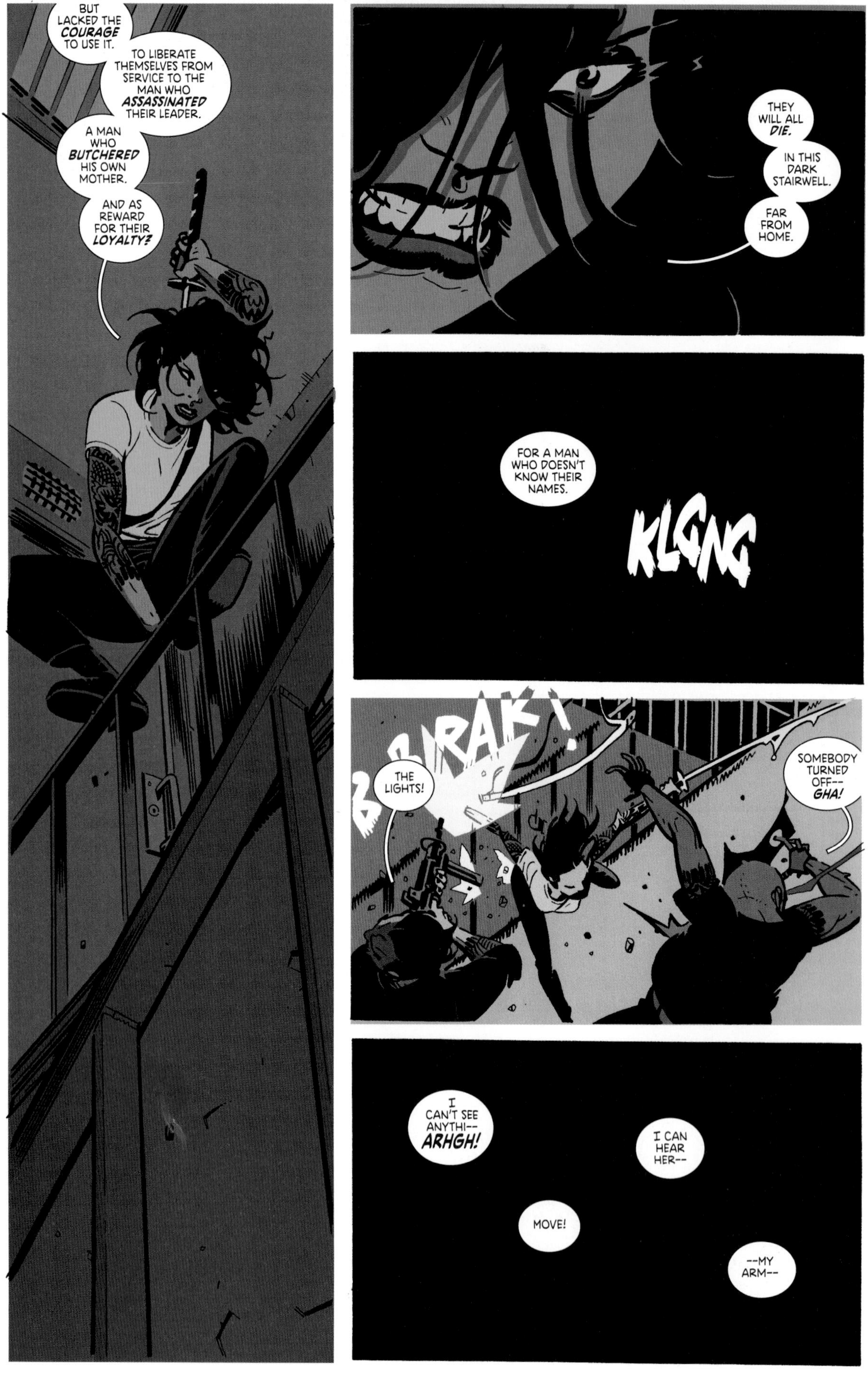

BUT LACKED THE COURAGE TO USE IT.
TO LIBERATE THEMSELVES FROM SERVICE TO THE MAN WHO ASSASSINATED THEIR LEADER.
A MAN WHO BUTCHERED HIS OWN MOTHER.
AND AS REWARD FOR THEIR LOYALTY?
THEY WILL ALL DIE.
IN THIS DARK STAIRWELL.
FAR FROM HOME.
FOR A MAN WHO DOESN'T KNOW THEIR NAMES.
KLGNG
BRRAK!
THE LIGHTS!
SOMEBODY TURNED OFF-- GHA!
I CAN'T SEE ANYTHI-- ARHGH!
I CAN HEAR HER--
MOVE!
--MY ARM--

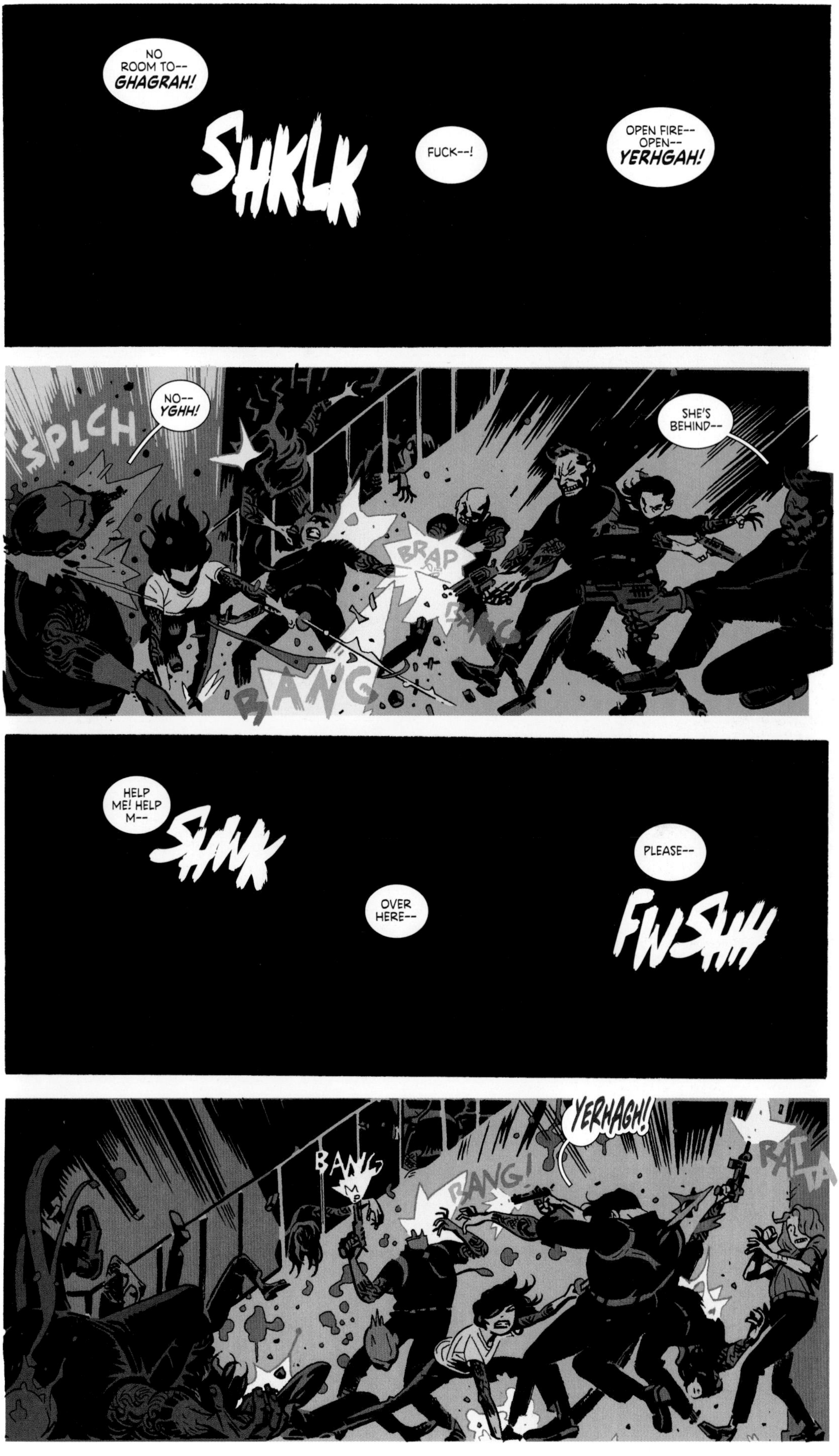
NO ROOM TO-- GHAGRAH!
SHKLK
FUCK--!
OPEN FIRE-- OPEN-- YERHGAH!
SPLCH
NO-- YGHH!
BRAP
BANG
BANG
SHE'S BEHIND--
HELP ME! HELP M--
SHNK
OVER HERE--
PLEASE--
FWSHH
YERHAGH!
BANG!

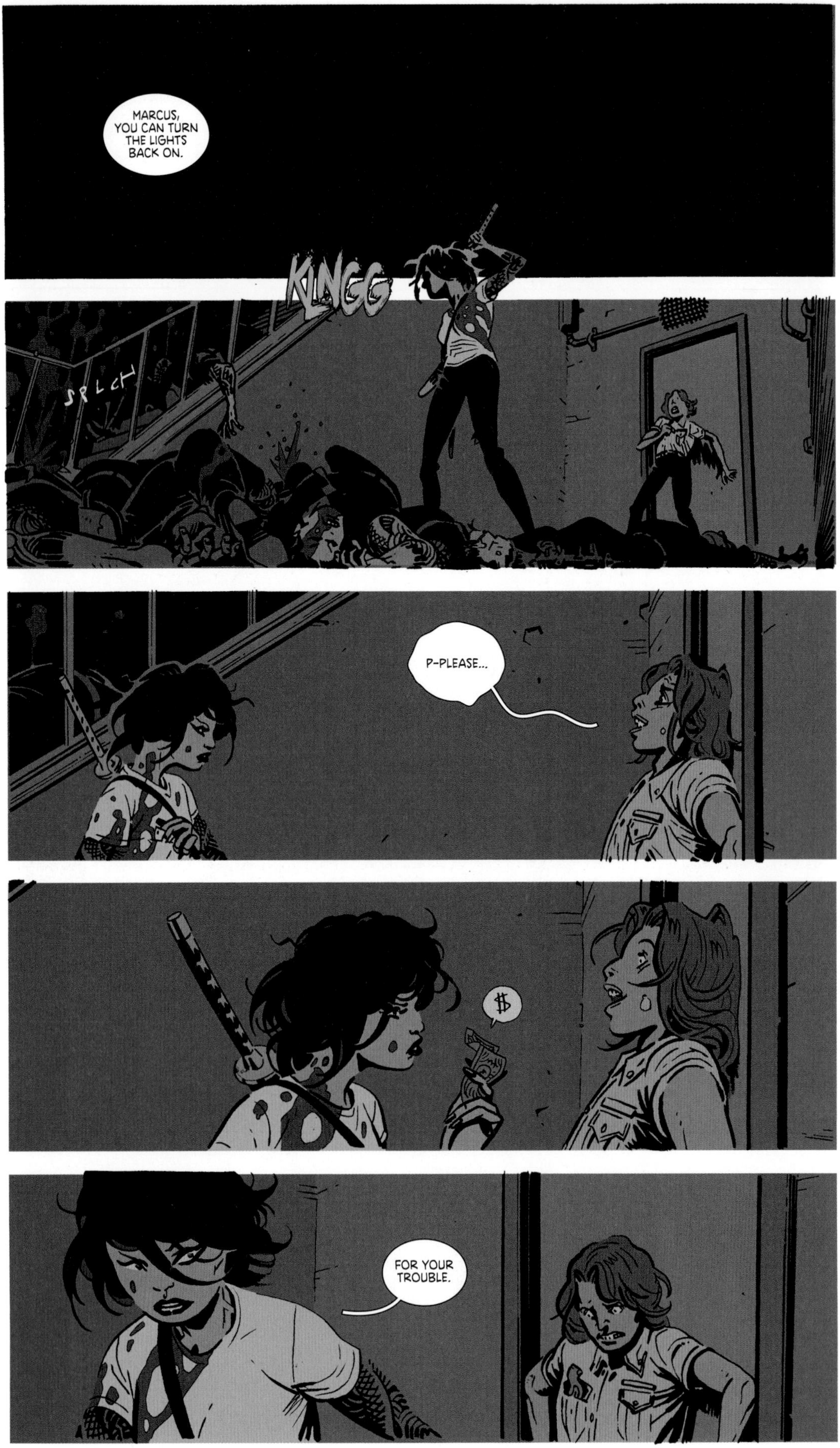
MARCUS, YOU CAN TURN THE LIGHTS BACK ON.
KLNGG
SPLCH
P-PLEASE...
$
FOR YOUR TROUBLE.

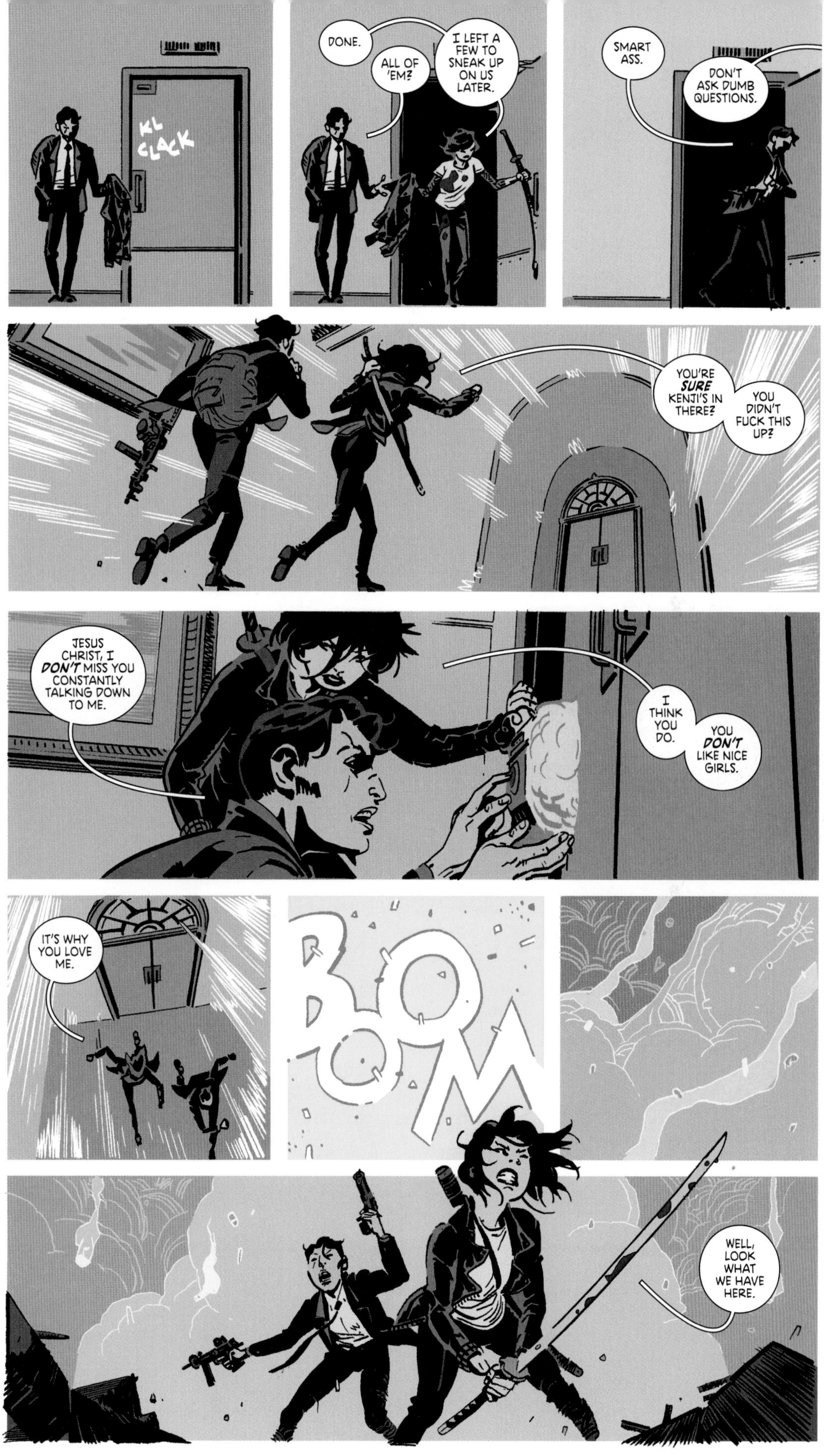
KL CLACK
DONE.
ALL OF 'EM?
I LEFT A FEW TO SNEAK UP ON US LATER.
SMART ASS.
DON'T ASK DUMB QUESTIONS.
YOU'RE SURE KENJI'S IN THERE?
YOU DIDN'T FUCK THIS UP?
JESUS CHRIST, I DON'T MISS YOU CONSTANTLY TALKING DOWN TO ME.
I THINK YOU DO.
YOU DON'T LIKE NICE GIRLS.
IT'S WHY YOU LOVE ME.
BOOM
WELL, LOOK WHAT WE HAVE HERE.

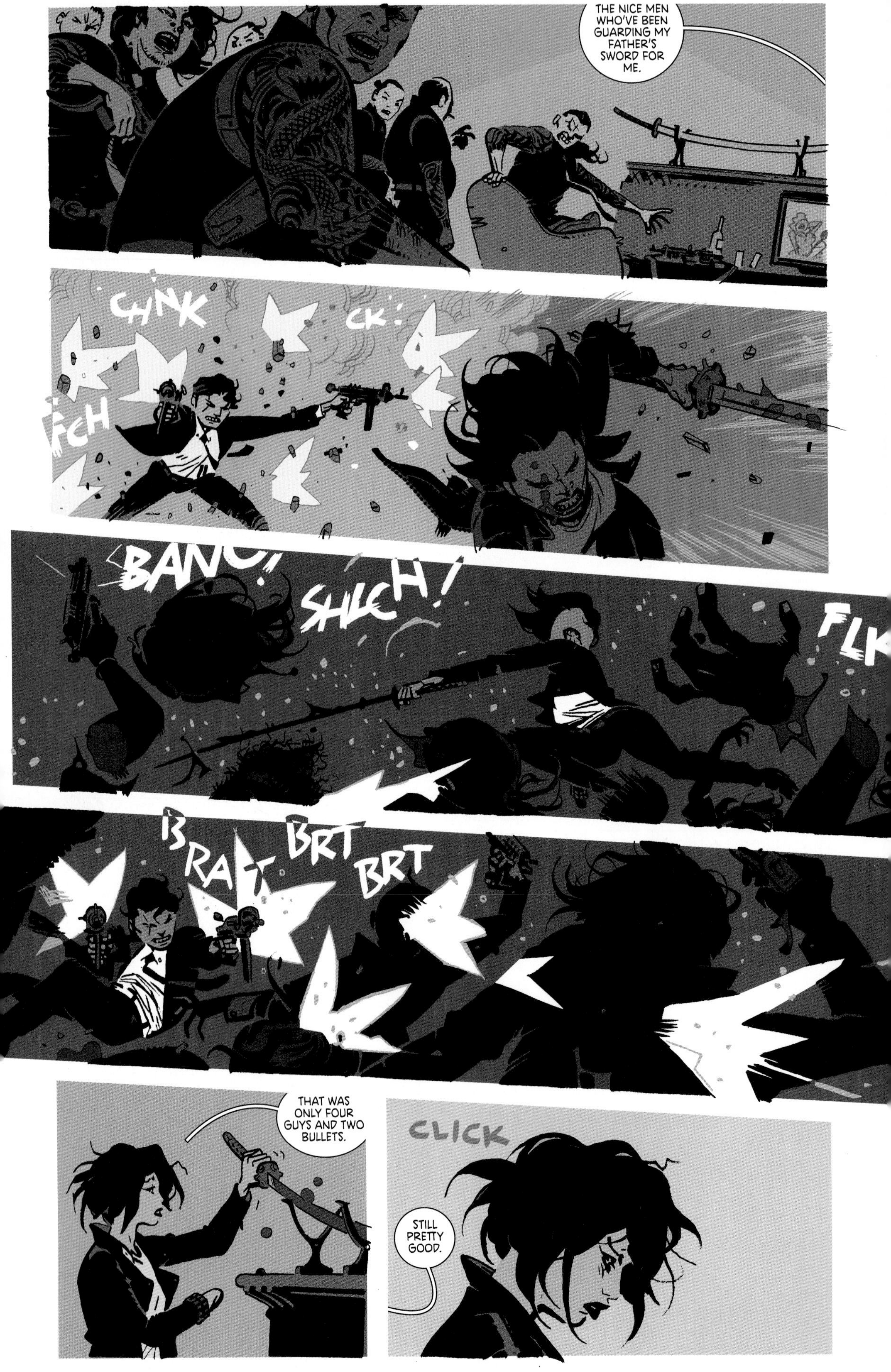
THE NICE MEN WHO'VE BEEN GUARDING MY FATHER'S SWORD FOR ME.
CHINK
CK!
FCH
BANG!
SHLCH!
FLK
BRAT
BRT
BRT
THAT WAS ONLY FOUR GUYS AND TWO BULLETS.
CLICK
STILL PRETTY GOOD.

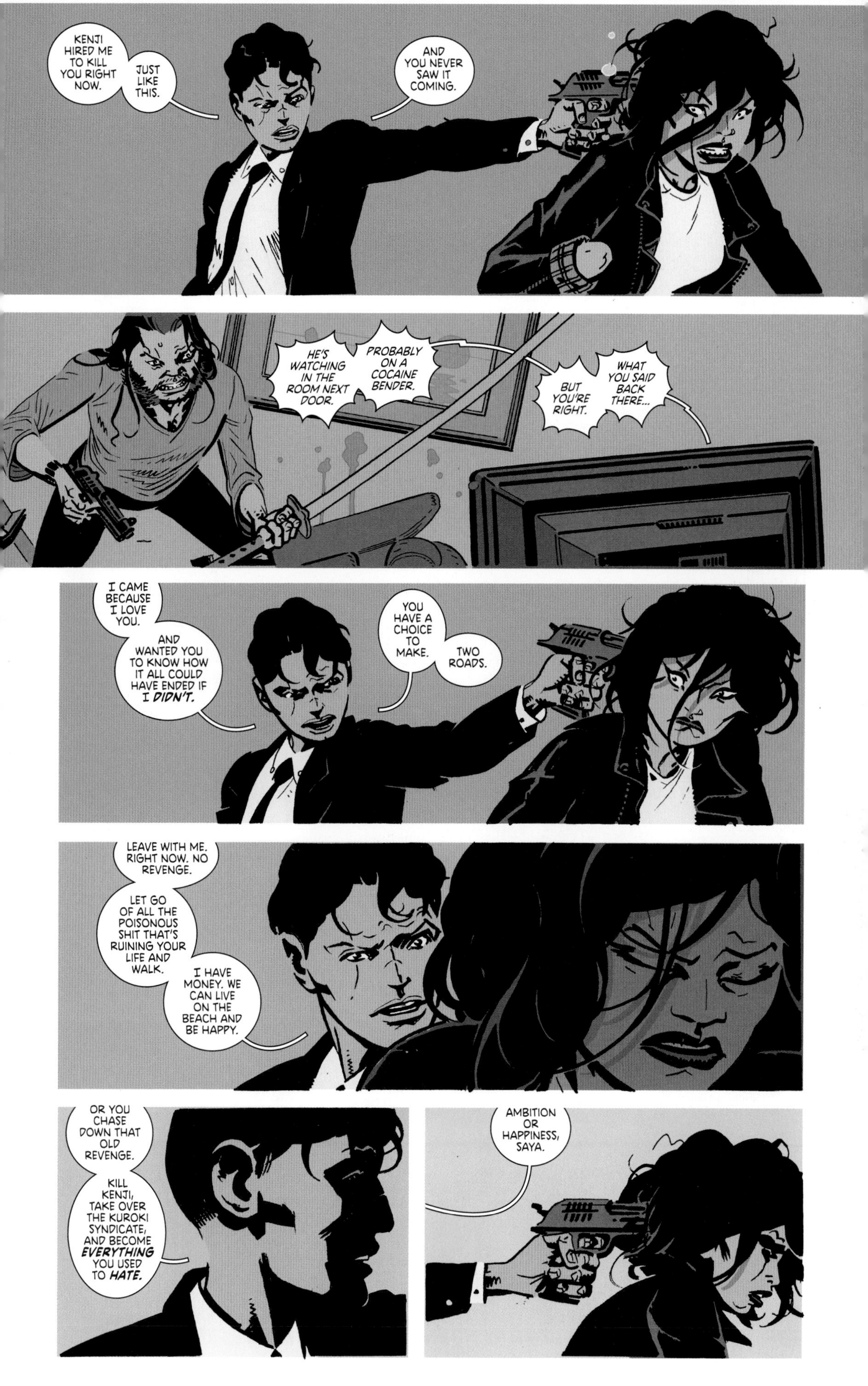
KENJI HIRED ME TO KILL YOU RIGHT NOW.
JUST LIKE THIS.
AND YOU NEVER SAW IT COMING.
HE'S WATCHING IN THE ROOM NEXT DOOR.
PROBABLY ON A COCAINE BENDER.
BUT YOU'RE RIGHT.
WHAT YOU SAID BACK THERE...
I CAME BECAUSE I LOVE YOU.
AND WANTED YOU TO KNOW HOW IT ALL COULD HAVE ENDED IF I *DIDN'T.*
YOU HAVE A CHOICE TO MAKE.
TWO ROADS.
LEAVE WITH ME. RIGHT NOW. NO REVENGE.
LET GO OF ALL THE POISONOUS SHIT THAT'S RUINING YOUR LIFE AND WALK.
I HAVE MONEY. WE CAN LIVE ON THE BEACH AND BE HAPPY.
OR YOU CHASE DOWN THAT OLD REVENGE.
KILL KENJI, TAKE OVER THE KUROKI SYNDICATE, AND BECOME ***EVERYTHING*** YOU USED TO ***HATE.***
AMBITION OR HAPPINESS, SAYA.

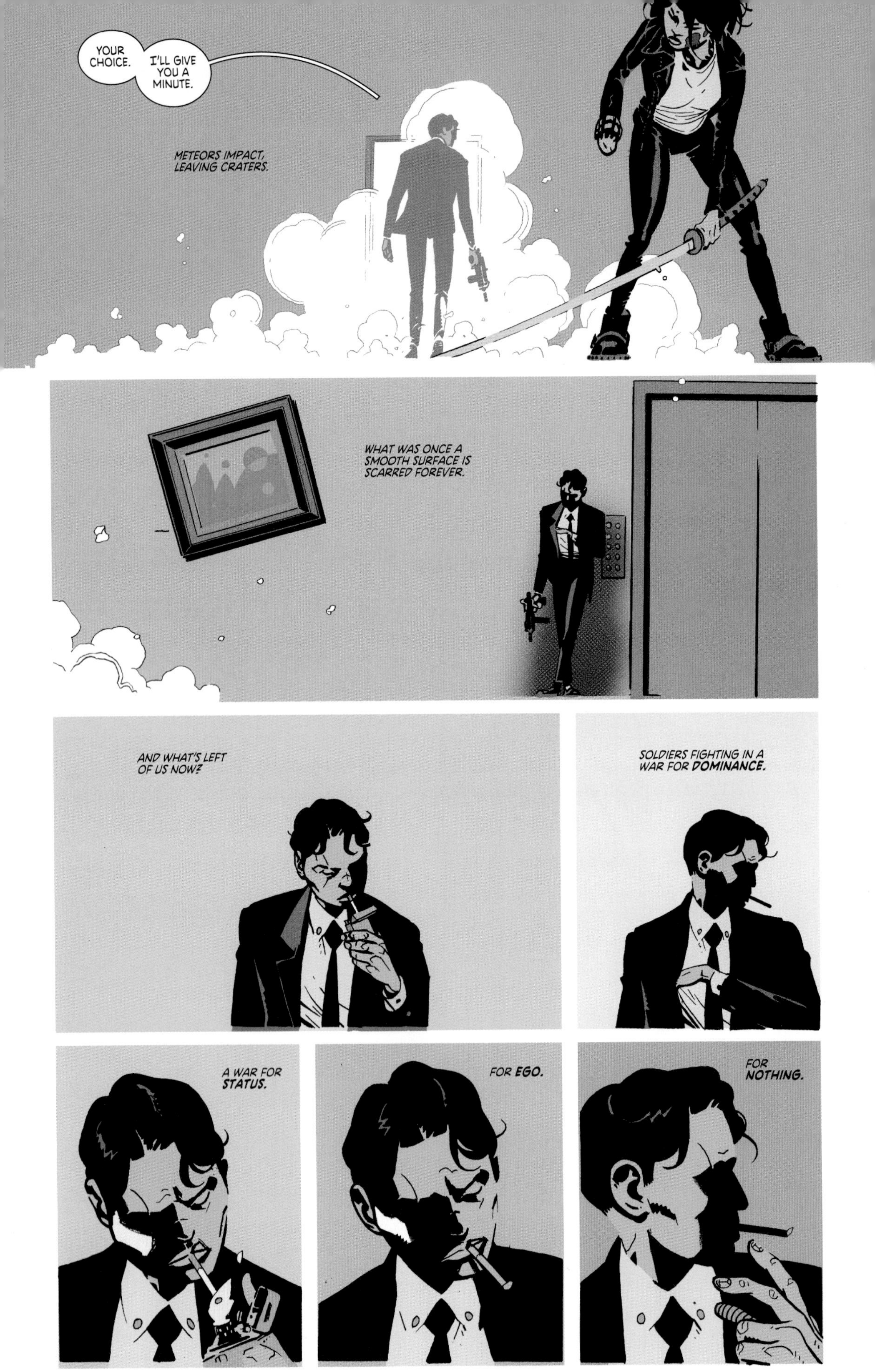
YOUR CHOICE.
I'LL GIVE YOU A MINUTE.
METEORS IMPACT, LEAVING CRATERS.
WHAT WAS ONCE A SMOOTH SURFACE IS SCARRED FOREVER.
AND WHAT'S LEFT OF US NOW?
SOLDIERS FIGHTING IN A WAR FOR DOMINANCE.
A WAR FOR STATUS.
FOR EGO.
FOR NOTHING.

EXHAUSTEDLY RUNNING A RACE STARTED A MILLION YEARS AGO.

BY A YOUNGER PERSON.

A *MUCH* DIFFERENT PERSON.

TO WIN A HEART-SHAPED AWARD.

TO DISPROVE EVERY NEGATIVE VOICE.

AND WHEN **ONE** SINGULAR DESIRE DRIVES US FOR **SO LONG**...

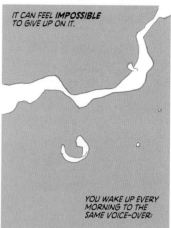

IT CAN FEEL **IMPOSSIBLE** TO GIVE UP ON IT.

YOU WAKE UP EVERY MORNING TO THE SAME VOICE-OVER:

"**WHAT** ARE YOU FIGHTING FOR?"

"*DO* YOU STILL CARE ABOUT **ANY** OF THIS?"

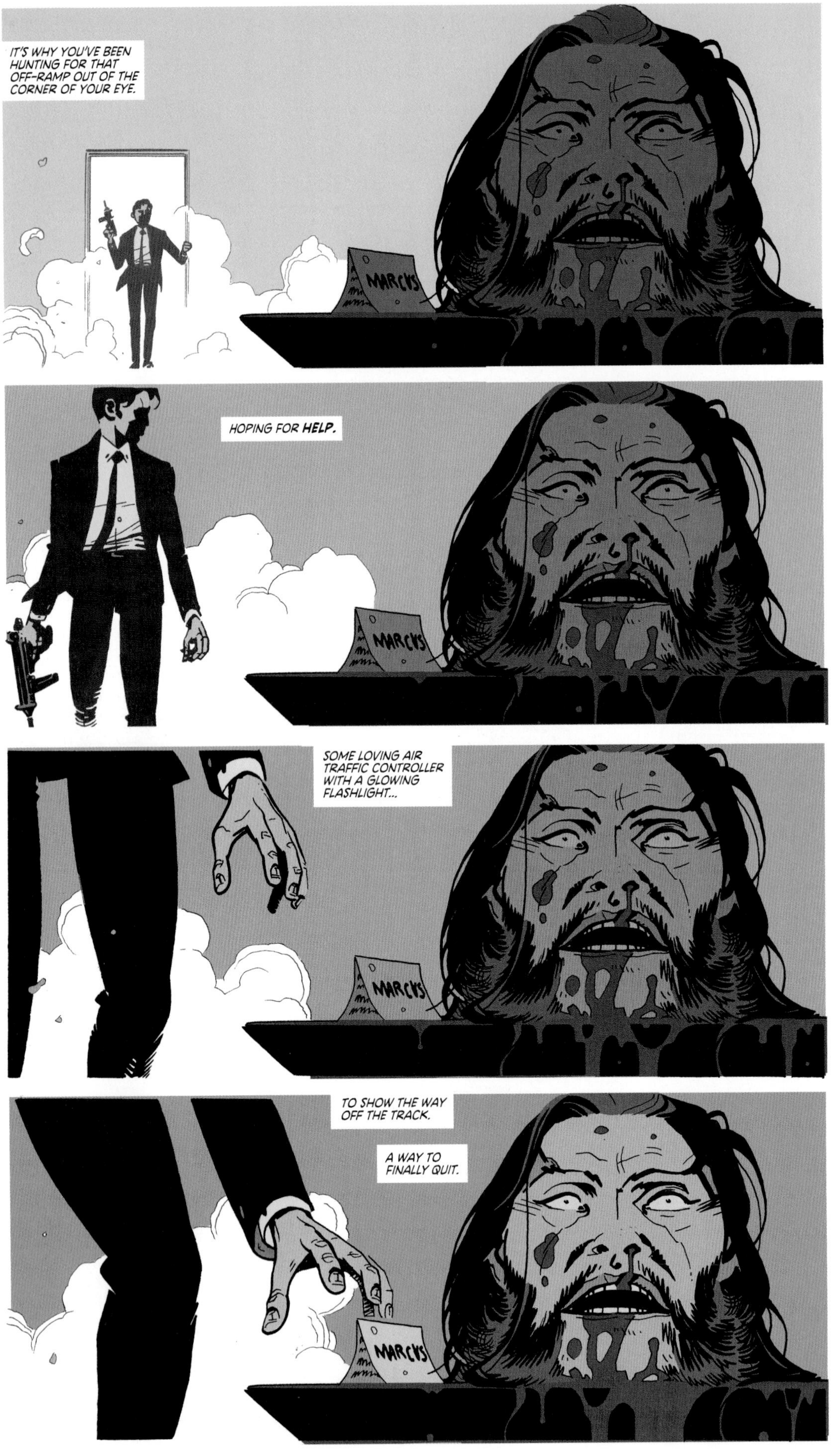
IT'S WHY YOU'VE BEEN HUNTING FOR THAT OFF-RAMP OUT OF THE CORNER OF YOUR EYE.
MARCUS
HOPING FOR **HELP.**
MARCUS
SOME LOVING AIR TRAFFIC CONTROLLER WITH A GLOWING FLASHLIGHT...
MARCUS
TO SHOW THE WAY OFF THE TRACK.
A WAY TO FINALLY QUIT.
MARCUS

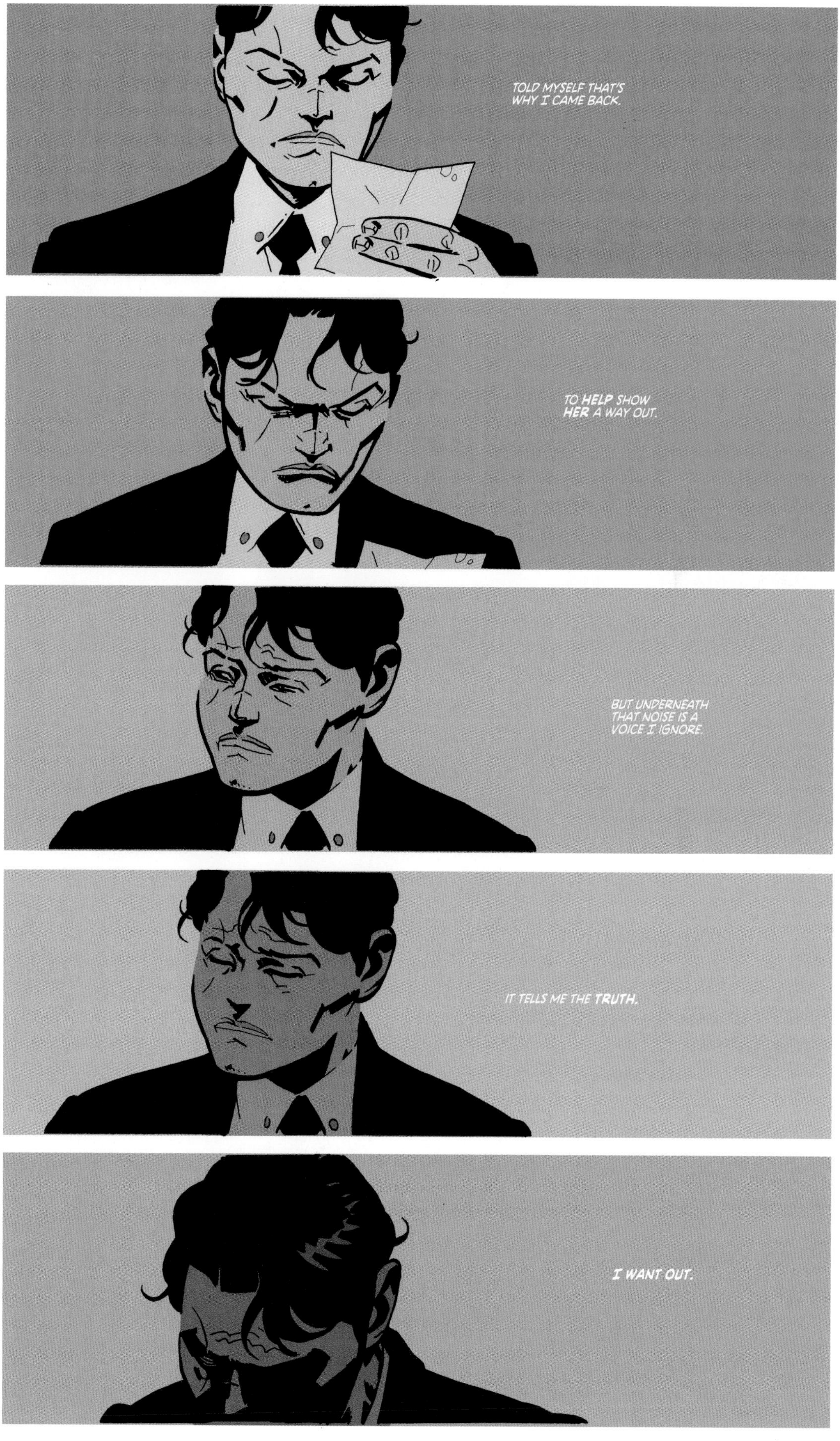
TOLD MYSELF THAT'S WHY I CAME BACK.
TO HELP SHOW HER A WAY OUT.
BUT UNDERNEATH THAT NOISE IS A VOICE I IGNORE.
IT TELLS ME THE TRUTH.
I WANT OUT.

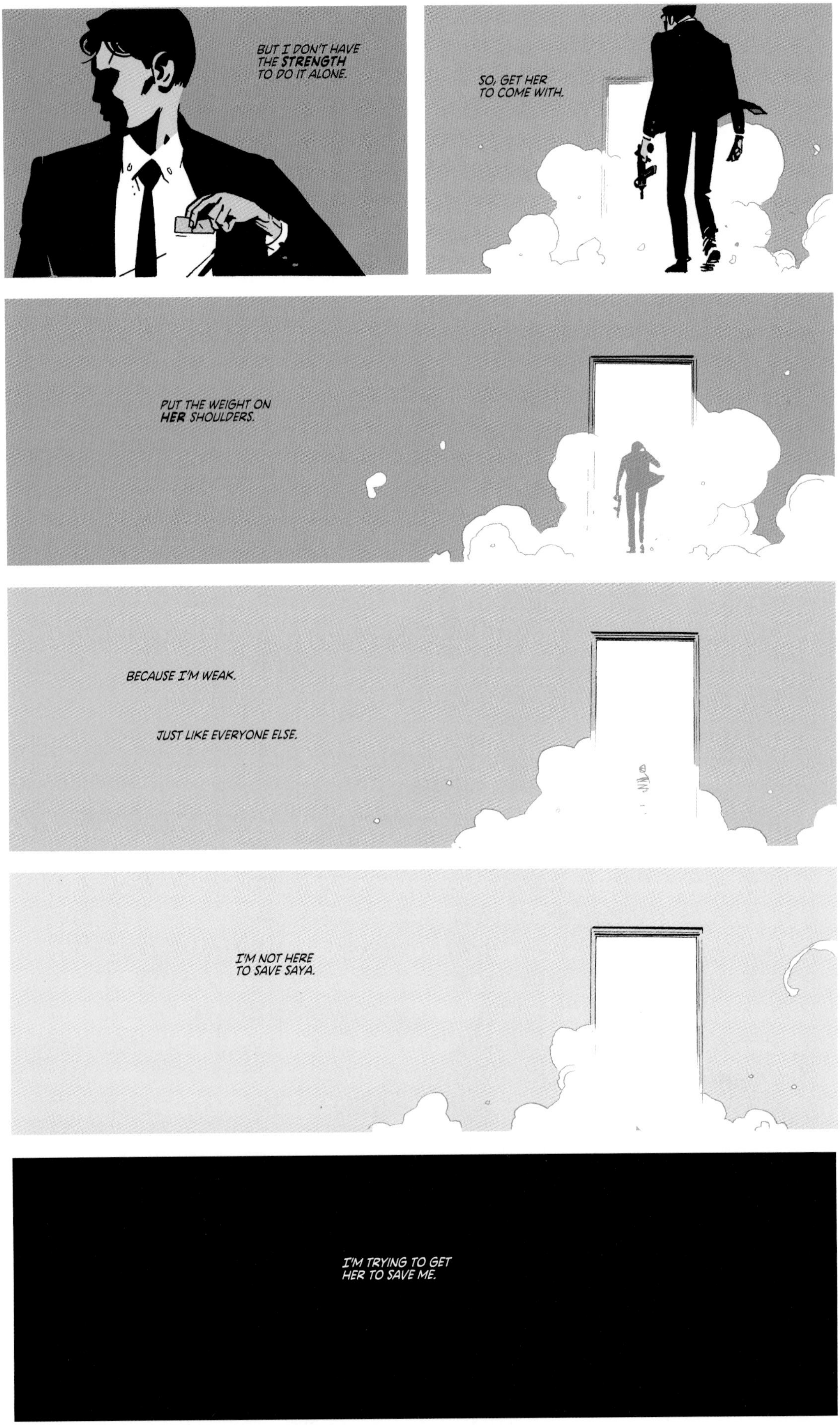
BUT I DON'T HAVE THE STRENGTH TO DO IT ALONE.
SO, GET HER TO COME WITH.
PUT THE WEIGHT ON HER SHOULDERS.
BECAUSE I'M WEAK.
JUST LIKE EVERYONE ELSE.
I'M NOT HERE TO SAVE SAYA.
I'M TRYING TO GET HER TO SAVE ME.

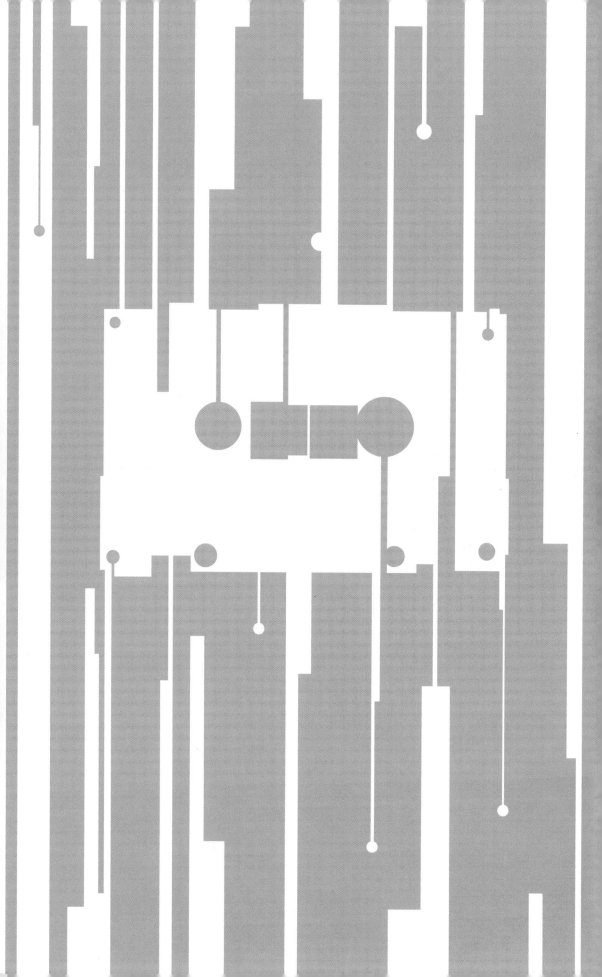

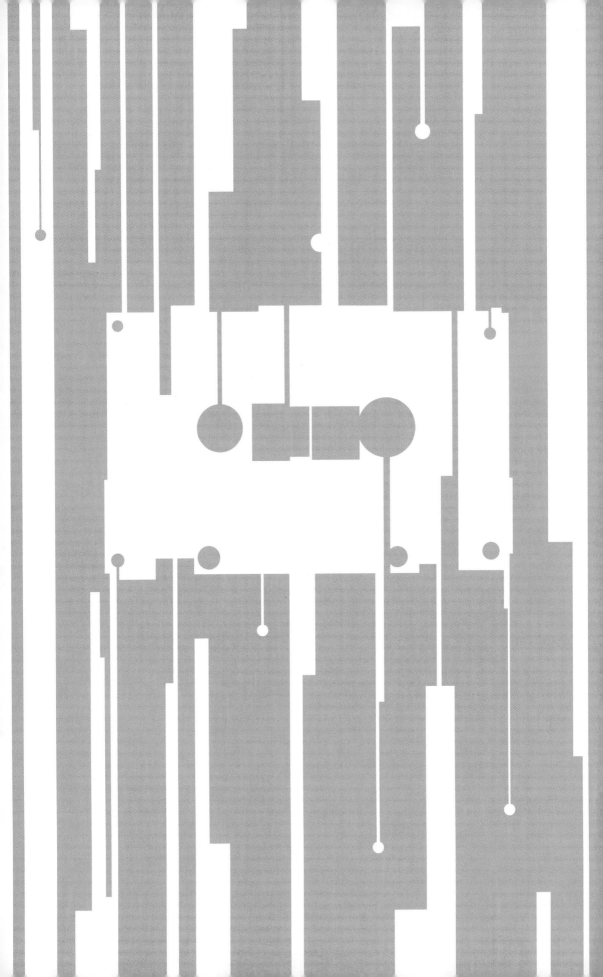

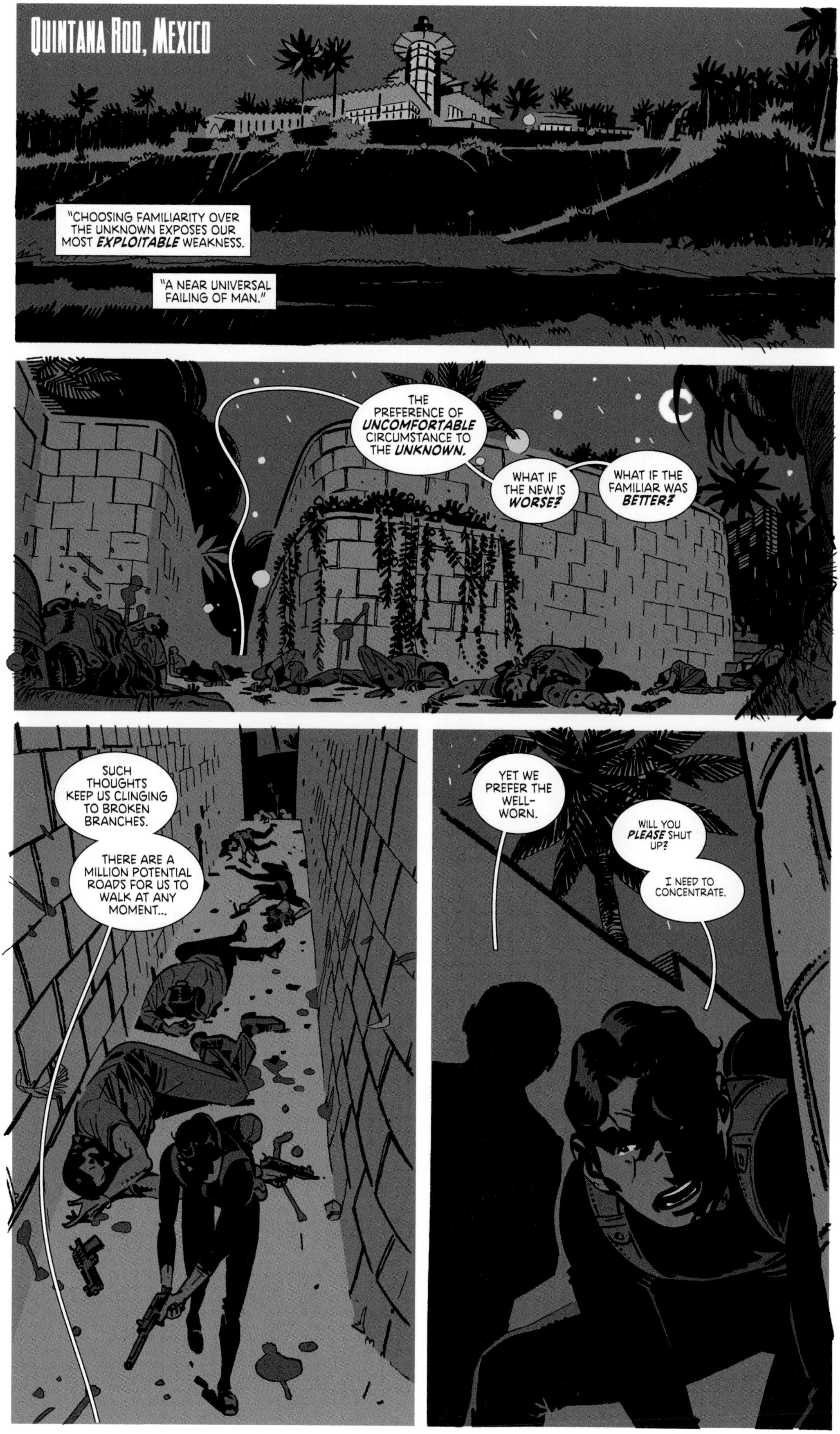
QUINTANA ROO, MEXICO
"CHOOSING FAMILIARITY OVER THE UNKNOWN EXPOSES OUR MOST EXPLOITABLE WEAKNESS.
"A NEAR UNIVERSAL FAILING OF MAN."
THE PREFERENCE OF UNCOMFORTABLE CIRCUMSTANCE TO THE UNKNOWN.
WHAT IF THE NEW IS WORSE?
WHAT IF THE FAMILIAR WAS BETTER?
SUCH THOUGHTS KEEP US CLINGING TO BROKEN BRANCHES.
THERE ARE A MILLION POTENTIAL ROADS FOR US TO WALK AT ANY MOMENT...
YET WE PREFER THE WELL-WORN.
WILL YOU PLEASE SHUT UP?
I NEED TO CONCENTRATE.

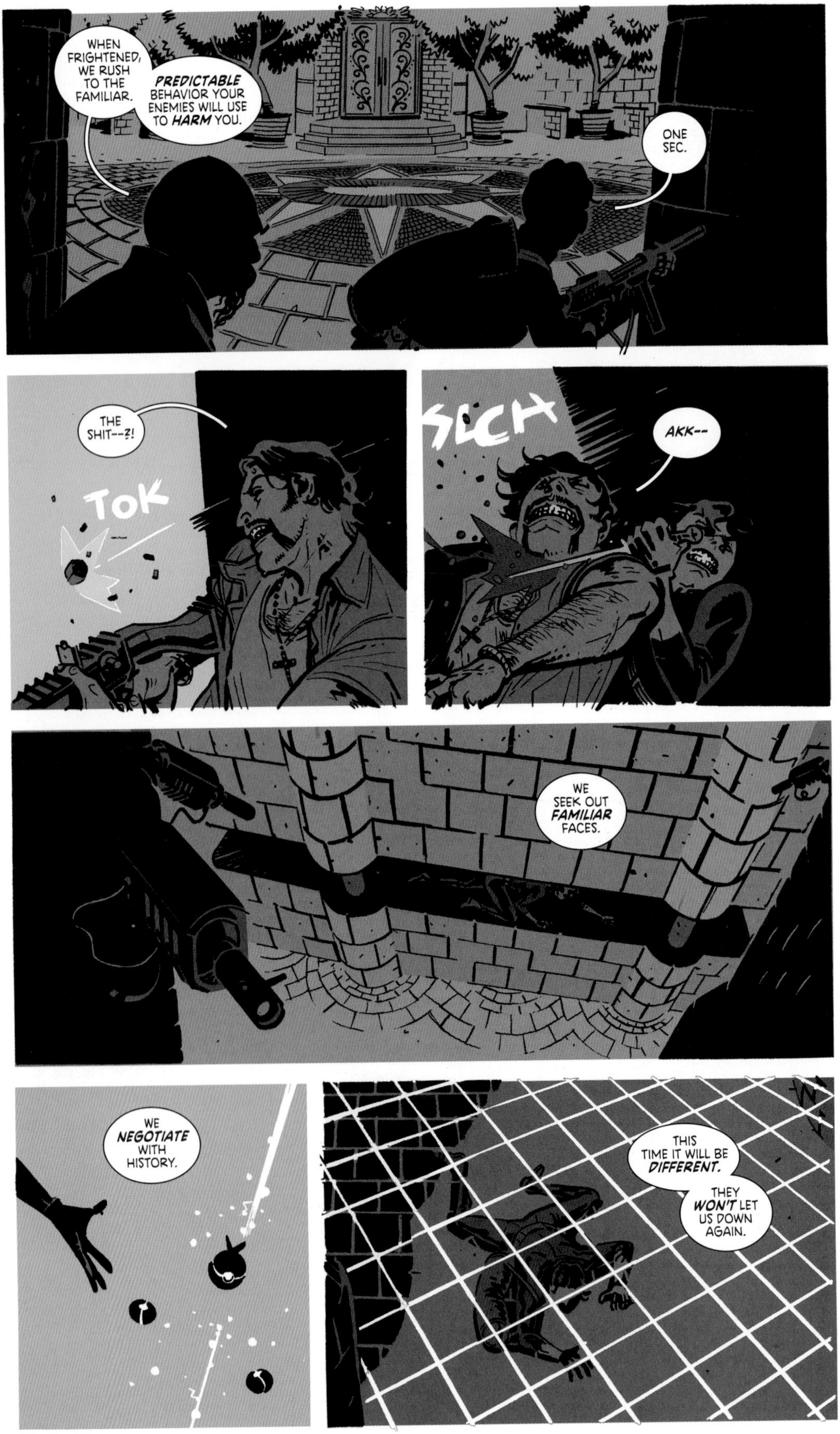
WHEN FRIGHTENED, WE RUSH TO THE FAMILIAR.
PREDICTABLE BEHAVIOR YOUR ENEMIES WILL USE TO HARM YOU.
ONE SEC.
THE SHIT--?!
TOK
SLCH
AKK--
WE SEEK OUT FAMILIAR FACES.
WE NEGOTIATE WITH HISTORY.
THIS TIME IT WILL BE DIFFERENT.
THEY WON'T LET US DOWN AGAIN.

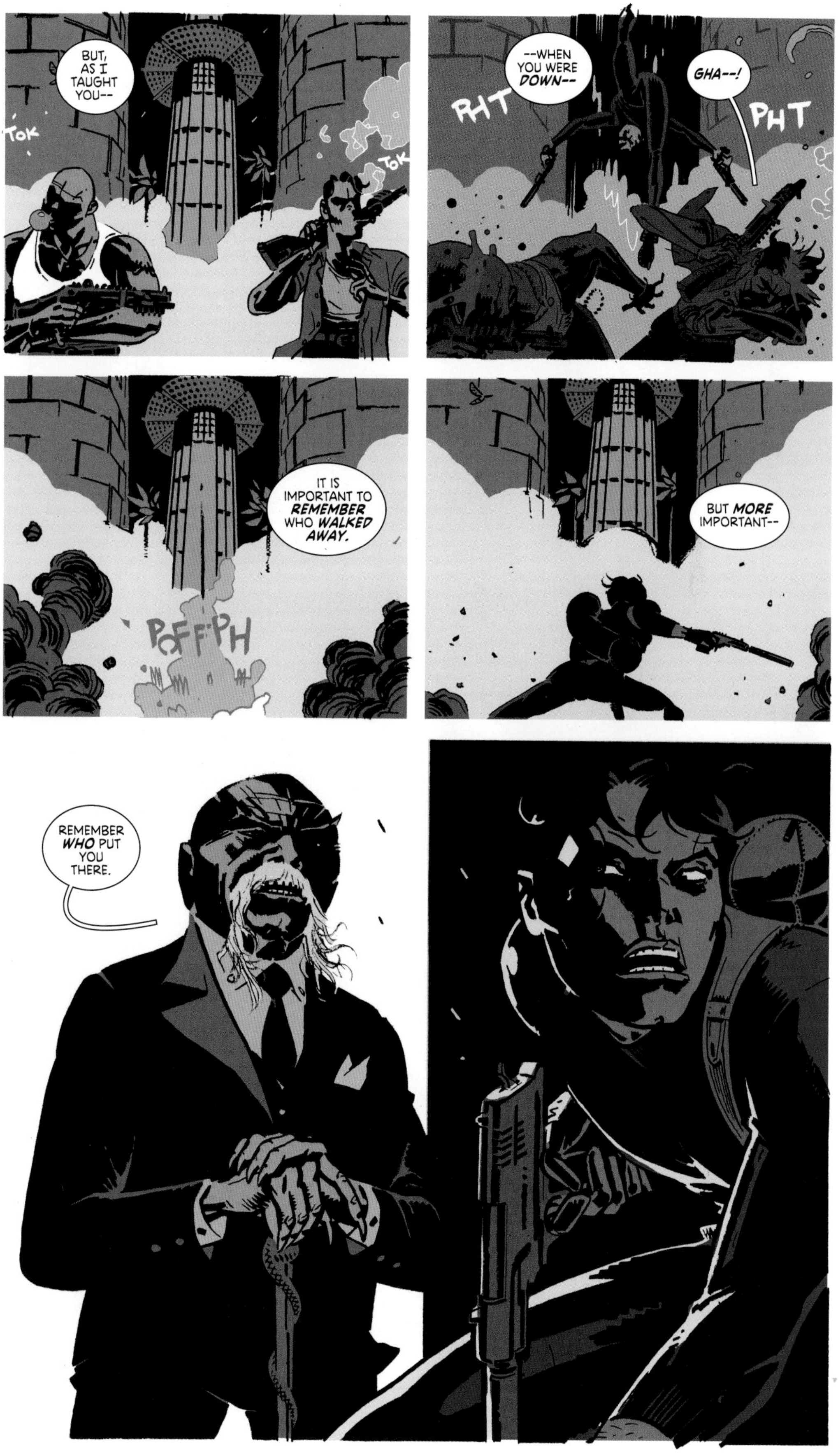
BUT, AS I TAUGHT YOU--
TOK
TOK
--WHEN YOU WERE *DOWN*--
GHA--!
PHT
PHT
IT IS IMPORTANT TO *REMEMBER* WHO *WALKED AWAY.*
POFF-PH
BUT *MORE* IMPORTANT--
REMEMBER *WHO* PUT YOU THERE.

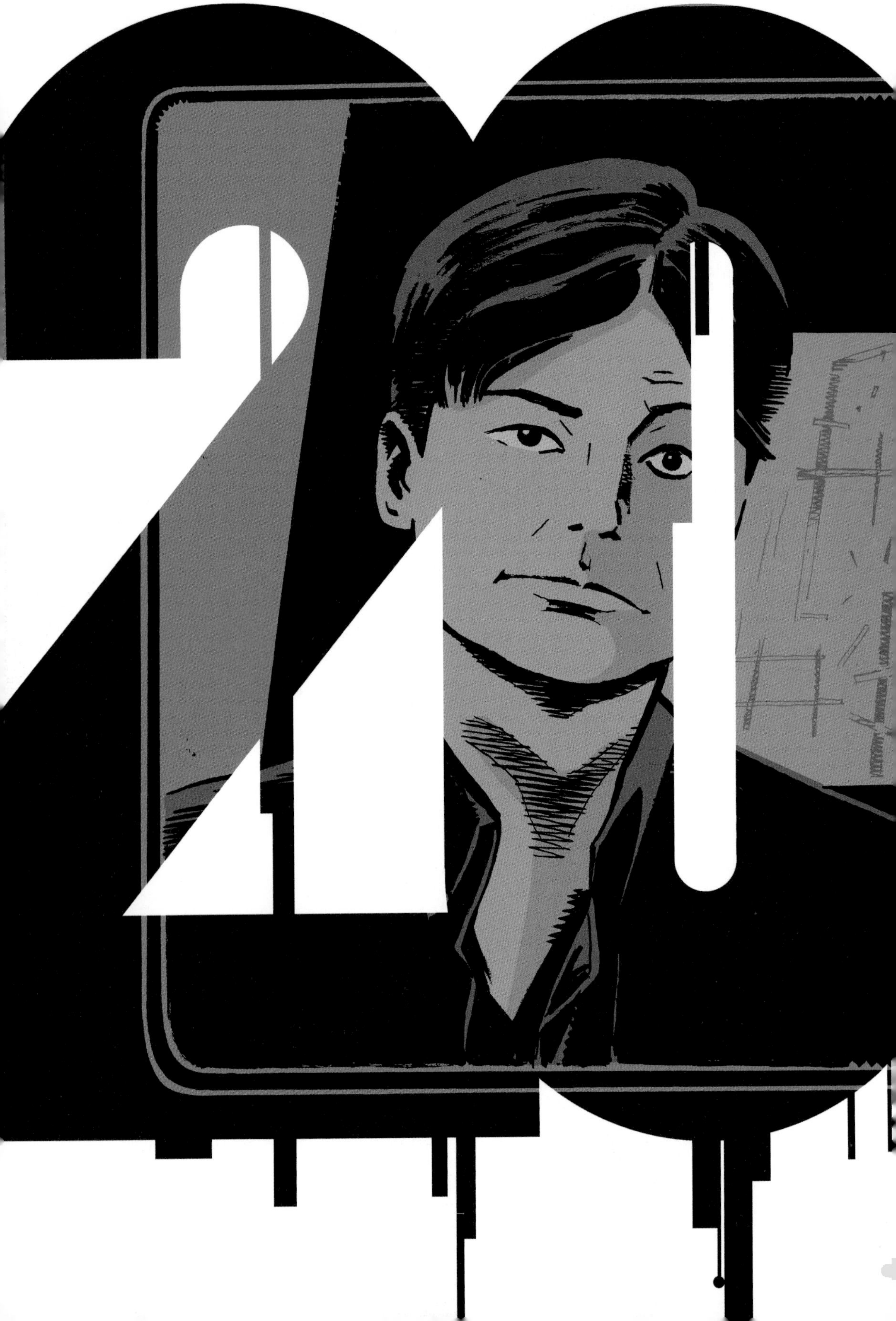

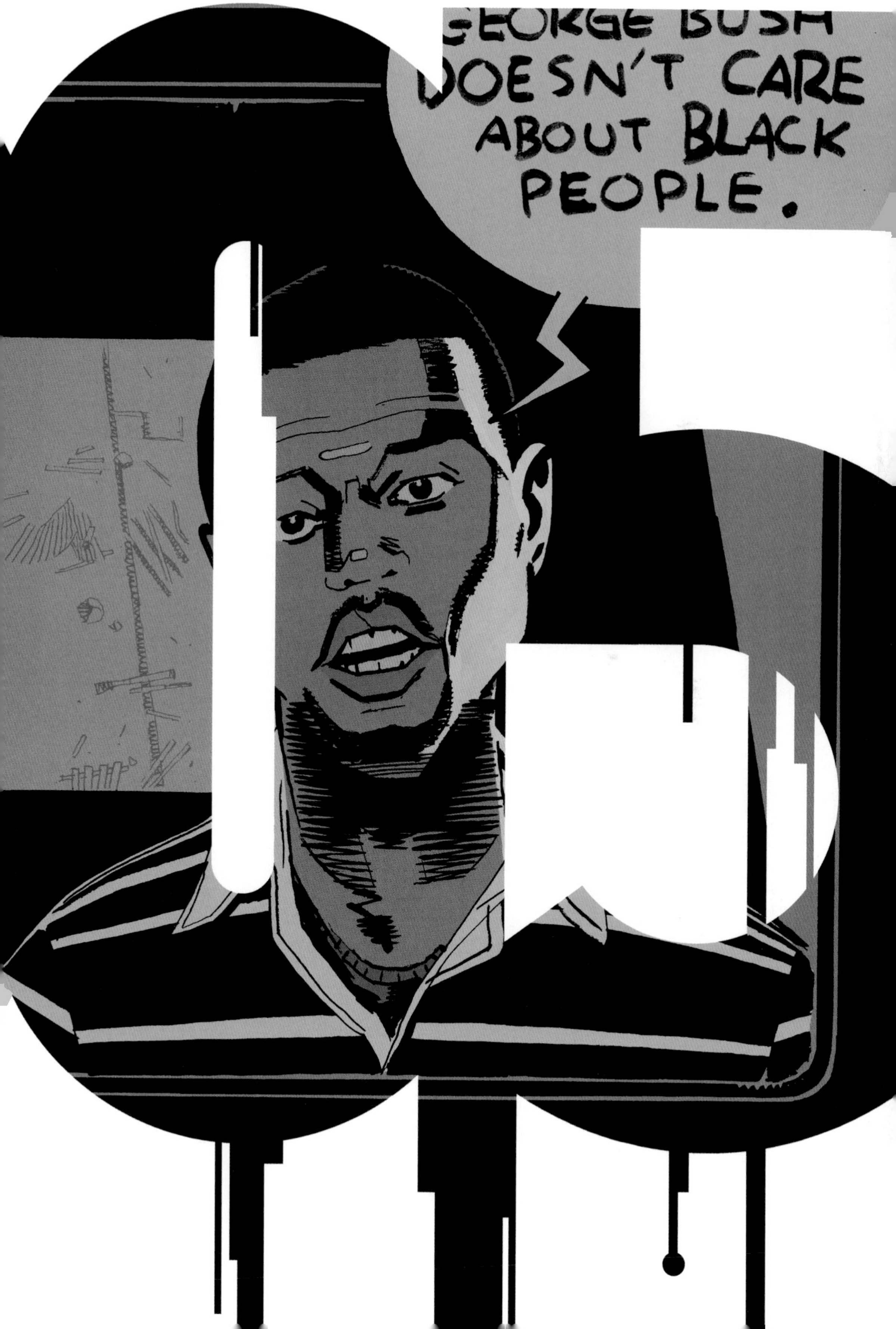
GEORGE BUSH DOESN'T CARE ABOUT BLACK PEOPLE.

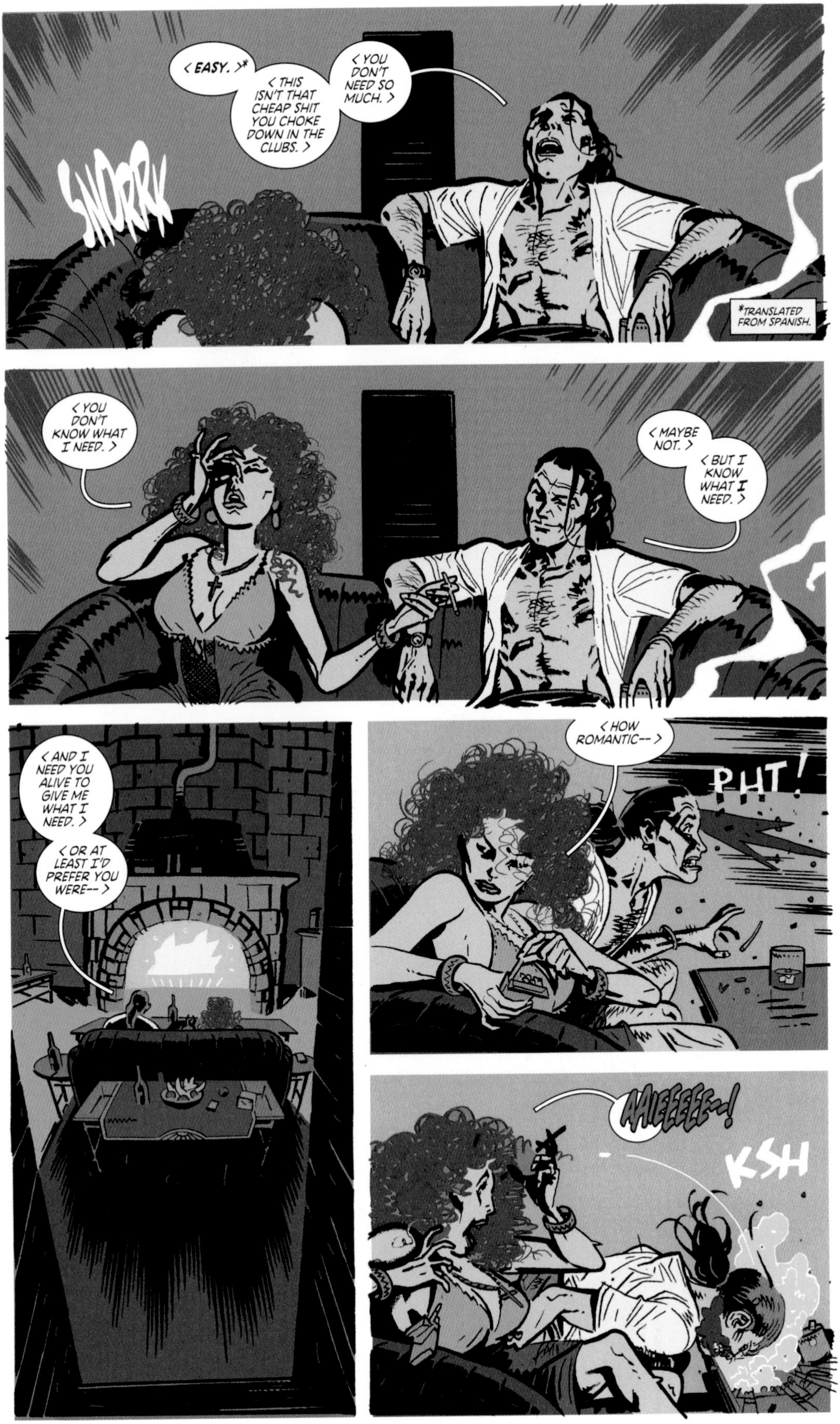
< EASY. >*
< THIS ISN'T THAT CHEAP SHIT YOU CHOKE DOWN IN THE CLUBS. >
< YOU DON'T NEED SO MUCH. >
SNORRK
*TRANSLATED FROM SPANISH.
< YOU DON'T KNOW WHAT I NEED. >
< MAYBE NOT. >
< BUT I KNOW WHAT I NEED. >
< AND I NEED YOU ALIVE TO GIVE ME WHAT I NEED. >
< OR AT LEAST I'D PREFER YOU WERE-- >
< HOW ROMANTIC-- >
PHT!
AAIEEEEEE--!
KSH

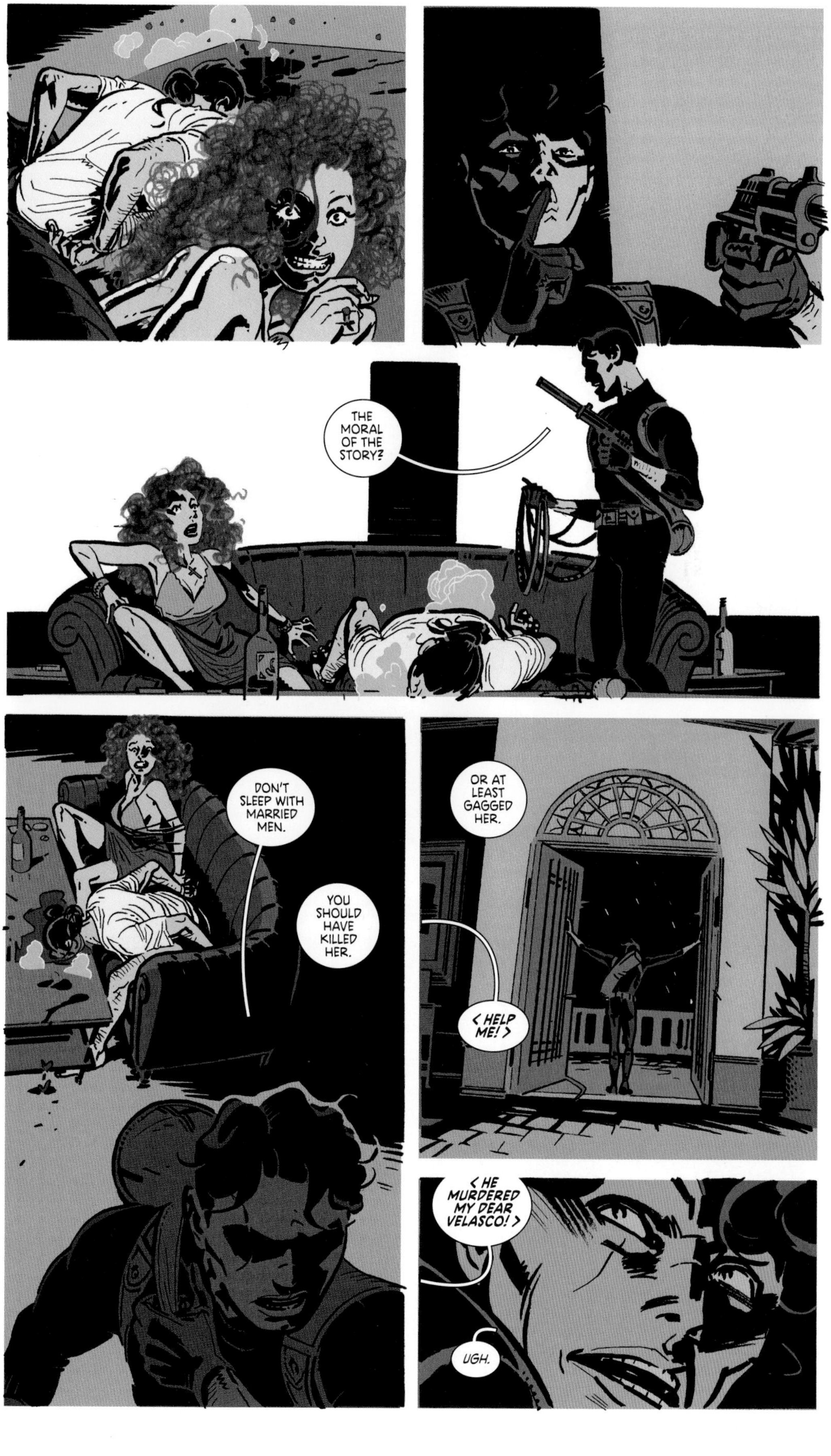
THE MORAL OF THE STORY?
DON'T SLEEP WITH MARRIED MEN.
YOU SHOULD HAVE KILLED HER.
OR AT LEAST GAGGED HER.
< HELP ME! >
< HE MURDERED MY DEAR VELASCO! >
UGH.

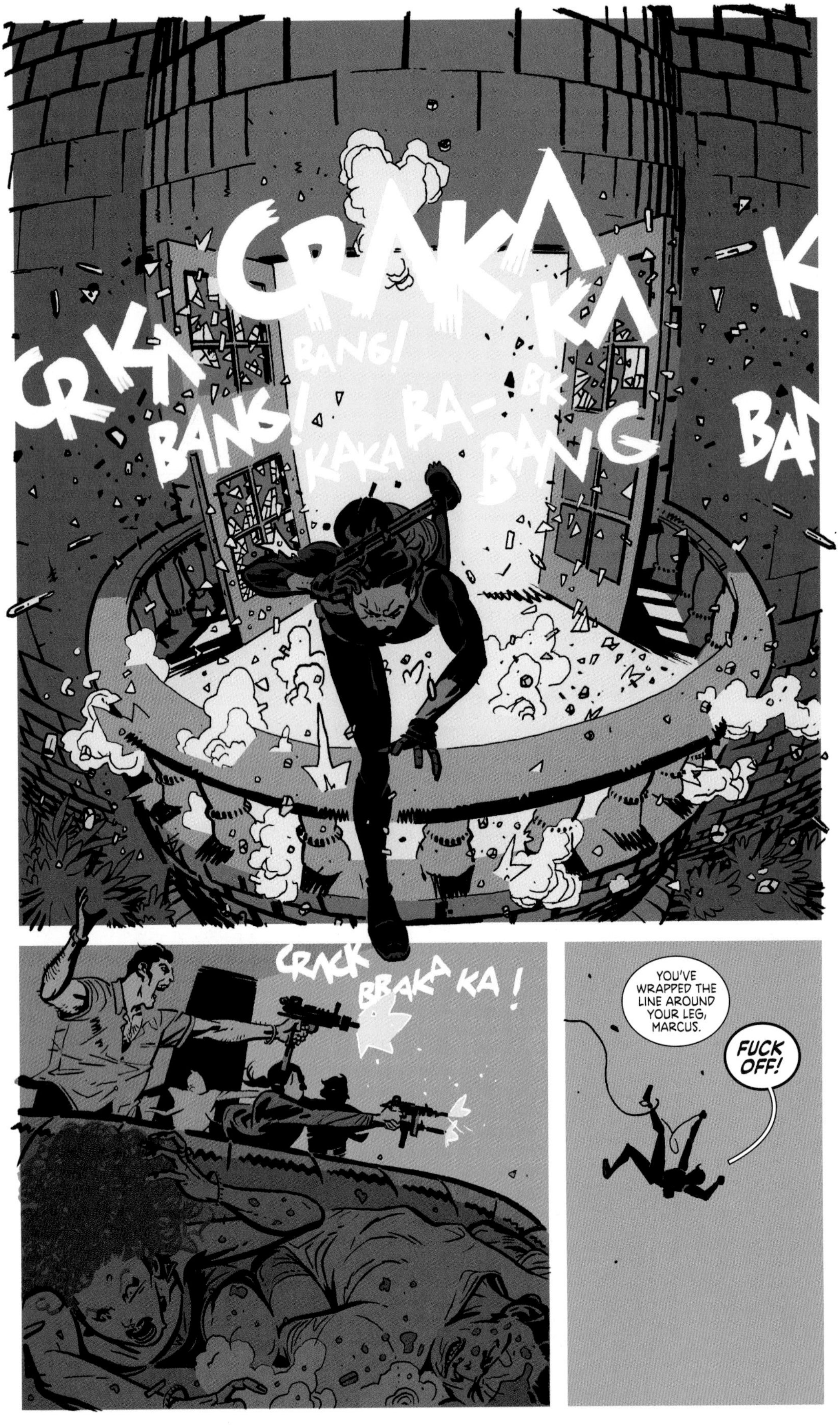
CRAKA
CRKA
BANG!
BANG!
KAKA
BA-
BK
BANG
CRACK
BRAKA KA !
YOU'VE WRAPPED THE LINE AROUND YOUR LEG, MARCUS.
FUCK OFF!

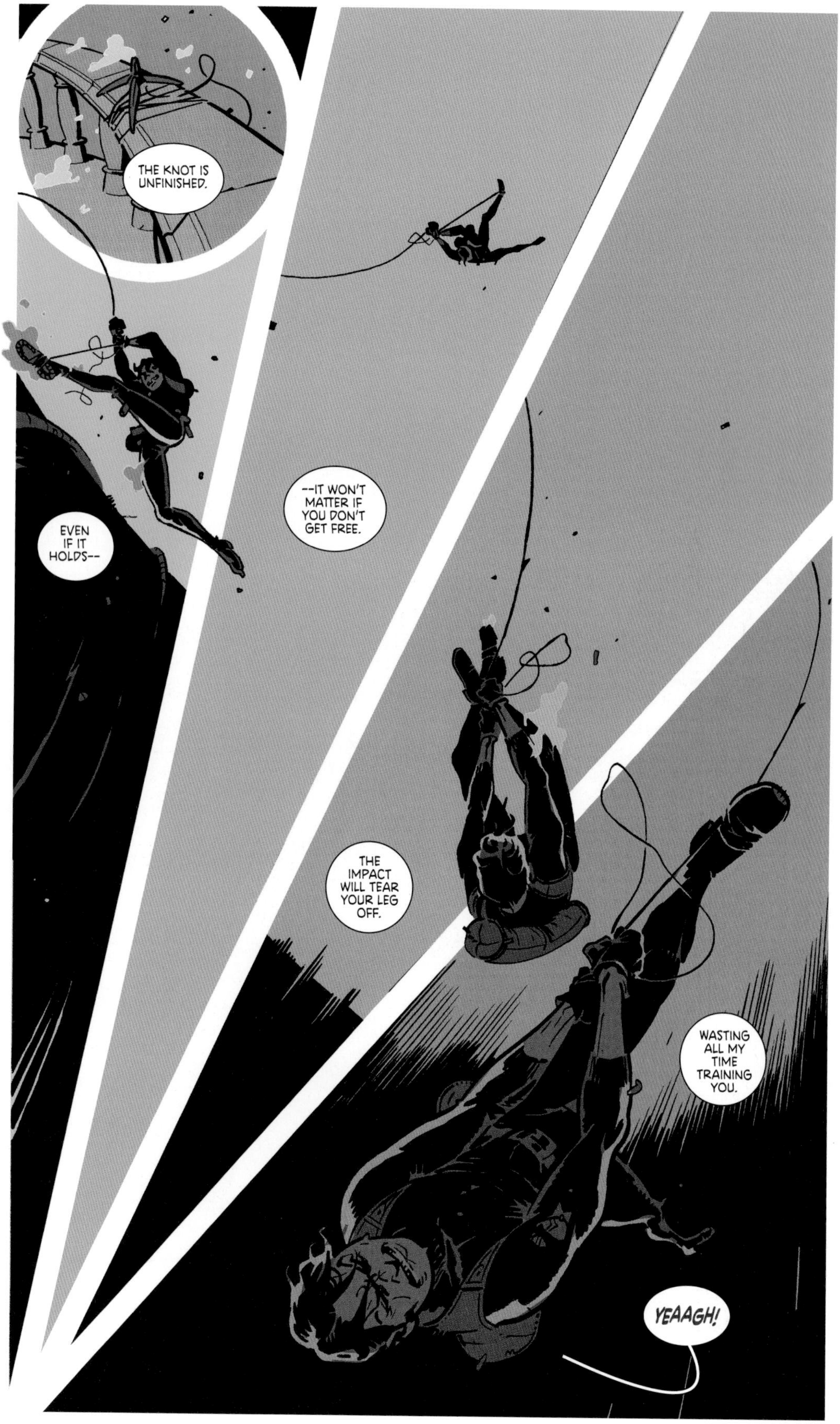
THE KNOT IS UNFINISHED.
EVEN IF IT HOLDS--
--IT WON'T MATTER IF YOU DON'T GET FREE.
THE IMPACT WILL TEAR YOUR LEG OFF.
WASTING ALL MY TIME TRAINING YOU.
YEAAGH!

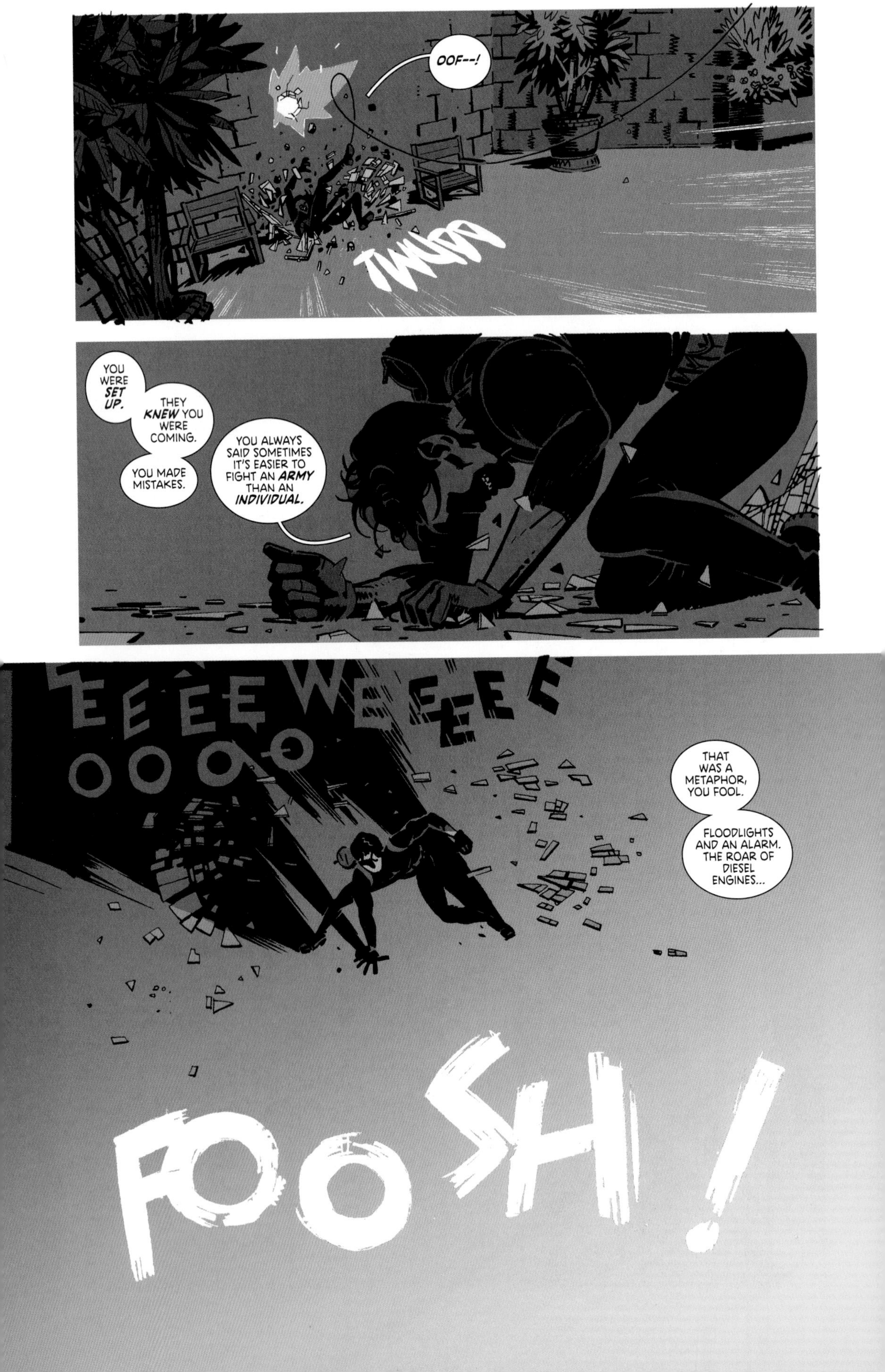

OOF--!
TWUDD
YOU WERE **SET UP.**
THEY **KNEW** YOU WERE COMING.
YOU MADE MISTAKES.
YOU ALWAYS SAID SOMETIMES IT'S EASIER TO FIGHT AN **ARMY** THAN AN **INDIVIDUAL.**
EEEE WEEEEE
OOOO
THAT WAS A METAPHOR, YOU FOOL.
FLOODLIGHTS AND AN ALARM. THE ROAR OF DIESEL ENGINES...
FOOSH!

"...VELASCO'S ARMY HAS BEEN ACTIVATED."

SKREEEECH

< GO! >

< THE GRINGO'S THIS WAY! >

< HE KILLED MR. VELASCO! >

< I DON'T SEE SHIT! >

< WHERE IS HE? >

< THE FUCK DO I KNOW?! >

< FAN OUT AND FIND HIM! >

< IF HE'S NOT DEAD IN TEN MINUTES, YOU WILL BE! >

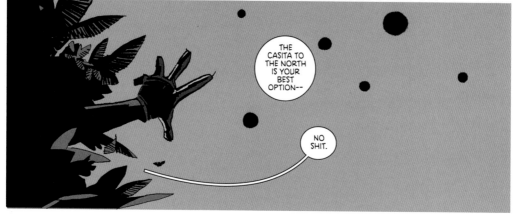

THE CASITA TO THE NORTH IS YOUR BEST OPTION--

NO SHIT.

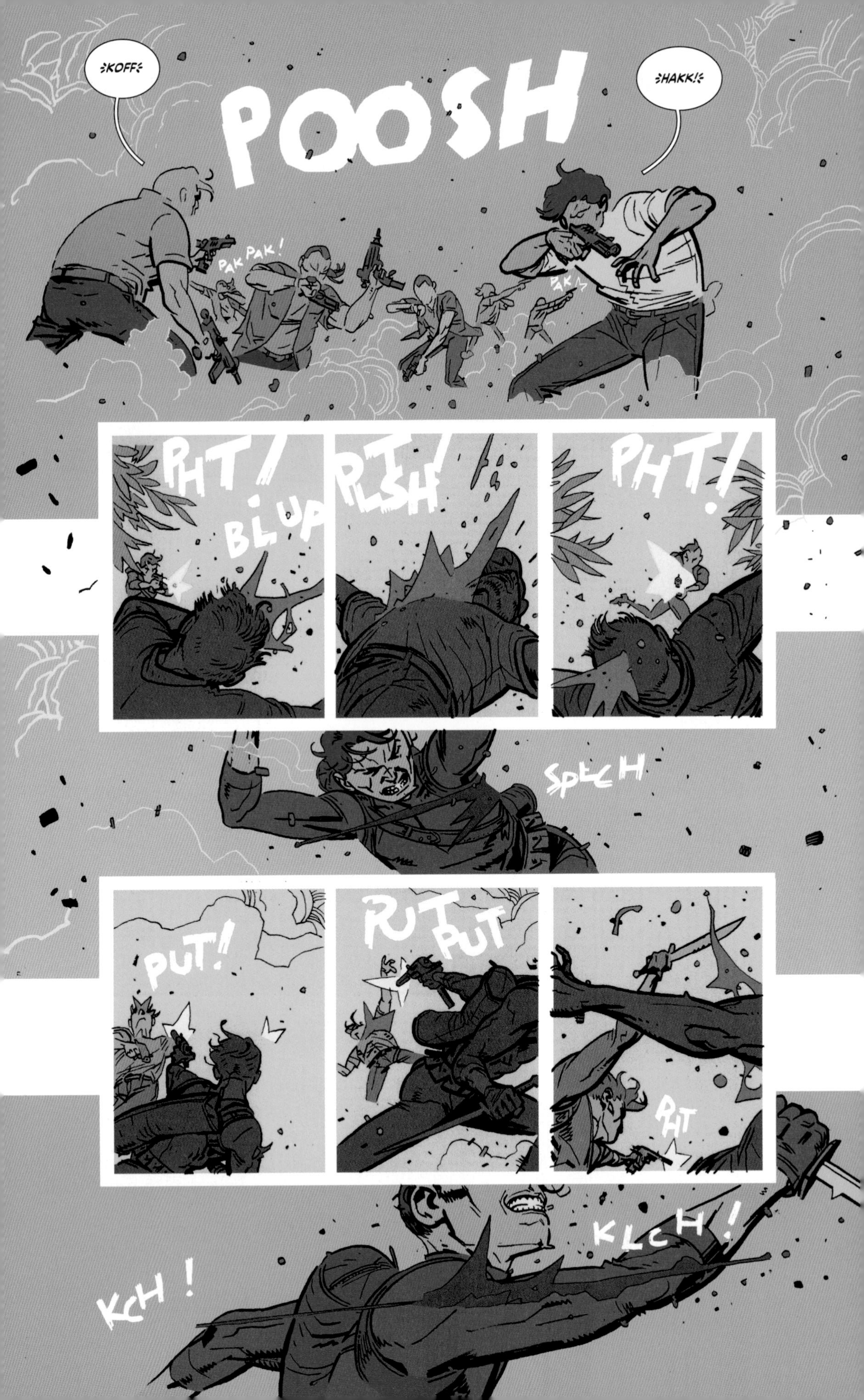

KOFF
POOSH
HAKK!
PAK PAK!
PAK
PHT!
BLUP
PHT!
PLSH
PHT!
SPLCH
PUT!
PUT
PUT
PHT
KLCH!
KCH!

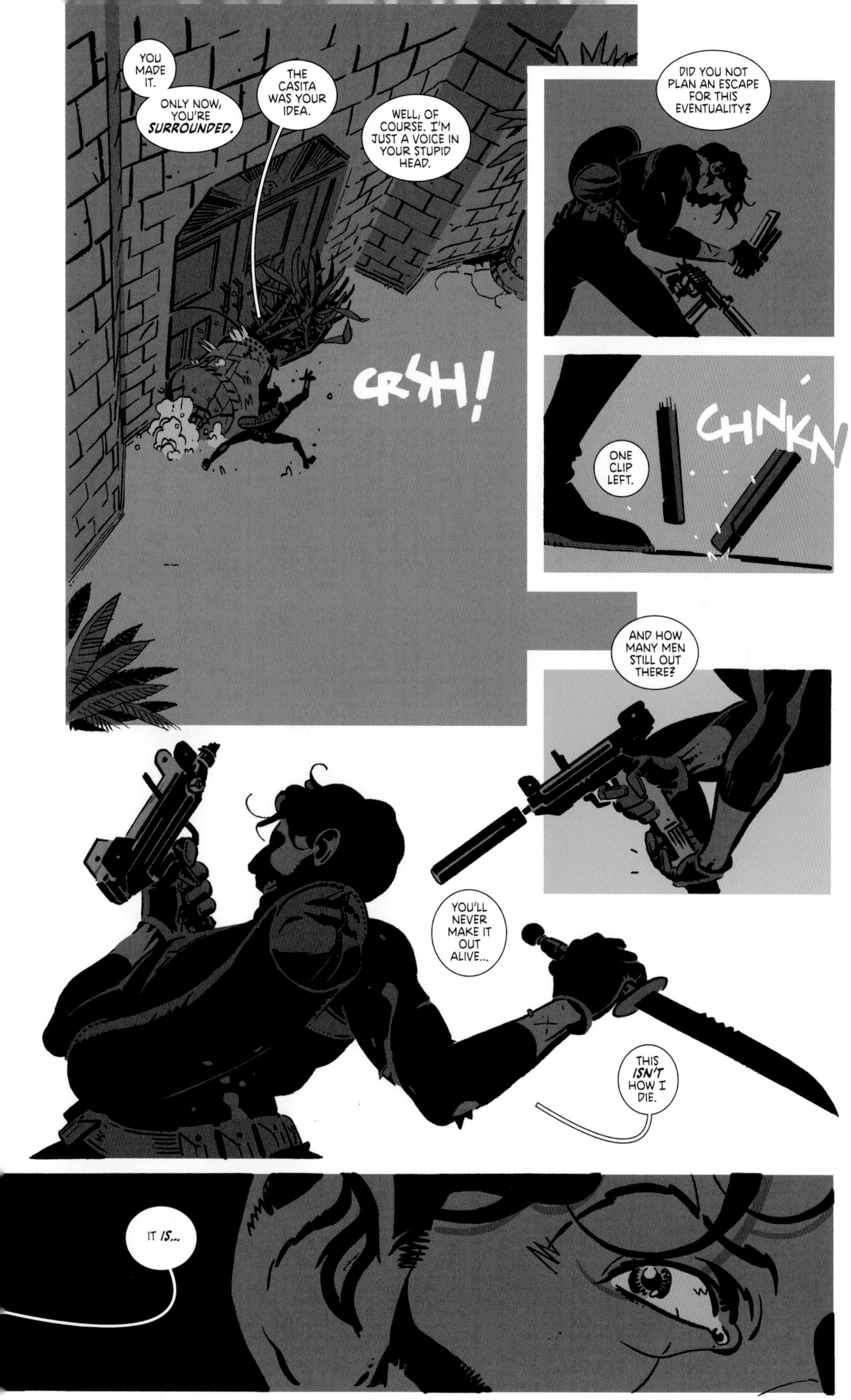
YOU MADE IT.
ONLY NOW, YOU'RE *SURROUNDED.*
THE CASITA WAS YOUR IDEA.
WELL, OF COURSE. I'M JUST A VOICE IN YOUR STUPID HEAD.
CRSH!
DID YOU NOT PLAN AN ESCAPE FOR THIS EVENTUALITY?
ONE CLIP LEFT.
CHNKN
AND HOW MANY MEN STILL OUT THERE?
YOU'LL NEVER MAKE IT OUT ALIVE...
THIS *ISN'T* HOW I DIE.
IT *IS...*

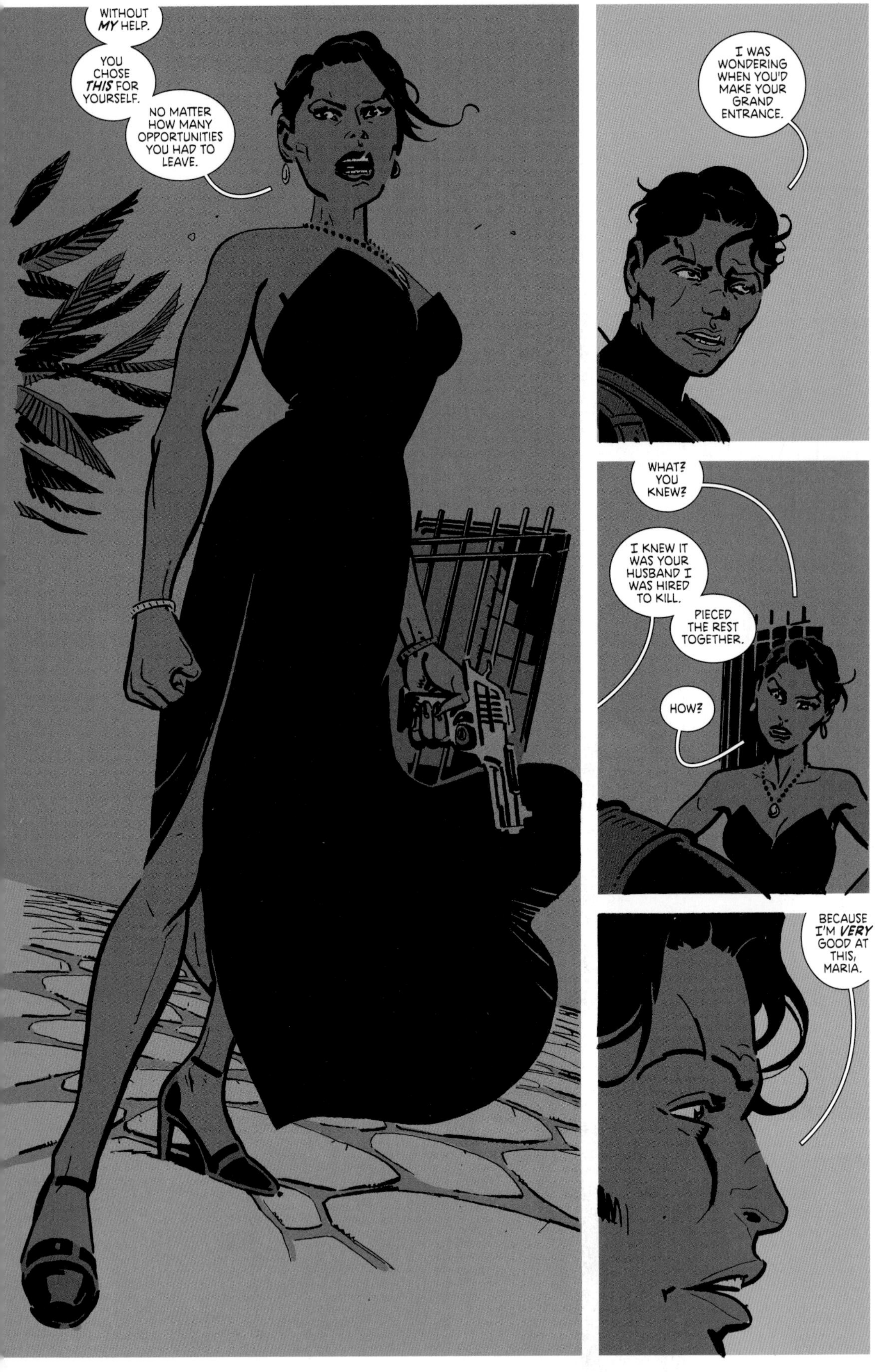
WITHOUT MY HELP.
YOU CHOSE THIS FOR YOURSELF.
NO MATTER HOW MANY OPPORTUNITIES YOU HAD TO LEAVE.
I WAS WONDERING WHEN YOU'D MAKE YOUR GRAND ENTRANCE.
WHAT? YOU KNEW?
I KNEW IT WAS YOUR HUSBAND I WAS HIRED TO KILL.
PIECED THE REST TOGETHER.
HOW?
BECAUSE I'M VERY GOOD AT THIS, MARIA.

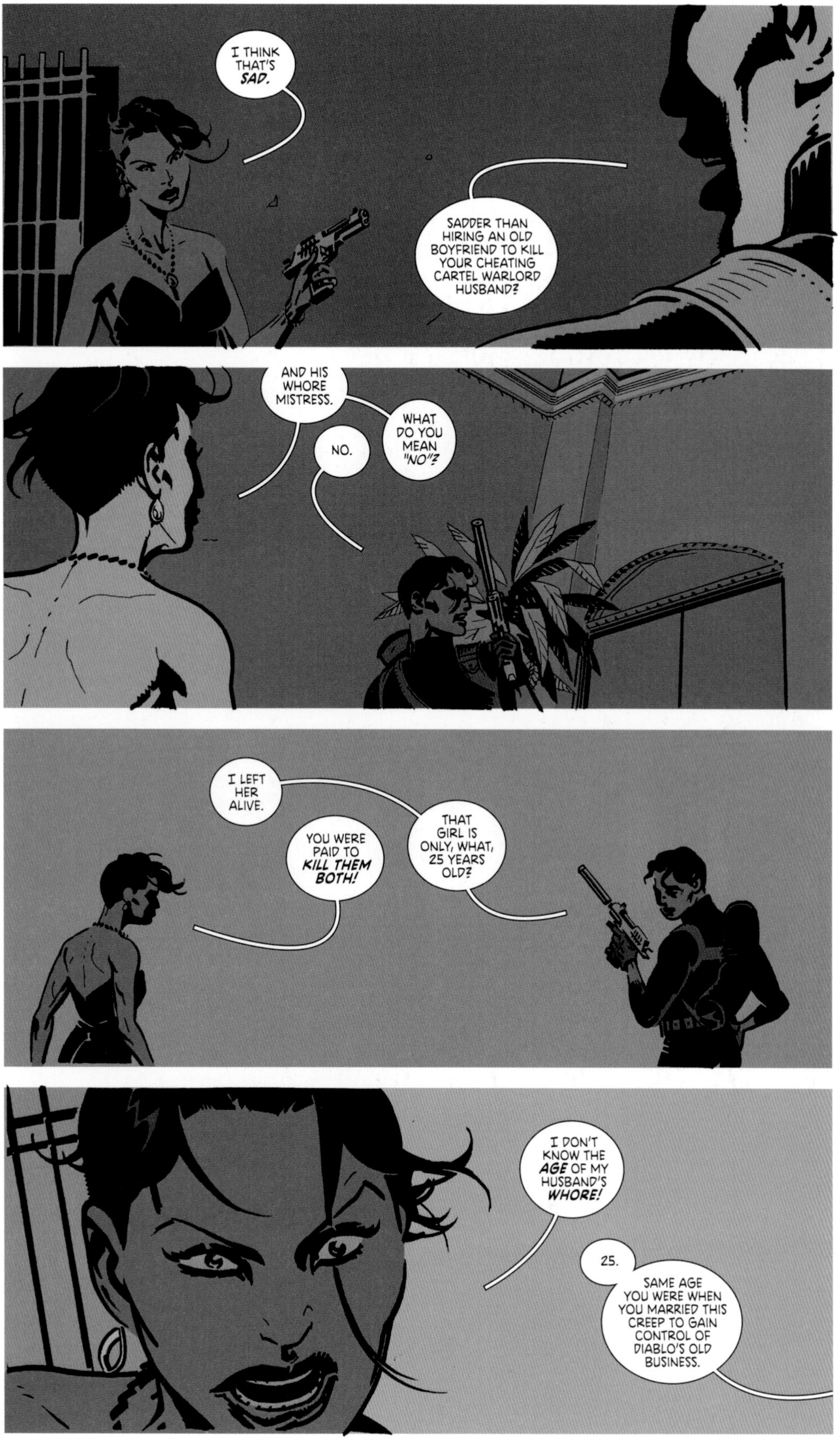

I THINK THAT'S SAD.
SADDER THAN HIRING AN OLD BOYFRIEND TO KILL YOUR CHEATING CARTEL WARLORD HUSBAND?
AND HIS WHORE MISTRESS.
WHAT DO YOU MEAN "NO"?
NO.
I LEFT HER ALIVE.
YOU WERE PAID TO KILL THEM BOTH!
THAT GIRL IS ONLY, WHAT, 25 YEARS OLD?
I DON'T KNOW THE AGE OF MY HUSBAND'S WHORE!
25.
SAME AGE YOU WERE WHEN YOU MARRIED THIS CREEP TO GAIN CONTROL OF DIABLO'S OLD BUSINESS.

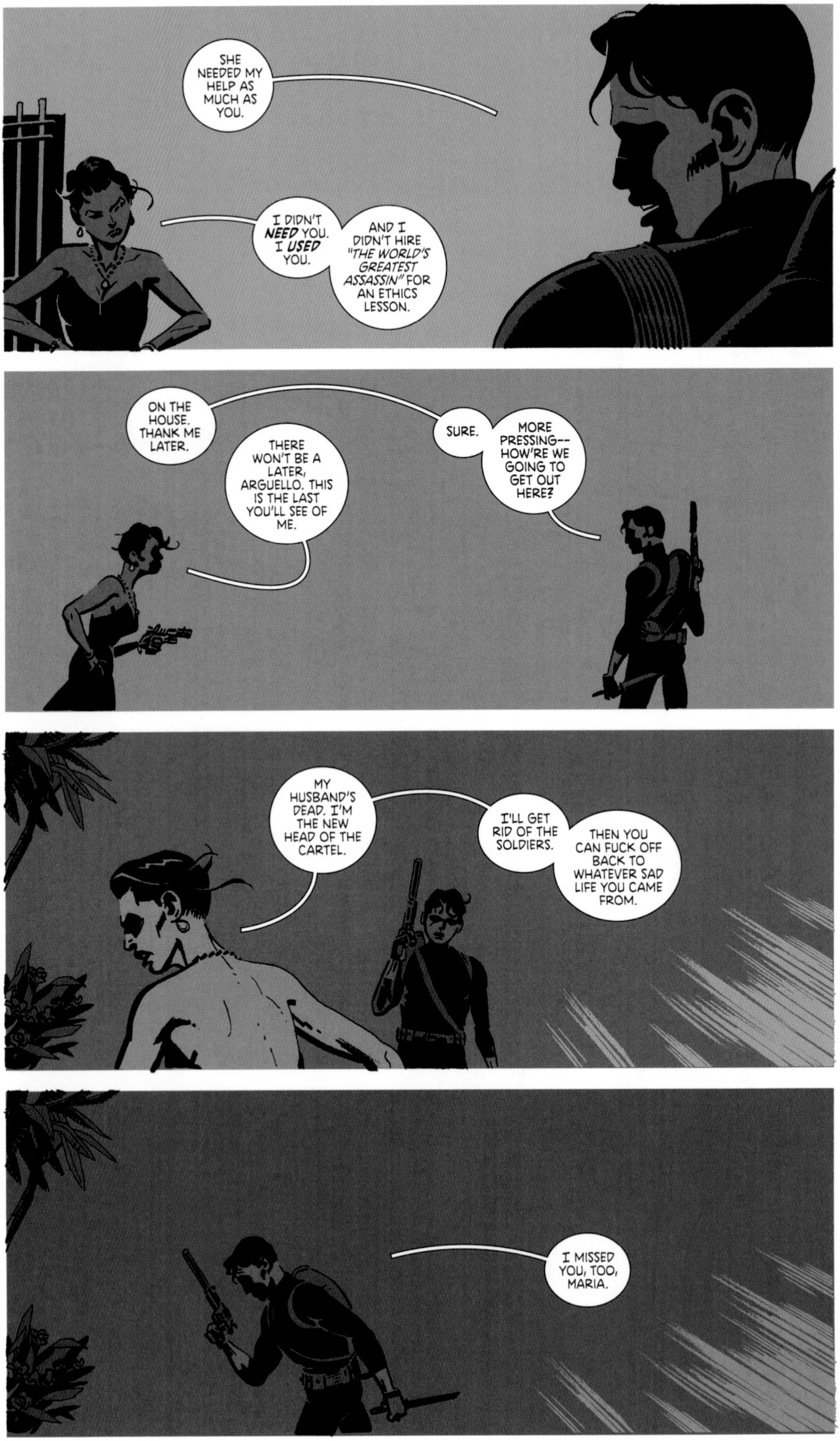
SHE NEEDED MY HELP AS MUCH AS YOU.
I DIDN'T **NEED** YOU. I **USED** YOU.
AND I DIDN'T HIRE *"THE WORLD'S GREATEST ASSASSIN"* FOR AN ETHICS LESSON.
ON THE HOUSE. THANK ME LATER.
THERE WON'T BE A LATER, ARGUELLO. THIS IS THE LAST YOU'LL SEE OF ME.
SURE.
MORE PRESSING-- HOW'RE WE GOING TO GET OUT HERE?
MY HUSBAND'S DEAD. I'M THE NEW HEAD OF THE CARTEL.
I'LL GET RID OF THE SOLDIERS.
THEN YOU CAN FUCK OFF BACK TO WHATEVER SAD LIFE YOU CAME FROM.
I MISSED YOU, TOO, MARIA.

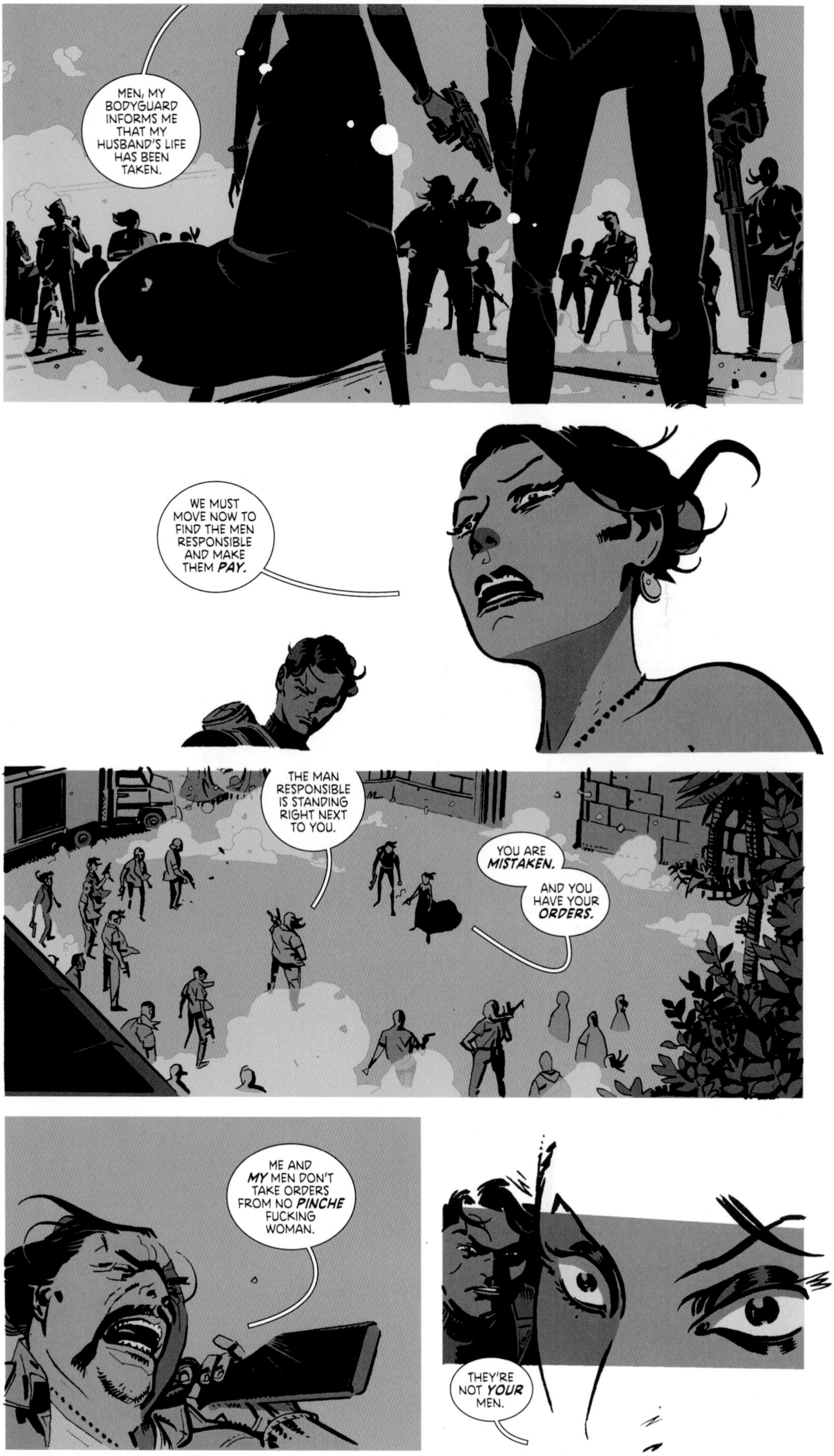
MEN, MY BODYGUARD INFORMS ME THAT MY HUSBAND'S LIFE HAS BEEN TAKEN.
WE MUST MOVE NOW TO FIND THE MEN RESPONSIBLE AND MAKE THEM *PAY.*
THE MAN RESPONSIBLE IS STANDING RIGHT NEXT TO YOU.
YOU ARE *MISTAKEN.*
AND YOU HAVE YOUR *ORDERS.*
ME AND *MY* MEN DON'T TAKE ORDERS FROM NO *PINCHE* FUCKING WOMAN.
THEY'RE NOT *YOUR* MEN.

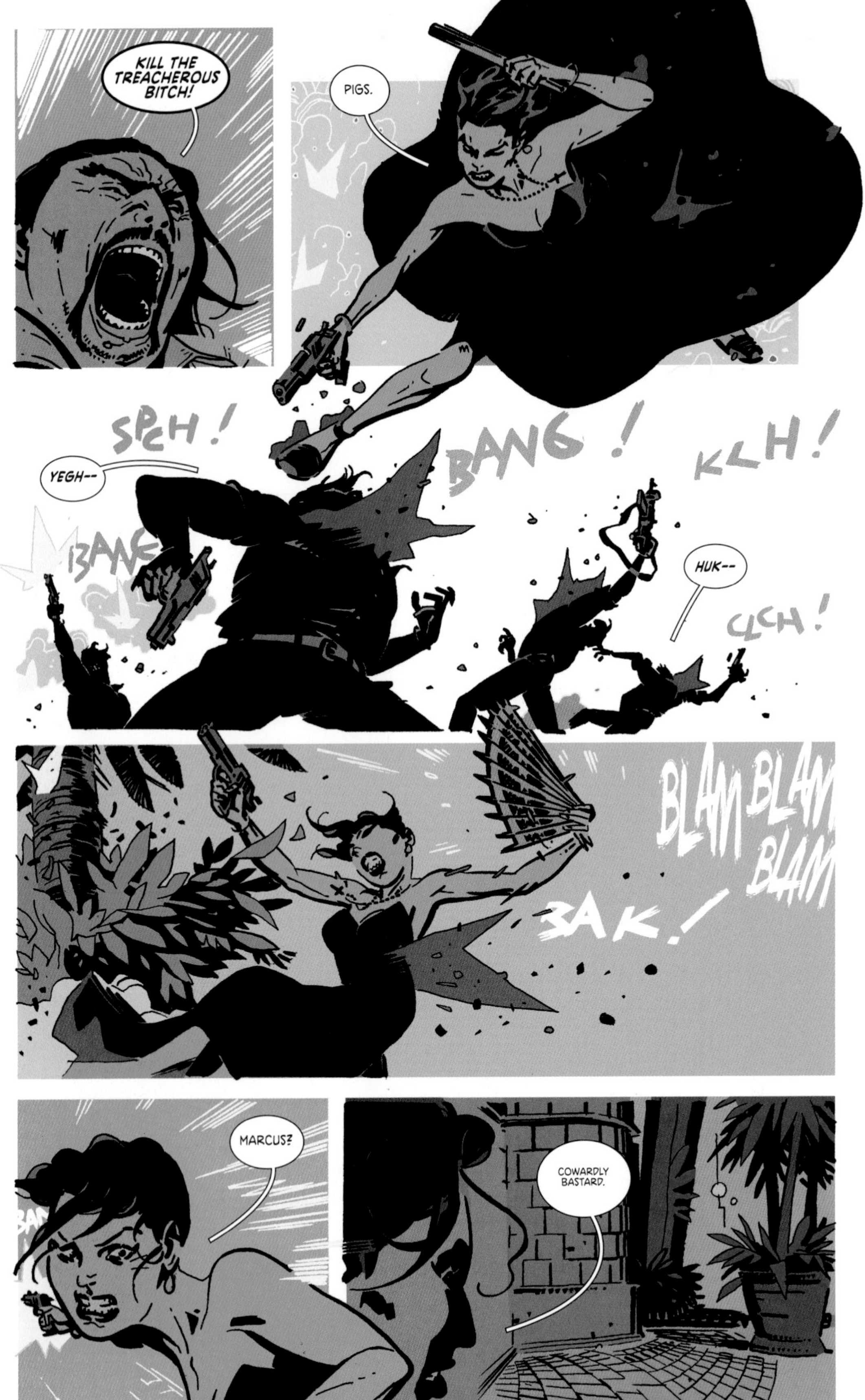
KILL THE TREACHEROUS BITCH!
PIGS.
SPCH!
BANG!
KLH!
YEGH--
BANG
HUK--
CLCH!
BLAM BLAM BLAM
BAK!
MARCUS?
COWARDLY BASTARD.

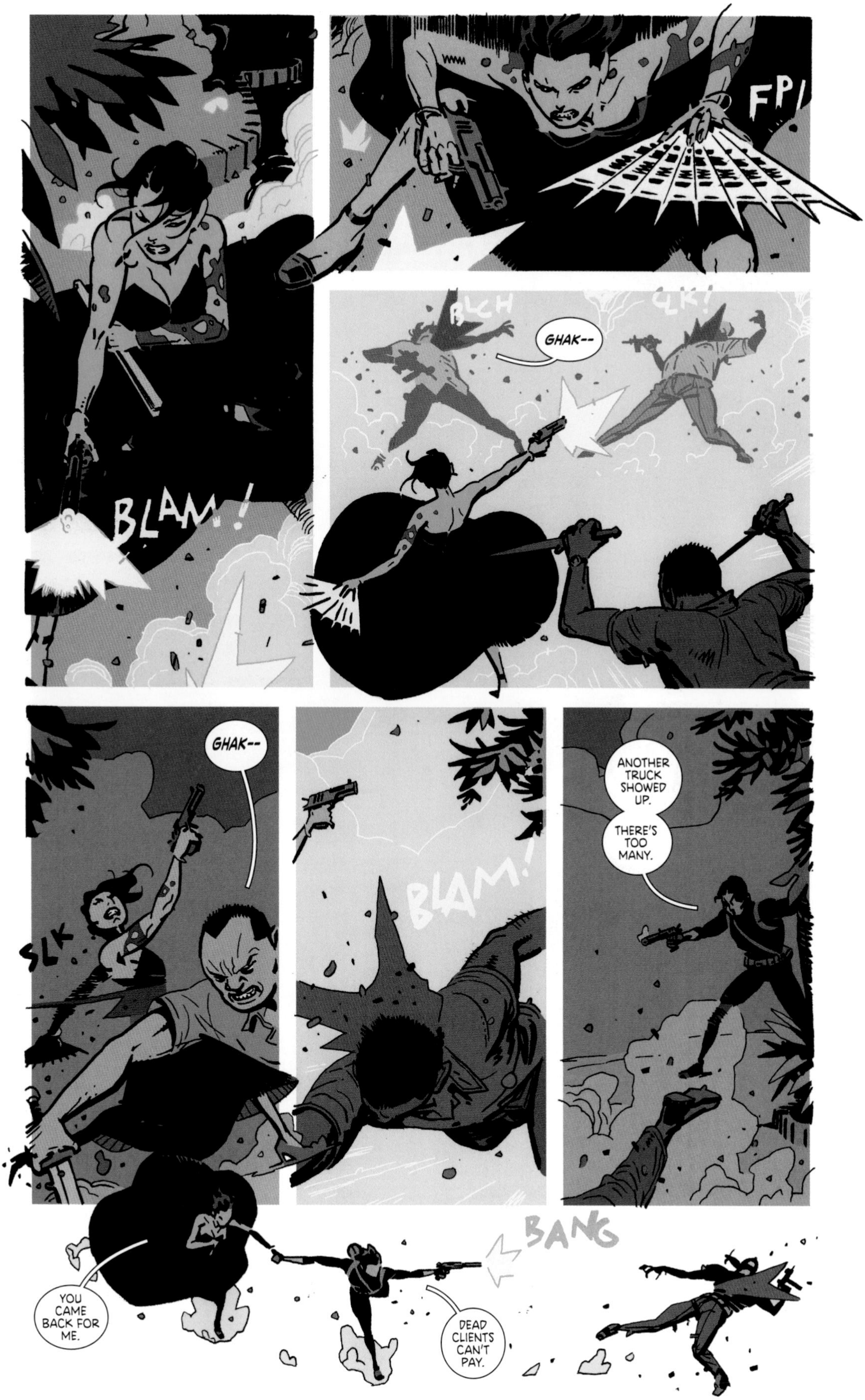
FP!
BLAM!
BLCH
CLK!
GHAK--
GHAK--
SLK
BLAM!
ANOTHER TRUCK SHOWED UP.
THERE'S TOO MANY.
BANG
YOU CAME BACK FOR ME.
DEAD CLIENTS CAN'T PAY.

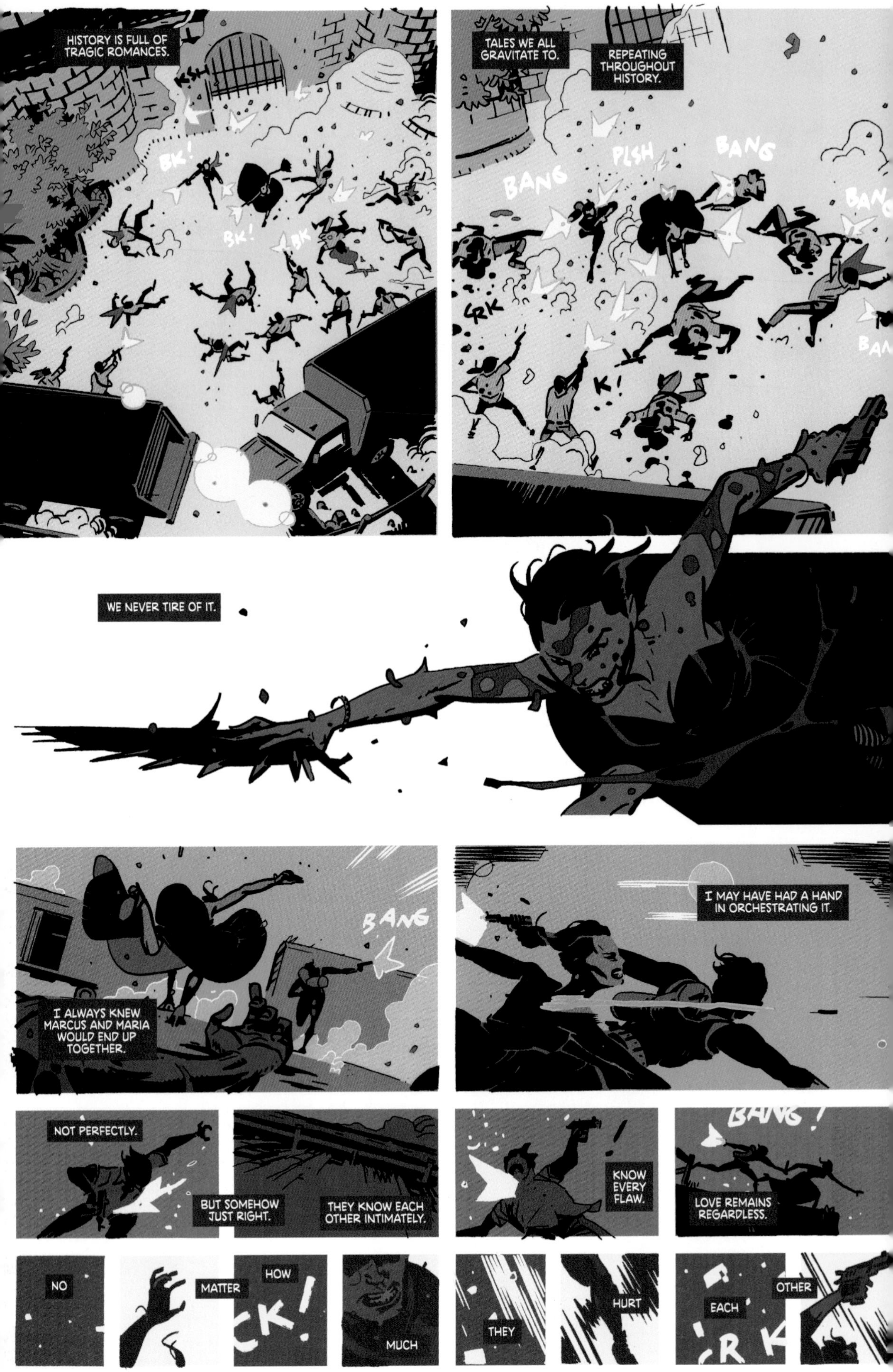
HISTORY IS FULL OF TRAGIC ROMANCES.
BK!
BK!
BK
TALES WE ALL GRAVITATE TO.
REPEATING THROUGHOUT HISTORY.
BANG
PLSH
BANG
BANG
CRK
K!
WE NEVER TIRE OF IT.
BANG
I ALWAYS KNEW MARCUS AND MARIA WOULD END UP TOGETHER.
I MAY HAVE HAD A HAND IN ORCHESTRATING IT.
NOT PERFECTLY.
BUT SOMEHOW JUST RIGHT.
THEY KNOW EACH OTHER INTIMATELY.
KNOW EVERY FLAW.
BANG!
LOVE REMAINS REGARDLESS.
NO
MATTER
HOW
CK!
MUCH
THEY
HURT
EACH
OTHER
CRK

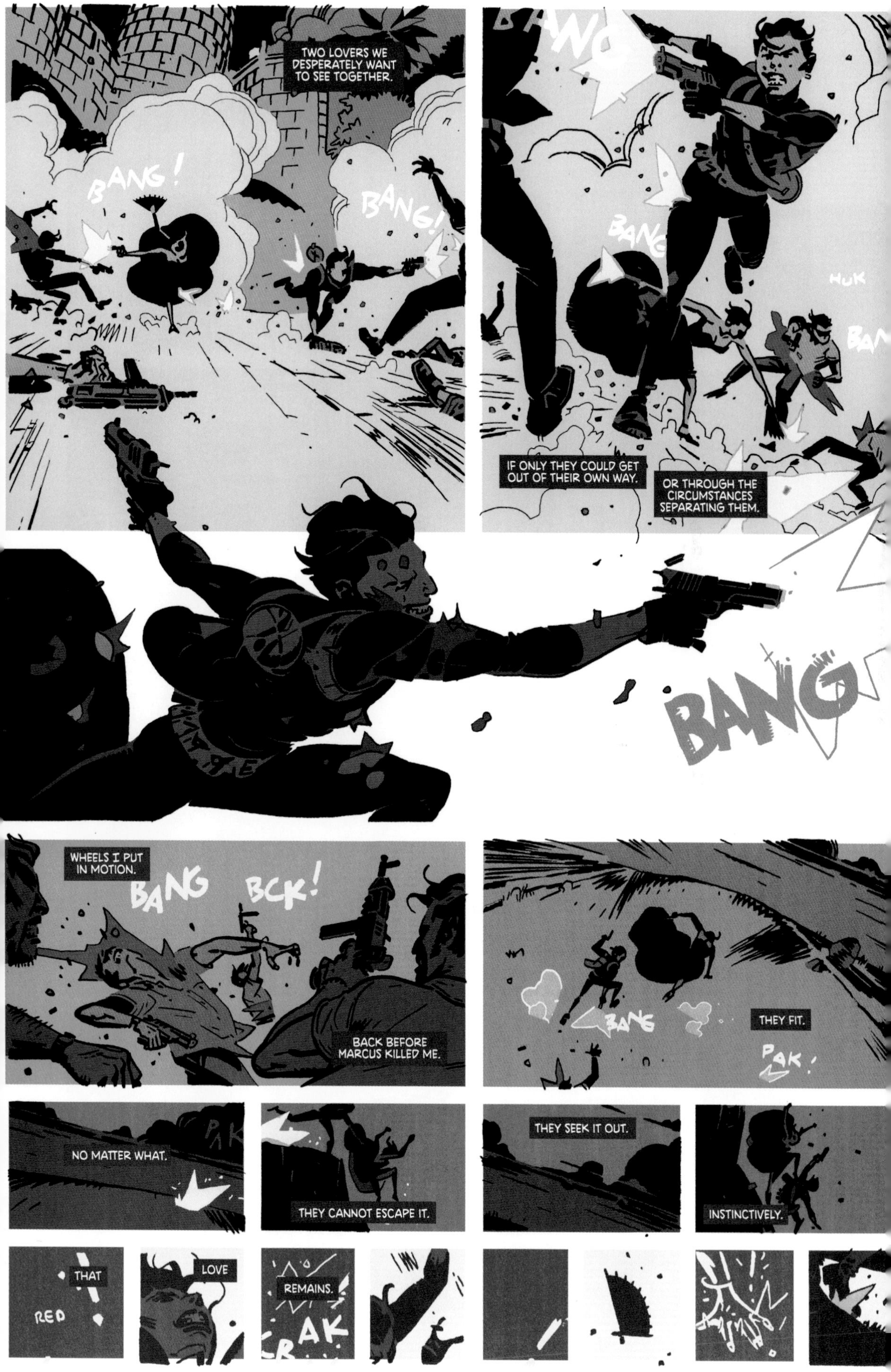
TWO LOVERS WE DESPERATELY WANT TO SEE TOGETHER.
BANG!
BANG!
BANG
HUK
IF ONLY THEY COULD GET OUT OF THEIR OWN WAY.
OR THROUGH THE CIRCUMSTANCES SEPARATING THEM.
BANG
WHEELS I PUT IN MOTION.
BANG
BCK!
BACK BEFORE MARCUS KILLED ME.
BANG
THEY FIT.
PAK!
NO MATTER WHAT.
THEY CANNOT ESCAPE IT.
THEY SEEK IT OUT.
INSTINCTIVELY.
THAT
RED
LOVE
REMAINS.
CRAK

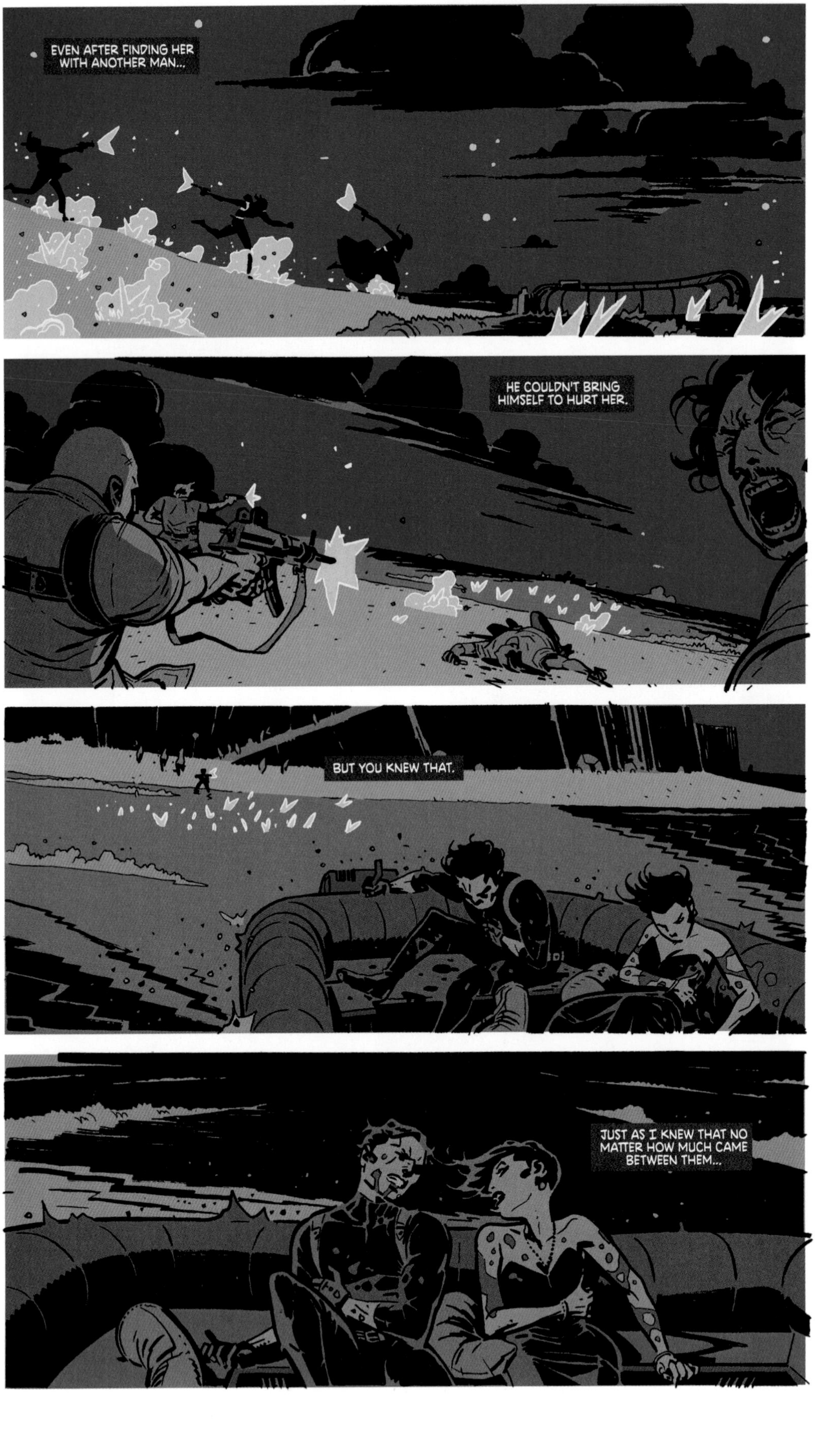
EVEN AFTER FINDING HER WITH ANOTHER MAN...
HE COULDN'T BRING HIMSELF TO HURT HER.
BUT YOU KNEW THAT.
JUST AS I KNEW THAT NO MATTER HOW MUCH CAME BETWEEN THEM...

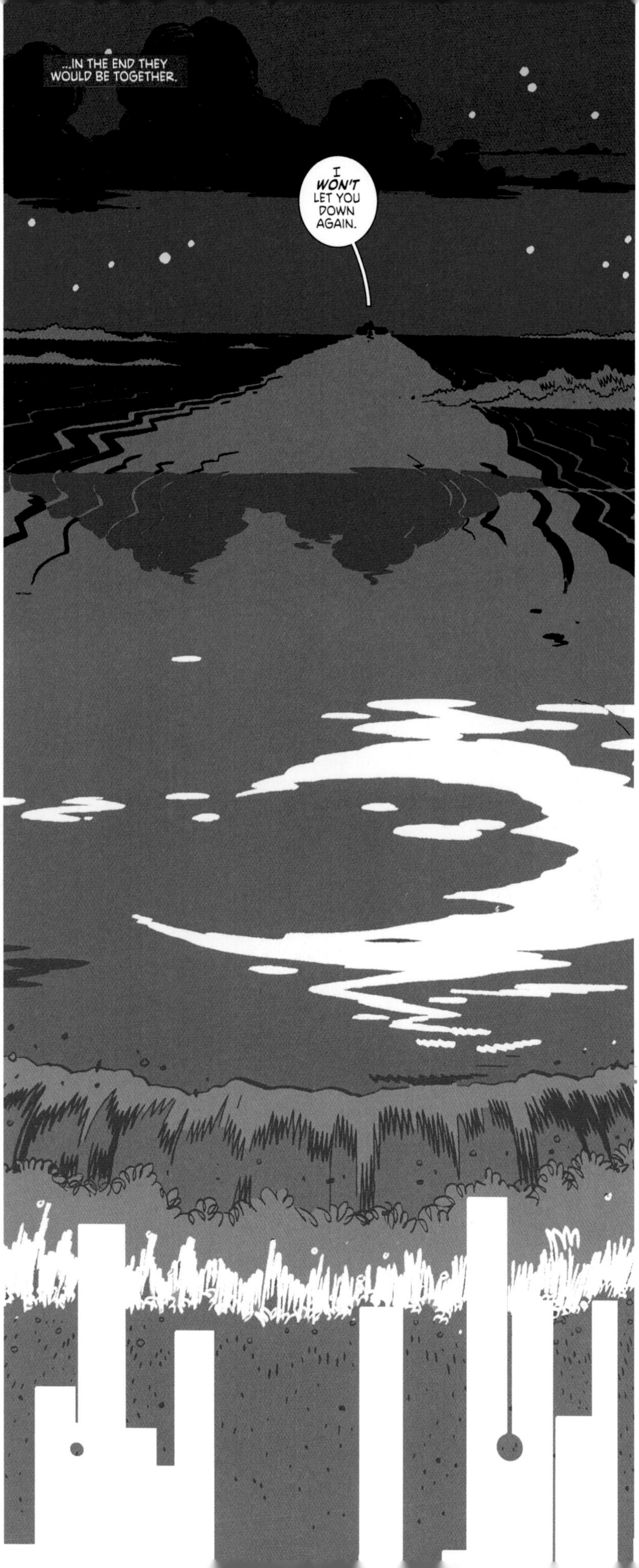
...IN THE END THEY WOULD BE TOGETHER.
I *WON'T* LET YOU DOWN AGAIN.

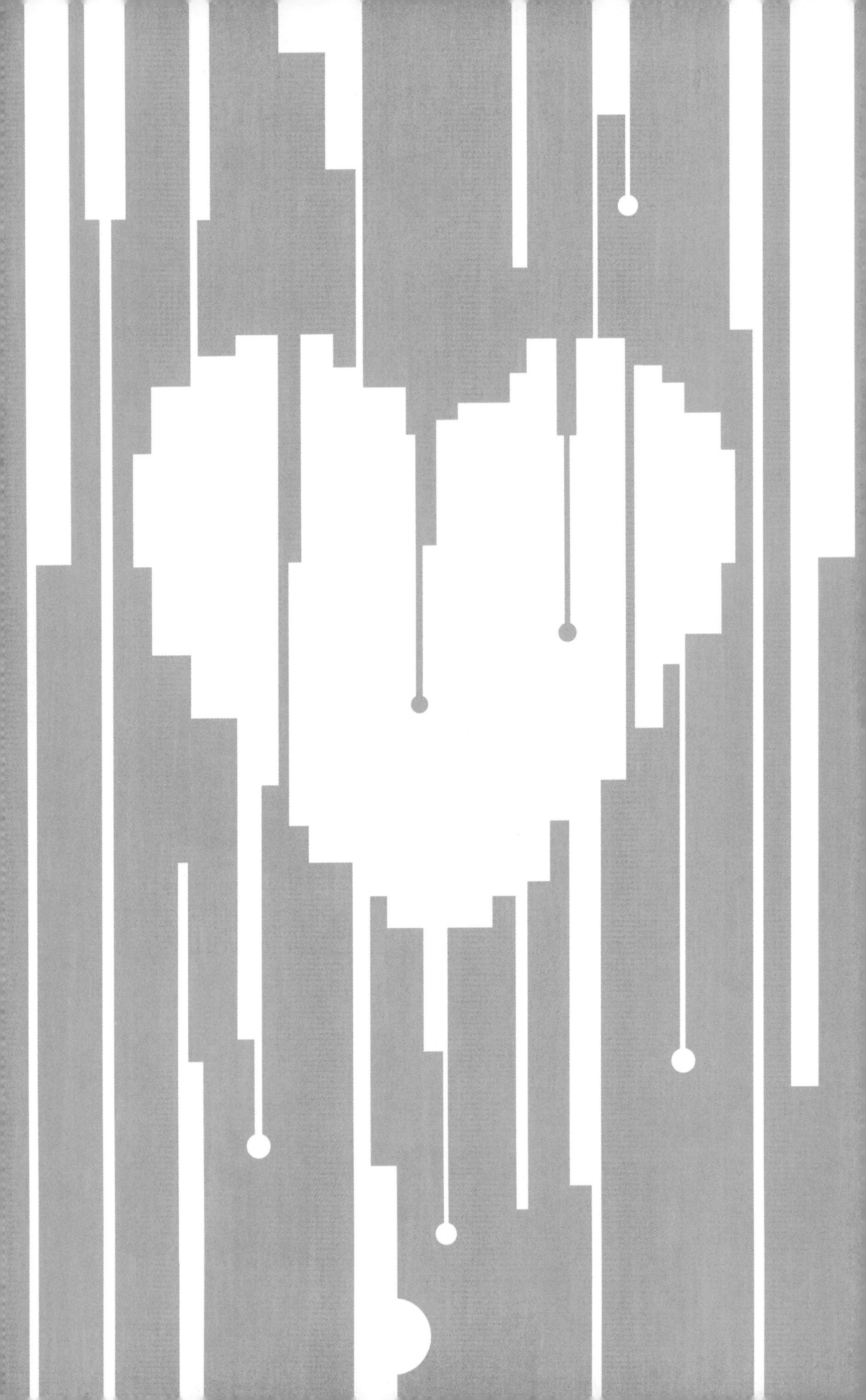

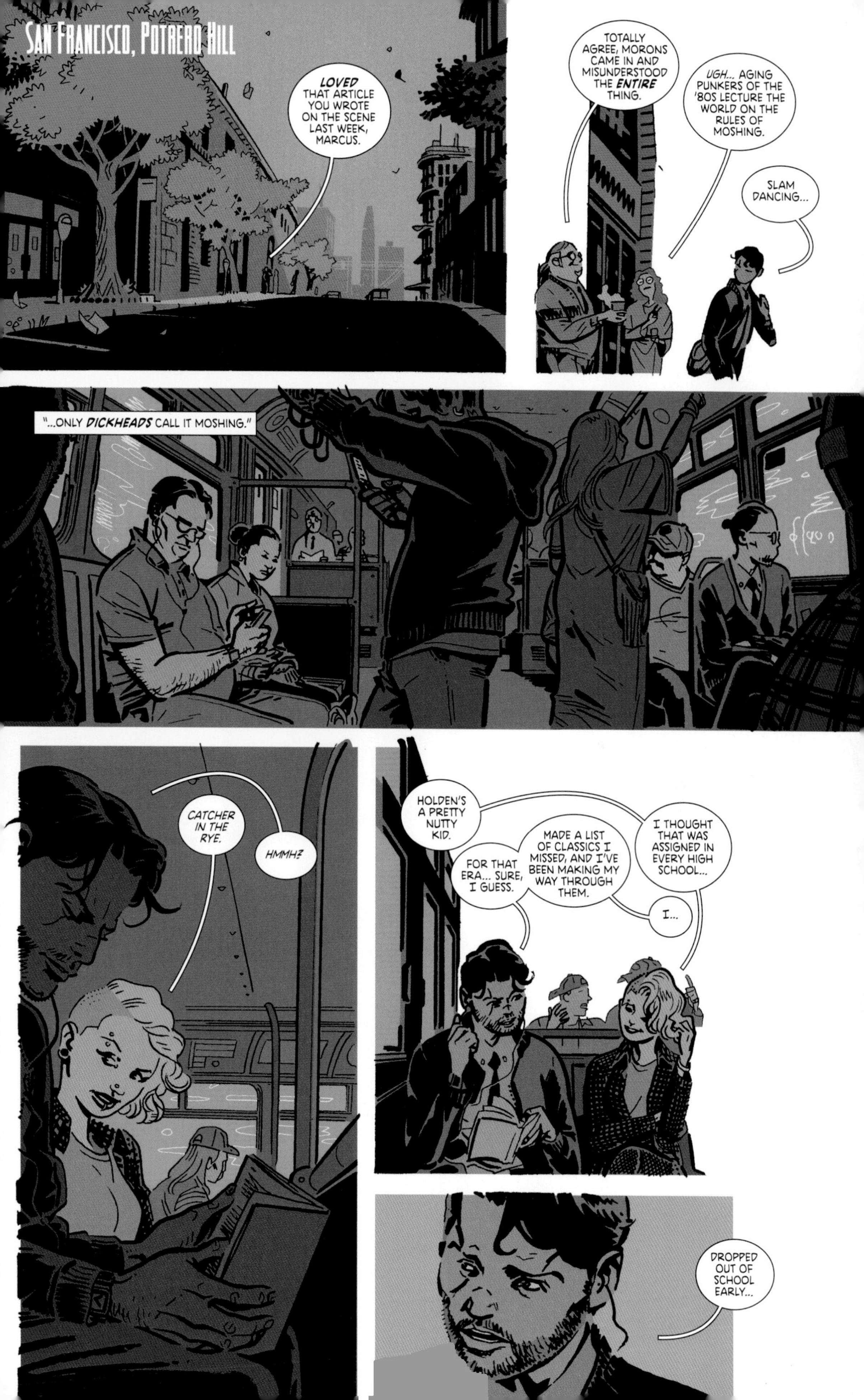
SAN FRANCISCO, POTRERO HILL
LOVED THAT ARTICLE YOU WROTE ON THE SCENE LAST WEEK, MARCUS.
TOTALLY AGREE, MORONS CAME IN AND MISUNDERSTOOD THE ENTIRE THING.
UGH... AGING PUNKERS OF THE '80S LECTURE THE WORLD ON THE RULES OF MOSHING.
SLAM DANCING...
"...ONLY DICKHEADS CALL IT MOSHING."
CATCHER IN THE RYE.
HMMH?
HOLDEN'S A PRETTY NUTTY KID.
I THOUGHT THAT WAS ASSIGNED IN EVERY HIGH SCHOOL...
I...
MADE A LIST OF CLASSICS I MISSED, AND I'VE BEEN MAKING MY WAY THROUGH THEM.
FOR THAT ERA... SURE, I GUESS.
DROPPED OUT OF SCHOOL EARLY...

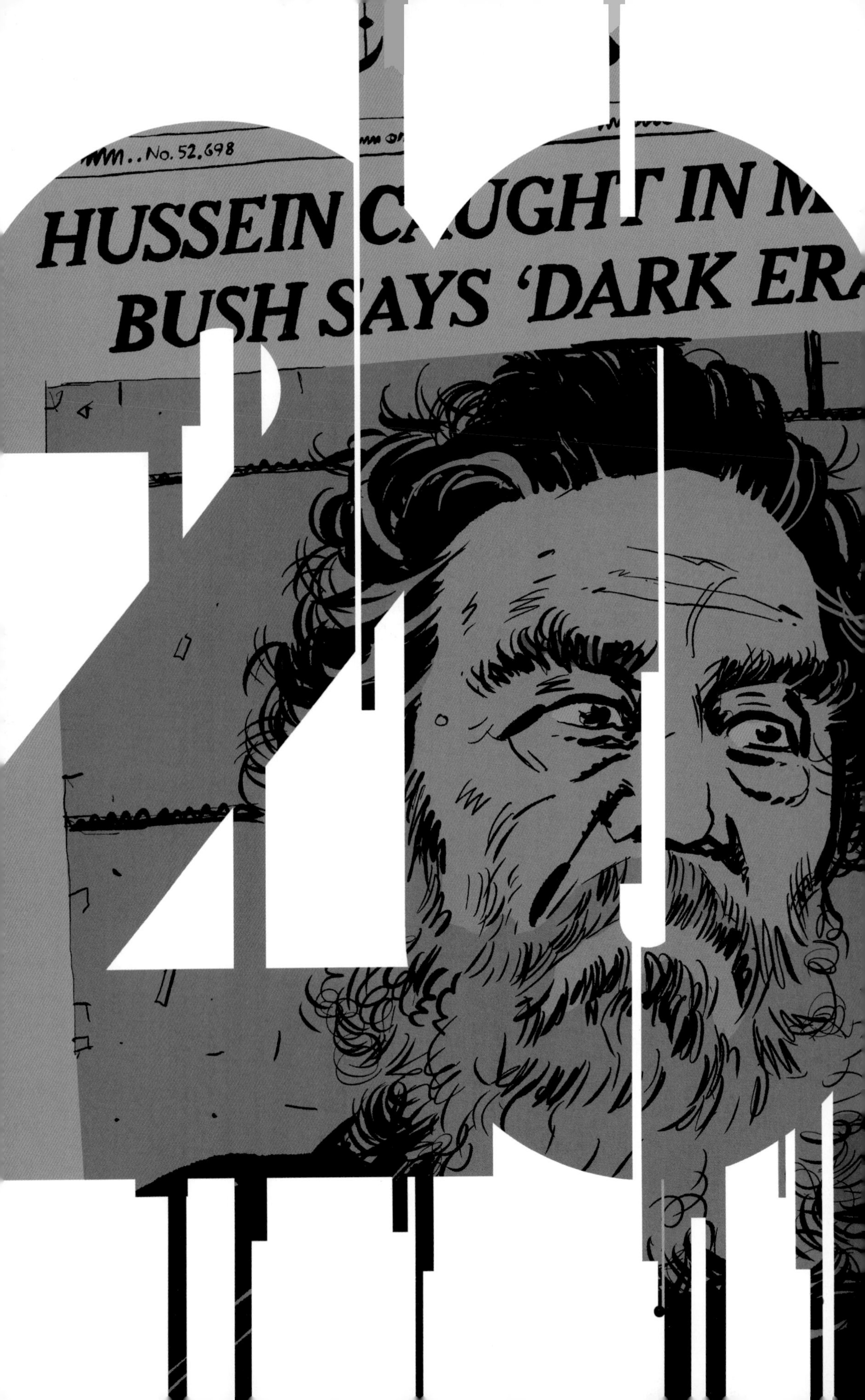
No. 52,698
HUSSEIN CAUGHT IN M
BUSH SAYS 'DARK ERA

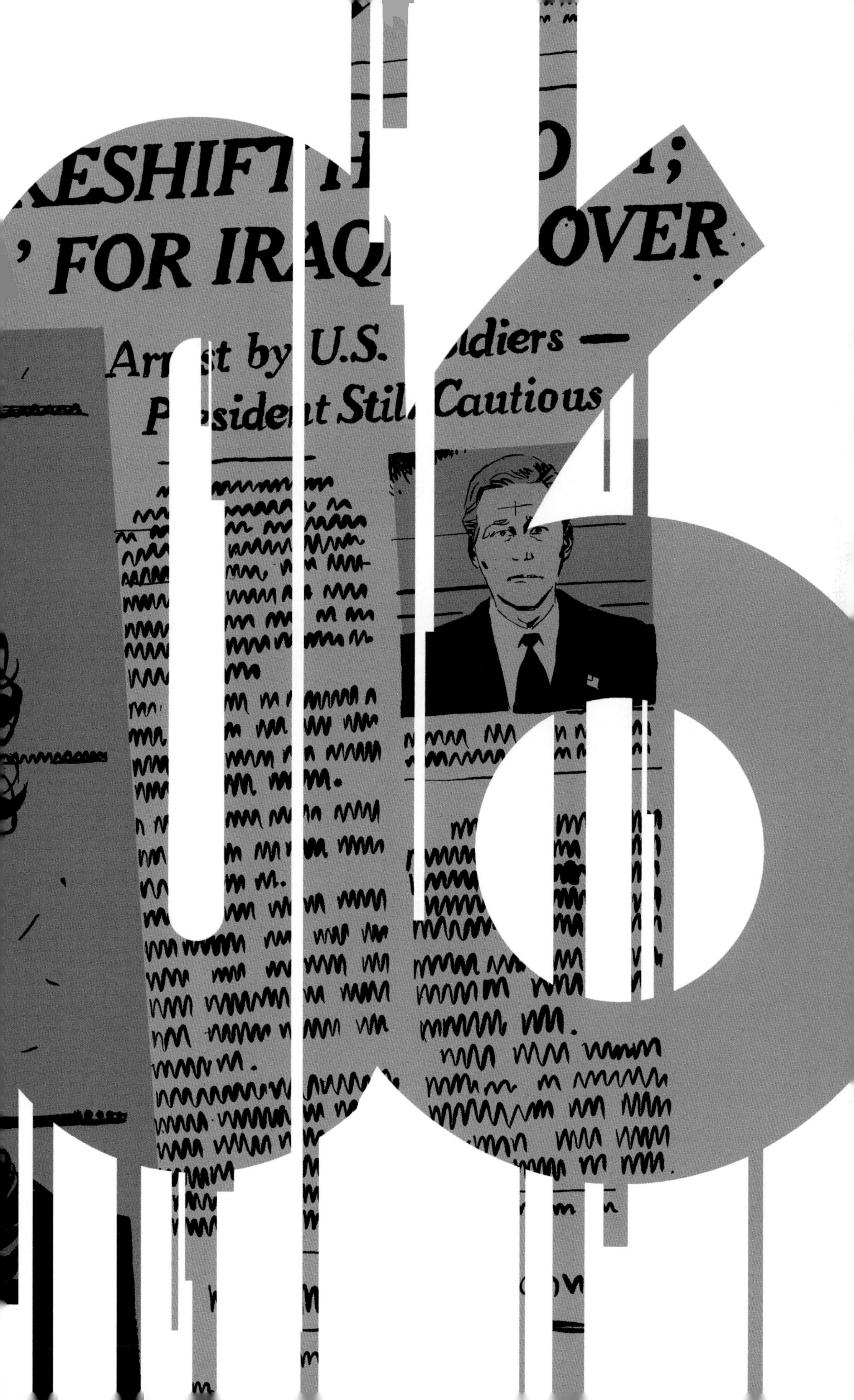

ESHIFT TH O I;
' FOR IRAQ OVER
Arr st by U.S. ldiers —
P sident Stil Cautious

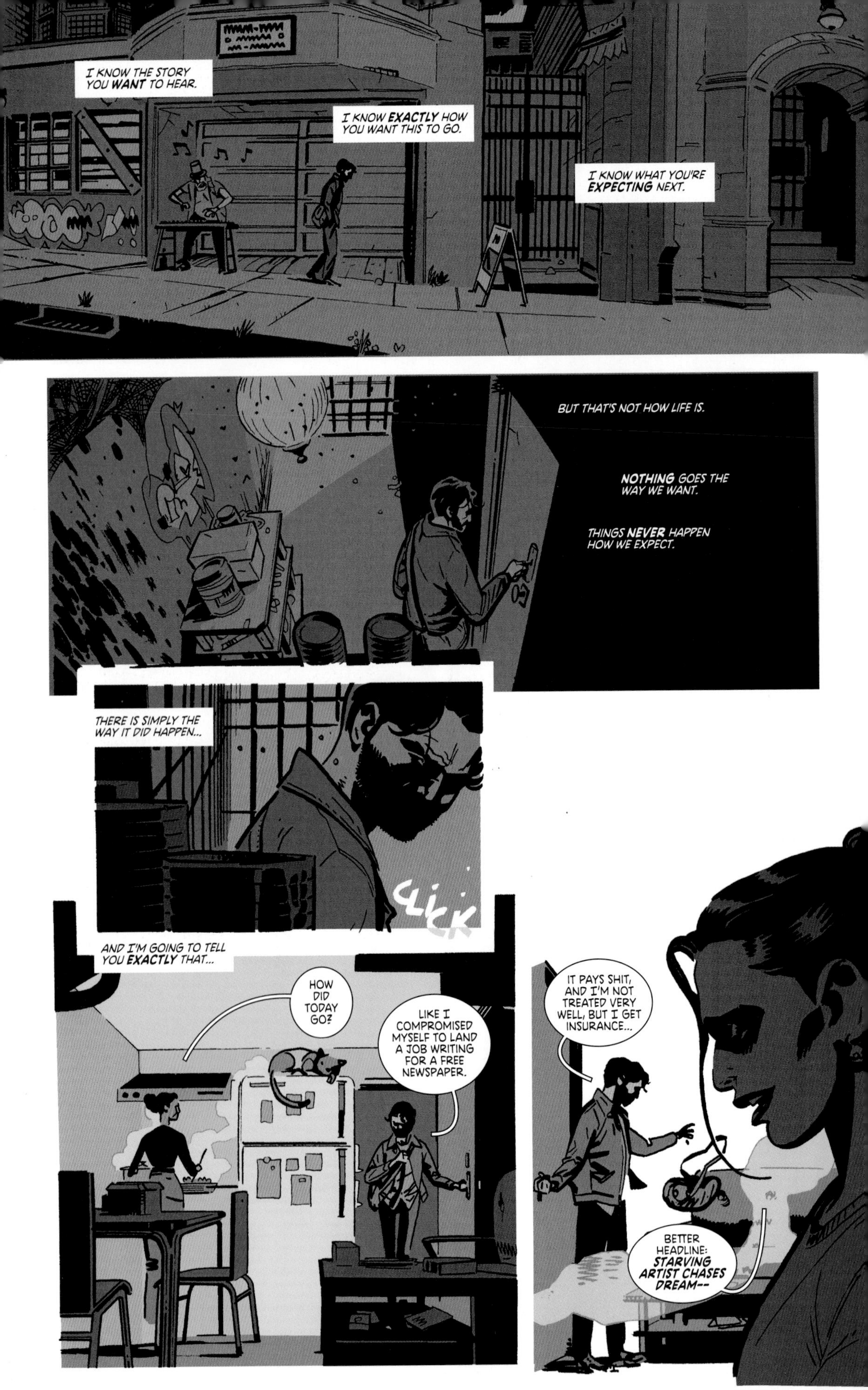
I KNOW THE STORY YOU WANT TO HEAR.
I KNOW EXACTLY HOW YOU WANT THIS TO GO.
I KNOW WHAT YOU'RE EXPECTING NEXT.
BUT THAT'S NOT HOW LIFE IS.
NOTHING GOES THE WAY WE WANT.
THINGS NEVER HAPPEN HOW WE EXPECT.
THERE IS SIMPLY THE WAY IT DID HAPPEN...
CLICK
AND I'M GOING TO TELL YOU EXACTLY THAT...
HOW DID TODAY GO?
LIKE I COMPROMISED MYSELF TO LAND A JOB WRITING FOR A FREE NEWSPAPER.
IT PAYS SHIT, AND I'M NOT TREATED VERY WELL, BUT I GET INSURANCE...
BETTER HEADLINE: STARVING ARTIST CHASES DREAM--

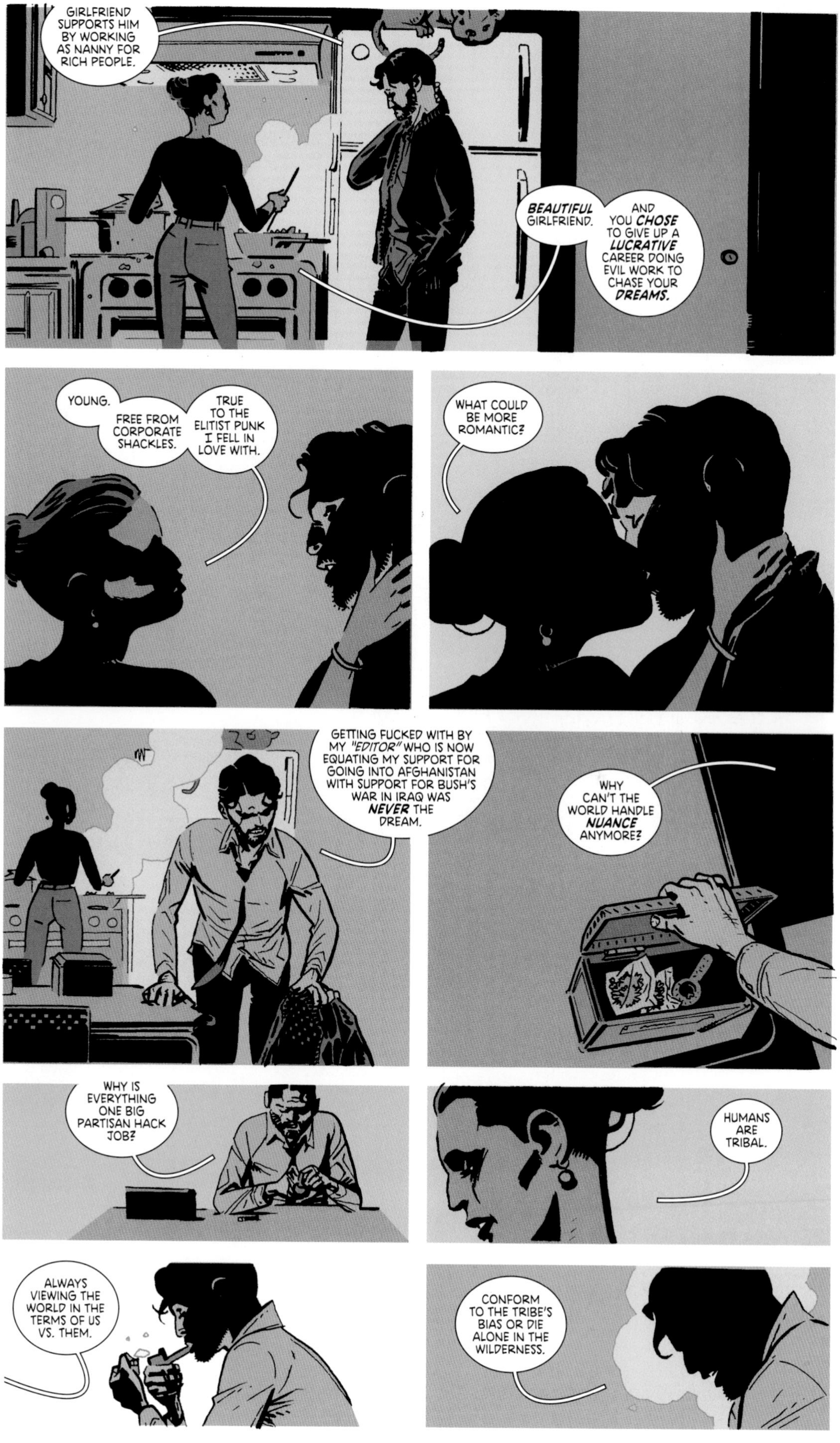
GIRLFRIEND SUPPORTS HIM BY WORKING AS NANNY FOR RICH PEOPLE.
BEAUTIFUL GIRLFRIEND.
AND YOU CHOSE TO GIVE UP A LUCRATIVE CAREER DOING EVIL WORK TO CHASE YOUR DREAMS.
YOUNG.
FREE FROM CORPORATE SHACKLES.
TRUE TO THE ELITIST PUNK I FELL IN LOVE WITH.
WHAT COULD BE MORE ROMANTIC?
GETTING FUCKED WITH BY MY "EDITOR" WHO IS NOW EQUATING MY SUPPORT FOR GOING INTO AFGHANISTAN WITH SUPPORT FOR BUSH'S WAR IN IRAQ WAS NEVER THE DREAM.
WHY CAN'T THE WORLD HANDLE NUANCE ANYMORE?
WHY IS EVERYTHING ONE BIG PARTISAN HACK JOB?
HUMANS ARE TRIBAL.
ALWAYS VIEWING THE WORLD IN THE TERMS OF US VS. THEM.
CONFORM TO THE TRIBE'S BIAS OR DIE ALONE IN THE WILDERNESS.

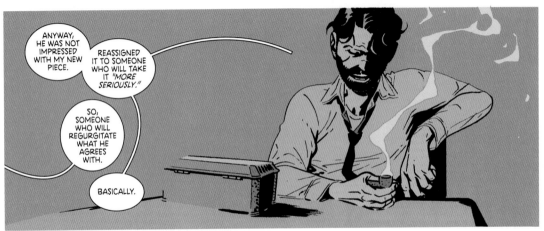

ANYWAY, HE WAS NOT IMPRESSED WITH MY NEW PIECE.

REASSIGNED IT TO SOMEONE WHO WILL TAKE IT *"MORE SERIOUSLY."*

SO, SOMEONE WHO WILL REGURGITATE WHAT HE AGREES WITH.

BASICALLY.

WOULDN'T EVEN DISCUSS IT.

WOULDN'T *CONSIDER* THAT THERE'S A DIFFERENCE BETWEEN HUNTING THE GUY WHO ORGANIZED 9-11 AND STARTING A RANDOM WAR WITH A COUNTRY THAT HAD NOTHING TO DO WITH IT.

MADE A JOKE THAT I'M RIGHT-WING ADJACENT.

THE LOOK IN HIS EYES... *BILE* AND *STUPIDITY.*

NOT EVERYONE IS GOING TO LIKE YOU.

SURE. SHIT, I'M FULLY OKAY IF SOMEONE EVEN *HATES* ME...

BUT I JUST WANT TO BE HATED FOR THINGS THAT ARE *TRUE.*

NOT MISUNDER-STANDINGS OR SLANDER OR CONCOCTED BULLSHIT.

THEY *DON'T* CARE ABOUT YOU, SO *DON'T* LET THEM RENT SPACE IN YOUR HEAD.

LIFE IS *QUICK* AND *IMPERMANENT* AND COMES DOWN TO SIMPLY ENJOYING WHO YOU SPEND YOUR TIME WITH--

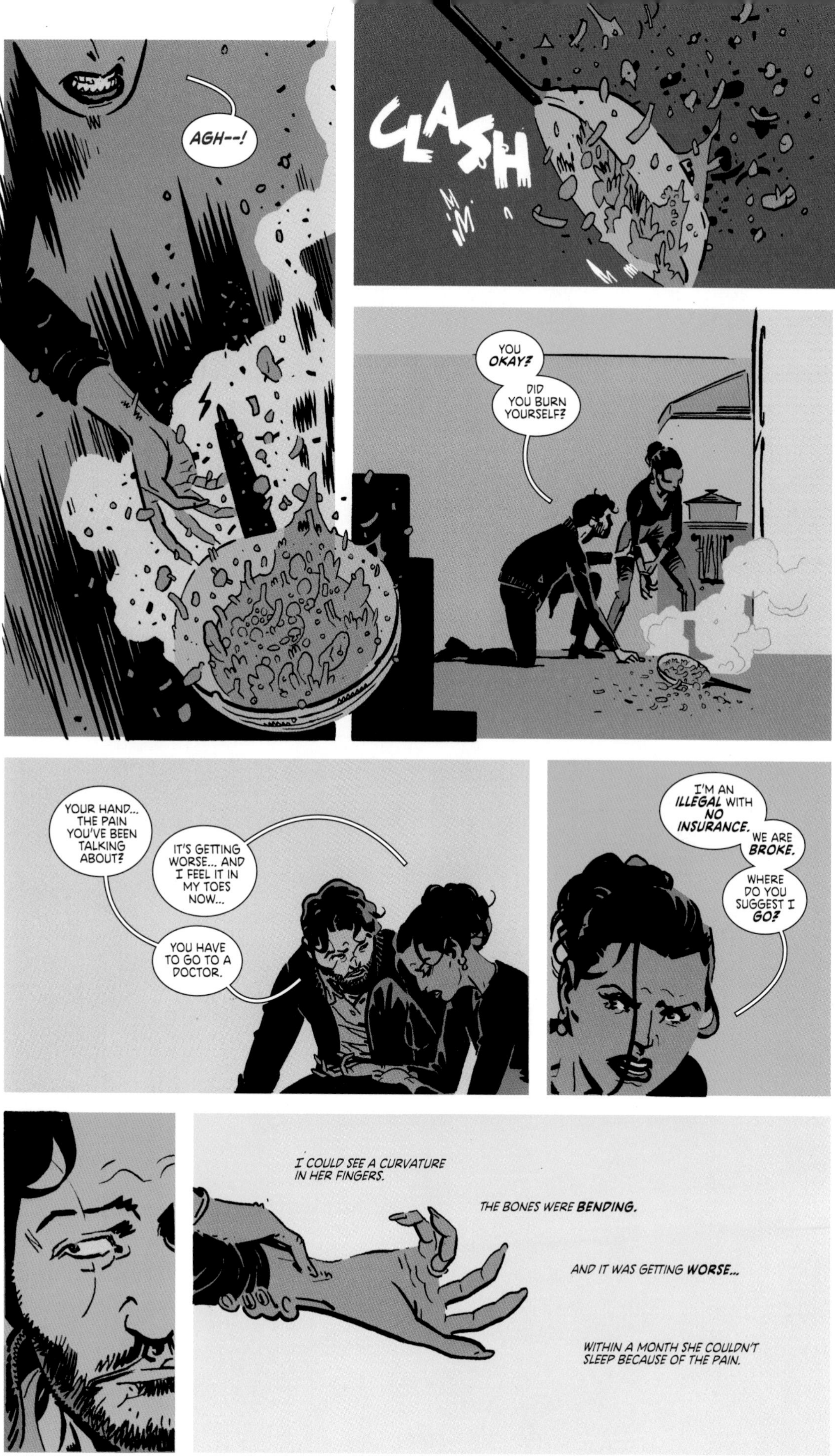
AGH--!
CLASH
YOU OKAY?
DID YOU BURN YOURSELF?
YOUR HAND... THE PAIN YOU'VE BEEN TALKING ABOUT?
IT'S GETTING WORSE... AND I FEEL IT IN MY TOES NOW...
YOU HAVE TO GO TO A DOCTOR.
I'M AN ILLEGAL WITH NO INSURANCE.
WE ARE BROKE.
WHERE DO YOU SUGGEST I GO?
I COULD SEE A CURVATURE IN HER FINGERS.
THE BONES WERE BENDING.
AND IT WAS GETTING WORSE...
WITHIN A MONTH SHE COULDN'T SLEEP BECAUSE OF THE PAIN.

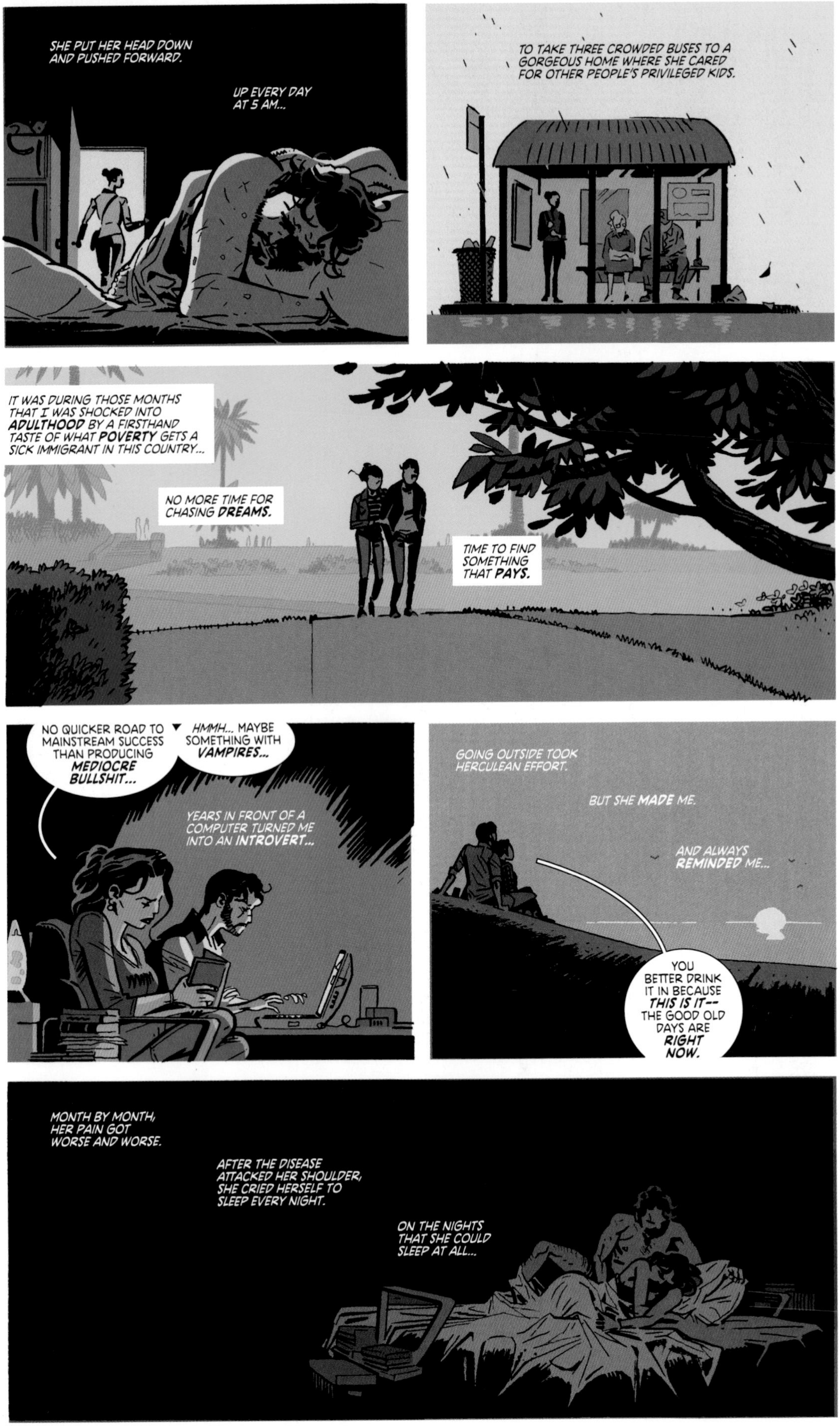
SHE PUT HER HEAD DOWN AND PUSHED FORWARD.
UP EVERY DAY AT 5 AM...
TO TAKE THREE CROWDED BUSES TO A GORGEOUS HOME WHERE SHE CARED FOR OTHER PEOPLE'S PRIVILEGED KIDS.
IT WAS DURING THOSE MONTHS THAT I WAS SHOCKED INTO ADULTHOOD BY A FIRSTHAND TASTE OF WHAT POVERTY GETS A SICK IMMIGRANT IN THIS COUNTRY...
NO MORE TIME FOR CHASING DREAMS.
TIME TO FIND SOMETHING THAT PAYS.
NO QUICKER ROAD TO MAINSTREAM SUCCESS THAN PRODUCING MEDIOCRE BULLSHIT...
HMMH... MAYBE SOMETHING WITH VAMPIRES...
YEARS IN FRONT OF A COMPUTER TURNED ME INTO AN INTROVERT...
GOING OUTSIDE TOOK HERCULEAN EFFORT.
BUT SHE MADE ME.
AND ALWAYS REMINDED ME...
YOU BETTER DRINK IT IN BECAUSE THIS IS IT-- THE GOOD OLD DAYS ARE RIGHT NOW.
MONTH BY MONTH, HER PAIN GOT WORSE AND WORSE.
AFTER THE DISEASE ATTACKED HER SHOULDER, SHE CRIED HERSELF TO SLEEP EVERY NIGHT.
ON THE NIGHTS THAT SHE COULD SLEEP AT ALL...

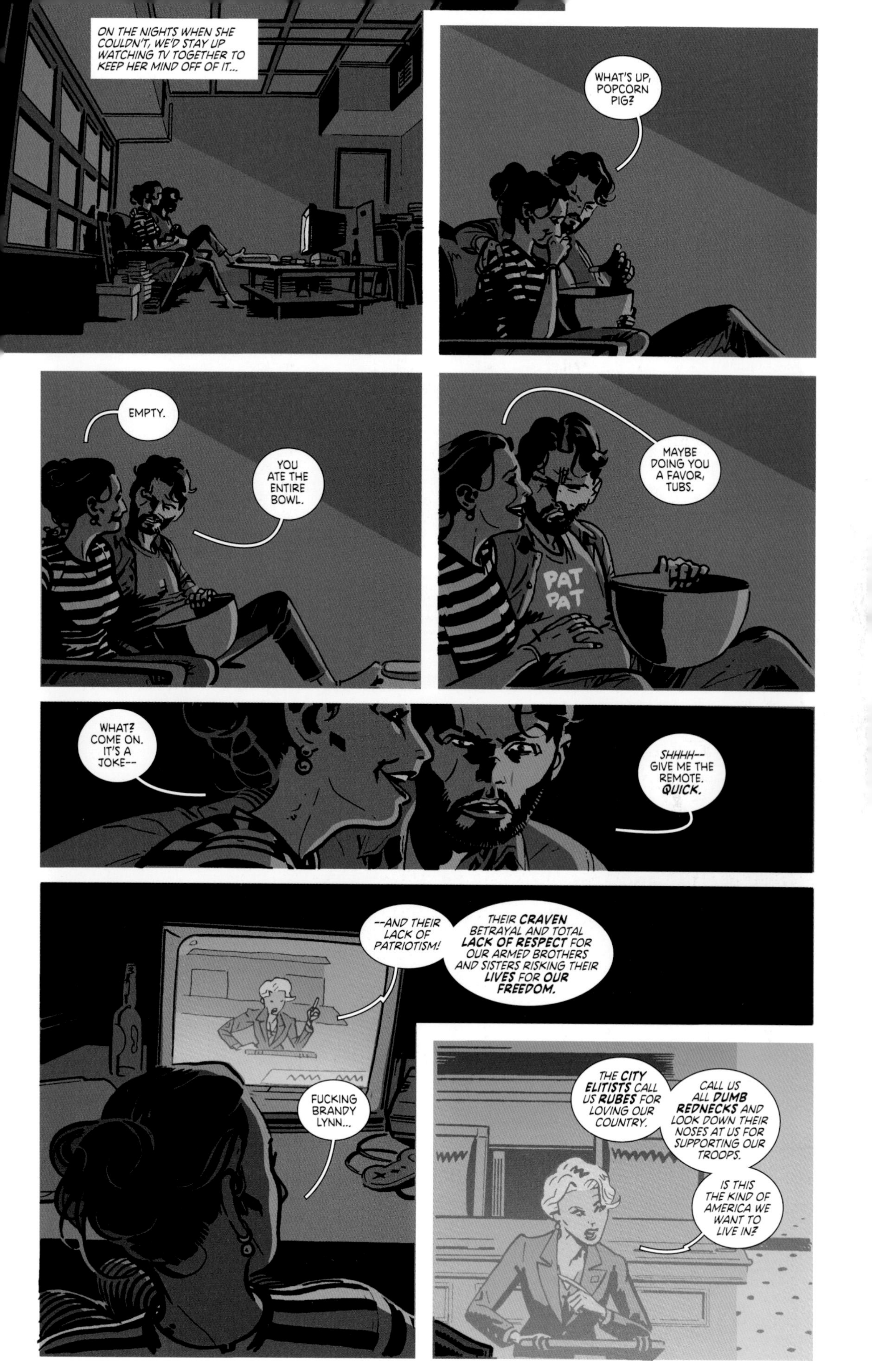
ON THE NIGHTS WHEN SHE COULDN'T, WE'D STAY UP WATCHING TV TOGETHER TO KEEP HER MIND OFF OF IT...
WHAT'S UP, POPCORN PIG?
EMPTY.
YOU ATE THE ENTIRE BOWL.
MAYBE DOING YOU A FAVOR, TUBS.
PAT PAT
WHAT? COME ON. IT'S A JOKE--
SHHHH-- GIVE ME THE REMOTE. QUICK.
--AND THEIR LACK OF PATRIOTISM!
THEIR CRAVEN BETRAYAL AND TOTAL LACK OF RESPECT FOR OUR ARMED BROTHERS AND SISTERS RISKING THEIR LIVES FOR OUR FREEDOM.
FUCKING BRANDY LYNN...
THE CITY ELITISTS CALL US RUBES FOR LOVING OUR COUNTRY.
CALL US ALL DUMB REDNECKS AND LOOK DOWN THEIR NOSES AT US FOR SUPPORTING OUR TROOPS.
IS THIS THE KIND OF AMERICA WE WANT TO LIVE IN?

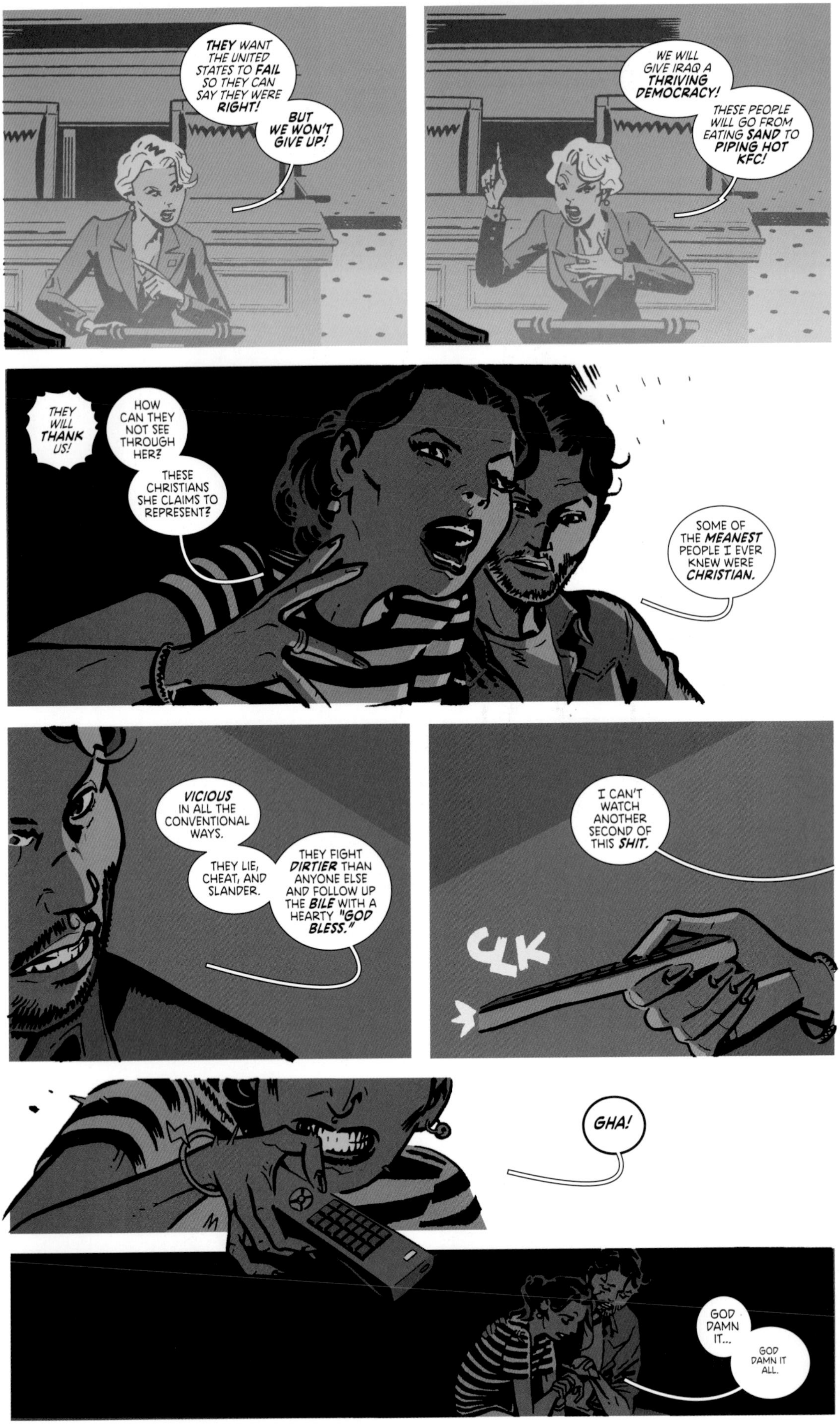
THEY WANT THE UNITED STATES TO FAIL SO THEY CAN SAY THEY WERE RIGHT!
BUT WE WON'T GIVE UP!
WE WILL GIVE IRAQ A THRIVING DEMOCRACY!
THESE PEOPLE WILL GO FROM EATING SAND TO PIPING HOT KFC!
THEY WILL THANK US!
HOW CAN THEY NOT SEE THROUGH HER?
THESE CHRISTIANS SHE CLAIMS TO REPRESENT?
SOME OF THE MEANEST PEOPLE I EVER KNEW WERE CHRISTIAN.
VICIOUS IN ALL THE CONVENTIONAL WAYS.
THEY LIE, CHEAT, AND SLANDER.
THEY FIGHT DIRTIER THAN ANYONE ELSE AND FOLLOW UP THE BILE WITH A HEARTY "GOD BLESS."
I CAN'T WATCH ANOTHER SECOND OF THIS SHIT.
CLK
GHA!
GOD DAMN IT...
GOD DAMN IT ALL.

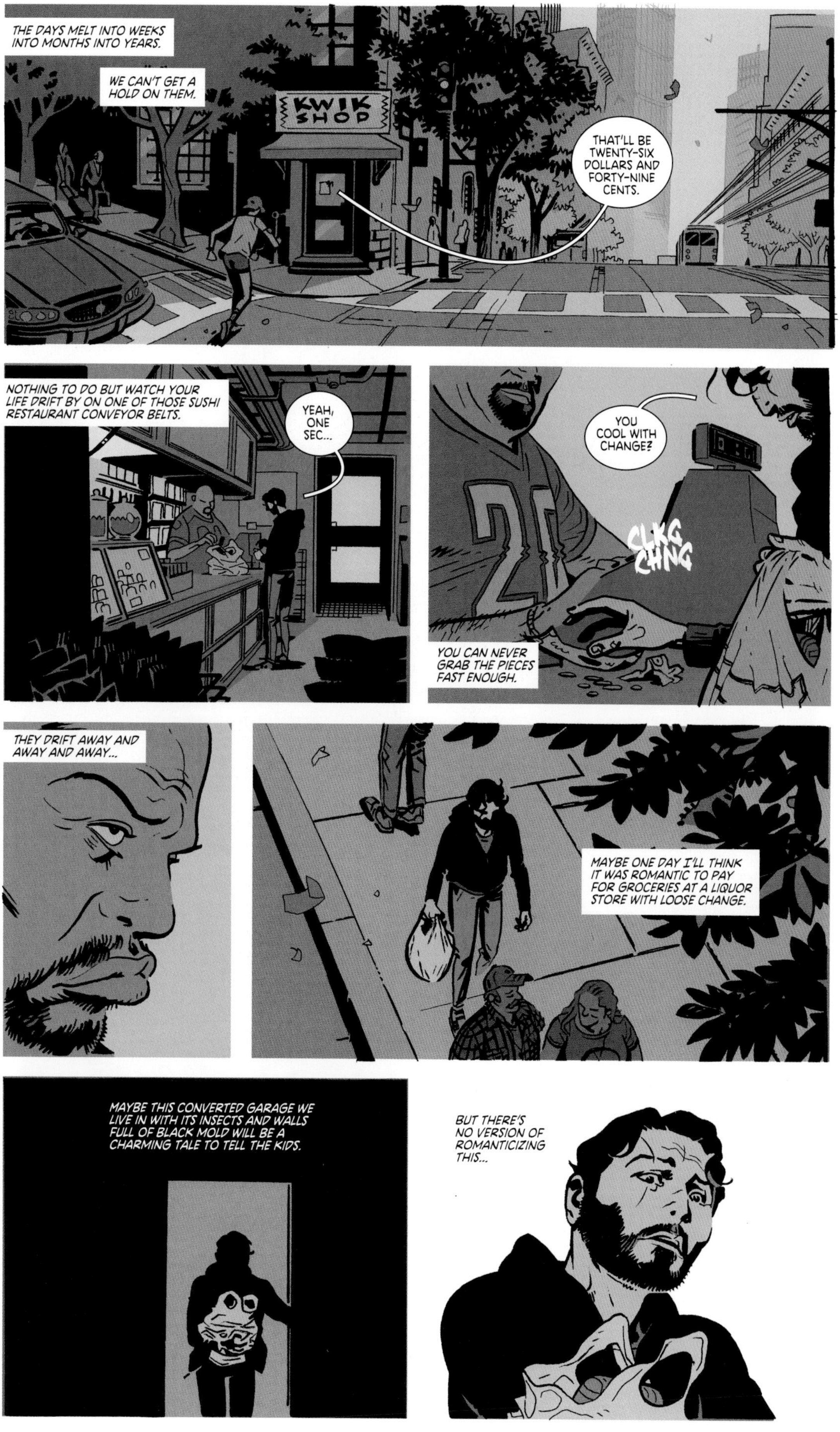
THE DAYS MELT INTO WEEKS INTO MONTHS INTO YEARS.
WE CAN'T GET A HOLD ON THEM.
KWIK SHOP
THAT'LL BE TWENTY-SIX DOLLARS AND FORTY-NINE CENTS.
NOTHING TO DO BUT WATCH YOUR LIFE DRIFT BY ON ONE OF THOSE SUSHI RESTAURANT CONVEYOR BELTS.
YEAH, ONE SEC...
YOU COOL WITH CHANGE?
CLKG CHNG
YOU CAN NEVER GRAB THE PIECES FAST ENOUGH.
THEY DRIFT AWAY AND AWAY AND AWAY...
MAYBE ONE DAY I'LL THINK IT WAS ROMANTIC TO PAY FOR GROCERIES AT A LIQUOR STORE WITH LOOSE CHANGE.
MAYBE THIS CONVERTED GARAGE WE LIVE IN WITH ITS INSECTS AND WALLS FULL OF BLACK MOLD WILL BE A CHARMING TALE TO TELL THE KIDS.
BUT THERE'S NO VERSION OF ROMANTICIZING THIS...

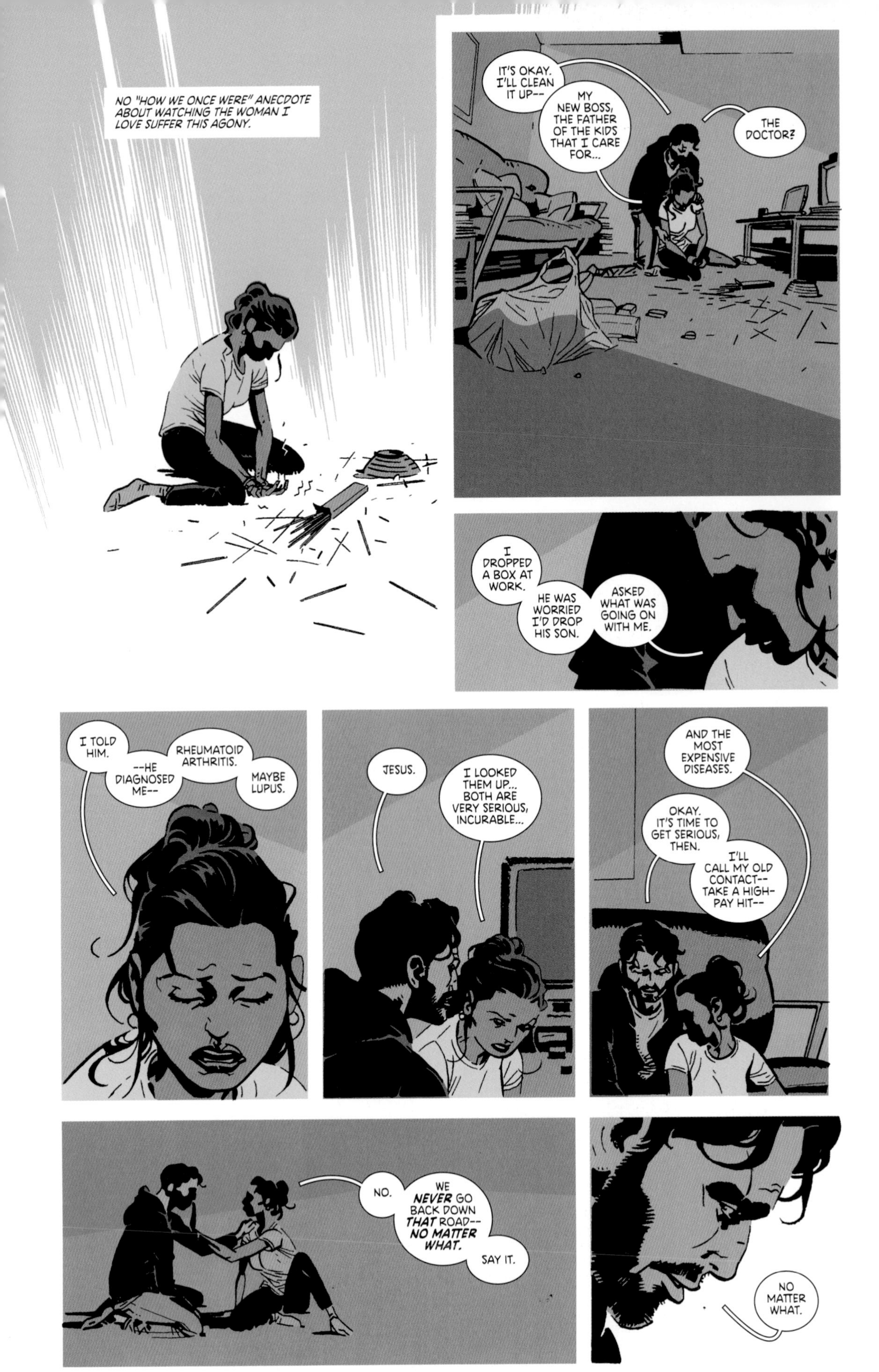
NO "HOW WE ONCE WERE" ANECDOTE ABOUT WATCHING THE WOMAN I LOVE SUFFER THIS AGONY.
IT'S OKAY. I'LL CLEAN IT UP--
MY NEW BOSS, THE FATHER OF THE KIDS THAT I CARE FOR...
THE DOCTOR?
I DROPPED A BOX AT WORK.
HE WAS WORRIED I'D DROP HIS SON.
ASKED WHAT WAS GOING ON WITH ME.
I TOLD HIM.
--HE DIAGNOSED ME--
RHEUMATOID ARTHRITIS.
MAYBE LUPUS.
JESUS.
I LOOKED THEM UP... BOTH ARE VERY SERIOUS, INCURABLE...
AND THE MOST EXPENSIVE DISEASES.
OKAY. IT'S TIME TO GET SERIOUS, THEN.
I'LL CALL MY OLD CONTACT-- TAKE A HIGH-PAY HIT--
NO.
WE **NEVER** GO BACK DOWN ***THAT*** ROAD-- ***NO MATTER WHAT.***
SAY IT.
NO MATTER WHAT.

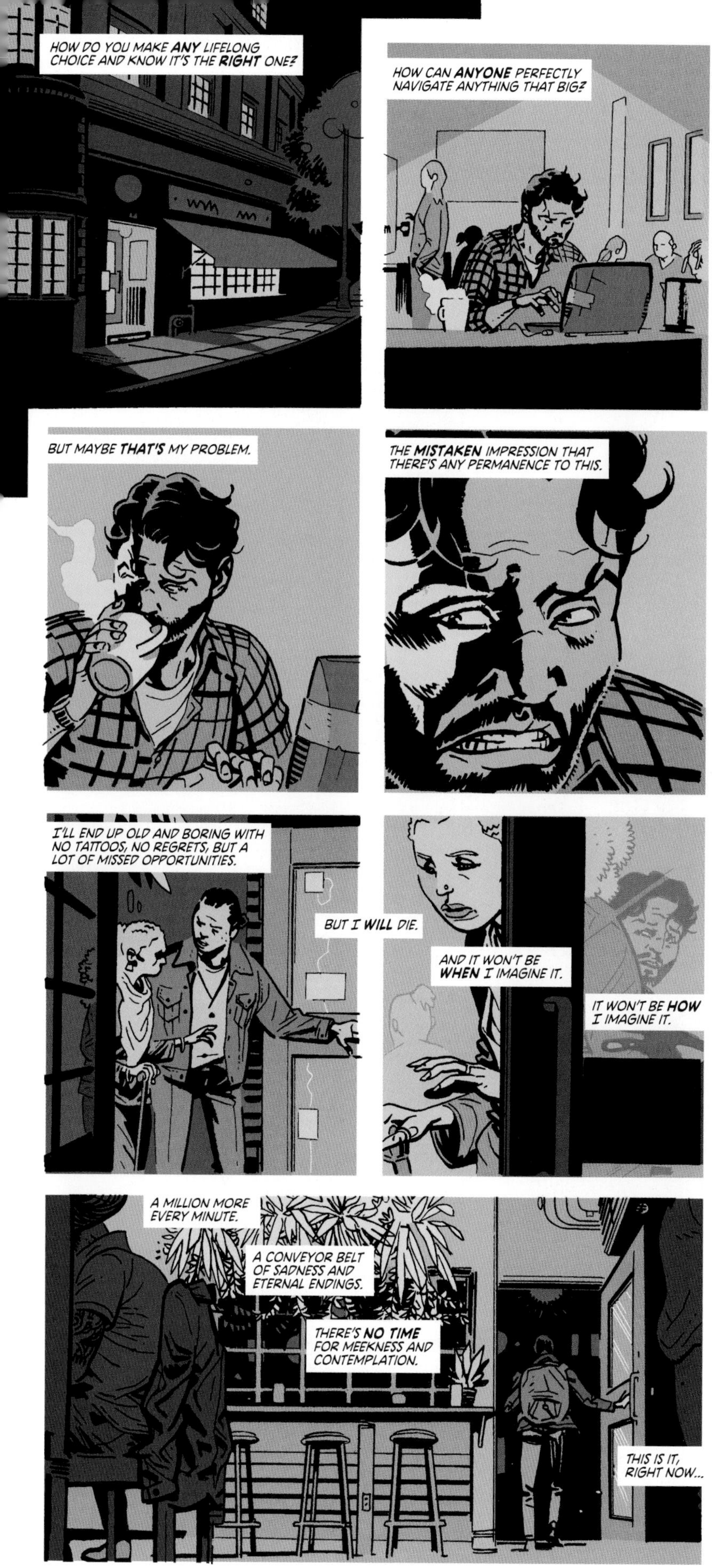
HOW DO YOU MAKE **ANY** LIFELONG CHOICE AND KNOW IT'S THE **RIGHT** ONE?
HOW CAN **ANYONE** PERFECTLY NAVIGATE ANYTHING THAT BIG?
BUT MAYBE **THAT'S** MY PROBLEM.
THE **MISTAKEN** IMPRESSION THAT THERE'S ANY PERMANENCE TO THIS.
I'LL END UP OLD AND BORING WITH NO TATTOOS, NO REGRETS, BUT A LOT OF MISSED OPPORTUNITIES.
BUT I **WILL** DIE.
AND IT WON'T BE **WHEN** I IMAGINE IT.
IT WON'T BE **HOW** I IMAGINE IT.
A MILLION MORE EVERY MINUTE.
A CONVEYOR BELT OF SADNESS AND ETERNAL ENDINGS.
THERE'S **NO TIME** FOR MEEKNESS AND CONTEMPLATION.
THIS IS IT, RIGHT NOW...

IT'S WHY I NEVER GOT A TATTOO.

THE ART THAT I FIND APPEALING RIGHT NOW MAY BE SOME PLAYED-OUT BULLSHIT BY THE TIME I'M 40.

WHY TAKE THE RISK AND FIND OUT?

I COULD HAVE A TON OF BAD TATTOOS AND MAYBE ALL THEY'D ADD UP TO IS MEMORIES OF WHEN I GOT THEM, THE TIMES I LIVED THROUGH.

INSTEAD I'M BECOMING THE GUY WHO SITS AROUND WORRYING ABOUT THE FUTURE SO MUCH THAT I NEVER TAKE ANY ACTION.

NEVER MAKE ANY CHOICES.

NEVER RISK A MISTAKE.

THERE IS NO PERFECT LIFE.

NO WAY TO BE SO CAUTIOUS YOU AVOID HEARTBREAK.

THERE ARE A MILLION BROKEN HEARTS RIGHT NOW, PEOPLE WHO LOST SOMEONE THEY LOVED.

TIME FOR ACTION.

# JUNE 6TH, 2006

I'M WRITING THIS TODAY FOR MY KIDS, WHO I IMAGINE WILL BE SURPRISED TO BE ADDRESSED GIVEN WE HAVEN'T HAD YOU YET.

STILL, YOU PROBABLY SHOULDN'T HAVE READ THESE; THERE'S A LOT OF UNCOMFORTABLE TRUTH BEING PROCESSED HERE. UNVARNISHED TRUTH IS UGLY IN HINDSIGHT. TRUTH IS UGLY ANYTIME, ACTUALLY.

BUT THERE ARE A FEW TRUTHS I'D LIKE TO SHARE FROM MY ENCYCLOPEDIA OF PERSONAL PERSPECTIVES.

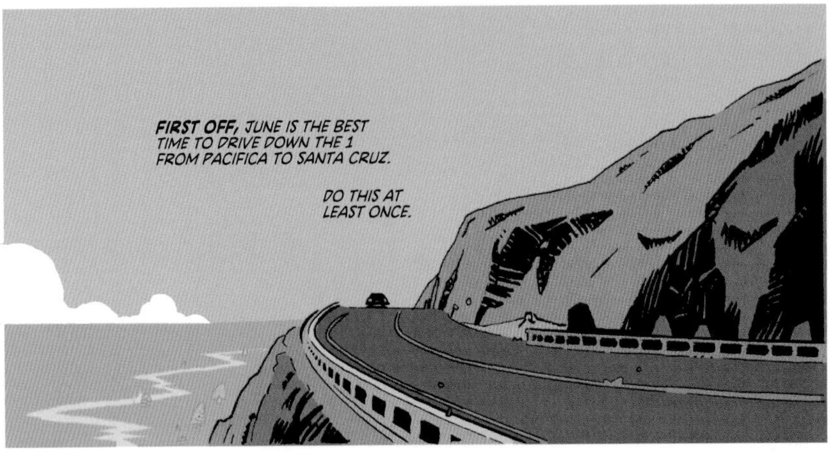
**FIRST OFF,** JUNE IS THE BEST TIME TO DRIVE DOWN THE 1 FROM PACIFICA TO SANTA CRUZ.
DO THIS AT LEAST ONCE.

FIGHT **ANYONE** WHO TELLS YOU HOW YOU'RE **ALLOWED** TO EXPRESS YOURSELF. ACCEPT NO MORAL AUTHORITY.

THINK LESS ABOUT WHAT YOU WANT TO **REMOVE** FROM THE WORLD AND MORE WHAT YOU WANT TO **ADD** TO IT.

IF YOU'RE **PROUD** OF AN ACCOMPLISHMENT, **HIDE IT** OR YOU'LL MAKE OTHER PEOPLE RESENTFUL.

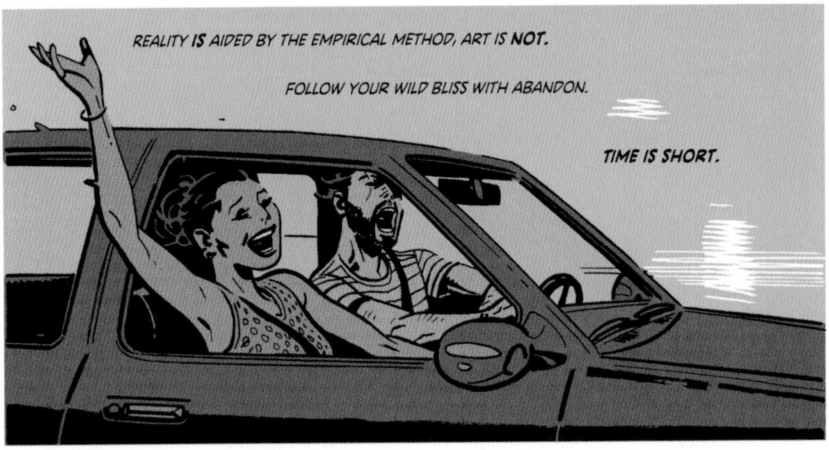
REALITY **IS** AIDED BY THE EMPIRICAL METHOD, ART IS **NOT.**
FOLLOW YOUR WILD BLISS WITH ABANDON.
**TIME IS SHORT.**

IF YOU'RE **NOT** WORRIED THAT **YOU'RE NO GOOD...** YOU'RE PROBABLY NO GOOD. IMPOSTER SYNDROME IS HEALTHY. IT KEEPS YOU **HUMBLE** AND **HARD-WORKING.**

FIND WHERE YOU BELONG AND BE OKAY THERE. IT'S BETTER TO PLAY YOUR OWN SONG IN A CLUB TO FIFTY PEOPLE THAN PLAY BULLSHIT TO AN ARENA OF TEN THOUSAND.

**AVOID** THE COMFORT OF **CONFORMING** TO **MASS IMITATION.** "BE YOURSELF" IS AN OLD PLATITUDE, BUT THE BEST ONE.

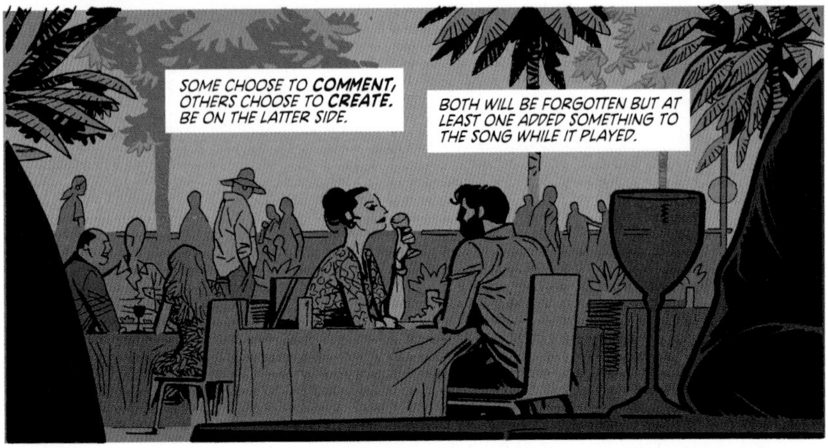
SOME CHOOSE TO **COMMENT,** OTHERS CHOOSE TO **CREATE.** BE ON THE LATTER SIDE.
BOTH WILL BE FORGOTTEN BUT AT LEAST ONE ADDED SOMETHING TO THE SONG WHILE IT PLAYED.

KNOW **WHAT** PROPELS YOU.

POPCORN IS DIFFERENT FROM A BOWL OF CREAMED CORN BECAUSE OF THE TYPE OF HEAT IT WAS PREPARED UNDER.

THE FUEL SOURCE OF YOUR MOTIVATION MATTERS.

KNOW WHAT YOU WANT, AND WHY, AND MAKE SURE IT'S **GOOD FOR YOU.**

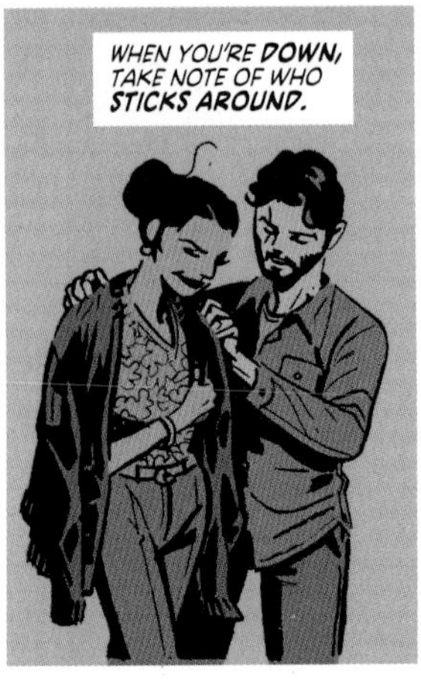
WHEN YOU'RE **DOWN,** TAKE NOTE OF WHO **STICKS AROUND.**

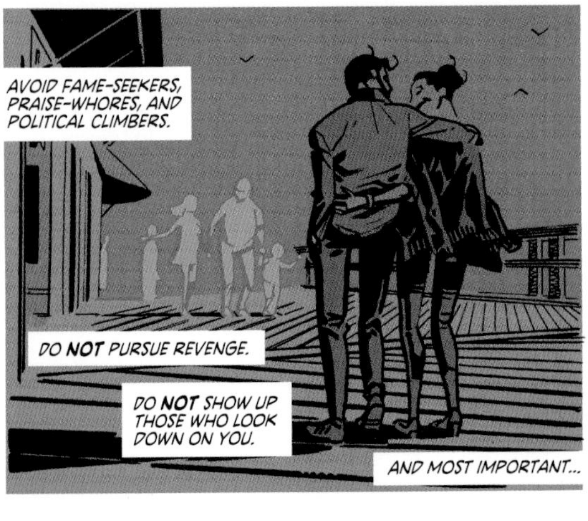
AVOID FAME-SEEKERS, PRAISE-WHORES, AND POLITICAL CLIMBERS.
DO **NOT** PURSUE REVENGE.
DO **NOT** SHOW UP THOSE WHO LOOK DOWN ON YOU.
AND MOST IMPORTANT...

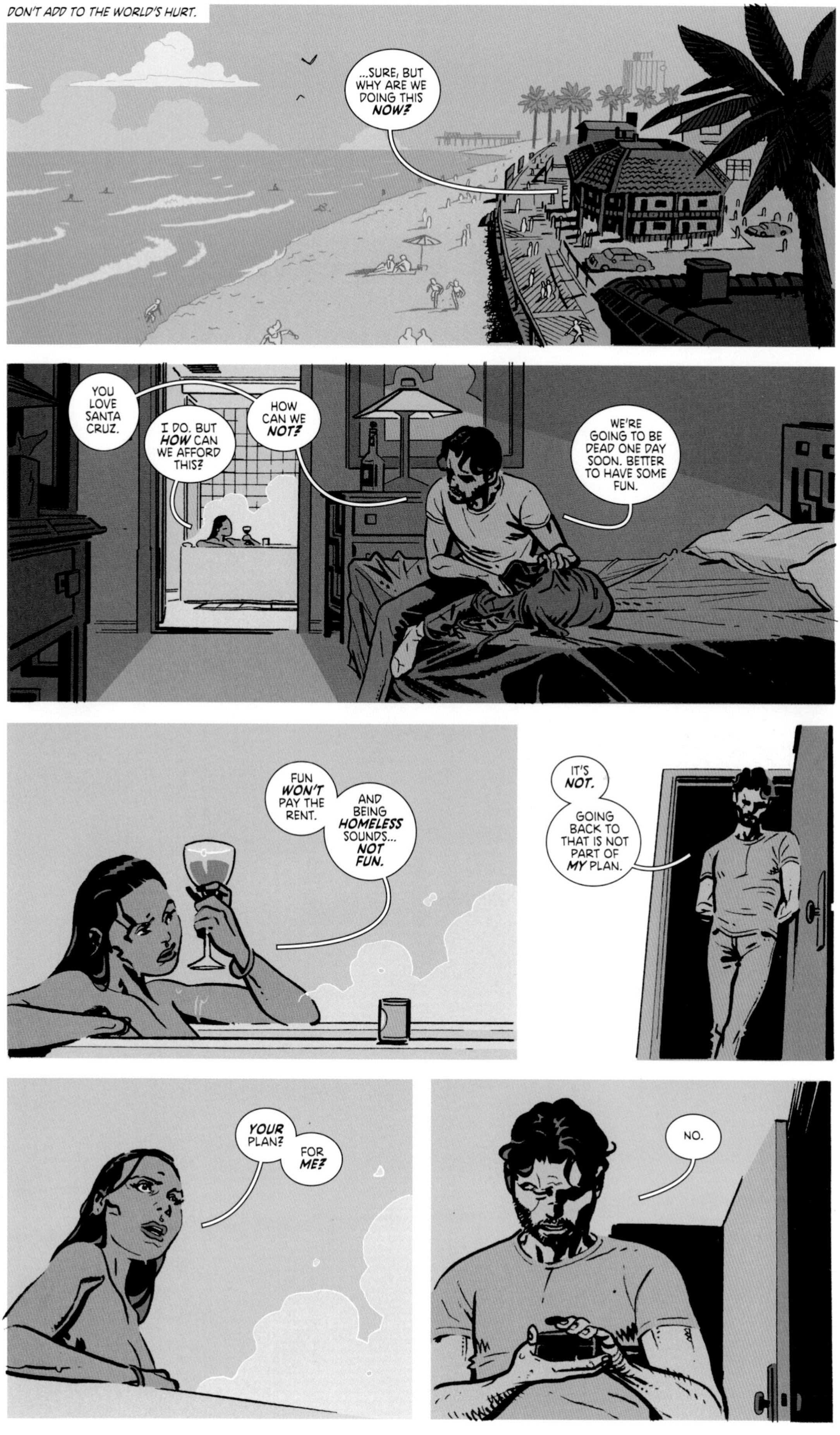
DON'T ADD TO THE WORLD'S HURT.
...SURE, BUT WHY ARE WE DOING THIS NOW?
YOU LOVE SANTA CRUZ.
I DO. BUT HOW CAN WE AFFORD THIS?
HOW CAN WE NOT?
WE'RE GOING TO BE DEAD ONE DAY SOON. BETTER TO HAVE SOME FUN.
FUN WON'T PAY THE RENT.
AND BEING HOMELESS SOUNDS... NOT FUN.
IT'S NOT.
GOING BACK TO THAT IS NOT PART OF MY PLAN.
YOUR PLAN?
FOR ME?
NO.

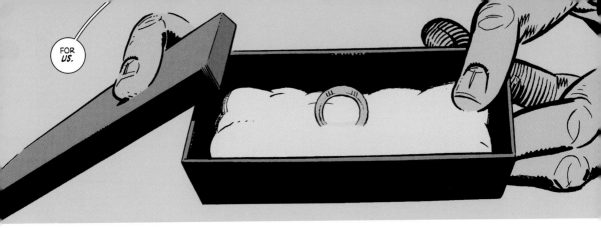

FOR *US.*

WHY NOW?

BECAUSE I'M SICK?

BECAUSE I LOVE YOU.

AND I WOULD HAVE DONE IT EVENTUALLY ANYWAY.

EVEN THOUGH I MAY BE CRIPPLED?

DON'T TALK LIKE THAT.

DON'T FOOL YOURSELF. WHICHEVER AUTOIMMUNE DISEASE I HAVE...

MY LIFE IS GOING TO LOOK DIFFERENT THAN NORMAL.

CONSIDER WHAT THAT *MEANS.*

ALL I KNOW IS, IT'S DARK WITHOUT YOU.

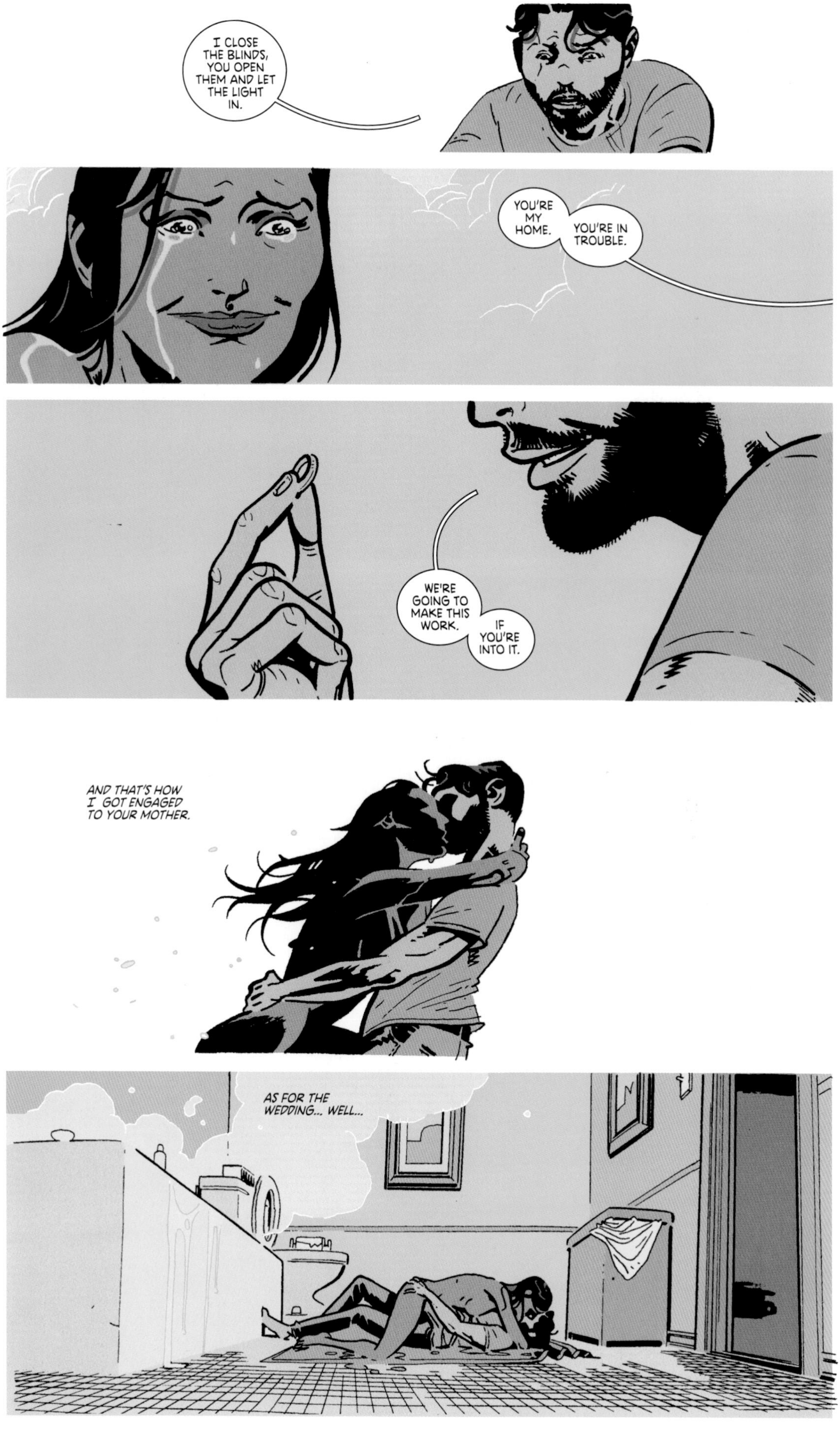
I CLOSE THE BLINDS, YOU OPEN THEM AND LET THE LIGHT IN.
YOU'RE MY HOME.
YOU'RE IN TROUBLE.
WE'RE GOING TO MAKE THIS WORK.
IF YOU'RE INTO IT.
AND THAT'S HOW I GOT ENGAGED TO YOUR MOTHER.
AS FOR THE WEDDING... WELL...

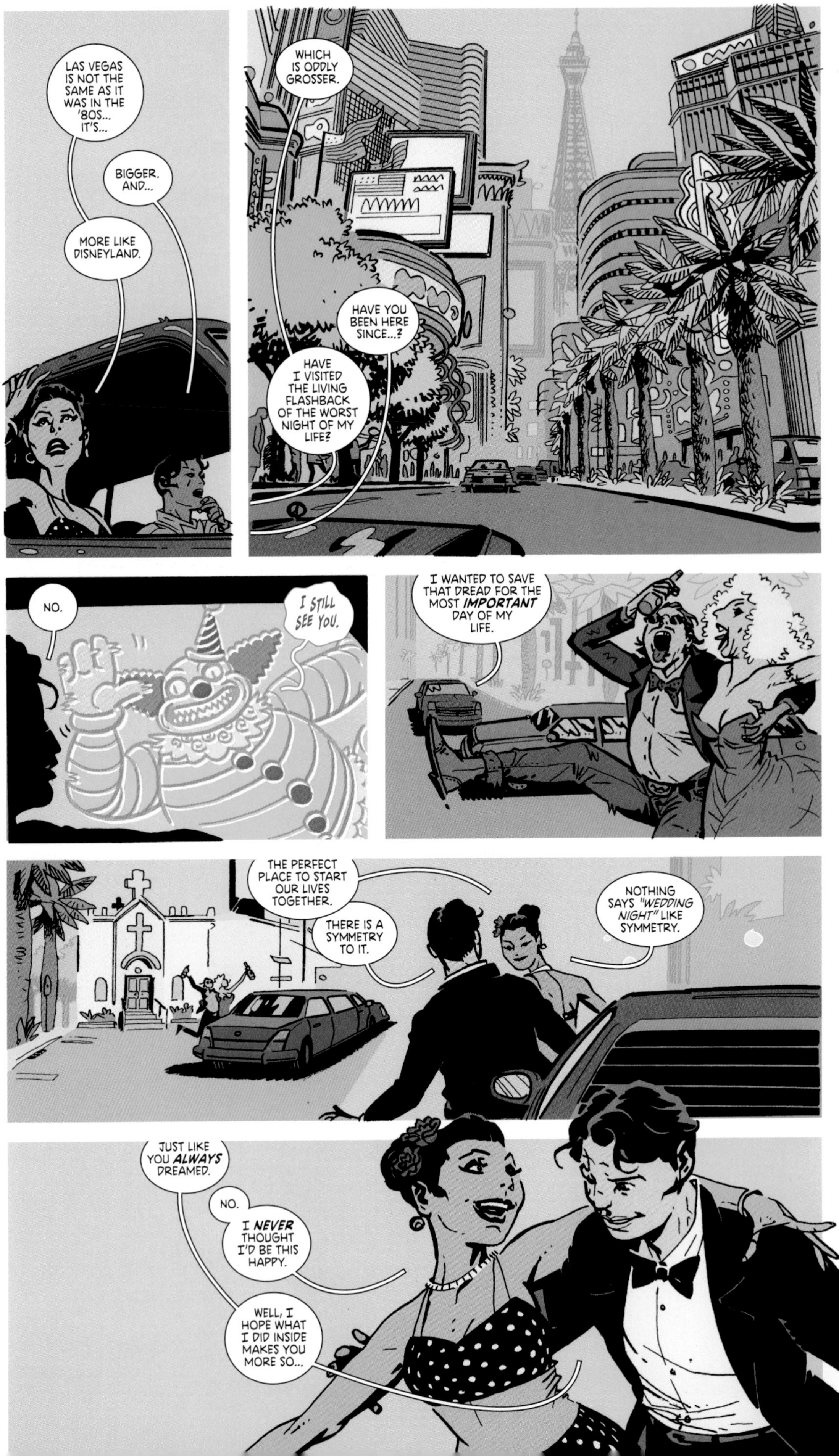
LAS VEGAS IS NOT THE SAME AS IT WAS IN THE '80S... IT'S...
BIGGER. AND...
MORE LIKE DISNEYLAND.
WHICH IS ODDLY GROSSER.
HAVE YOU BEEN HERE SINCE...?
HAVE I VISITED THE LIVING FLASHBACK OF THE WORST NIGHT OF MY LIFE?
NO.
I STILL SEE YOU.
I WANTED TO SAVE THAT DREAD FOR THE MOST IMPORTANT DAY OF MY LIFE.
THE PERFECT PLACE TO START OUR LIVES TOGETHER.
THERE IS A SYMMETRY TO IT.
NOTHING SAYS "WEDDING NIGHT" LIKE SYMMETRY.
JUST LIKE YOU ALWAYS DREAMED.
NO.
I NEVER THOUGHT I'D BE THIS HAPPY.
WELL, I HOPE WHAT I DID INSIDE MAKES YOU MORE SO...

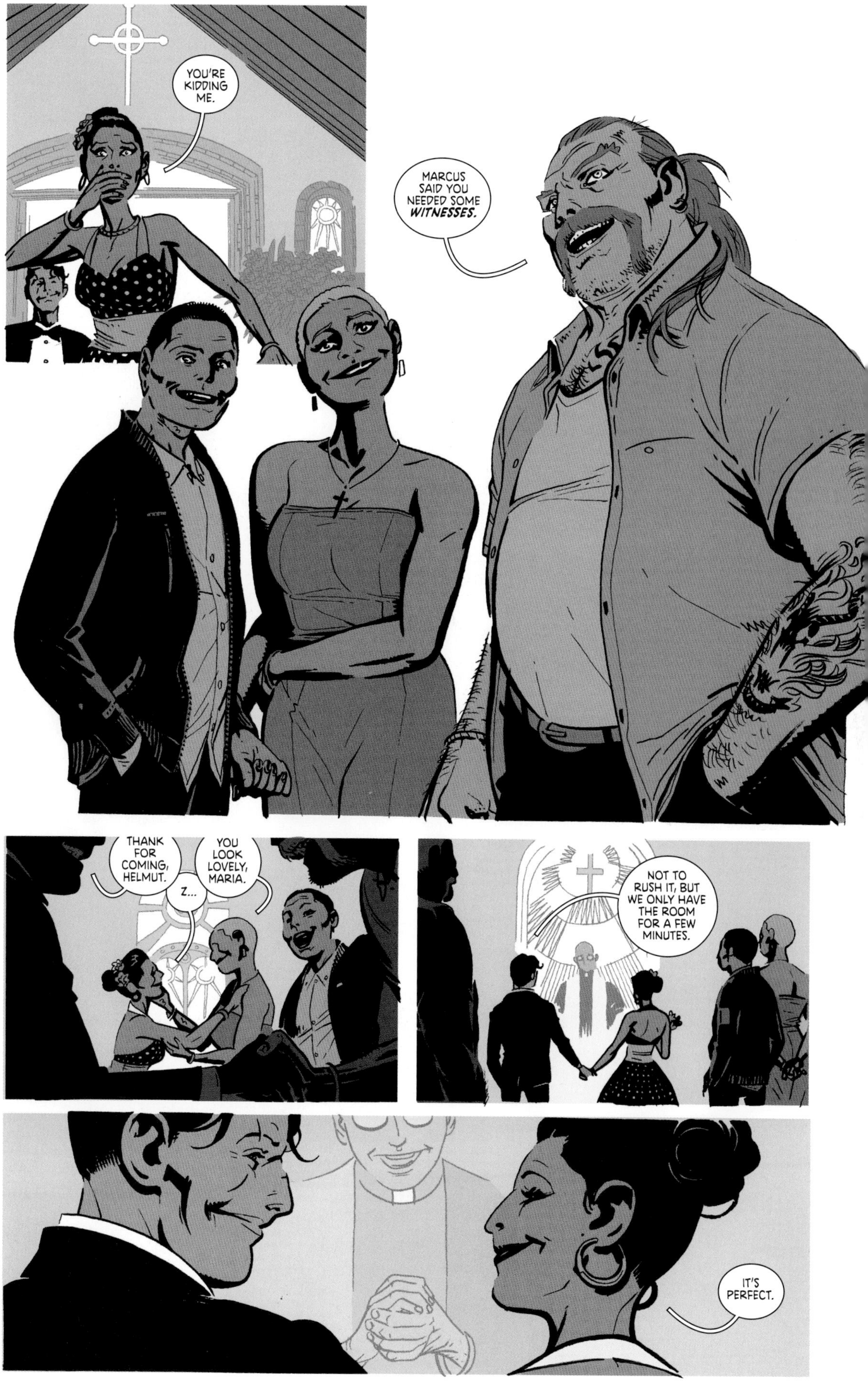

YOU'RE KIDDING ME.
MARCUS SAID YOU NEEDED SOME *WITNESSES.*
THANK FOR COMING, HELMUT.
Z...
YOU LOOK LOVELY, MARIA.
NOT TO RUSH IT, BUT WE ONLY HAVE THE ROOM FOR A FEW MINUTES.
IT'S PERFECT.

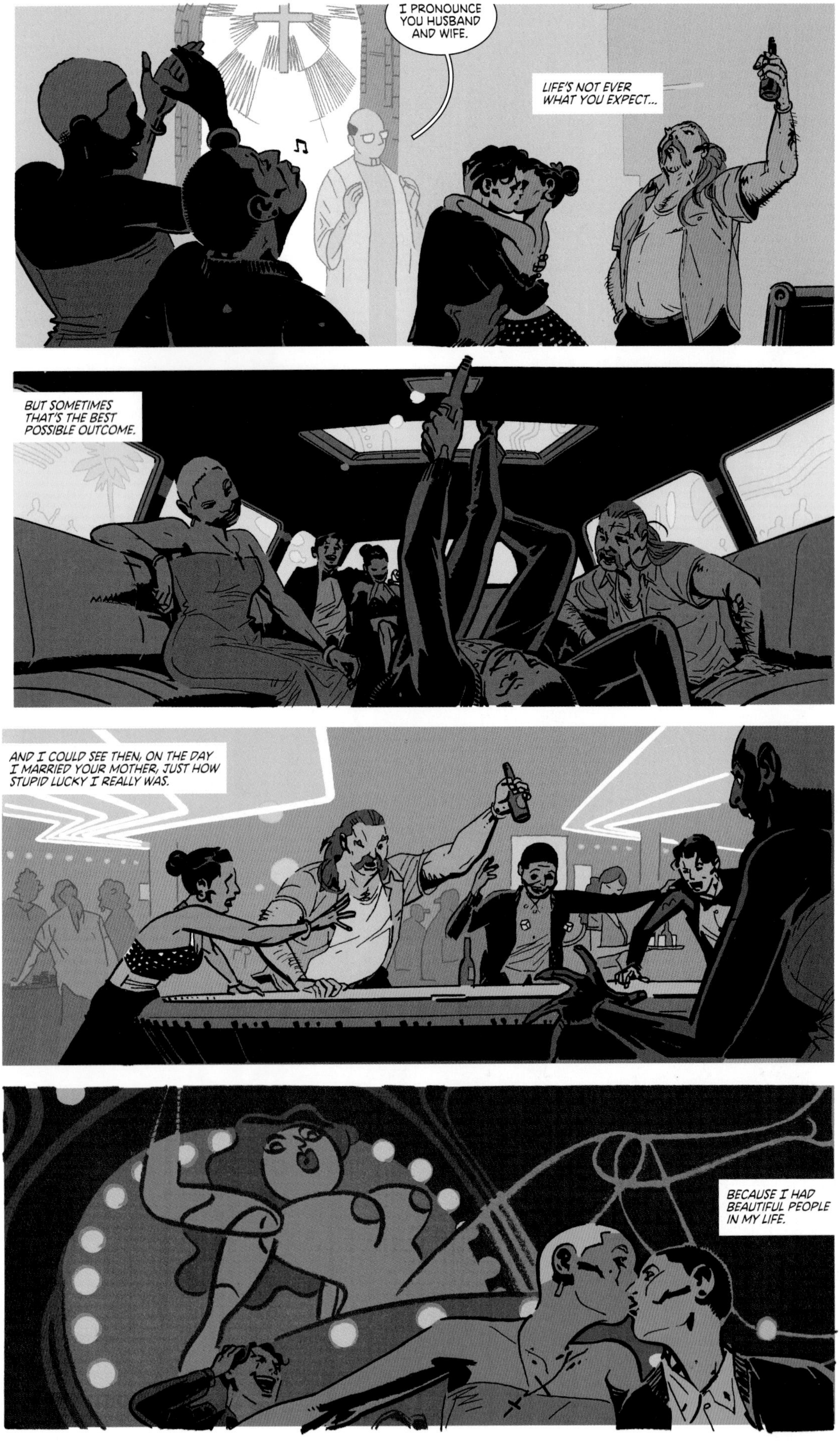
I PRONOUNCE YOU HUSBAND AND WIFE.
LIFE'S NOT EVER WHAT YOU EXPECT...
BUT SOMETIMES THAT'S THE BEST POSSIBLE OUTCOME.
AND I COULD SEE THEN, ON THE DAY I MARRIED YOUR MOTHER, JUST HOW STUPID LUCKY I REALLY WAS.
BECAUSE I HAD BEAUTIFUL PEOPLE IN MY LIFE.

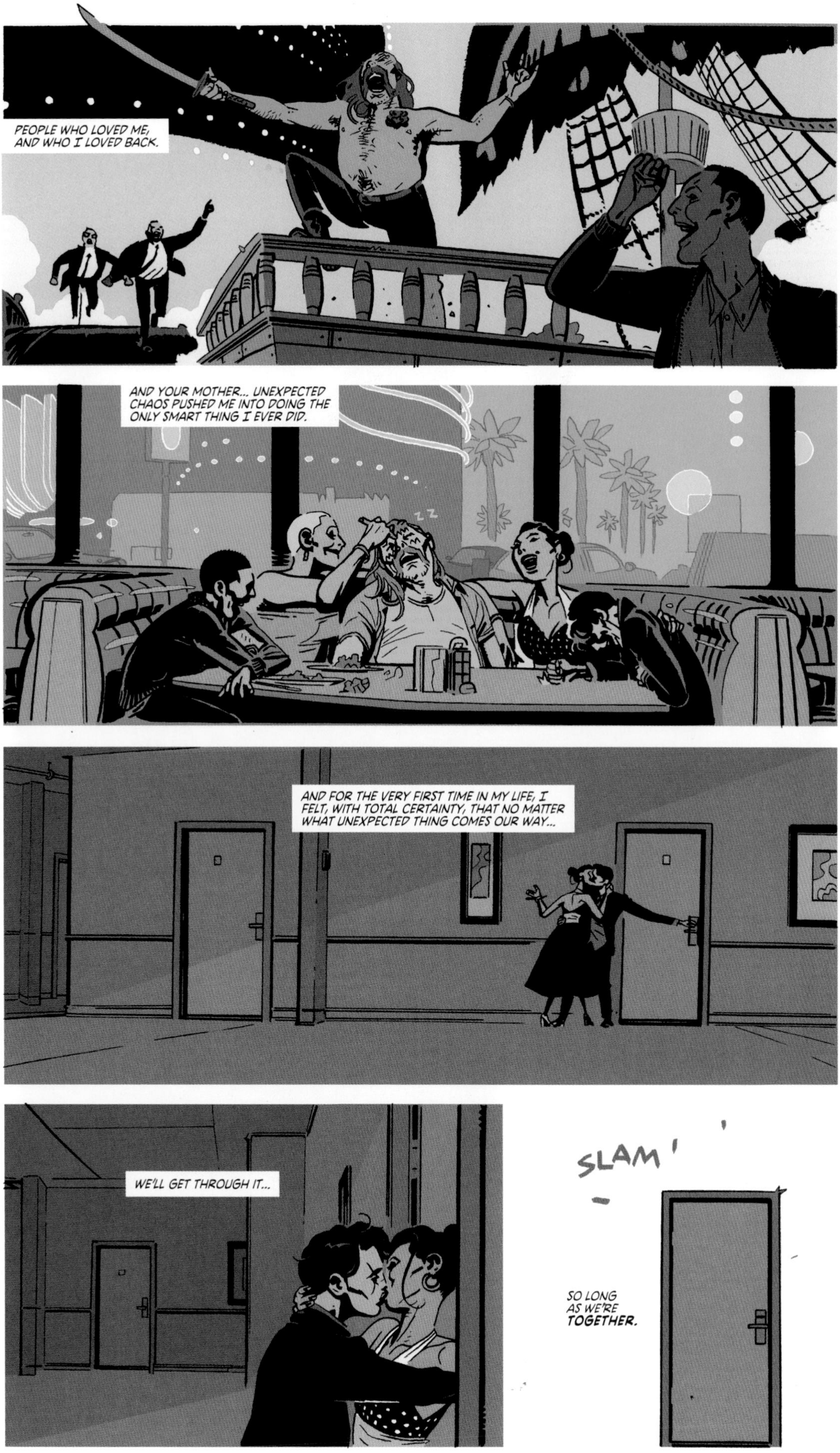
PEOPLE WHO LOVED ME, AND WHO I LOVED BACK.
AND YOUR MOTHER... UNEXPECTED CHAOS PUSHED ME INTO DOING THE ONLY SMART THING I EVER DID.
ZZZ
AND FOR THE VERY FIRST TIME IN MY LIFE, I FELT, WITH TOTAL CERTAINTY, THAT NO MATTER WHAT UNEXPECTED THING COMES OUR WAY...
WE'LL GET THROUGH IT...
SLAM!
SO LONG AS WE'RE TOGETHER.

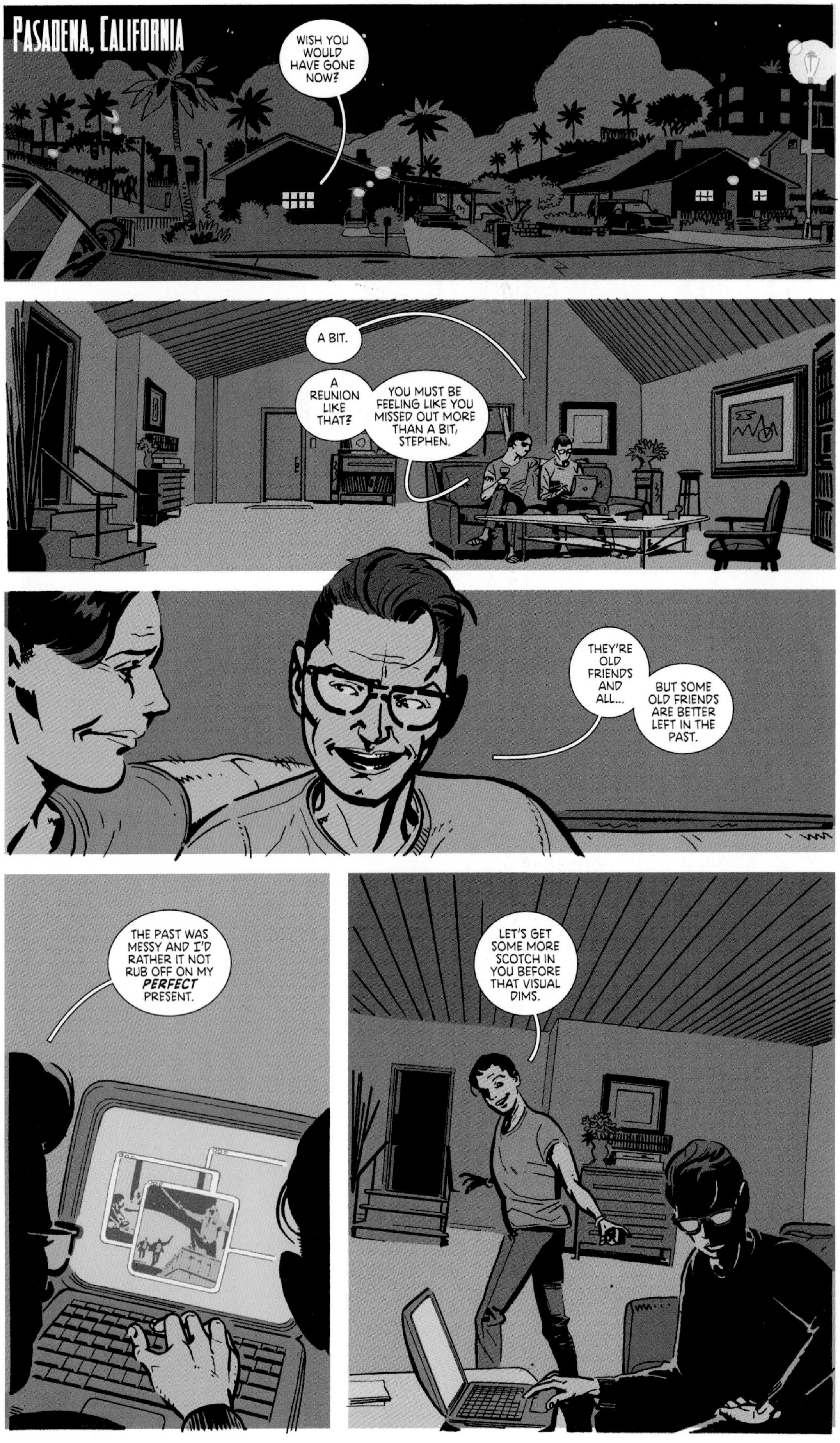
PASADENA, CALIFORNIA
WISH YOU WOULD HAVE GONE NOW?
A BIT.
A REUNION LIKE THAT?
YOU MUST BE FEELING LIKE YOU MISSED OUT MORE THAN A BIT, STEPHEN.
THEY'RE OLD FRIENDS AND ALL...
BUT SOME OLD FRIENDS ARE BETTER LEFT IN THE PAST.
THE PAST WAS MESSY AND I'D RATHER IT NOT RUB OFF ON MY PERFECT PRESENT.
LET'S GET SOME MORE SCOTCH IN YOU BEFORE THAT VISUAL DIMS.

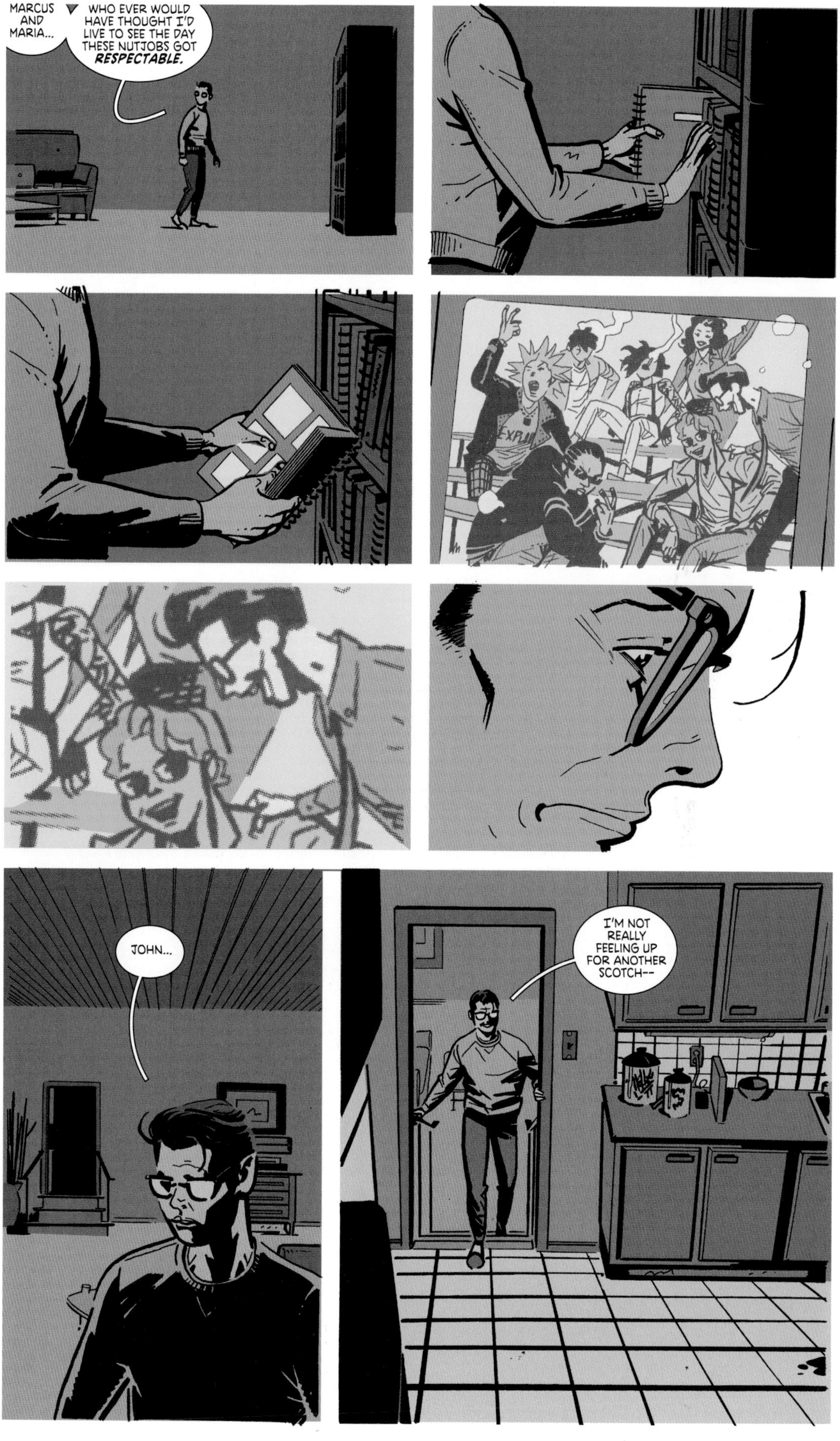
MARCUS AND MARIA...
WHO EVER WOULD HAVE THOUGHT I'D LIVE TO SEE THE DAY THESE NUTJOBS GOT **RESPECTABLE.**
JOHN...
I'M NOT REALLY FEELING UP FOR ANOTHER SCOTCH--

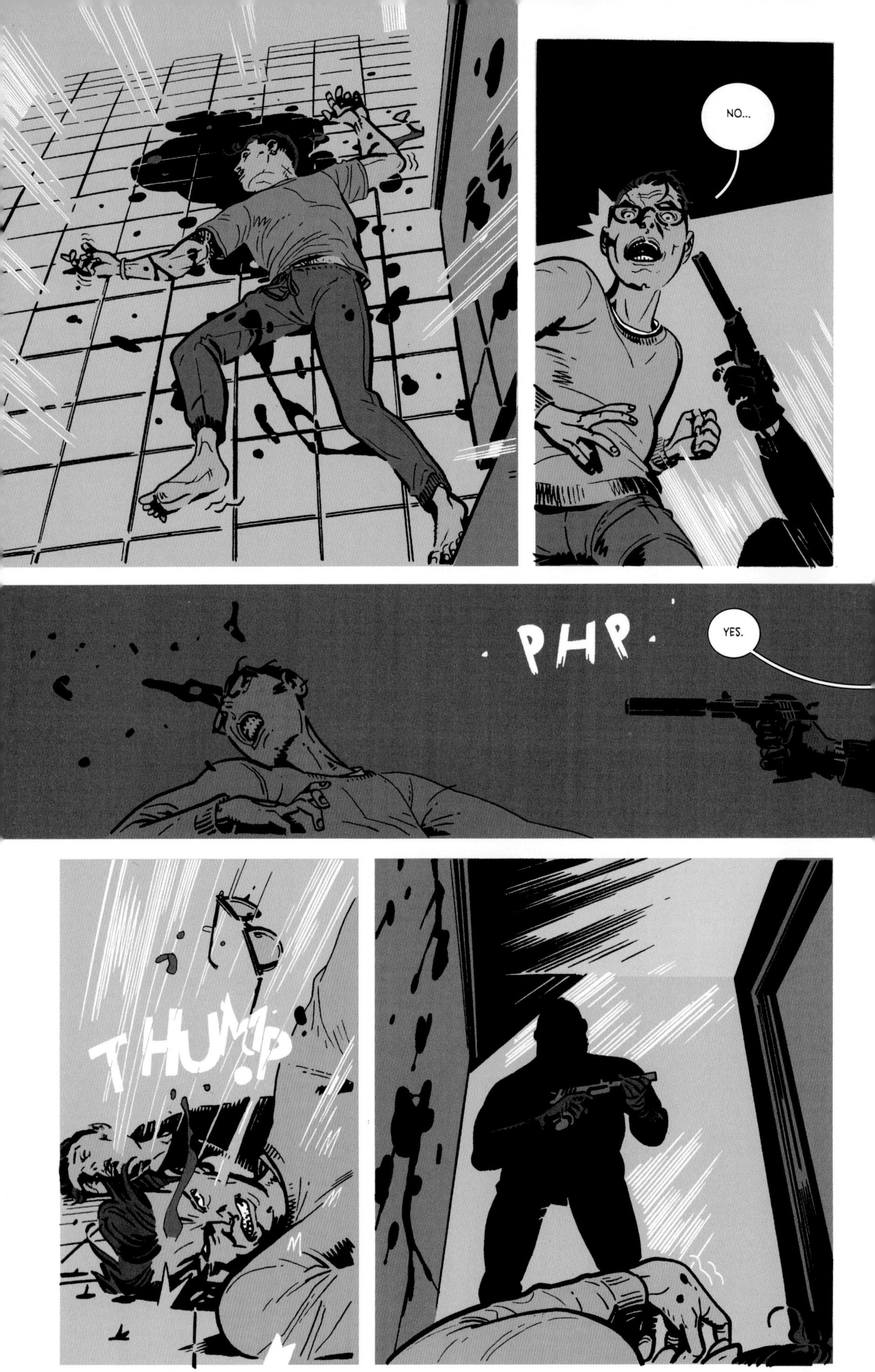
NO...
PHP
YES.
THUMP

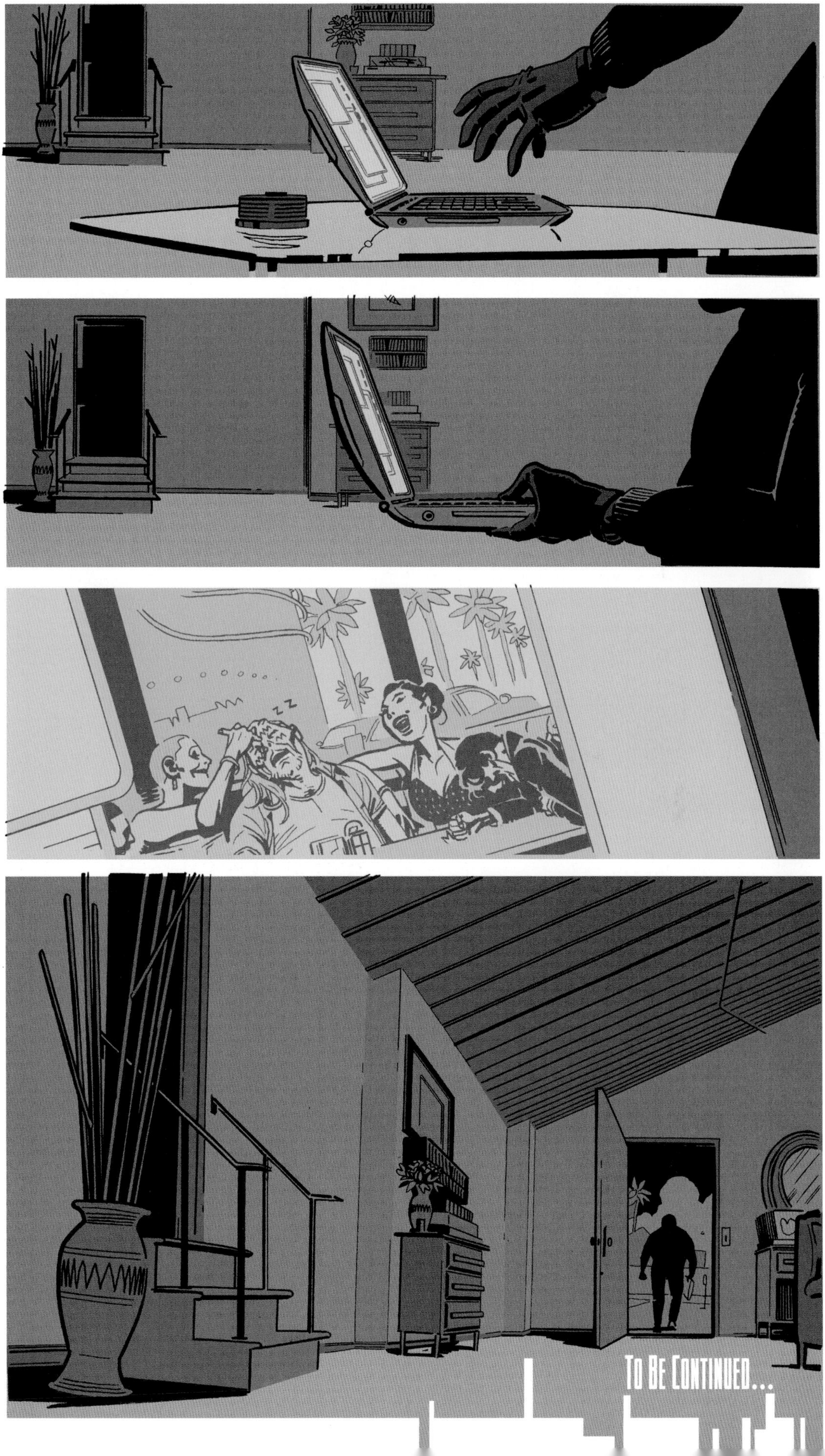

Z Z
To Be Continued...

EST 1637

IN VITAM MORTEM

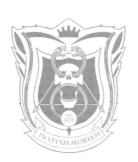

COVER GALLERY

#49 COVER BY **WES CRAIG**

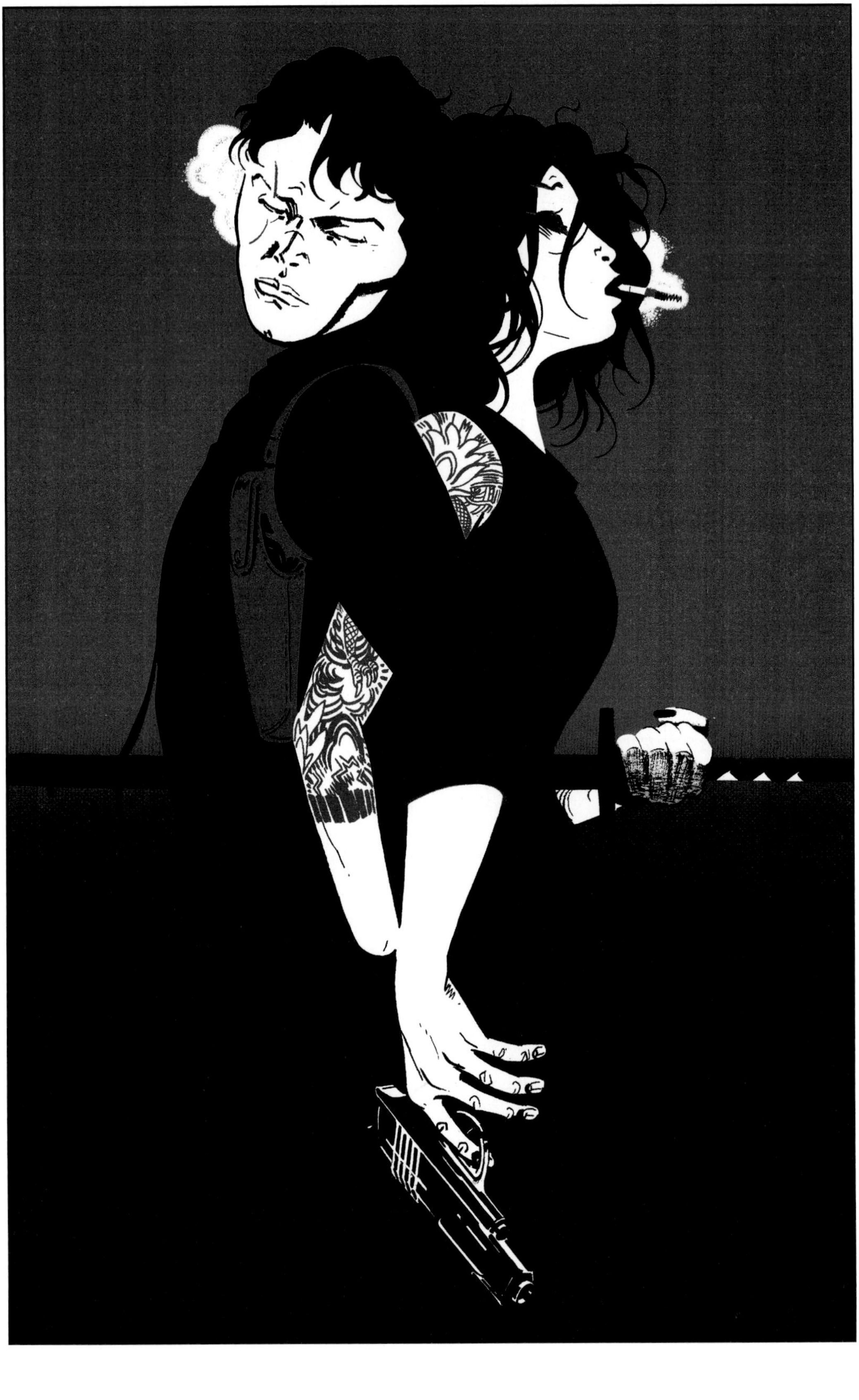

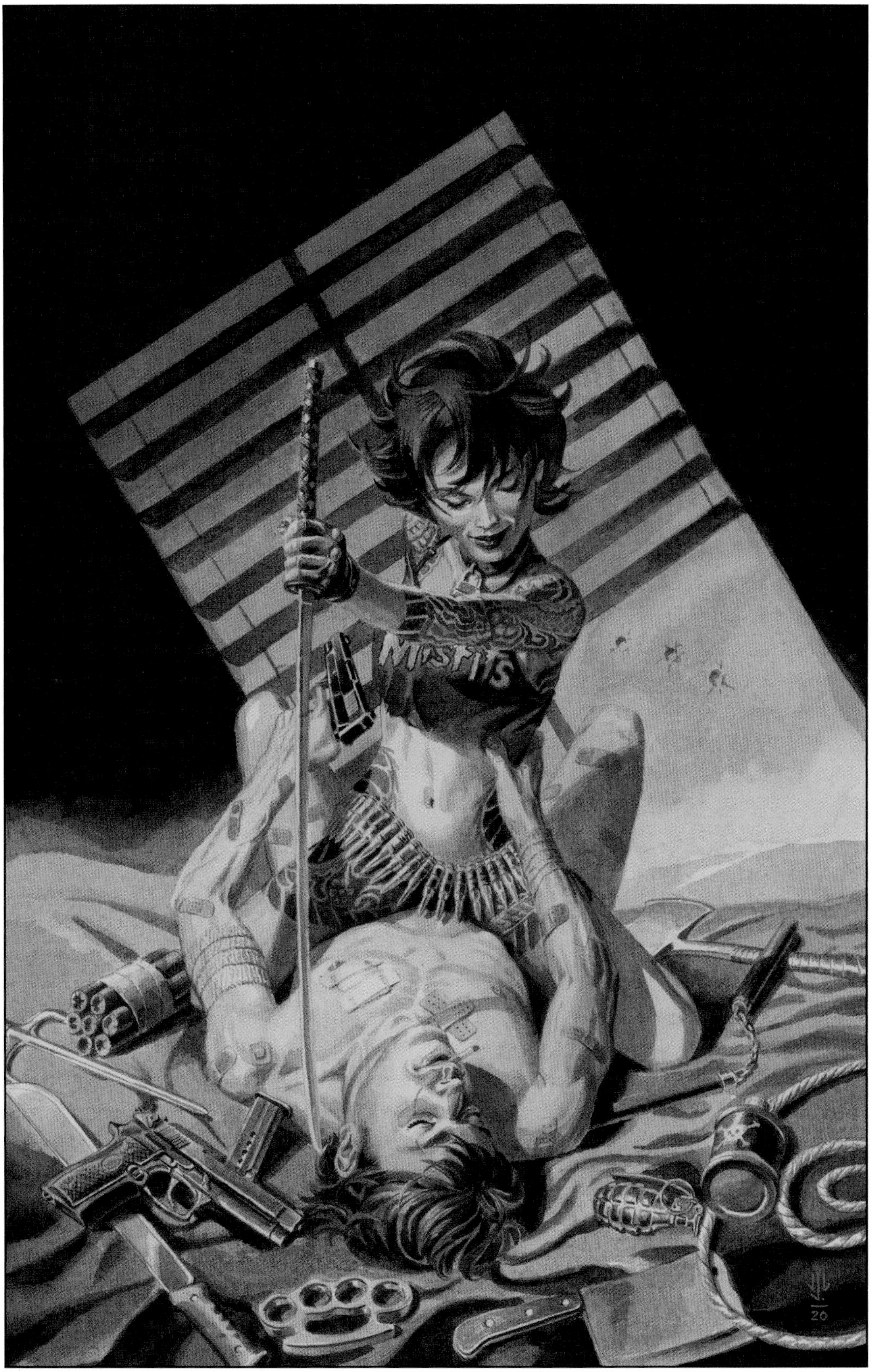
MISFITS

#49 VARIANT BY **J.G. JONES**

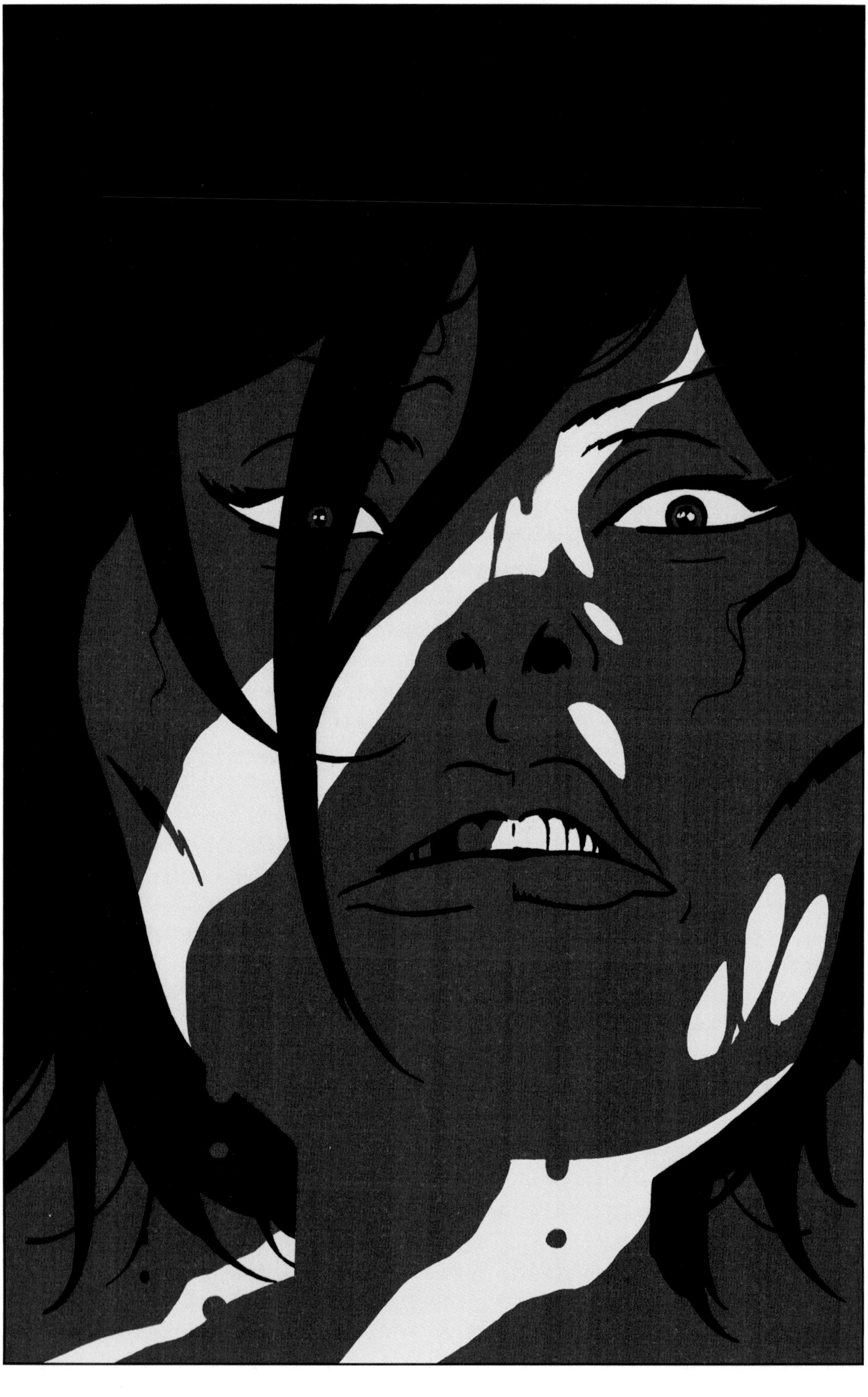

#50 COVER BY **WES CRAIG**

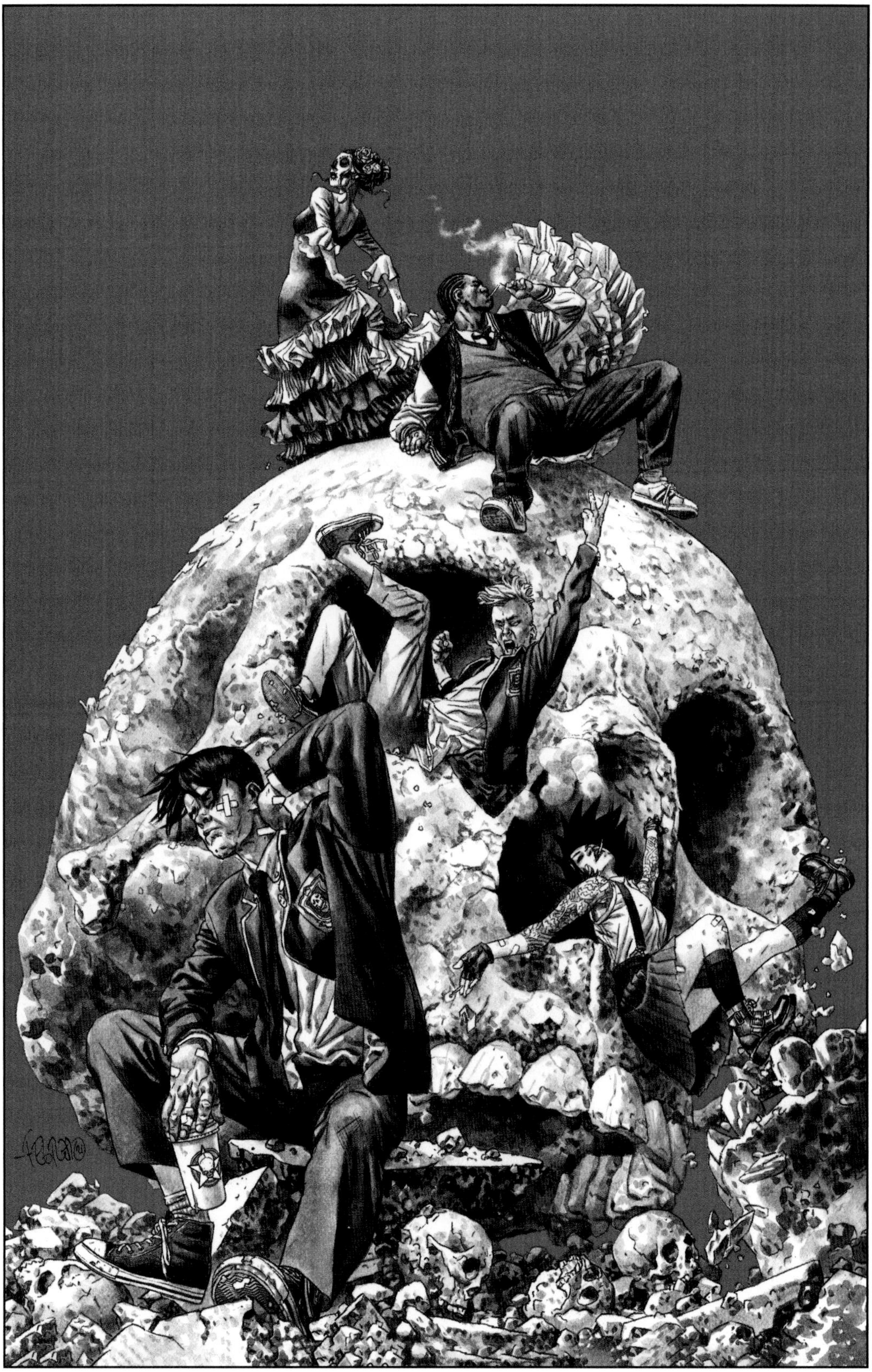

#50 VARIANT BY **DUNCAN FEGREDO**

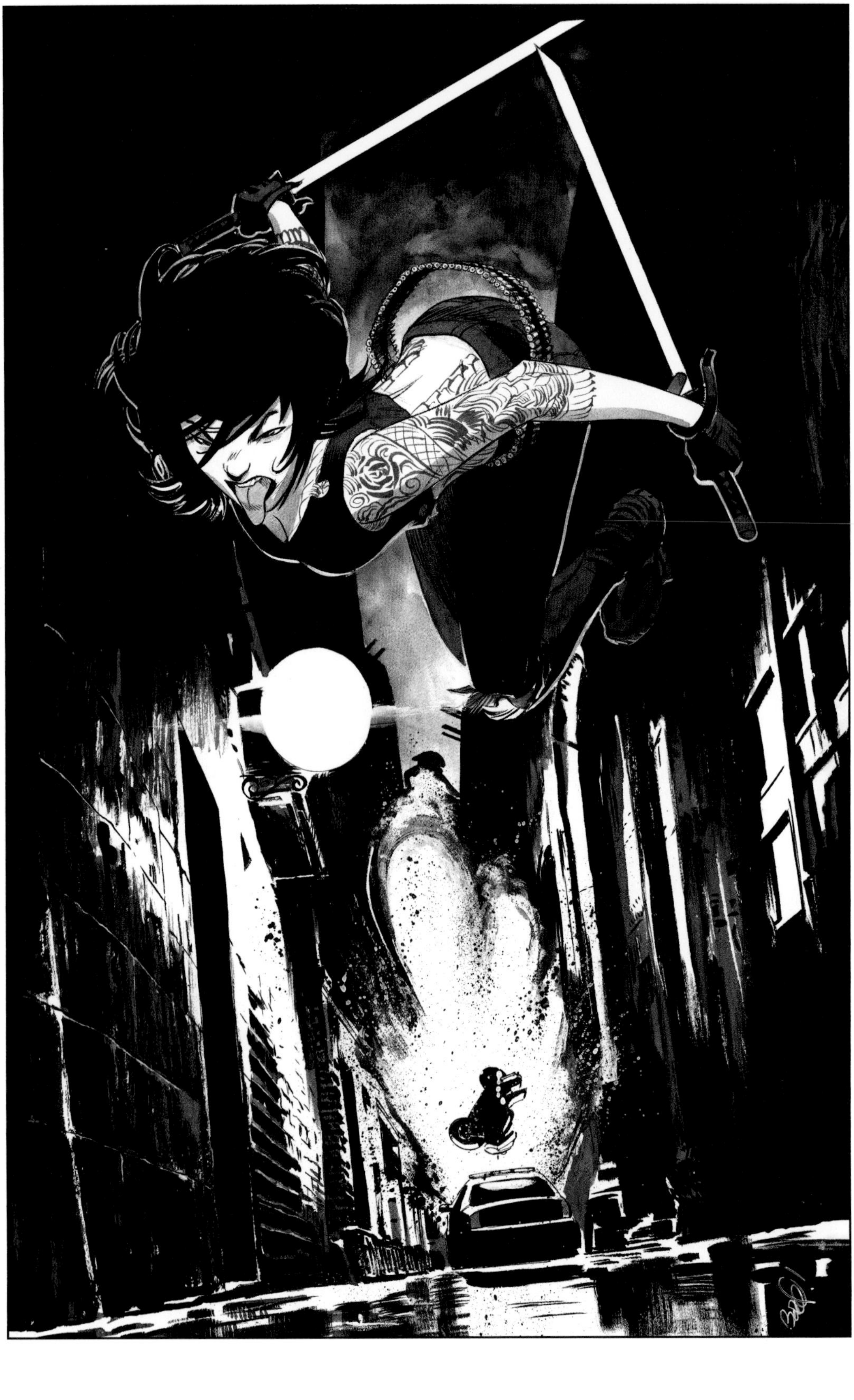

#50 VARIANT BY **BOB QUINN**

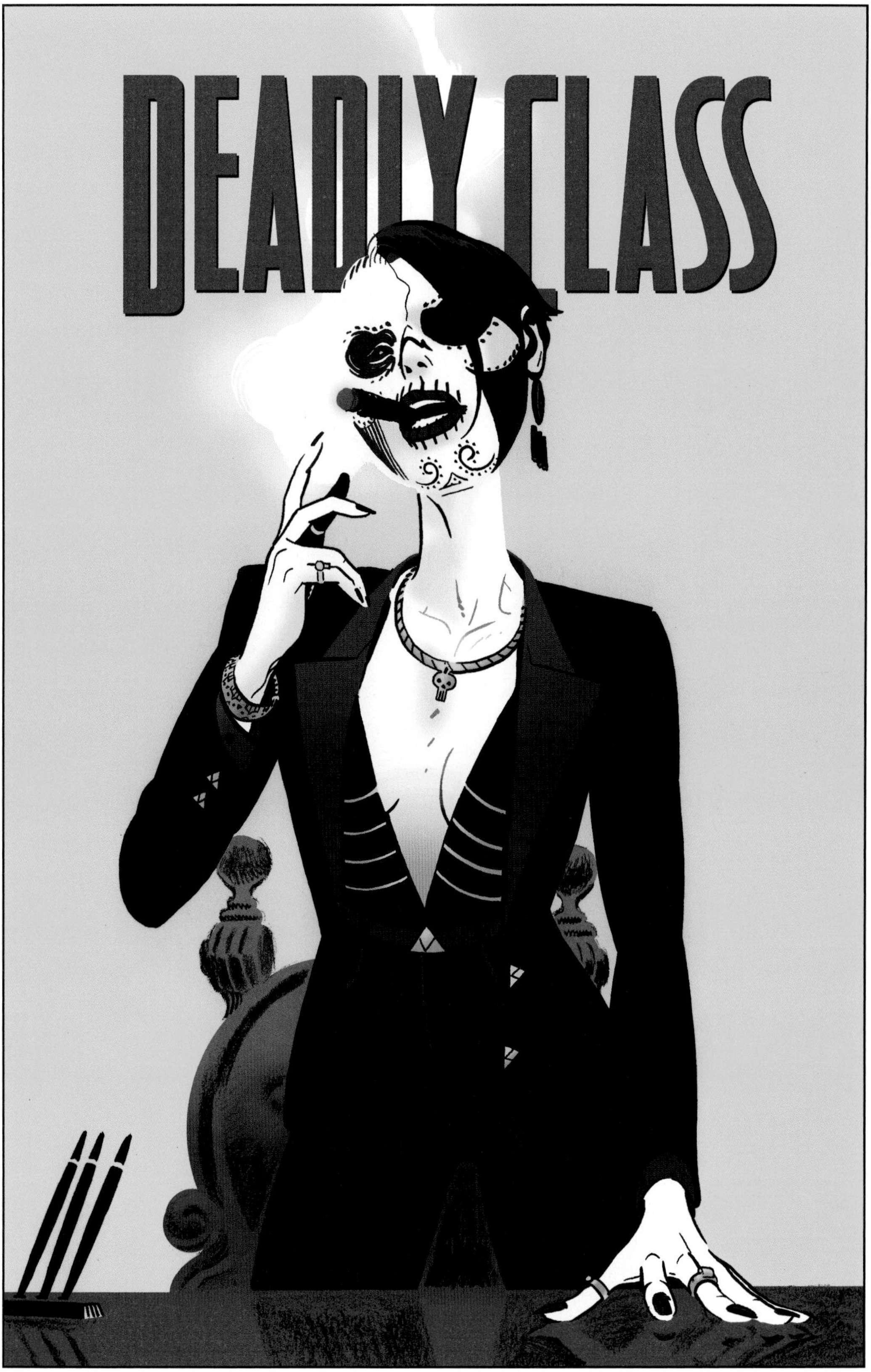
DEADLY CLASS

#51 COVER BY **WES CRAIG**

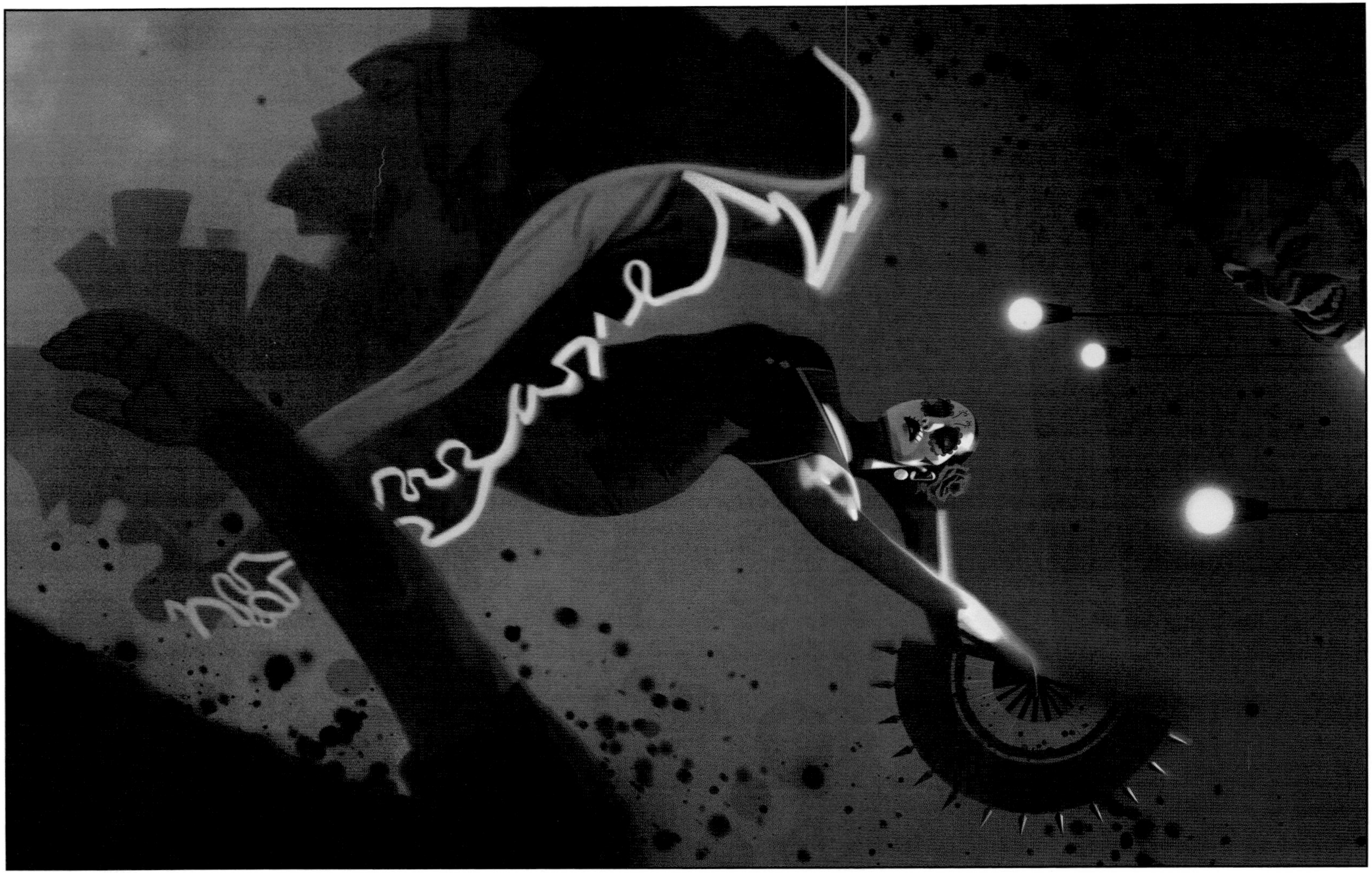

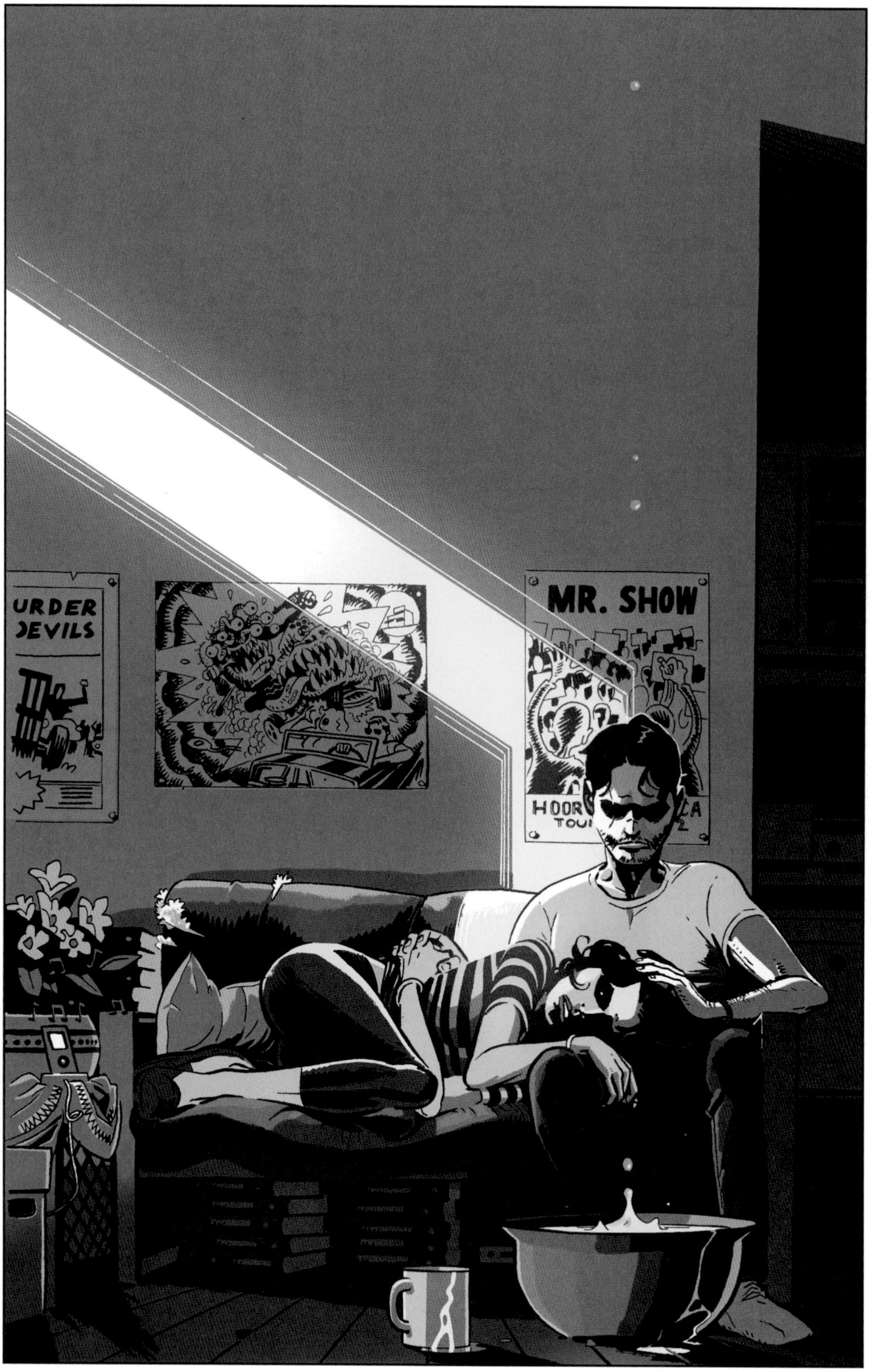
MR. SHOW

#52 COVER BY **WES CRAIG**

#52 VARIANT BY **CHUMA HILL**

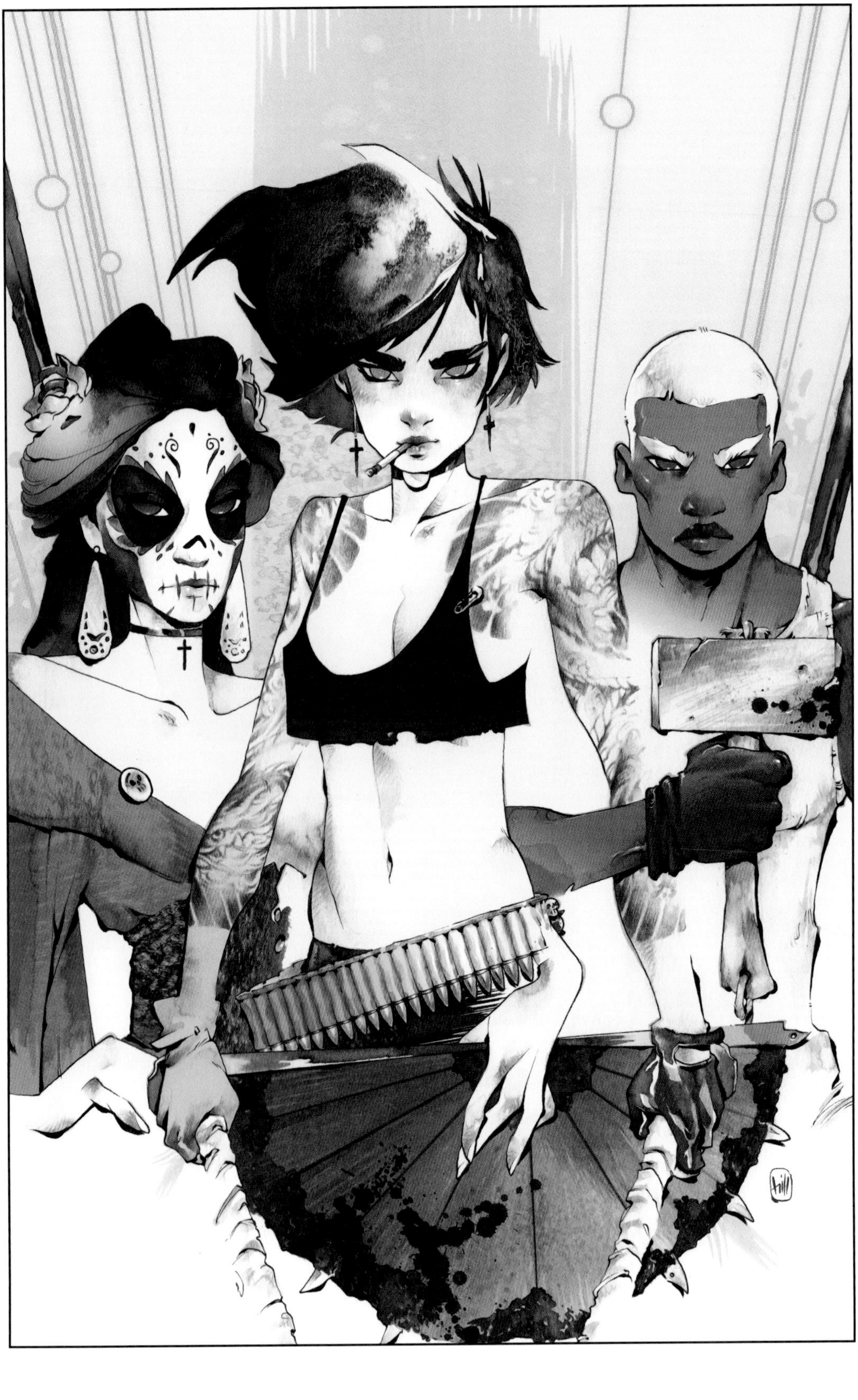

ISSUE #49 PROCESS

#49 INTERIOR ROUGHS BY **WES CRAIG**

DC 49 (11.1)

SAYA
+
MARCUS

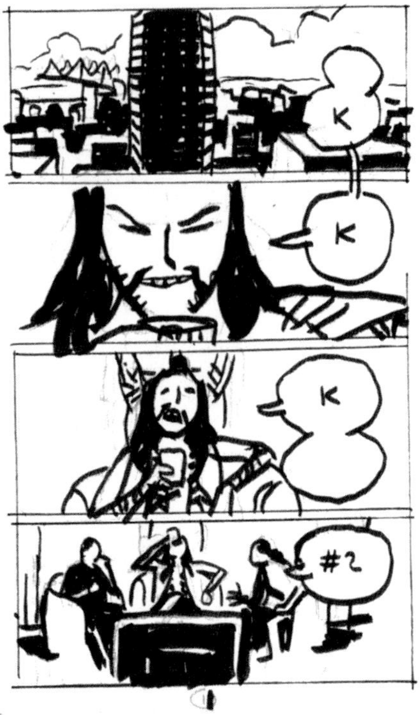
K
K
K
#2
1

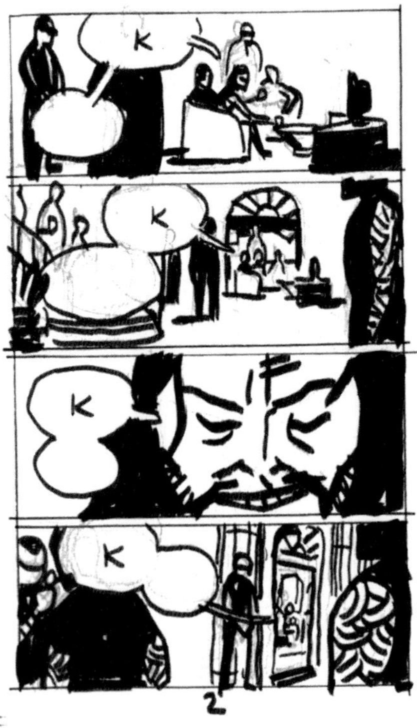
K
K
K
K
2

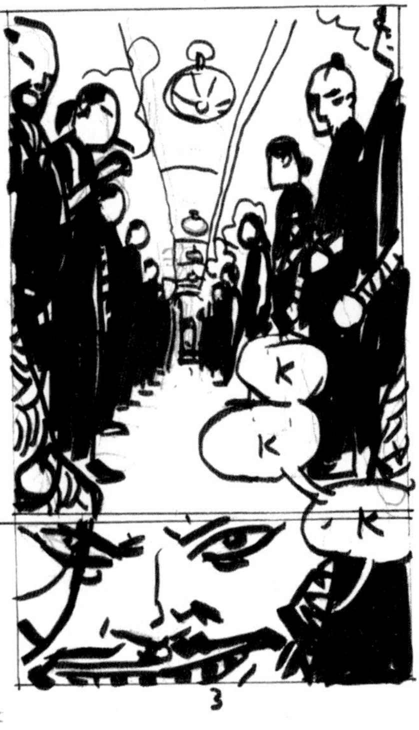
K
K
K
3

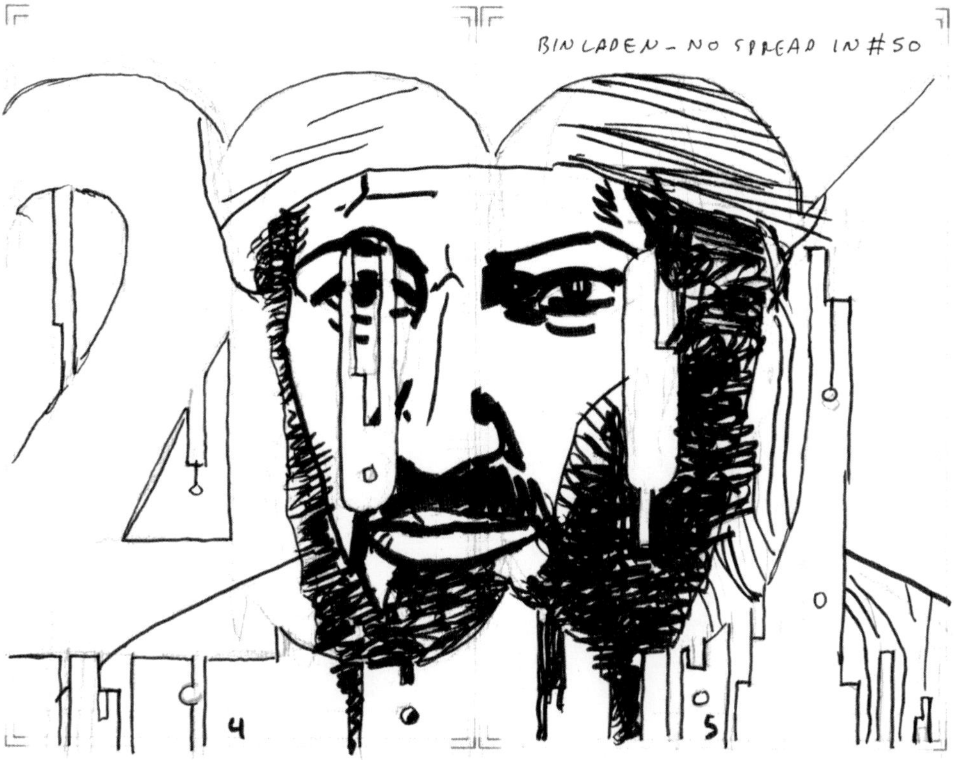
BIN LADEN - NO SPREAD IN #50
4
5

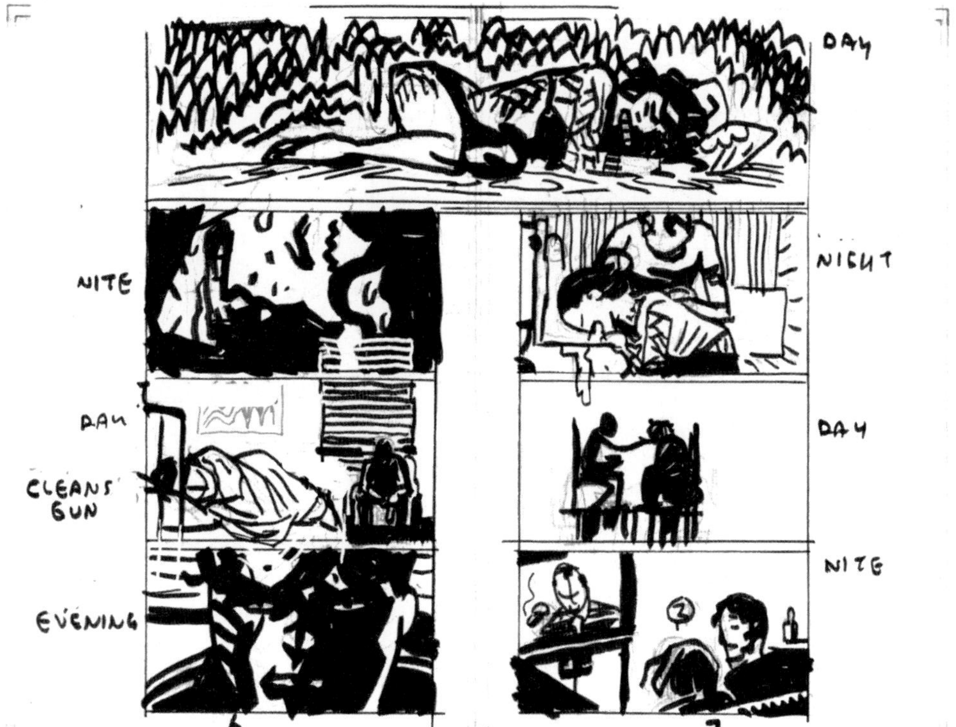
DAY
NITE
NIGHT
DAY
CLEANS GUN
DAY
EVENING
NITE
6
7

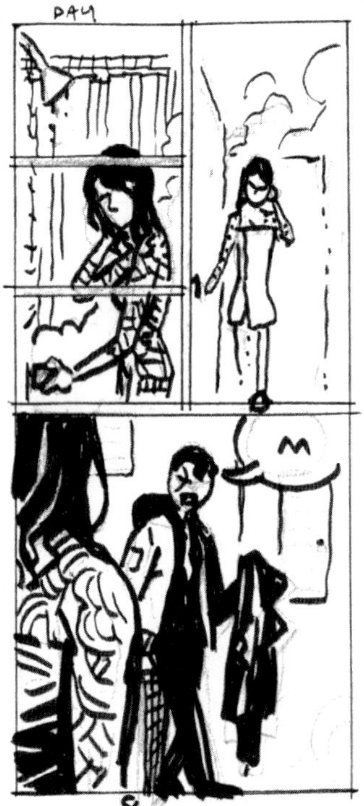
DAY
M

8

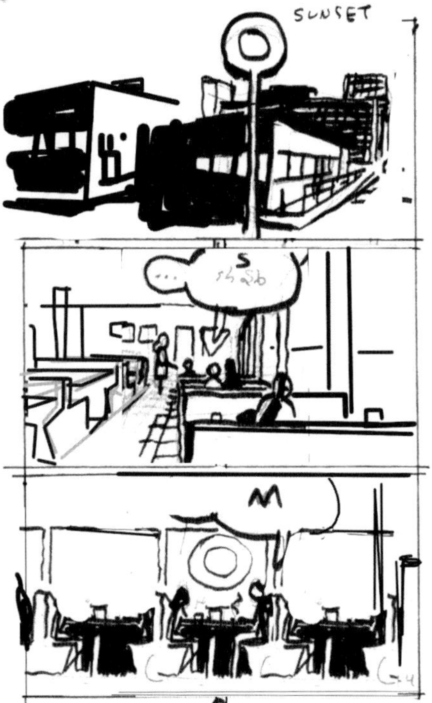
SUNSET
...
S
M

9

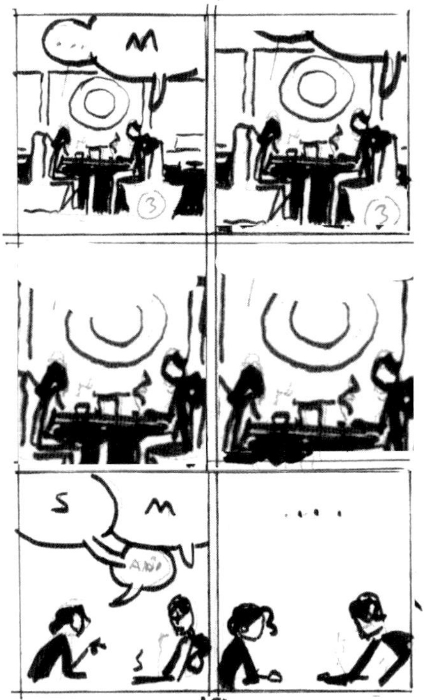
...
M
S
M
AND
....

10

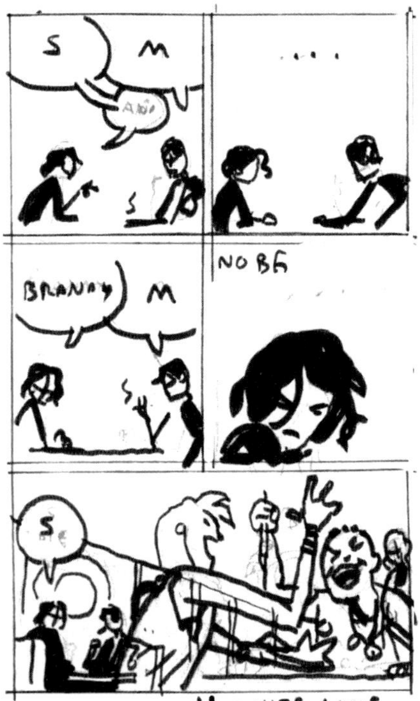
S
M
AND
....
BRANDY
M
NO BG
S

11 WHITE LINE

M
S
S
M
S
M
W
S

12

S
S
S
M
M

13

S
M
M
M
S
M
M
SO FUCKING BORING

14

JUNKY? M
S
S
NO BS
...
...

15

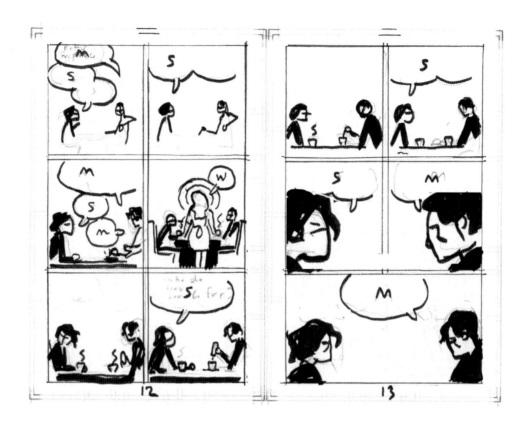

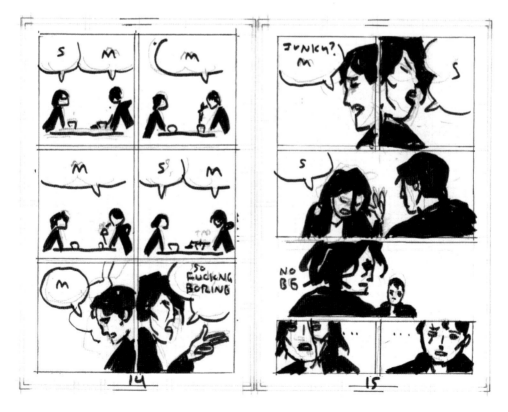

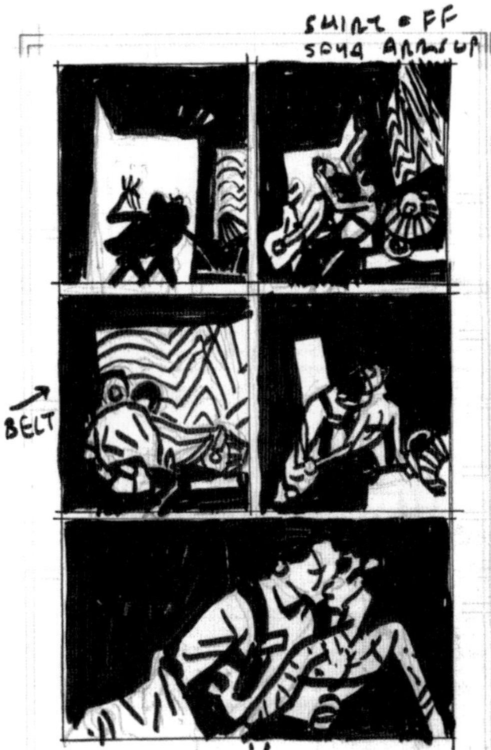
SHIRT OFF
ARMS UP
BELT

16

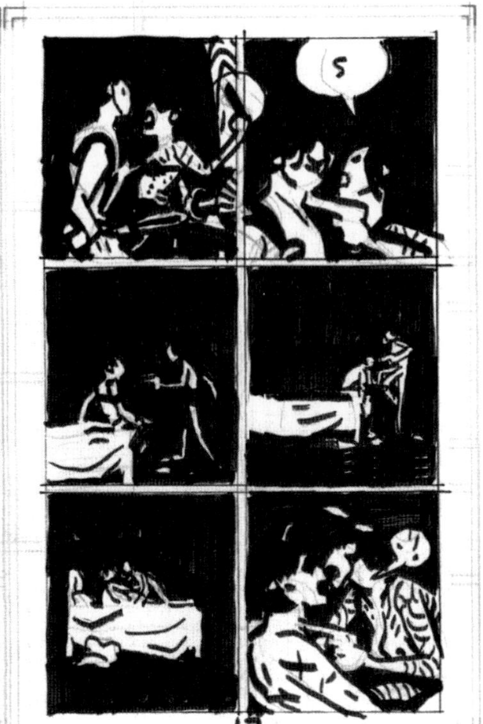
S

17

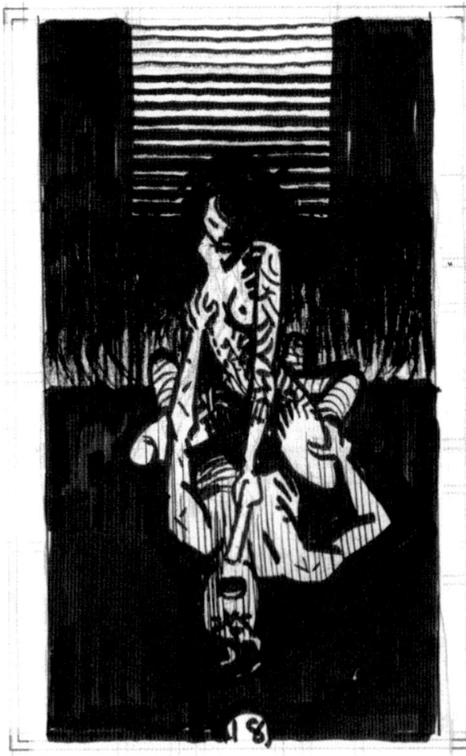

18

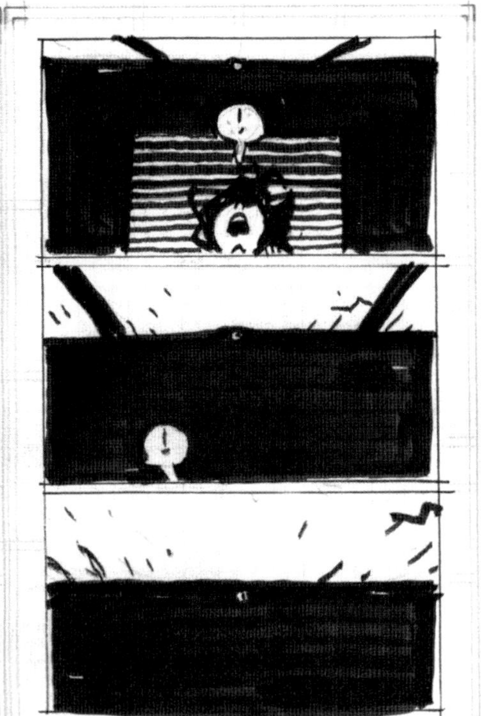
!
!

19

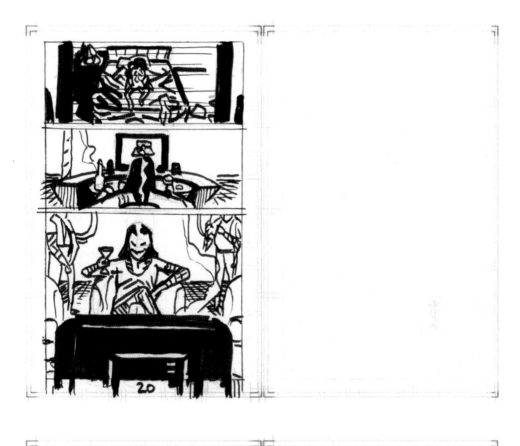

20

PAGE 16 PENCILS BY **WES CRAIG**

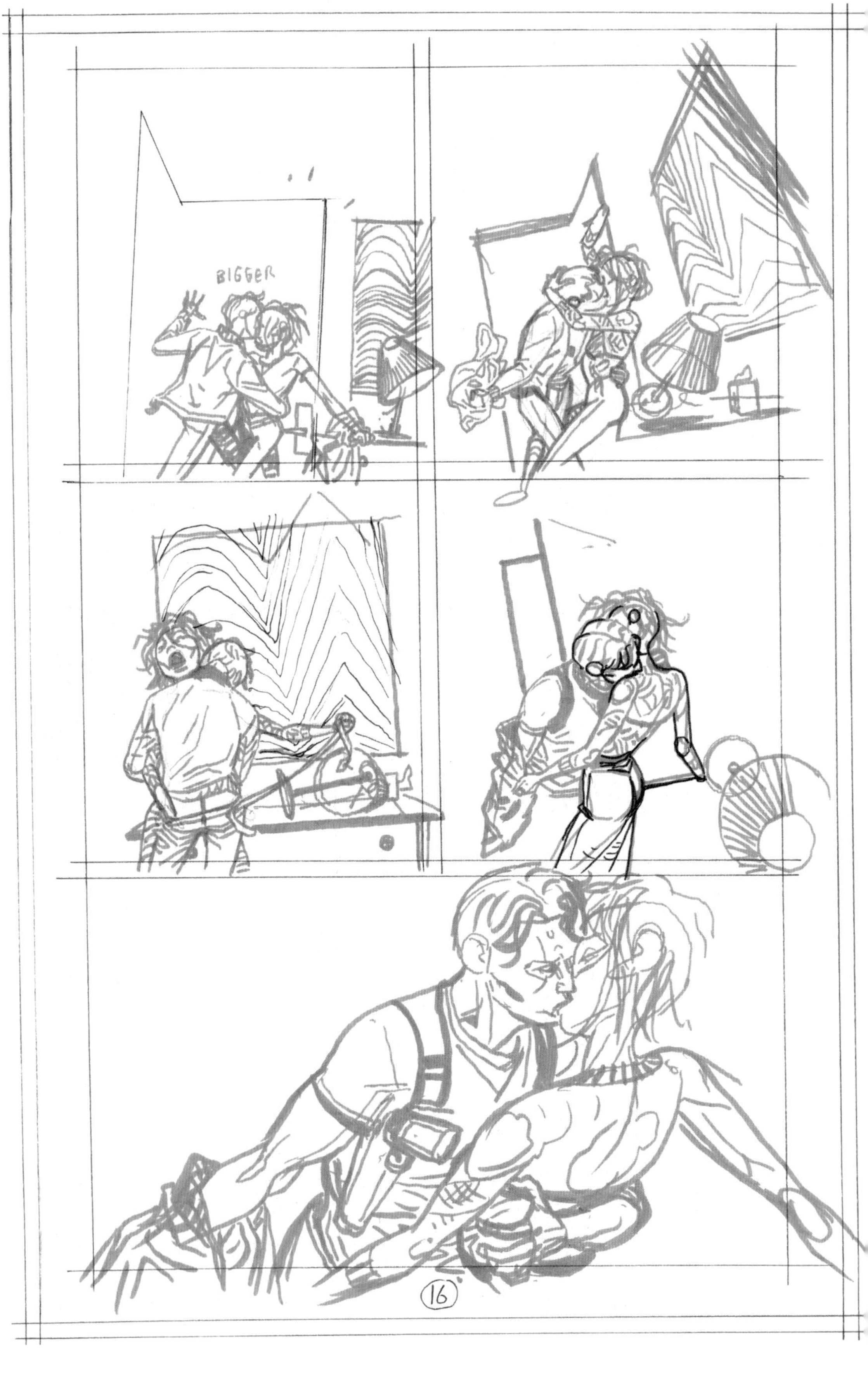
BIGGER
16

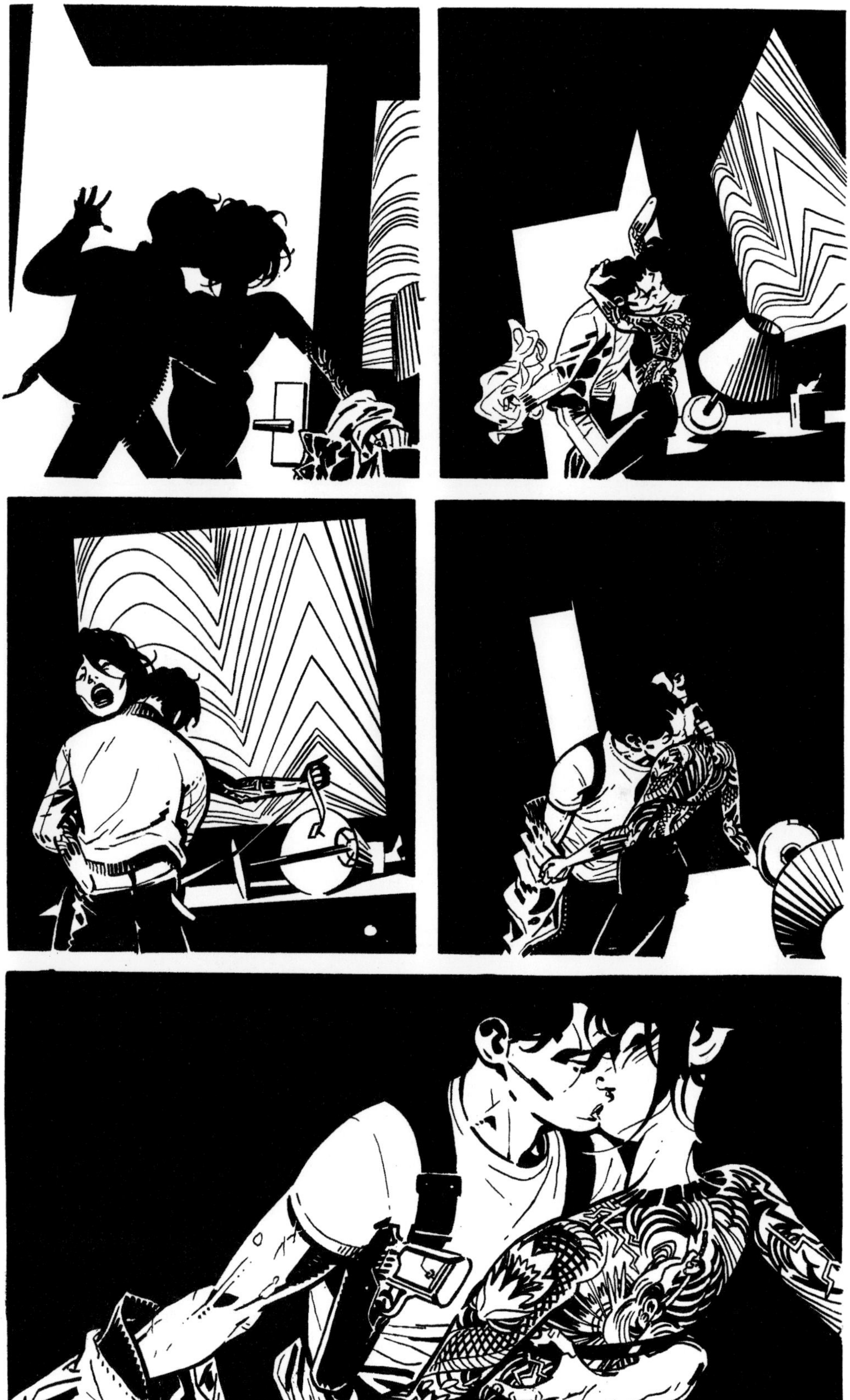

PAGE 16 INKS BY **WES CRAIG**

PAGE 17 PENCILS BY **WES CRAIG**

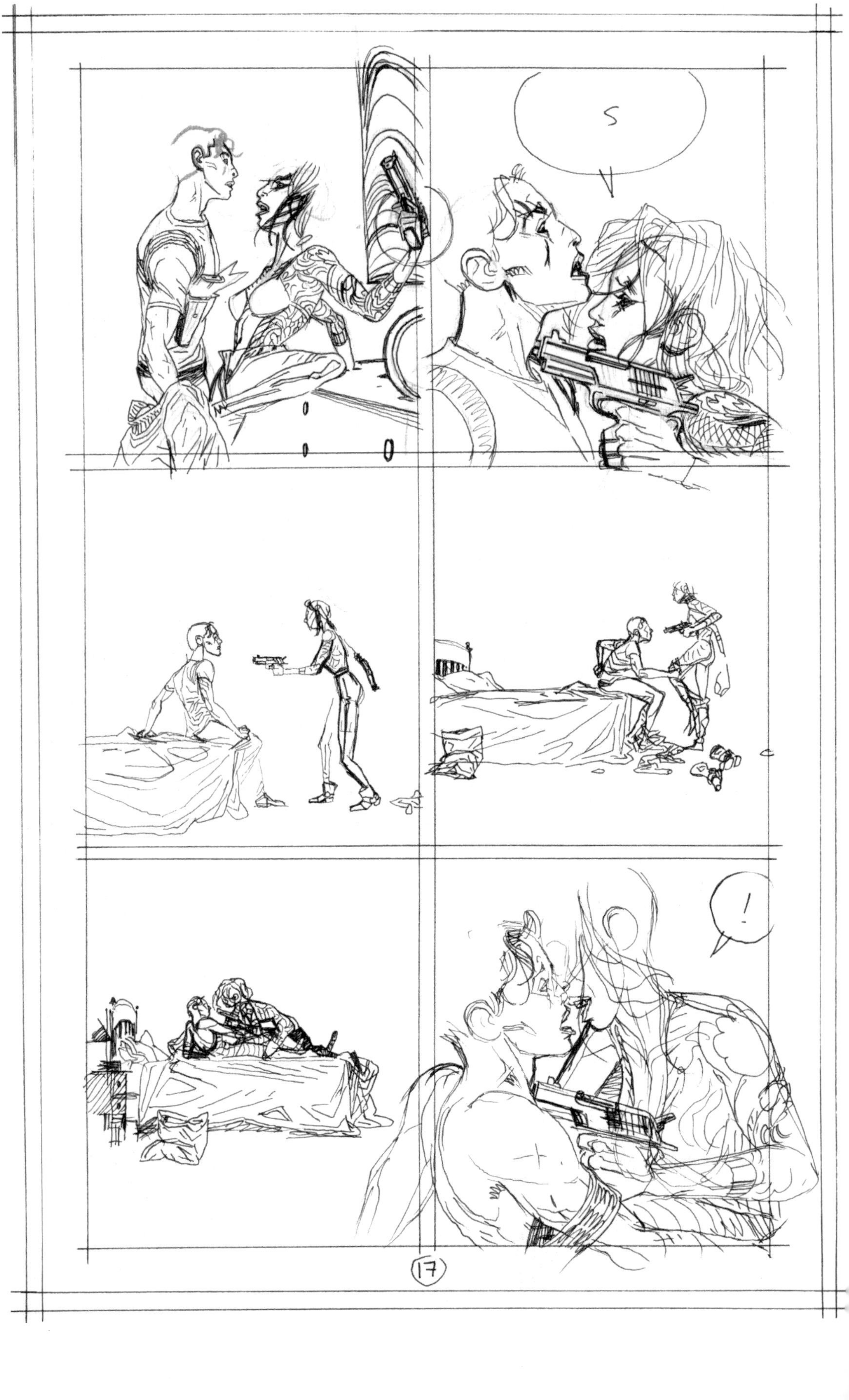
S
!
17

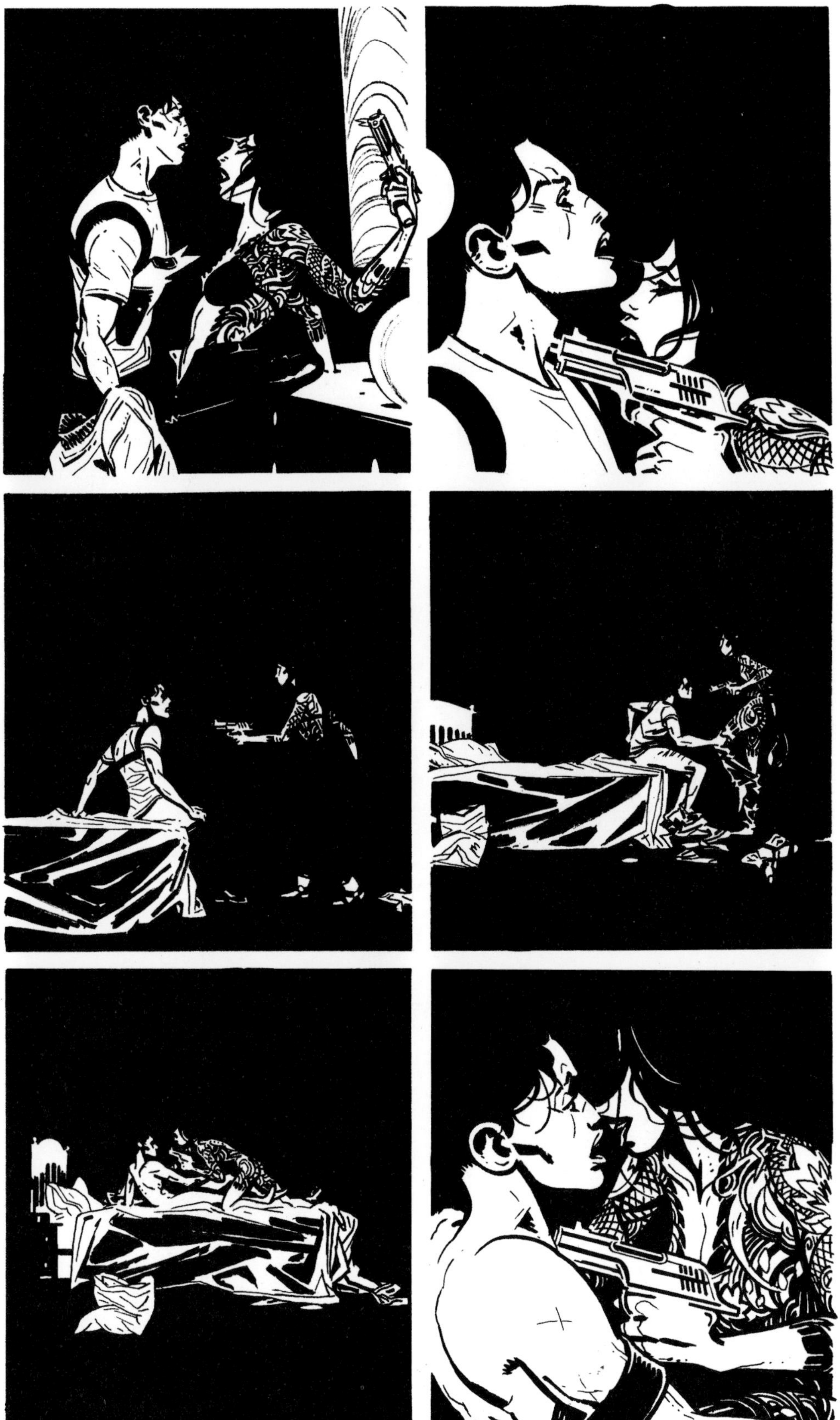

PAGE 17 INKS BY **WES CRAIG**

PAGE 18 PENCILS BY **WES CRAIG**

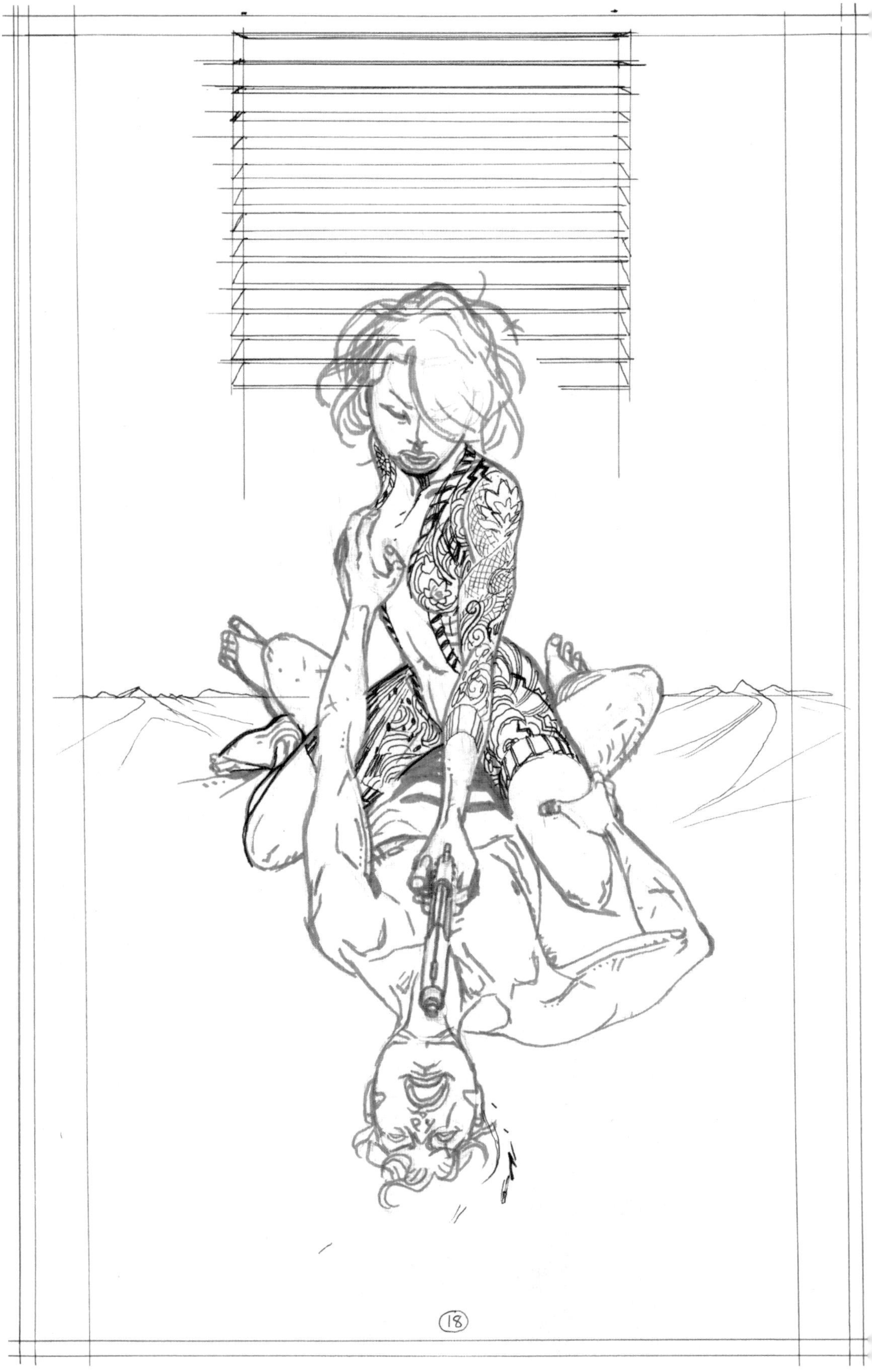

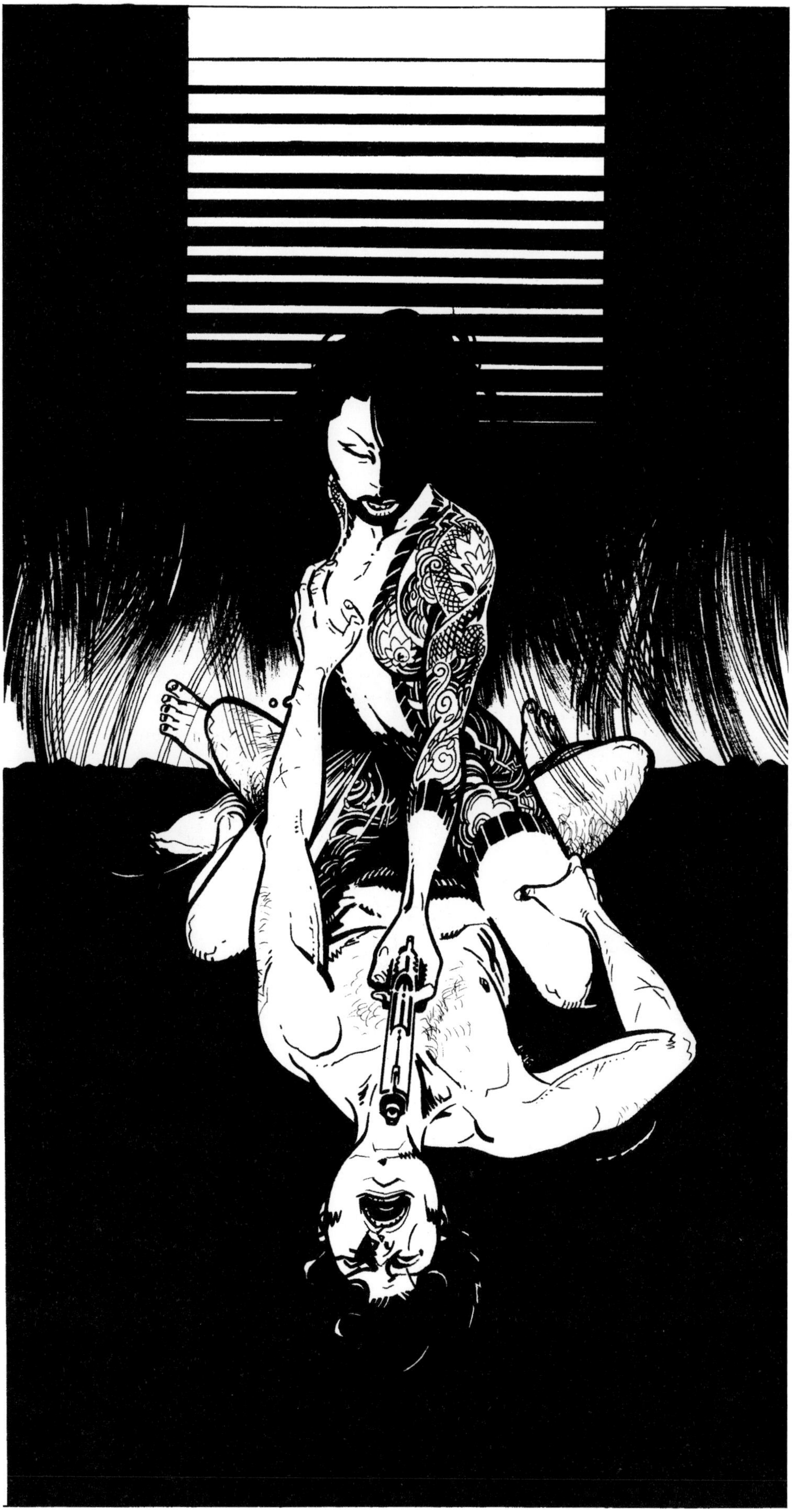

PAGE 18 INKS BY **WES CRAIG**

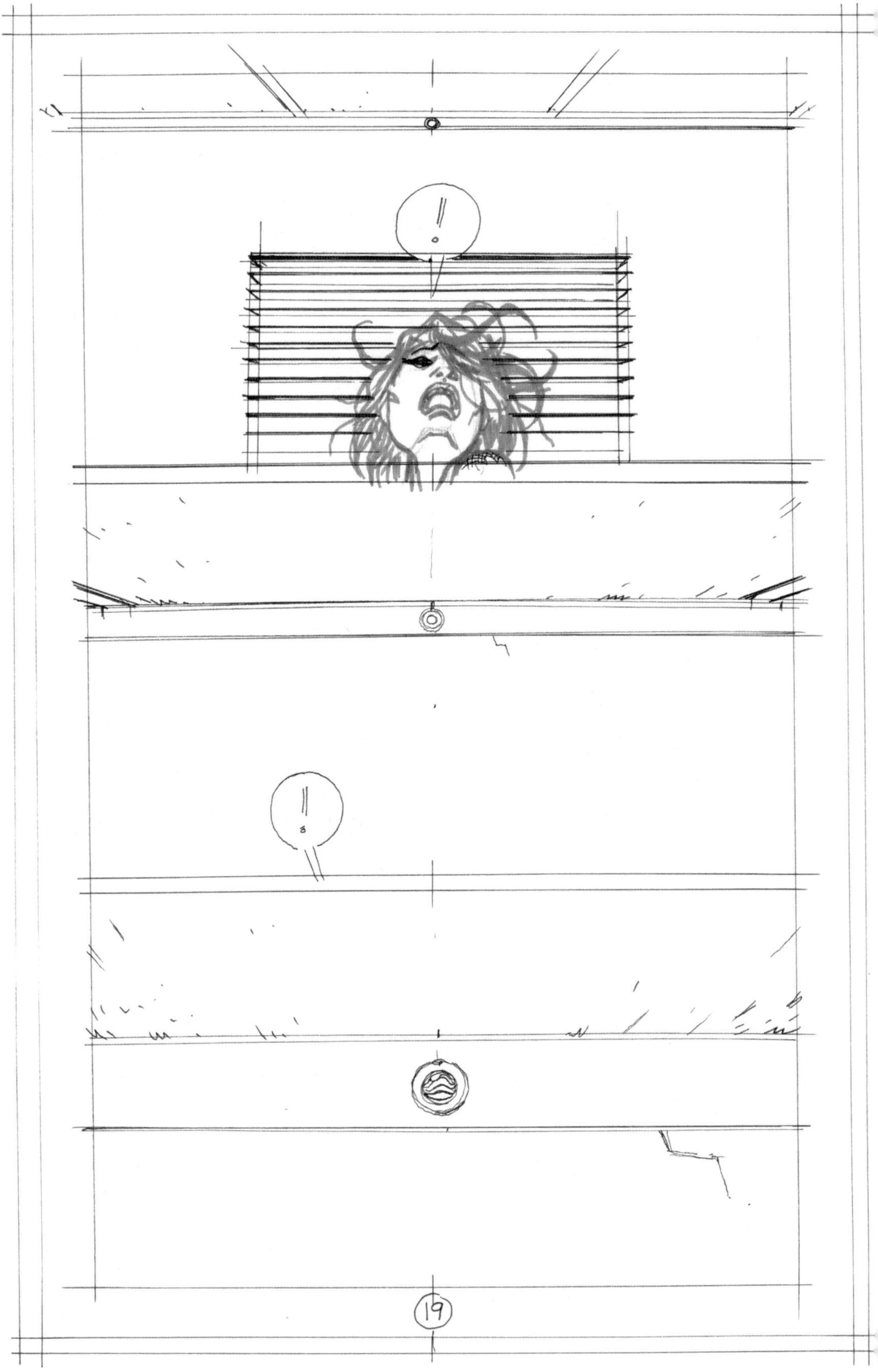


PAGE 19 PENCILS BY **WES CRAIG**

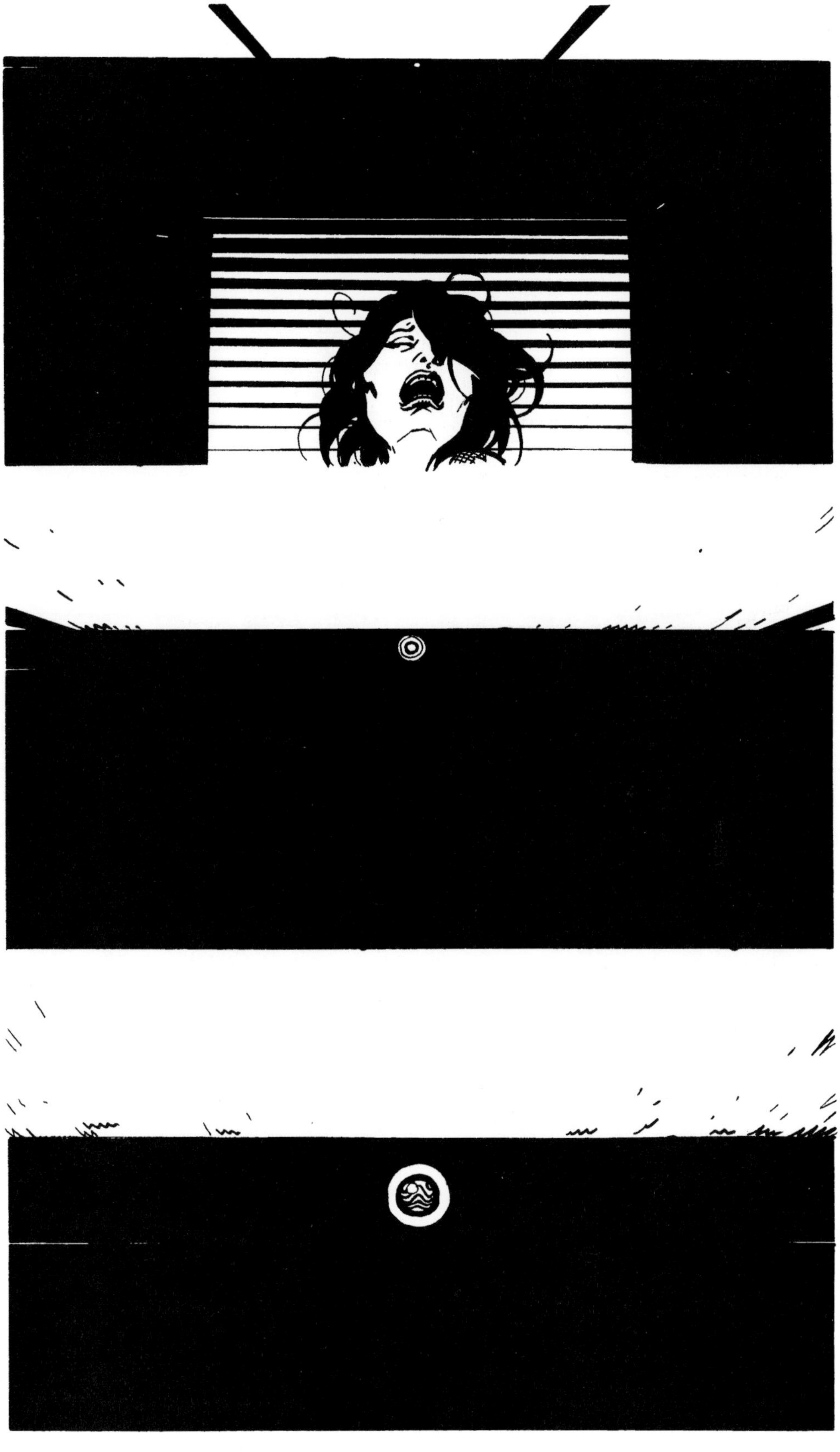

PAGE 19 INKS BY **WES CRAIG**

PAGE 20 PENCILS BY **WES CRAIG**

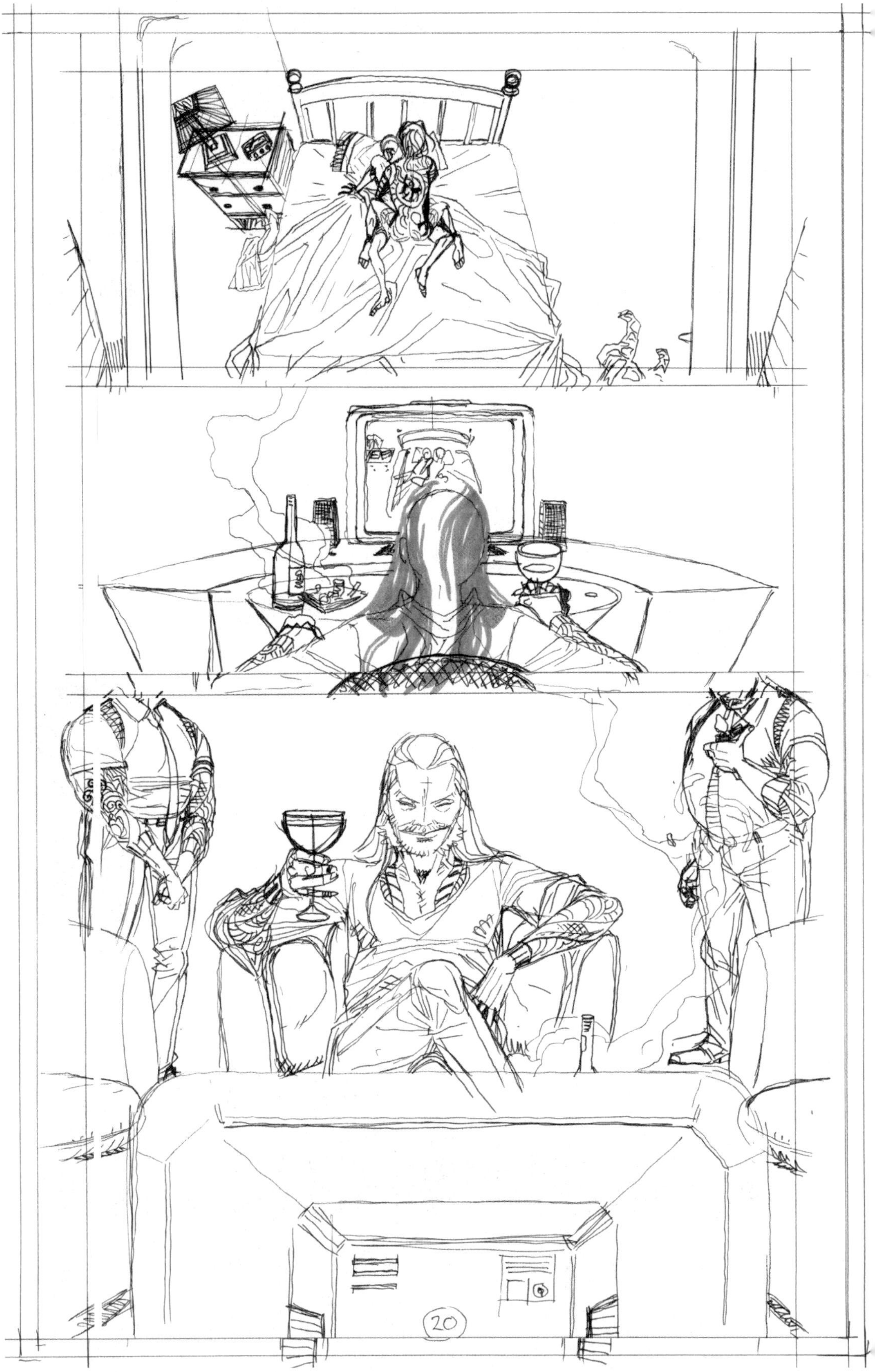
20

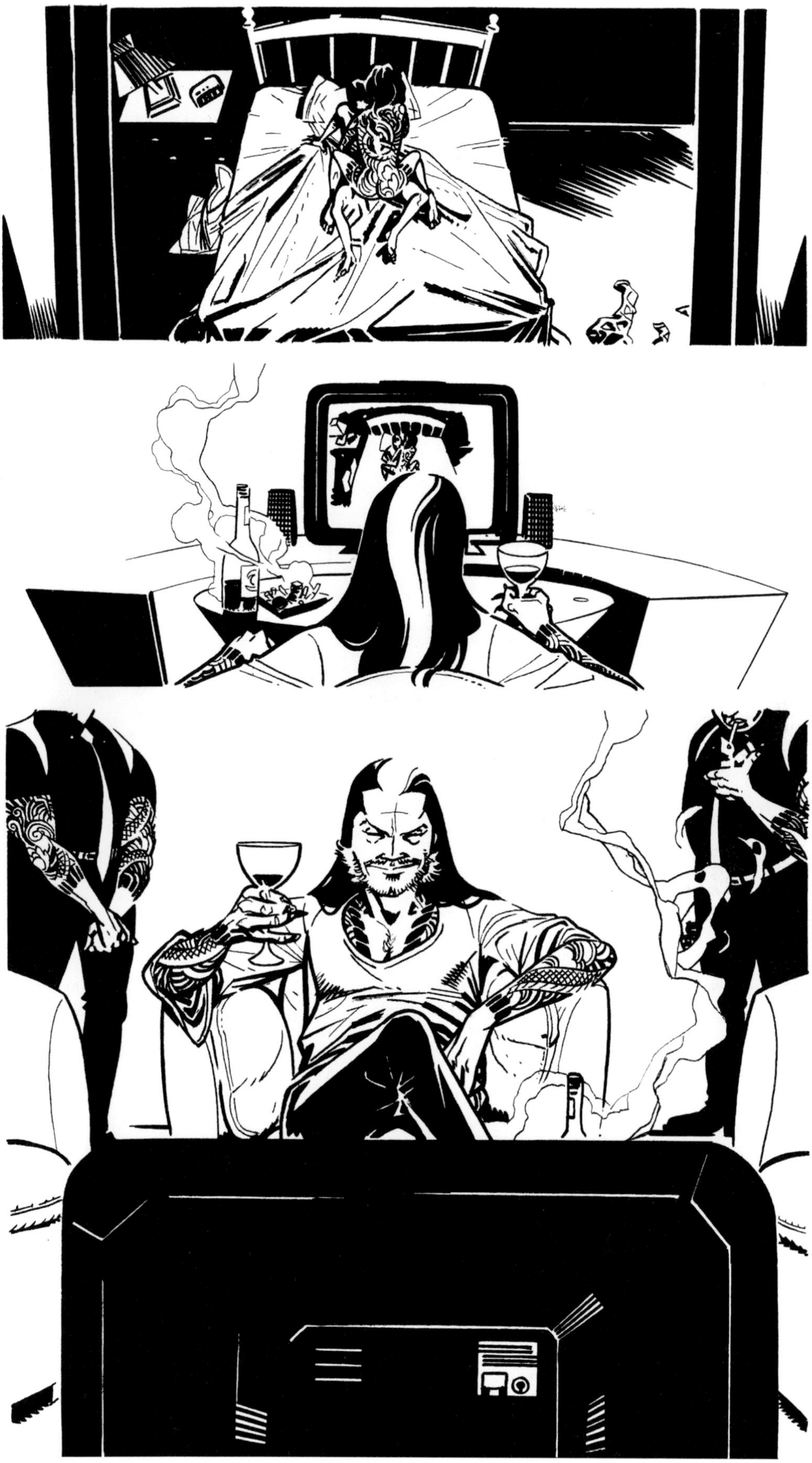

PAGE 20 INKS BY **WES CRAIG**

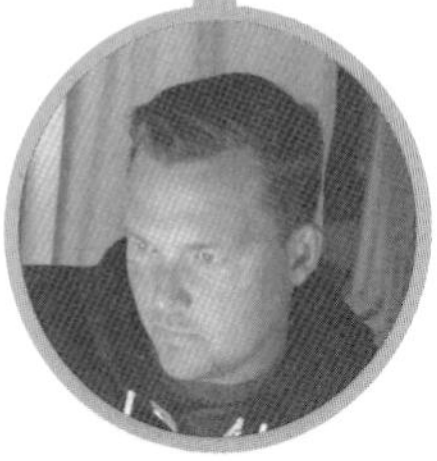

**RICK REMENDER** is the co-creator of *Deadly Class*, *Black Science*, *Seven to Eternity*, *LOW*, *The Scumbag*, *Fear Agent*, *Tokyo Ghost*, and more for Image Comics. His work at Marvel Comics is the basis for major elements of *Avengers: Endgame*, *The Falcon and the Winter Soldier*, and *Deadpool 2*. He's written and developed several sci-fi games for Electronic Arts, including the universally acclaimed survival horror title *Dead Space*, and he has worked alongside the Russo brothers as co-showrunner of *Deadly Class*'s Sony Pictures television adaptation. Currently, he's writing the film adaptation of *Tokyo Ghost* for Cary Fukunaga and Legendary Entertainment and curating his publishing imprint, Giant Generator.

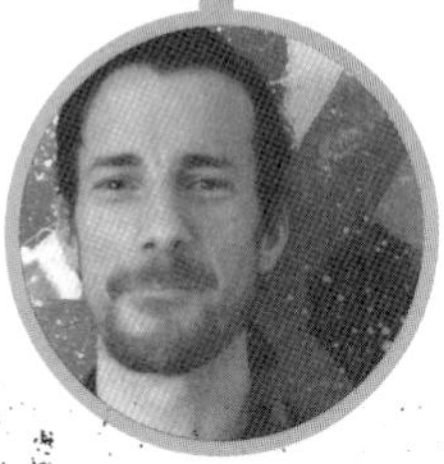

**WES CRAIG** is the artist and co-creator of *Deadly Class*, the writer and co-creator of *The Gravediggers Union*, and the writer-artist of *Kaya*, debuting fall 2022, all from Image Comics. He has also worked on *Superman*, *Batman*, and *The Flash* for DC Comics, and *Guardians of the Galaxy* for Marvel. He lives in Montreal, Quebec with his family.

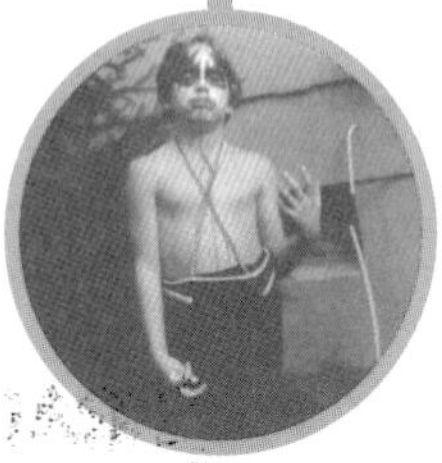

**LEE LOUGHRIDGE** has been in the comic industry for over 20 years working on hundreds of titles. Lee is far more handsome than any other member of the *Deadly Class* team. The last fact was the basis for his previous departure from the book. He resides in Southern California longing for the days when his testosterone count was considerably higher.